Theorizing Literature

Erik Schilling

Theorizing Literature

Literary Theory in Contemporary
Novels – and Their Analysis

Erik Schilling
Faculty of Linguistics and Literature
University of Munich (LMU)
München, Bayern, Germany

ISBN 978-3-031-53325-9   ISBN 978-3-031-53326-6   (eBook)
https://doi.org/10.1007/978-3-031-53326-6

© The Editor(s) (if applicable) and The Author(s), under exclusive license to Springer Nature Switzerland AG 2024

This work is subject to copyright. All rights are solely and exclusively licensed by the Publisher, whether the whole or part of the material is concerned, specifically the rights of translation, reprinting, reuse of illustrations, recitation, broadcasting, reproduction on microfilms or in any other physical way, and transmission or information storage and retrieval, electronic adaptation, computer software, or by similar or dissimilar methodology now known or hereafter developed.

The use of general descriptive names, registered names, trademarks, service marks, etc. in this publication does not imply, even in the absence of a specific statement, that such names are exempt from the relevant protective laws and regulations and therefore free for general use.

The publisher, the authors, and the editors are safe to assume that the advice and information in this book are believed to be true and accurate at the date of publication. Neither the publisher nor the authors or the editors give a warranty, expressed or implied, with respect to the material contained herein or for any errors or omissions that may have been made. The publisher remains neutral with regard to jurisdictional claims in published maps and institutional affiliations.

This Palgrave Macmillan imprint is published by the registered company Springer Nature Switzerland AG.
The registered company address is: Gewerbestrasse 11, 6330 Cham, Switzerland

Paper in this product is recyclable.

Preface

Theorizing literature is not a topic destined to win the popularity contest among literature students. For many, literary theory feels like a maze designed by sadistic professors, full of words that seem to do nothing more than decorate academic papers. "Why should we care about the death of the author—or is it the resurrection?", they ask. "Is theory just a highbrow game made for ivory towers or does it have something to do with the real world? Are we just surfing an endless wave of signs to nowhere? Basically, is theory here to enlighten us or just to make our lives even more complicated?"

Fortunately, many contemporary authors seem to have experienced this distress as well and have dealt with it creatively: by inventing theorizing *literature*. In several literary works, they pick up elements of theory and present them in a narrative context. In doing so, they adopt theory and test its suitability for 'real life', for example, by having their characters act according to a theoretical concept. They test the limits of theory by looking at the resistance of some phenomena to being placed in theoretical categories. They make fun of the castles in the air built by theorists. But they also work productively with theory: they refine elements of theory within their fiction, they shed light on dark spots in theory, and they use the tools of fiction, such as ambiguity or irony, to approach theory in 'non-theoretical' ways.

Therefore, literary texts dealing with theory ideally achieve two things at once: they actively participate in theoretical debates and they deliver a powerful story that reaches its audience on more than just a theoretical level. Reading these texts offers a twofold experience: first, the intellectual pleasure of identifying elements of theory in a literary text and understanding how and why they are used in the context of fiction. And, second, the emotional pleasure of being presented with a good story. Umberto Eco's novel *The Name of the Rose*, for example, may be enjoyed for its clever integration of semiotic theories into the narrative world of a fourteenth-century monastery, but also for the novel's intricate story of intrigue and deduction, in which a spate of murders forms the basis for a medieval detective mystery.

Some of the novels discussed below can be read as introductions to literary theory, either to theory in general (David Lodge's *Small World*) or to a particular theoretical approach (Mithu Sanyal's *Identitti* on critical race theory). Others tell the history of literary theory (Laurent Binet's *The 7th Function of Language*) or focus on a central topic (such as authorship in Patricia Duncker's *Hallucinating Foucault* or Daniel Kehlmann's *F*). In all these cases, however, seemingly dull literary theory becomes quite graphic when it forms part of a narrative world.

Since the literary texts in question offer both a cunning presentation of theory and an exciting story, their analysis needs to be (at least) twofold: it has to offer a theoretical concept for *theorizing* literature and it has to use it for interpretations of theorizing *literature*. Therefore, this book looks at its textual corpus from both a theoretical and a literary point of view: it offers some ideas on how to deal with 'theory-informed' texts in a theoretically informed way, and it—hopefully—provides some convincing interpretations of these texts that go beyond their intertextual comparison with theory and treat them as holistic literary works of art. The basis for this is a second-order literary theory as proposed in the methodological chapter, looking at mode, level, function, and a possible extrapolation of theory in/from literature.

This book could not have been written without the support of many people. First and foremost, I would like to thank my students in Bern, Bielefeld, and Munich for their great interest in the topic and their challenging questions. Invitations to conferences and lectures allowed me to work on various aspects of this book. For specific discussions, ideas, and suggestions, I would like to thank Sibylle Baumbach, Michael Bies, Klaus Birnstiel, Chiara Conterno, Nicolas Detering, Isabelle Dolezalek, Carolin Duttlinger, Ulrike Draesner, Patrick Durdel, Alexander Edlich, Walter Erhart, Michael Gamper, Matthew Hines, Achim Hölter, Thomas Kempf, Felix Kraft, Elias Kreuzmair, Tobias Krüger, Jakob Lenz, Solvejg Nitzke, Ronja Rieger, Michael Schilling, Thorsten Schilling, Hendrik Schlieper,

Monika Schmitz-Emans, Tim Sommer, Magdalena Specht, Alexander Sperling, Carlos Spoerhase, Susanne Strätling, and Kathrin Wittler. Sebastian Matzner came up with the perfect title for the book, Alastair Smith made important linguistic improvements to the manuscript.

In terms of institutional support, I am grateful to Palgrave Macmillan for organizing an efficient peer-review and for a very smooth publication process. Moreover, I would like to thank the German Research Foundation (DFG), which facilitated writing this book with a Heisenberg Fellowship. The *Junge Akademie* of The Berlin-Brandenburg Academy of Sciences and Humanities and the German National Academy of Sciences Leopoldina allowed me two helpful writing retreats.

Munich, Germany   Erik Schilling

Contents

1 Theory Permeating Literature 1

2 Second-Order Literary Theory 17

3 Narrating Literary Theory 51

4 Topics in/of Theory 77

5 The Fragile Relationship of Author, Reader, and Text 109

6 Creating and Interpreting Fictional Worlds 143

7 Beyond Novels—Beyond Theory? 163

8 Theory Extrapolated from Literature 179

Name Index 199

Subject Index 203

LIST OF FIGURES

Fig. 2.1　The four dimensions of second-order literary theory (overview)　18
Fig. 2.2　Modeling the observation process (first alternative)　20
Fig. 2.3　Modeling the observation process (second alternative)　22
Fig. 2.4　Modes of theory within literature (*intertextual dimension*)　24
Fig. 2.5　Levels of theory within literature (*narratological dimension*)　30
Fig. 2.6　Functions of theory within literature (*hermeneutical dimension*)　36
Fig. 2.7　Extrapolation of theory from literature (*theoretical dimension*)　43
Fig. 2.8　The four dimensions of second-order literary theory (detailed)　47
Fig. 8.1　Extrapolation of theory from literature: authorship concepts　181

LIST OF TABLES

Table 2.1	Examples for different modes of theory in literature	28
Table 2.2	Examples for different levels of theory in literature	35
Table 2.3	Examples for different functions of theory in literature	42
Table 2.4	Examples for different extrapolations of theory from literature	46

CHAPTER 1

Theory Permeating Literature

The ambiguity of the title *Theorizing Literature* captures the two key aspects of this book: it theorizes literature and it focuses on literature that itself 'theorizes', that is, engages with literary theory. In doing so, this book deals with a striking phenomenon: many influential literary texts of the last fifty years draw on contemporary literary theory. They present theory in a narrative form, have their characters act according to theoretical premises, use irony to point out unresolved problems of theory, and actively contribute to theoretical discourses.

Reading these books may feel like watching Christopher Nolan's film *Inception*: there is theory invented to analyze literature, literature that uses this theory, another theory needed to analyze 'theory-informed' literature, and so on. This leads to an interlocking of theory and literature that may seem as unstable as the interwoven dream worlds of *Inception*. In what follows, however, I will try to unravel this by looking at a representative selection of this kind of literature—along with theoretical reflections on how to engage with these texts. In doing so, this book offers a meta-perspective on the connection between theory and literature through a 'second-order literary theory'.

Literary theory has been among the most influential developments in the humanities since the Second World War.[1] The difference between author and text, the role of signs and the reader, and the introduction of new perspectives on gender, colonialism, migration, and the environment have all stood at the center of famous theoretical debates. Intellectuals working on 'theory' became the rockstars of literature and philosophy departments: Michel Foucault and Roland Barthes, Julia Kristeva and Susan Sontag, Jacques Derrida and Paul de Man, Judith Butler and Shoshana Felman.

These are stories that have been told many times.[2] In 1983, Terry Eagleton wrote a famous introduction to the field of literary theory before going on to proclaim a time *After Theory* in 2003.[3] There is a broad range of introductions to theory for students or encyclopedias that give an overview of its key terms and concepts.[4] Therefore, I do not intend to provide another résumé of the difference between hermeneutics and deconstruction or the arbitrariness of the sign. Instead, I will move from the side of theory to the side of literature and turn my attention to postmodern and contemporary novels that take up literary theory as a topic to be integrated into their fictional world.

David Lodge's *Small World* creates an academic world with different characters allegorically representing different theories. Christoph Ransmayr's *The Last World* and Daniel Kehlmann's *F* present and question the hermeneutic model of author, reader, and text. In *Hallucinating Foucault*, Patricia Duncker draws on thoughts from psychoanalysis, queer studies, and discourse analysis. Italo Calvino's *If on a Winter's Night a Traveler* and Umberto Eco's *Foucault's Pendulum* adopt post-structuralist, deconstructivist, and semiotic concepts. Ulrike Draesner's *Dowry* tells the story of an intersex protagonist, reflecting the genders of people and texts. Mithu Sanyal's *Identitti* and Bernadine Evaristo's *Girl, Woman, Other*

---

[1] By 'theory', I mainly refer to the forms of literary theory developed and popularized in the second half of the twentieth century. In front of all, this is the so-called French theory with its different currents of (post-)structuralism, deconstruction, etc.

[2] Habib (2008); Felsch (2015); Birnstiel (2016); Bittner (2020).

[3] Eagleton (1983); Eagleton (2003). In the late 1980s, however, Olsen (1987) already proclaimed *The End of Literary Theory*. Other publications in the last twenty years take the same line, e.g., Kablitz (2013); Felski (2015); Geisenhanslüke (2015); North (2017); Poppenberg (2018).

[4] Wellbery (1985); Culler (1997); Jahraus (2002); Waugh (2006); Cuddon (2013); Klages (2017); Rivkin and Ryan (2017).

work with critical race theory. Juli Zeh, in her novel *Dark Matter*, compares quantum physics and fiction theory. And in *The 7th Function of Language*, Laurent Binet has Roland Barthes murdered in Paris, inflicting upon him the 'death of the author'.

In this book, I intend to show that the literary texts in question do not simply engage with elements of theory for the sake of literary play or intertextuality. Instead, they work productively with theory: they elaborate the contradictions and tensions between different theoretical approaches, inhabit the blind spots that theory ignores, and propose inventive solutions for widely discussed questions in theory. For example, they further discussions on the role of author and reader, on dealing with gender or race biases, or on confronting the quest for meaning with the infinite drift of signs. Other novels tell the history of theory, either by using Barthes, Foucault, Kristeva, etc. as fictional characters or by creating characters who represent key elements of theory. Thus, this book deals with texts that reflect upon the possibilities and limits of their own 'interpretability'.

THE INTRICATE RELATIONSHIP OF THEORY AND LITERATURE

In her book *The Novel after Theory*, Judith Ryan identifies elements of theory in literary texts, especially by postmodern authors.[5] Her focus lies on the intertextual comparison between theory and literature: "My discussion of the novels attempts to capture this complex intertextual relation between narrative fiction and post-structuralist ideas."[6] Observing this intertextuality is the first indispensable step for interpreting the literary texts in question because it is this comparative approach that allows the relationship between a given text and a given theory to be properly ascertained.

Another important perspective to consider is that of a 'theory of theory',[7] which seeks to bring various theories into the scope of its analytical standpoint.[8] This is grounded in the history of science, discourse analysis, and sociology. Like the intertextual comparison of theory and literature,

---

[5] Ryan (2011); see also Schilling (2012a); Kreuzmair (2020).
[6] Ryan (2011, 17). Sorensen (2010) focuses on postcolonial studies and literature. Kreuzmair (2020) works in a similar way with a particular emphasis on pop literature and its groundings in theory. Solte-Gresser and Schmeling (2016) offer a variety of perspectives on the phenomenon.
[7] Elliott and Attridge (2011).
[8] Müller Nielaba and Previšič (2010); Grizelj and Jahraus (2011); Jahraus (2011).

the questions raised by theories of theory are indispensable for arriving at an analytical standpoint on theory, before going on to look at the texts that integrate it into their own literary project. It is precisely this metaperspective that allows theory to be treated not (only) as an analytical tool, but as a discourse represented in texts—which may then be adopted by literature.

A third perspective in research is taken by those who use the theory reflected upon in a literary text for the analysis of the text itself.[9] This was the approach often taken for the paradigm of theory-informed novels: Umberto Eco's *The Name of the Rose*, whereby the novel was frequently understood through a comparison with semiotics.[10] Eco's protagonist William is able to describe a runaway horse on the basis of traces, signs, and deductions without ever having seen it.[11] This is what Eco's narrated theory looks like—and it can be understood by returning to semiotics for an interpretive framework. However, it cannot be assumed that the theory integrated into the literary text is especially useful for its interpretation—it may even be that the opposite is true, for example, when theory is used with an ironic twist.

A fourth approach in research is to discuss the novels in question with regard to aesthetic or literary characteristics not linked to the elements of theory in particular. Linda Hutcheon, for example, reads several texts relevant for the topic of theory in literature against the background of postmodernism as a cultural movement.[12] Other contributions undertake similar readings of other novels or topics.[13]

Despite this variety of useful approaches to theory in literature, a systematic analysis of the phenomenon is lacking. Some of the unresolved questions include: how and where exactly does literature incorporate theory? Do the various modes and levels of theory in literature alter the understanding of a text? What precisely is the function of theory in literature? Is an awareness of the current trends in theory merely a pretext for an intellectual game? Or does literature continue the debates taking place in theory? And, if so, what kind of theoretical elements do the literary texts develop? Can (new) theory be extrapolated from literary texts? In

[9] See Jaeger (2000) on both.
[10] Bennett (1988); Schick (1989); Micskey (1992); Schilling (2021). Accordingly, Mersch (1993, 7–8) writes that Eco's novels are to be understood as 'narrative semiotics'.
[11] See Schilling (2012b) for details.
[12] Hutcheon (1988).
[13] Regn (1992); Zima (2001); Nünning (2003); Schilling (2012a).

addition, there are questions regarding the interpretation of a literary text on the basis of a theory found in it: can a theory embedded in a novel be used for its analysis? What if the novel, through an ironic treatment of theory, shows itself to be critically aware of the limits of its 'interpretability'?

By formulating a second-order literary theory, this book aims to answer as many of these questions as possible. In doing so, it proposes new perspectives on literary theory, sheds light on self-reflexivity, and, last but not least, offers an analysis of some of the most exciting and challenging books of the last fifty years. My key idea is that the literary texts in question actively develop important aspects of theory. Literary criticism is therefore not finished as soon as the crucial intertextual references are identified or the fictional story is compared to important moments in the history of theory. Instead, literary texts have to be taken seriously as original contributions to the debates on literary theory themselves. This approach has been used for so-called artistic research[14] but not yet for theory in literature.

Thus, literature does not only adopt theory, but it also creates theory and proposes solutions for unresolved problems in the field. Both will be my focus in this book. I follow three main hypotheses:

1. Literary texts fill gaps in theory. Due to their fictional approach to important questions (e.g., the construction of authorship, the role of the reader, the perception of gender or race), they shed new light on seemingly well-discussed topics.
2. Since literary texts usually eschew the conventional academic format of thesis, argument, and evidential support, they engage with theoretical concepts through devices predominant in fiction, such as irony, self-reflexivity, or ambiguity. The literary form equips these texts to illuminate specific phenomena in ways often unattainable within the confines of 'traditional' theoretical discourse.
3. Despite their contributions to theoretical discourse, the texts under consideration remain literary works. As such, an examination of their literary elements is necessary, in addition to scrutinizing their theoretical claims. However, conventional methodologies for textual analysis may falter when texts possess an intrinsic 'awareness' of

[14] For some introductory remarks on 'artistic research', see Schwab et al. (2014); Butt (2017).

the interpretive tools being applied to them. To address this analytical challenge, I advocate for a 'second-order literary theory'. This approach is designed to analyze 'theory-informed' texts along four dimensions: the mode and level at which theory is integrated; the function it serves within the text; and the potential for extrapolating theory from the literary text.

Earlier Forms of 'Theory' in Literature

The phenomenon discussed in this book is by no means a new one. Since antiquity, there have been representations of interpretive processes in literature and, therefore, fictional treatments of 'theory'.[15] In his famous 'Allegory of the Cave', for example, Plato frames an interpretive process within a narrative scenario. The person who leaves the cave and gets to see the sun does not only gain a deeper insight into the difference between phenomena and ideas, but is also forced to acknowledge the conditions of their own interpretations. A similar allegory can be seen in Virgil's ekphrasis of the shield of Aeneas, on whose surface key episodes of the future Roman history are depicted and analyzed—for both Aeneas himself and for the 'modern' (i.e., Roman) reader.

Equally as long as the history of hermeneutics is the history of fictional presentations of hermeneutic processes. In late antiquity and the Middle Ages, the four senses of Scripture became part not only of the interpretation of the Bible, but also of literary texts. In his *Divine Comedy* (c. 1308–1321), for example, Dante engages in the representation of interpretive processes by having Virgil explain the significance of the various punishments in Hell and the allegorical structure of Hell in general. The second part of Miguel de Cervantes's *Don Quixote* (1605/1615) presents several characters reading about Quixote's adventures of the first part— and in doing so also their understandings of, and reactions to, the novel. And Laurence Sterne's novel *Tristram Shandy* (1759–1767) deals with the problems of language, harking back to John Locke's epistemological *Essay Concerning Human Understanding*. For instance, the protagonist's name is subject to a complex series of interpretations within the novel, reaching from connotations with the Medieval hero Tristan to the mystic figure Hermes Trismegistus and the Latin word 'tristis' (for 'sad').

---

[15] For an overview, see Harland (1999). Bray (2019) analyzes nineteenth-century French novels with a focus on elements of theory.

Modern hermeneutics is closely linked to literature as well. Friedrich Schlegel and Friedrich Schleiermacher did not only live together for some time in a Berlin apartment, but also responded to each other in their writings. Schlegel, in his novel *Lucinde* (1799), describes various forms of love with the help of hermeneutic processes; Schleiermacher, in his *Confidential Letters on Schlegel's Lucinde* (1800), directly reacts to the text by subjecting it to a hermeneutic analysis in an epistolary novel. In the early twentieth century, various literary texts take up psychoanalytical hermeneutics. For example, in his *Dream Story* (1925/26), turned into the film *Eyes Wide Shut* by Stanley Kubrick, Arthur Schnitzler presents an analysis of the sexual fantasies of a couple using Freud's terminology and concepts.

Despite this long tradition, which has only been briefly sketched here, this book deals with literary texts from the last fifty years that deal primarily with twentieth-century literary theory. There are two reasons for this, one pragmatic, the other heuristic. First, limiting the scope to a certain period allows for a more detailed and systematic understanding of the phenomenon. Second, the variety of literary theories developed in the second half of the twentieth century makes it possible to analyze different methods of interpretation, something that a history of hermeneutic processes in literary texts does not do—which is not to say that such a history would not be worth writing or reading.

The Self-Presentation of 'Theory-Informed' Literature

Essential to this book is the understanding that literary theory is not separate from literature, but inextricably linked to it. In this spirit, the book offers a new perspective on the literature of the last fifty years and a new way of thinking about theory. Thus, it not only presents various layers and forms of an interesting literary phenomenon, but also examines its implications for literary theory.

Many of the books analyzed here outwardly proclaim their connection to literary theory on their covers, in their blurbs, or in other paratexts. This is often combined with the explicit announcement of a detective story. Binet's *7th Function of Language*, for example, asks on its cover: "Who has killed Roland Barthes?"[16] The question "whodunit" is explicitly

---

[16] "Qui a tué Roland Barthes?" (https://www.livredepoche.com/livre/la-septieme-fonction-du-langage-9782253066248).

linked to Barthes's 'death of the author'—at least for readers who are familiar with theory, who may then also see the irony in applying Barthes's conceptual idea to a real death. The blurb goes on to say that, in order to find the killer, one must delve into the intellectual spheres of Parisian life, where everyone is a suspect.[17]

Duncker's *Hallucinating Foucault* is presented as "a literary thriller that explores [...] the passionate relationship between reader and writer, between the factual and the fictional", likewise linking theory to thriller. The blurb of Eco's *Foucault's Pendulum* announces three editors dabbling in occult sciences who come up with a plan—"but someone takes them seriously".[18] Again, it is just a small step from the literary scene to a thriller element. And the film *Stranger than Fiction* is even more outspoken in this respect: "I.R.S. auditor Harold Crick suddenly finds his mundane Chicago life to be the subject of narration only he can hear: narration that begins to affect his entire existence, from his work to his love life to his death".[19]

There may be (at least) two reasons for linking theory to the thriller: first, as I argued in the preface to this book, because theory itself may seem a rather boring subject. By combining it with the suspense of a murder mystery, and explicitly emphasizing this in the book's presentation, the text may attract a larger audience than a mere narrative of theory. Second, the connection between theorizing literature and detective fiction can also be explained structurally. Theory provides concepts that allow hypotheses to organize phenomena in a plausible, perhaps even empirically verifiable, way. The investigator in a detective story does exactly the same thing: there are certain pieces of evidence that can be organized according to particular methods in order to present a convincing hypothesis about the guilty party.

---

[17] "Pour retrouver l'assassin, ils vont devoir plonger dans les hautes sphères intellectuelles de la vie Parisienne. Quelle n'est pas leur surprise de découvrir que tout le monde est suspect ! Un roman drôle, intelligent et d'inventif qui se lit comme un polar" (https://editionsgabelire.com/catalogue/la-septieme-fonction-du-langage/).

[18] "[T]re redattori editoriali, a Milano, dopo avere frequentato troppo a lungo autori [...] che si dilettano di scienze occulte, società segrete e complotti cosmici, decidono di inventare, senza alcun senso di responsabilità, un Piano. Ma qualcuno li prende sul serio" (https://lanaveditesco.eu/portfolio/il-pendolo-di-foucault/).

[19] https://www.imdb.com/title/tt0420223/.

Shedding New Light on Theory in Literature

In what follows, I will dwell on this connection between theory and an exciting story, attempting in particular to tease out the links between the two. In a methodological chapter, I first present four dimensions of theorizing literature. These dimensions comprise *mode, level, function,* and an *extrapolation* of theory in/from literature.

Analyzing the mode serves to facilitate a discussion of literary texts vis-à-vis the different currents of theory they emerge from and thereby illustrates how elements of theory become part of literature (the *intertextual dimension*). With regard to the mode, for example, theory may be directly referred to or seen as a structural similarity. In addition, I look at the levels of integrating theory into literature (the *narratological dimension*) and its function within the fictional world (the *hermeneutical dimension*). In terms of the level, theory may, for instance, be present diegetically (e.g., as the history of or a story about theory) or on other narrative levels (e.g., within dialogues between characters or as a characteristics of the narrator). Its function may, for example, be affirmative or critical with regard to a certain methodological approach or toward theory in general. Finally, I look at elements of theory developed in literature. In doing so, I analyze the texts with regard to their 'doing theory' (the *theoretical dimension*). An extrapolation of theory from literature may identify elements of theory within literature that can play a role in new concepts of theory.

On a self-reflexive level, I also ask what it means for a theoretically informed analysis to deal with literary texts which are 'aware' of theory. Does it support or compromise a certain methodological approach if the text 'knows' about and reacts to it beforehand? What does the readers' awareness of the texts' awareness of theory mean for interpretation as a result? In successively presenting and substantiating these perspectives, I offer some ideas for a second-order literary theory that allows for texts dealing with theory to be multifariously analyzed.[20]

In the chapters following this methodological foundation, I analyze literary texts (and one film) from the last fifty years that work with, and offer innovative ideas for, literary theory. My textual analysis starts with a chapter on two novels that *narrate (and ironize) the history of literary*

---

[20] Of course, this is an infinite regress: I hope to see a writer picking up the idea of a second-order literary theory in order to integrate and work on it in a literary text—possibly resulting in the need for a third-order literary theory.

theory. David Lodge's *Small World* (1984) has different characters represent important filiations of theory: an English professor mostly working on a hermeneutic basis, a French post-structuralist, an Italian Marxist, a German reader-response theorist, and a US deconstructivist all feature in the novel's cast of characters. Early forms of feminist theory and digital humanities also make an appearance. Laurent Binet's *The 7th Function of Language* (*La septième fonction du langage*, 2015) is a historical novel set in 1980s France and has Roland Barthes murdered in Paris. A French policeman asks a PhD student to assist him with the investigation, as he requires expertise on the intellectual scene. During the investigation, the two meet important representatives of twentieth-century theory who appear in partially authentic, partially ironic ways (Foucault in a gay sauna, Kristeva working for the Bulgarian secret service, Searle and Derrida arguing about the performativity of language, etc.). Lodge and Binet therefore stand for the idea of presenting a narration of literary theory in literature, as a 'novel of ideas' in the first case and as a historical novel in the latter.

The subject of the following chapter is topics in/of theory in literature. It deals with novels that *incorporate thematically oriented forms of theory*. Patricia Duncker's *Hallucinating Foucault* (1996) sets out from Michel Foucault's discourse analysis, linking it to queer theory. In addition, the topic of authorship is central to the novel. While the protagonist tracks down Paul Michel, a gay author living in a French asylum, questions discussed in Foucault's works arise, for example those of *Madness and Civilization* or *The History of Sexuality*. Ulrike Draesner's *Dowry* (*Mitgift*, 2002) presents an intersex protagonist whose gender transition is a key part of the narrative. At the same time, gender fluidity is reflected upon by the novel as a fictional work, which is set between the genres of novel, novella, and drama. The novel thus questions categorizations of *genus*—of gender and genre—in general. Mithu Sanyal's *Identitti* (2021) offers various perspectives on race, linking them to corresponding theories and, at the same time, illustrating the theories' limits. The examples of Duncker, Draesner, and Sanyal, therefore, represent novels that adopt specific literary theories and test out their limits within a fictional context.

The next chapter looks at three novels that *deal with the fragile relationship of author, reader, and text*. They each part from a 'traditional' hermeneutic understanding of the reception process, reflecting upon it, and subverting it instead. In Daniel Kehlmann's novel *F* (2013), each of the main characters serves as an author. By presenting authorships of fiction, faith, financial fraud, and forged art, the novel multiplies authorship, offering multiple ideas for an extrapolation of theory. Italo Calvino's *If on a Winter's Night a Traveler* (*Se una notte d'inverno un viaggiatore*, 1979), in contrast, multiplies the reader. It features a fictional character reading Calvino's novel. In various phases of his reading process, the reader meets other readers with different views on reading—and even a reader who, in the end, becomes his wife. Again, the novel might be used for an extrapolation of theory: for a typology of reader types. Christoph Ransmayr's *The Last World* (*Die letzte Welt*, 1988) starts with an author and a reader within the fictional world. However, the reader cannot trace the author, only being able to access his fiction. In addition, the fiction is not clearly separated from the world surrounding the reader, but forms an integral part of it, so that, in the end, everything—the novel, its fictional world, and even the constructions of reader and author—turns out to be text. Kehlmann, Calvino, and Ransmayr, therefore, transform debates of literary theory into fiction: are authors relevant for interpretation at all—and if so: how to get hold of them? What kind of readers exist—and to what extent does the interpretation of a text depend on them? Where are the borders of a text—or is the whole world a giant text?

A further chapter examines the creation and interpretation of fiction in general, as seen in novels that *deal with (fictional) worlds, their norms, and their interpretation*. Umberto Eco's novel *Foucault's Pendulum* (*Il pendolo di Foucault*, 1988) sees its protagonists, three editors working for a Milanese publisher, inventing a playful alternate history of the world. When secret societies start to believe in the inventions, however, made-up aspects suddenly become reality. Both the editors and the members of the secret societies perform various interpretations of signs, each according to their norms and preferences. This is extended to the question of how to differentiate good and bad interpretations in general. Juli Zeh's *Dark Matter* (*Schilf*, 2007) has its protagonists—two theoretical physicists—acting out a murder according to the laws of quantum theory. In doing so, they seemingly create a parallel world within their own, a world whose norms they control—just as every fictional work creates norms and conditions of its own.

Another chapter goes beyond theory in novels by looking at a poetry collection and a film. Jan Wagner's collection *The Owl Haters in the Hall Houses* (*Die Eulenhasser in den Hallenhäusern*, 2012) presents three fictitious poets, their poems, and typical instruments of literary scholarship that make the poets and their work accessible, such as a glossary of terms, a commentary, and remarks on the various poetic genres the poets use.

Thus, Wagner does not only publish poems (all written by himself), but also the first—partially ironic, partially useful—steps toward their own literary criticism. Marc Forster's film *Stranger than Fiction* (2006) can be considered a cinematic presentation of literary theory, dealing with the link between narrator, character, and reader—and metaleptically crossing the borders between the three.

The final chapter of this book works both as a résumé and as an extrapolation of theory from literature. Since almost all literary texts analyzed here deal with authorship, I look at the texts again, reflecting on what they—implicitly or explicitly—contribute to a theoretical perspective on authorship. Thus, the fragility of the analytical concept 'authorship' is pointed out—and restored within specific contexts, such as taking on a sociological or juridical perspective on literary texts.

THIS BOOK—AND BEYOND

Of course, the texts analyzed here do not cover the phenomenon in total. Many others could also be considered. Umberto Eco's *The Name of the Rose* (*Il nome della rosa*, 1980), for example, has its protagonist, the medieval monk William of Baskerville, perform a murder investigation in a Benedictine abbey. The interpretation of signs he has to perform is gradually extended to a theory of interpretive conclusions in general. Juli Zeh's *Gaming Instinct* (*Spieltrieb*, 2004) has its protagonists exemplifying an experiment from game theory, the prisoners' dilemma. Two high school students trick one of their teachers into a compromising situation and blackmail him afterward.

J.J. Abrams and Doug Dorst's *Ship of Theseus* (2013) does not only contain a literary text (supposedly by another author, V.M. Straka), but also the marginal notes of two readers of the book, 'written' next to the novel's text. The two readers start to communicate using the book as a material basis for their conversation. The first one annotates certain things, the second one answers, etc. Observing this seemingly real interpretive process offers insights into various aspects of the reading process (academic annotations, personal experiences similar to the ones in the book, considerations triggered by the book, etc.). In addition, the book crosses the border into material studies by not only presenting a seemingly antiquarian book with marginal notes, but also other documents within the book accompanying the reading processes (comments, information from literary archives, newspaper articles, etc.).

Other books one could consider are Thomas Meinecke's *Tomboy* (1998), Jasper Fforde's series of Thursday Next novels (starting with *The Eyre Affair*, 2001), Pola Oloixarac's *Savage Theories* (*Las teorías salvajes*, 2008), Jefferey Eugenides's *The Marriage Plot* (2011), or Dionne Brand's *Theory* (2018).[21] Moreover, the integration of interpretive theory into non-literary artworks would also be an interesting test case—for example, when the observer's perspective is integrated into an artwork, providing guiding cues or contextual information as to how to interpret the piece.

But, taken together, the books in question here allow for a varied look at the reception and production of theory in literature. They rewrite the history of theory, span across traditional aspects of literature (author, reader, text), cover specific interpretive perspectives (sexual orientation, gender, race), observe the interpretive process and the characteristics of fictional worlds in general, and create theory within fiction. Therefore, they may serve as the detailed basis for a second-order literary theory observing how theory in literature works and how it can be analyzed.

In addition, the book follows a comparative approach by looking at novels from different languages and contexts. I analyze American, Austrian, British, French, German, and Italian texts, thereby capturing the international phenomenon of literary theory through a comparative perspective on the literature that deals with it. As a result, this book may hopefully be of interest to readers from different linguistic and cultural backgrounds, linked by their common interest in literary theory.

Bibliography

Bennett, Helen T. (1988): Sign and De-Sign: Medieval and Modern Semiotics in Umberto Eco's "The Name of the Rose". In: M. Thomas Inge, ed.: *Naming the Rose. Essays on Eco's "The Name of the Rose"*. Jackson, 119–129.
Birnstiel, Klaus (2016): *Wie am Meeresufer ein Gesicht im Sand: Eine kurze Geschichte des Poststrukturalismus*. Paderborn.
Bittner, Jacob (2020): *The Emergence of Literature: An Archaeology of Modern Literary Theory*. New York.
Bray, Patrick M. (2019): *The Price of Literature: The French Novel's Theoretical Turn*. Evanston.
Butt, Danny (2017): *Artistic Research in the Future Academy*. Bristol/Chicago.

---

[21] Friedrich Kittler's recently republished detective short story *Neuntöter* would also be an interesting test case, since it develops a 'model for literature', as Horn (2022, 102) puts it.

Cuddon, John A. (2013): *A Dictionary of Literary Terms and Literary Theory*. 5th ed. Rev. by Rafey Habib. Chichester.
Culler, Jonathan (1997): *Literary Theory: A Very Short Introduction*. Oxford.
Eagleton, Terry (1983): *Literary Theory: An Introduction*. Minneapolis.
Eagleton, Terry (2003): *After Theory*. New York.
Elliott, Jane, and Attridge, Derek, eds. (2011): *Theory after 'Theory'*. London/New York.
Felsch, Philipp (2015): *Der lange Sommer der Theorie: Geschichte einer Revolte, 1960–1990*. München.
Felski, Rita (2015): *The Limits of Critique*. Chicago/London.
Geisenhanslüke, Achim (2015): *Textkulturen: Literaturtheorie nach dem Ende der Theorie*. Paderborn.
Grizelj, Mario, and Jahraus, Oliver, eds. (2011): *Theorietheorie: Wider die Theoriemüdigkeit in den Geisteswissenschaften*. München.
Habib, Rafey (2008): *Modern Literary Criticism and Theory: A History*. Malden et al.
Harland, Richard (1999): *Literary Theory from Plato to Barthes: An Introductory History*. Basingstoke et al.
Horn, Eva (2022): Kittlers Rätselmaschine. Eine Kriminalgeschichte als Literaturmodell. In: *Zeitschrift für Ideengeschichte* 16, 101–110.
Hutcheon, Linda (1988): *A Poetics of Postmodernism: History, Theory, Fiction*. New York.
Jaeger, Stephan (2000): Postmodernes Lesevergnügen oder die Unlust des wissenschaftlichen Lesers: Umberto Ecos "Der Name der Rose". In: *Weimarer Beiträge* 46, 582–594.
Jahraus, Oliver, ed. (2002): *Kafkas "Urteil" und die Literaturtheorie: Zehn Modellanalysen*. Stuttgart.
Jahraus, Oliver (2011): Theorietheorie. In: Mario Grizelj and Oliver Jahraus, eds.: *Theorietheorie: Wider die Theoriemüdigkeit in den Geisteswissenschaften*. München, 17–39.
Kablitz, Andreas (2013): *Kunst des Möglichen: Theorie der Literatur*. Freiburg.
Klages, Mary (2017): *Literary Theory: The Complete Guide*. London et al.
Kreuzmair, Elias (2020): *Pop und Tod: Schreiben nach der Theorie*. Stuttgart.
Mersch, Dieter (1993): *Umberto Eco zur Einführung*. Hamburg.
Micskey, Koloman N. (1992): Zeichenräume des Geistes: Ecos Rosenroman als Zeichen der kairologischen Bestimmtheit geistiger und historischer Räume und der offenen Semiose. In: Wilfried Engemann and Rainer Volp, eds.: *Gib mir ein Zeichen: Zur Bedeutung der Semiotik für theologische Praxis- und Denkmodelle*. Berlin/New York, 123–146.
Müller Nielaba, Daniel, and Previšič, Boris (2010): Reflexion literarischer (Selbst-)Beobachtung: Skizzen zu einer radikalen Philologie. In: Boris Previšič, ed.: *Die Literatur der Literaturtheorie*. Bern et al., 9–19.

North, Joseph (2017): *Literary Criticism: A Concise Political History.* Cambridge/MA.

Nünning, Ansgar (2003): Die Rückkehr des sinnstiftenden Subjekts: Selbstreflexive Inszenierungen von historisierten Subjekten und subjektivierten Geschichten in britischen und postkolonialen historischen Romanen der Gegenwart. In: Stefan Deines et al., eds.: *Historisierte Subjekte – subjektivierte Historie: Zur Verfügbarkeit und Unverfügbarkeit von Geschichte.* Berlin, 239–261.

Olsen, Stein Haugom (1987): *The End of Literary Theory.* Cambridge et al.

Poppenberg, Gerhard (2018): *Herbst der Theorie: Erinnerungen an die alte Gelehrtenrepublik Deutschland.* Berlin.

Regn, Gerhard (1992): Postmoderne und Poetik der Oberfläche. In: Klaus W. Hempfer, ed.: *Poststrukturalismus – Dekonstruktion – Postmoderne.* Stuttgart, 52–74.

Rivkin, Julie, and Ryan, Michael (2017): *Literary Theory: An Anthology. Third edition.* Hoboken.

Ryan, Judith (2011): *The Novel After Theory.* New York.

Schick, Ursula (1989): Erzählte Semiotik oder intertextuelles Verwirrspiel? In: Burkhart Kroeber, ed.: *Zeichen in Umberto Ecos Roman "Der Name der Rose": Aufsätze aus Europa und Amerika.* München, 107–133.

Schilling, Erik (2012a): *Der historische Roman seit der Postmoderne: Umberto Eco und die deutsche Literatur.* Heidelberg.

Schilling, Erik (2012b): Umberto Eco zwischen Theorie und Literatur. In: Klaus Birnstiel and Erik Schilling, eds.: *Literatur und Theorie seit der Postmoderne. Mit einem Nachwort von Hans Ulrich Gumbrecht.* Stuttgart, 67–80.

Schilling, Erik (2021): "Der Name der Rose" ("Il nome della rosa"). In: Erik Schilling, ed.: *Umberto-Eco-Handbuch: Leben – Werk – Wirkung.* Stuttgart, 147–165.

Schwab, Michael et al., eds. (2014): *The Exposition of Artistic Research: Publishing Art in Academia.* Leiden.

Solte-Gresser, Christiane, and Schmeling, Manfred, eds. (2016): *Theorie erzählen. Raconter la théorie. Narrating theory: Fiktionalisierte Literaturtheorie im Roman.* Würzburg.

Sorensen, Eli Park (2010): *Postcolonial Studies and the Literary: Theory, Interpretation and the Novel.* Basingstoke et al.

Waugh, Patricia, ed. (2006): *Literary Theory and Criticism: An Oxford Guide.* Oxford et al.

Wellbery, David E., ed. (1985): *Positionen der Literaturwissenschaft: Acht Modellanalysen am Beispiel von Kleists "Das Erdbeben in Chili".* München.

Zima, Peter V. (2001): *Moderne – Postmoderne: Gesellschaft, Philosophie, Literatur.* Tübingen.

CHAPTER 2

Second-Order Literary Theory

This chapter offers ideas for a 'second-order' literary theory suited to the analysis of literary texts that work with literary theory. It looks at four aspects in order to identify the precise role of theory in literary texts: *how* is theory integrated into literature (*mode*)? *Where* in the texts are the elements of theory (*level*)? *Why* is theory integrated into literature (*function*)? And finally: *which* ideas developed in the literary text could be adopted in literary theory (*extrapolation*)? This conceptualization assumes a (potentially infinite) scale of observations: theory observes literature; literature observes theory observing literature; second-order literary theory observes literature observing theory observing literature, and so forth. Taken together, the four dimensions sketch out the steps necessary to understand better literary texts with elements of literary theory. While the discussion in the following is largely limited to literary theory, it would most likely work in an analogue way for other forms of theory as well.

With regard to the *mode*, elements of theory can be identified on a broad spectrum between a self-reflexive explicit mentioning of an intertextual relation in the text on the one hand and rather implicit similarities to another text or genre, (partially) constructed by the reader, on the other hand. In terms of the *level*, elements of theory can be used in a variety of

© The Author(s), under exclusive license to Springer Nature Switzerland AG 2024
E. Schilling, *Theorizing Literature*,
https://doi.org/10.1007/978-3-031-53326-6_2

conjunctions in the whole range of *histoire* and *discours*:[1] being narrated within clearly defined parts of the text, formed allegorically as a trait of a character, shaped as a particularity of the narrator or the literary form, etc. With regard to their *function*, elements of theory can be either simply presented, used for dynamizing the story, evaluated (in an affirmative, critical, or ironic way), or put into question in general by a focus on an immediate experience of the world that works without theory. At times, an *extrapolation* of theory from literature is possible: literary texts self-reflexively deal with the opportunities and limits of theory and contribute to debates in the field of theory by developing theoretical concepts or by providing answers to questions typically dealt with in theory. As a consequence, theory may also find inspiration in literature.

Sketching a second-order literary theory means providing tools for analyzing various forms of linking literature and theory together. Important elements of such a second-order literary theory are displayed in Fig. 2.1.

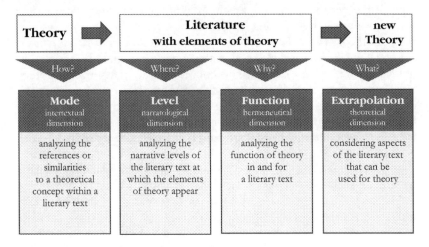

Fig. 2.1 The four dimensions of second-order literary theory (overview)

[1] In the following, I use the terms *histoire* and *discours* according to Genette (1980) and Genette (1982), who by *histoire* refers to the chronology of events told (a sequence of events) and by *discours* to the arrangement of events in the literary presentation (a sequence of signs). In the case studies, I also use 'story' and 'plot' (in an analogous function) for better readability in the English-language context. For a useful English introduction to narratology, see Bal (2017).

Reading for mode, level, function, and a possible extrapolation of theory in/from literature captures literary texts from various points of view. Looking at the mode raises questions of intertextuality. Analyzing the level deals with questions of structure and narratology. Asking for the function is related to a hermeneutical approach toward literature. And the extrapolation is part of working on theory itself.

By differentiating these elements and considering the conclusions they lead to, a second-order literary theory as proposed in this book arrives at a more precise and more organized way of (dealing with) theorizing literature. In addition, it contributes to a plural approach toward literature in general. In the following paragraphs, I provide an overview of mode, level, function, and extrapolation of theory within literature. Before doing so, however, I sketch a model of the observation process.

Modeling the Observation Process

This book is about observing and observations. It challenges the idea that there is an object to be observed (in this case: literature) and a neutral methodology or concept for the observation process (in this case: theory). Instead, the novels in question illustrate that there is no such clear boundary. Literature may take part in the theoretical discourse; theory may use narrative structures.

There are at least two ways of reacting to this interdependency of literature and theory. The first would be to renounce any differentiation between the two: theory observes literature, and literature observes theory; both, however, are presented as text and both may even be part of the same text (Fig. 2.2).

Should theory and literature coexist within the same textual framework, the question then arises: what necessitates their differentiation? One could regard it superfluous, given that all texts are simply that—texts. No less a scholar than Jürgen Habermas calls it an illusion to believe that Freud's and Joyce's texts can be sorted according to characteristics that inherently distinguish them as theory on the one hand and fiction on the other.[2] Such an argument holds merit, particularly because any act of categorization is a construct, fraught with simplifications and potential oversights. However, categorization remains an indispensable and efficacious tool in academic

[2] Habermas (1988, 243).

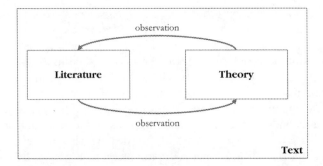

Fig. 2.2 Modeling the observation process (first alternative)

inquiry. In the absence of such categorical distinctions, we would lack the foundational concepts of genres, epochs, and thematic focuses that facilitate scholarly analysis and discussion.[3] Given that, the emphasis may shift from reconstructing essential characteristics of textual artifacts to understanding the epistemological implications of the categorization process itself.[4]

The second possible reaction to the unclear boundary between literature and theory in certain texts is to re-install the differentiation on a higher level. As Niklas Luhmann (among others) has shown,[5] the observer cannot be the object of the observation unless there is another observer observing the first observer—a second-order observation. I will argue that the literary texts discussed in this book operate just such a second-order observation: they observe theory, which itself works as an observer. As a consequence, this book ultimately takes the standpoint of a third-order observation: it observes literature observing theory observing literature. As this book analyzes literature that incorporates theory, its methodology may be termed second-order literary theory. Again, one may think of the

---

[3] Although I do agree with this first conceptualization—it is almost impossible to differentiate reliably between literature and theory—I consider some ideas of the second, now following a more promising one, because this approach relies on some basic procedures of literary analysis: it coins terms, concepts, and models that are not ontologically given, yet nonetheless helpful in describing certain phenomena.

[4] Accordingly, Michler (2015, 48–49) understands literary genres not as groups of texts with common characteristics, but classifications (groupings) of literary texts based on the attribution of common characteristics.

[5] Luhmann (1994).

film *Inception* for a very palpable illustration of such a multiply graded observation process.

Luhmann takes up a concept from George Spencer-Brown, elaborated in *Laws of Form*.[6] Spencer-Brown introduces the concept of re-entry for understanding the complexities of self-referential systems and distinctions. He elucidates how a distinction, once made, can be folded back into its own space, thereby introducing new levels of complexity. This process of re-entry serves as a theoretical framework that transcends simple binary oppositions, allowing for the examination of feedback loops and recursion in diverse domains ranging from mathematics to social systems. As an analytical concept, re-entry therefore allows for the investigation of the intertwined nature of self-reference and systemic complexity across various scientific and philosophical landscapes. Luhmann extends the concept beyond its mathematical origins to serve as a critical tool for analyzing social systems, capturing their ability to self-reproduce and self-regulate. The incorporation of re-entry into Luhmann's systems theory provides an analytical lens for interrogating self-referential social structures.

Following on from that, one may use the term 're-entry' to describe a specific phenomenon of the observation process: first, there is a differentiation between two or more categories (in this case: literature vs. theory). Second, the differentiation collapses when it is unable to describe certain phenomena usefully, especially that of the observation of the observer. Taking a different standpoint, though, the differentiation may re-enter the observation—and may also lead to new differentiations as a consequence of its re-entry.

The following model illustrates both the multiply graded observation process and the steps of differentiation, its collapse, and its re-entry. First, literature is observed using theoretical approaches. Theory, second, is observed by literature which incorporates elements of theory. Third, a second-order theory may be necessary for the analysis of theory-informed literature (and, of course, the process might be extended further by literary texts reacting to second-order theory, etc.). An observer observing theory analyzing literature operates from the difference of theory and literature. Literature integrating theory leads to a collapse of this differentiation. An observation of the respective literary texts from a different theoretical viewpoint (such as I will attempt in this book) may, however, lead to a 're-entry' of the differentiation (Fig. 2.3).

---

[6] Spencer-Brown (1969).

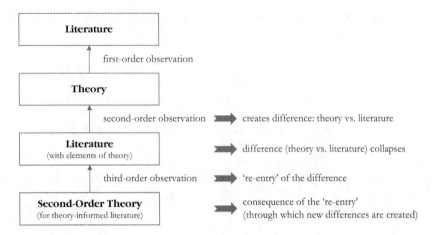

Fig. 2.3 Modeling the observation process (second alternative)

This conceptualization assumes a (potentially infinite) scale of observations: theory observes literature; literature observes theory observing literature; second-order theory observes literature observing theory observing literature, etc.[7] Either way, literature and theory do not form systemically separate spheres, but contain a series of interferences and feedbacks, resulting in a spiral of mutual influence, self-reflection, and modification. Depending on the observation at hand, the difference between literature and theory can collapse, be re-installed, collapse again, etc.

In the following, I propose theoretical patterns for such a potentially infinite scale of observations. In doing so, I offer ideas for how to deal with blind spots of theory in general and those of theory aiming at analyzing theory-informed texts in particular. If the integration of theory within literature is conceived of as proposed in this second model, then the differentiation between theory and literature is still operative—and it allows for a second-order theory to analyze literature containing elements of theory with regard to their mode, level, function, and a possible extrapolation of theory in/from literature.

---

[7] Agostini (2021, 16, 19) initially pursues a similar approach when she also speaks of a second-order theory that leads to an observation of an observation of an observation. In the following, however, her remarks concentrate on a meta-physics of literature (ibid., 26).

Modes of Theory in Literature

The first analytical step of dealing with theorizing literature is to look at the *mode* of theory in literature. This serves to identify theoretical texts that can be intertextually linked to the literary text in question and to differentiate various forms of references and/or similarities: where is the theoretical element from—and is this origin explicitly referred to (and maybe even explicated in its function), or does the reader require a certain knowledge in order to 'decipher' or even construct the implicit similarity?

The more the reader plays a crucial role in constructing an intertextual relation and ascribing a meaning to it, the more one could—as Jakob Lenz has proposed[8]—speak of *similarity* instead of *reference* (the latter implying a clearly identifiable quotation in the text or even a corresponding intention on part of the author). In contrast to the notion of reference, the concept of similarity serves as a more dynamic framework for capturing the relationships between texts. Unlike reference, which often implies a fixed, one-to-one correspondence, similarity operates on a continuum, accommodating a wider range of nuanced connections.

This can also be understood as increasingly adopting a comparative perspective on literary texts. A similarity between two texts can be intersubjectively proven, but it needs no evidence that the author intended it to be there. Yet this lack of evidence does not mean that diagnosing a similarity is less fruitful than following a reference; on the contrary, it can be even more enlightening, as it offers perspectives on the text that are not openly presented in it. However, it is an act of construction and as such it needs more argumentative foundation compared to staying with the explicit references. While explicit references to theory mostly allow for a clear differentiation between theory and literature, implicit similarities blur the boundaries between the two.[9]

Theory can be integrated into literature (and texts into other texts in general) in six ways, reaching from explicit references to implicit similarities (Fig. 2.4).

---

[8] Lenz and Schilling (2023, 94–95); see also Bhatti and Kimmich (2018).
[9] Cf. Wolf (1989, 20).

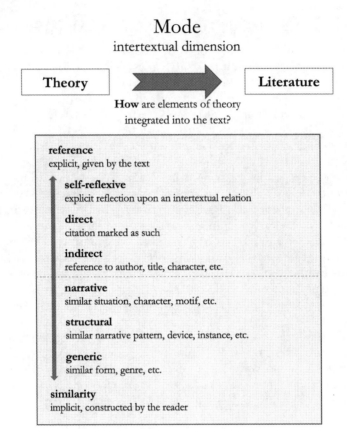

Fig. 2.4 Modes of theory within literature (*intertextual dimension*)

Self-Reflexive Reference: Explicit Reflection upon an Intertextual Relation

A *self-reflexive reference* is the most obvious form of an intertextual relation: it is marked and self-reflexively broached as an issue. In addition to forming a direct reference (the following form of intertextuality), a self-reflexive reference means some way of speaking about the fact that (and possibly how and why) a certain text is referred to. It is self-reflexive as the reference is not only there and laid open, but also spoken about in its function and making. This form of intertextuality may, therefore, enable the reader to learn something about the use of intertextuality in general—which is particularly interesting in the context of novels that deal with theory themselves. Among the texts analyzed in the following, Laurent Binet's *The 7th Function of Language* presents various concepts of literary theory, explicitly quoting, systematically locating and reflecting upon them.

Direct Reference: Citation Marked as Such

A *direct reference* is probably the most common way of integrating one text into another. A citation forms part of a text and is marked as such, mentioning its original context (author, text, source in general, etc.). This is standard in academic works, but also in some literary texts that disclose their sources and the material on which they are based, whether in the form of footnotes or in an appendix listing the texts used.[10] In contrast to a self-reflexive reference, however, there is 'just' the reference and its source, no further reflections upon the particular way the reference works or its function for the text it is integrated in. In her novel *Identitti*, for example, Mithu Sanyal uses several direct citations from theoretical works, providing full bibliographical information in an appendix.

Indirect Reference: Reference to Author, Title, Character, etc.

An *indirect reference* works with a clear denomination of an intertextual source as well, but it can be considered less detailed than a direct reference; just a mention of Shakespeare (without further details of a particular work or even line), for instance, or a reference to Odysseus or the *Odyssey*, without specifying what particular aspect of the character or the text is referred to. Thus, a gradual move toward a more active role of the recipients in ascribing a certain function to a reference (or, as in the following, similarity) is to be noted. Whereas in the case of self-reflexive or direct references, the source, the extent of the adoption, and its function are rather openly presented, in the case of an indirect reference there is a hint to a certain author or text, but no further specification—which, as a consequence, may become part of the readers' activities. In her novel *Hallucinating Foucault*, for example, Patricia Duncker works with various indirect references, alluding to Michel Foucault in the novel's title and story.

---

[10] This is what Pfister (1985) in a classical contribution to the debate on intertextuality calls 'Einzeltextreferenz', meaning a reference to one particular other text.

Narrative Similarity: Situation, Character, Motif, etc.

A *narrative similarity* can be noted between two texts regarding certain characters, situations, or constellations. For example, a novel in which a character commits adultery can be seen in an intertextual comparison to other texts about adultery, and, by identifying similarities and differences to these other texts, one can arrive at interpretive hypotheses on the text in question—and, potentially, also on the other texts. In this case, the similarity is usually noted on the diegetic level:[11] it may be a situation, character, etc. similar to the one narrated in another text. Ulrike Draesner's novel *Dowry*, for example, acts out the situation of a non-binary person as reflected upon in various texts of gender studies.

Structural Similarity: Narrative Pattern, Device, Instance, etc.

If the similarity is not (limited to) a specific diegetic situation, character, or constellation, but a fundamental aspect of the text in question, one can speak of a *structural similarity*. Such a similarity can be seen in a general 'building plan' of a literary text or certain narrative schemes. For example, a text may be narrated as a stream of consciousness similar to Molly's in the final chapter of James Joyce's *Ulysses*. Such an intertextual connection between a specific text and a fundamental pattern or narrative scheme is already an ascription on the part of the reader. Thus, the reader has to justify the link created by making it part of an interpretation that underlines the use of seeing the two texts in comparison. Whether or not the author thought of the same link while writing the text is irrelevant, for two reasons: first, it cannot be proven (even if the author says so, it might be a false memory or a lie); second, it is not relevant, as the gain of constructing an intertextual similarity is not to retrace some procedure in writing the novel but to use the similarity for a convincing interpretation of one (or both) text(s). Among the texts analyzed in the following, Daniel Kehlmann's novel *F* presents various forms of authorship (as narrative schemes) similar to concepts of authorship debated in theory.

---

[11] For the terminology of the various diegetic levels (exodiegetic, diegetic, and peridiegetic), see the following paragraph ('Levels of Theory in Literature').

Generic Similarity: Form, Genre, etc.

The ascription of a *generic similarity* is even more an act of interpretation than those of highlighting a narrative or structural one. It means that a text in big parts or even as a whole is compared to another text as an integral artwork—or even to a series of texts, such as a genre. For example, a text can be seen as generically similar to the scheme of the ancient Greek tragedy. While there have been vivid debates about whether or not genres are an entity existing per se or rather as constructs,[12] I argue for the latter, as the choice of picking certain aspects as fundamental for a specific genre (e.g., fourteen verses for a sonnet) is already an act of interpretation.[13] As a consequence, the integration of one specific text into a genre[14] also means constructing an intertextual similarity. It is not justified in itself, but useful only if made the starting point for an interpretation of a certain text (and other texts the specific one is intertextually linked to). Such a generic similarity can be noted for Italo Calvino's *If on a Winter's Night a Traveler*: the novel eliminates the 'whole' of a literary text, taking up the main ideas of deconstruction.

Overview of the Literary Texts in Terms of the Modes of Theory

To sum up, the intertextual references and/or similarities between theory and literature can be categorized from explicit self-reflexive references to ascribed generic similarities. Focusing on relevant contemporary novels, this is displayed in Table 2.1. With regard to theorizing literature in particular, the categorization of different intertextual connections proves useful as different consequences arise that impact the interpretation of the literary text (and a possible extrapolation of theory from it), depending on how the theory is integrated into it.

---

[12] The most famous extremes are probably the nihilistic standpoint of Croce (1902), who in a book on aesthetics renounces genres altogether, and the structuralist perspective of Hempfer (1973), who gives detailed criteria for which genres to differentiate and why.

[13] For an overview, a systematic reconstruction and a plea to understand genres as habitualized classification acts, see Michler (2015).

[14] This is what Pfister (1985, 52–53) calls 'Systemreferenz', meaning a reference (or rather 'similarity') between a single text and a 'system' of other texts, mostly that of a genre the text can be ascribed to.

Table 2.1 Examples for different modes of theory in literature

Mode	Example
Self-reflexive reference	*Binet*: presents various concepts of literary theory, (historically) locating and reflecting upon them
Direct reference	*Sanyal*: gives direct citations from theoretical works, providing full bibliographical information
Indirect reference	*Duncker*: alludes to Michel Foucault's name in the novel's title and story
Narrative similarity	*Draesner*: acts out the situation of a non-binary person as reflected upon in texts of gender studies
Structural similarity	*Kehlmann*: presents various forms of authorship similar to concepts of authorship debated in theory
Generic similarity	*Calvino*: eliminates the 'whole' of a literary text, taking up the main ideas of deconstruction

LEVELS OF THEORY IN LITERATURE

The second step of a second-order literary theory is to describe the position of an element of theory (identified by an intertextual comparison) within the literary text, with regard to the *level* it is situated at: is it, for example, referred to in a dialogue between characters? Does a character serve as an allegorical personification of theory? Does a similarity to a certain theory carry broader implications for narrative elements, for example, narrator or implied reader? Does the text offer any particularities in its form that may be linked to some theory?

Preliminary Remark: On the Various Diegetic Levels

In the following, I use the terms 'exodiegetic', 'diegetic', and 'endodiegetic' to differentiate the different narrative levels of a text, instead of Genette's terms 'extradiegetic', 'intradiegetic', and 'metadiegetic'.[15] Despite Genette's terminology being well established, it comes with three problems. It is not clear which level the differentiation starts from, and while there is just one step out of the intradiegetic level

[15] Intradiegetic (or diegetic) refers to the basic level of narration, extradiegetic is the level of the narrator, and metadiegetic is a narration within the narration on the (intra-)diegetic level. For details on these terms, see Genette (1980) and Genette (1982).

(extradiegetic), there is a potentially unlimited number of sub-narratives (metadiegetic, meta-metadiegetic, etc.). Moreover, '*meta*-diegetic' linguistically implies a change of perspective, from the inside of the text to seeing it from the outside, which is not the case in Genette's use of the term.

In contrast, I propose to call the level of a text where the main story of the narration is set *diegetic*. Determining this diegetic level is already an act of interpretation. Once the diegetic level is determined, one may find an unlimited number of *exo-* and *endodiegetic* levels above or below the diegetic one: on a first exodiegetic level, there may be a narrator, on a second one, there may be a (fictitious) editor, on a third one an implied author, etc. The same holds true for the endodiegetic levels: if a character on the diegetic level tells a story, there is a first endodiegetic level. In this, there may be a second endodiegetic level, and so forth. Both the exo- and endodiegetic levels may also be non-existent. A textual level that is completely detached from any diegetic aspect can be called *peridiegetic*.[16] Texts that accompany the narrative but are clearly separate from it can be called *paradiegetic*, following Genette's concept of 'paratext'. Moreover, in some circumstances, the text may actually contain a *metadiegetic* position: a narrative perspective that intersects one or more diegetic levels and provides a meta-commentary on them.

In any case, looking at the endo-/exodiegetic levels around a diegetic level defined in the interpretation allows for a clearer narratological grasp of the text. This also has the advantage of using just Greek-based terminology and just one metaphoric dimension (the three spatial aspects of one place with an inside and an outside) instead of Genette's mixing of languages (Latin and Greek) and concepts (logically, 'extra' and 'intra' stand on the same 'horizontal' level, whilst 'meta' implies jumping onto a different 'vertical' level). The analysis of the text along these structural-narratological dimensions can be visualized as follows (Fig. 2.5).

---

[16] The peridiegetic level of the text is built 'around' the narrative ('peri' being 'around' in Greek), referring to formal aspects. Using the term this way underlines the proximity of the peridiegetic level to Genette's concept of *discours* ('dis-currere' in Latin, meaning 'to run around'). Lang (2014, 369), in contrast, calls 'peridiegetic' narrators those who "are marked by the fact that they cannot have been involved in the event".

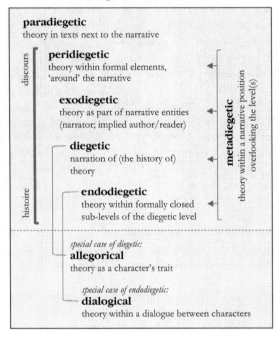

Fig. 2.5 Levels of theory within literature (*narratological dimension*)

Paradiegetic: Theory in Text Next to the Narrative

As noted in Chapter 1, the occupation of literary texts with theory begins in the paratexts: on their covers, in their blurbs, or in other material provided by authors, editors, or publishers. This can be seen as a 'paradiegetic' level of the text itself: in the paratext there is a narrative in its own right, but it is completely detached from the diegetic level of the book in question. Therefore, to integrate theory into a paratext is to use theory in a narrative way (and not in a formal way, as in the case of the peridiegetic level). For example, the English blurb for Eco's *Foucault's Pendulum* promises a "multi-layered semiotic adventure" that integrates theory into one of the novel's paratexts. Although the blurb is usually a very brief summary of the book, it can be seen as a narrative in its own right, into which theory is integrated.

Peridiegetic: Theory Within Formal Elements, 'Around' the Narrative

Some reflections on theory can be seen within *peridiegetic* elements of a certain text.[17] Such formal representations of theory are almost always implicit when it comes to *discours*. Nonetheless, they represent a preoccupation with theory, especially when formally executing a concept the corresponding theory describes. If, for instance, deconstructivist theory pursues the idea that there is no fixed center for narratives in particular and the construction of meaning in general, this idea is taken up, and executed by, novels that renounce a formally closed story by presenting fragmentary beginnings of stories without ever concluding them. Such an integration of theory into peridiegetic elements of the literary text can be noted for Calvino's *If on a Winter's Night* and its presentation of different novel beginnings. It can be considered a similarity to deconstructivist theory.

Exodiegetic: Theory as Part of Narrative Entities (Narrator, Implied Author/Reader)

On an 'intermediate' level between form and content, elements of theory can be part of *exodiegetic* patterns of the literary text, such as (implied) author, narrator, or (implied) reader.[18] Post-structuralist or deconstructivist ideas challenging the established narratological categories offer fertile ground for novels that themselves 'de-construct', for example, by questioning the notions of author or narrator as useful categories for analysis and interpretation. Texts expanding the power of the narrative to

---

[17] This is a narrative device that has also been used in earlier forms of literature. For example, theoretically informed texts of early Romanticism in German literature work with the idea of the fragment as a structuring force (Ceserani and Zanotti 2008).

[18] On the implied author/reader, see Booth (1961).

encompass the whole world may be considered an illustration of Derrida's famous postulation of the non-existent outside of the text. Christoph Ransmayr's *The Last World*, for instance, undertakes such a deconstruction of (implied) author and reader in favor of an all-embracing text.

Diegetic: Narration of (the History of) Theory

Probably the most common way in which theory can become part of a literary text is found on its *diegetic* level: through the narration of theory. Texts may place crucial (historical) figures, representing various forms of theory, among their casts of characters, or build a narrative around (the history of) important theoretical concepts. In narratives that offer a diegetic presentation of theory, theory is dealt with as a topic, just as any other (historical) topic might form the basis of a story. In this context, a narrative about inventing deconstruction is not functionally different from a narrative about inventing the theory of relativity. It does not necessarily (yet may) have implications for theory itself: Derrida can be the protagonist of a historical novel just like Einstein. Nonetheless, there is a chance that a literary text dealing with the history of theory will integrate theory on other levels of the narrative as well. The most prominent case of such a narration of theory is Binet's *7th Function of Language*, in which historical figures (Derrida, Foucault, Kristeva, etc.) appear as characters of the novel.

Endodiegetic: Theory Within Formally Closed Sub-Parts

An *endodiegetic* presentation of theory is an integration of theory into narratively closed sub-levels of the story (Genette would call these metadiegetic). This holds for structurally isolated elaborations on theory, for example, a talk given by one of the characters or a document dealing with theory that is integrated into the story as a whole. The talk can be understood as a new diegesis within the diegetic world of the narrative and thus an endodiegetic presentation of theory. This way of integrating theory into literature is probably the most obvious one and, at the same time, the one with the least problematic consequences for a differentiation between literature and theory. Endodiegetic theory usually 'remains' theory within literature, without raising questions as to the usefulness of the conceptional differences between the text genres. The characteristics of theory often do not change when theory is presented in a clearly defined part of literature.

In David Lodge's *Small World*, for example, one of the characters gives a lecture on deconstruction at an academic conference—this can be considered an endodiegetic presentation of theory in the context of the novel.

Metadiegetic: Theory Within a Narrative Position Overlooking the Level(s)

Finally, some texts may contain a *metadiegetic* position created by a narrative voice that steps out of the exo-/endo-/diegetic hierarchy in order to reflect upon it.[19] Such a position provides a meta-perspective: within its realm, one might encounter a narrator, commentator, or recipient who approaches the unfolding story from a detached point of view—the story either on all its diegetic levels or on particular ones. This metadiegetic position reflects upon or criticizes the mechanisms of storytelling on one or more diegetic levels, thereby adding a complex, multi-layered dimension to the text. Moreover, it potentially destabilizes the conventional hierarchies of narrative authority, questioning the assumptions and constructions underlying the text and its reception. For example, Jan Wagner's poetry collection *The Owl Haters in the Hall Houses* provides—within the realm of the literary text—a commentary on its poems, ironically questioning both the poems and theoretical approaches toward them.

The aforementioned categories cover all the levels of a narrative text. Nonetheless, I propose two sub-categories for special (very frequent) cases of presenting theory in literature, the first one on the diegetic level, the second one on the endodiegetic level.

Allegorical: Theory as a Character's Trait

The first is probably the most amusing form of presenting theory in literature: in an *allegorical* form, that is, built into a character's traits. For example, a character 'standing for' hermeneutics might look for a reason in everything. A structuralist might analyze everything with regard to underlying patterns. A gender theorist might see manifestations of gender roles

---

[19] This would be metadiegetic in the actual sense of 'meta', not in Genette's sense of a sub-level, but providing a narrative perspective that intersects the other diegetic levels—at a perpendicular angle, if you will.

in every instance of human interaction. And a deconstructivist might consider the whole world as one big game. If theory is allegorically presented as a character's trait, it may become quite palpable—leaving broad scope for amusing interactions between different theoretical approaches, such as two concepts competing in theory falling in love as personifications. In addition, an allegorical presentation of theory allows for certain aspects of theory to be understood by the actions associated with them, thereby breaking down theory into 'the real'. Draesner's *Dowry*, for example, features an intersex character representing central questions of gender studies, such as the difference between sex and gender and the existence of more than just two genders/sexes.

Dialogical: Theory Within a Dialogue Between Characters

The second special case is a *dialogical* presentation of theory within literature: a dialogue between characters that contains elements of theory, especially two (or more) competing theories. This dialogical presentation of theory may evolve in an argumentative debate, be it (explicitly) in the form of an academic dispute, or (rather implicitly) in the form of two (or more) characters elaborating arguments that go back to a particular theory without explicitly stating that their discussion is based on theory at all. The arguments of the debate form a diegesis of its own. Correspondingly, the process is the same as for endodiegetic theory: theory enters literature within a clearly defined unit of the narrative, not as an overall phenomenon. Duncker's *Hallucinating Foucault*, for example, has its protagonists discuss various elements of Foucault's discourse analysis, with some characters arguing in favor of the importance of authors for their works and others disputing that.

Overview of the Literary Texts in Terms of the Levels of Theory

Table 2.2 provides an overview of the literary texts to be discussed in this book with regard to the level on which theory is most prevalent within the text (although the texts in question often contain elements of theory on more than one level). As such, each text can serve as an example of a particular level of theory in literature.

Table 2.2 Examples for different levels of theory in literature

Level	Example
Paradiegetic	*Eco*: promises a "multi-layered semiotic adventure" in the novel's blurb, hinting at theory even outside the narrative
Peridiegetic	*Calvino*: presents different novel beginnings in combination with respective reader types
Exodiegetic	*Ransmayr*: deconstructs (implied) author and reader in favor of an all-embracing text
Diegetic	*Binet*: has historical figures (Foucault, Kristeva, etc.) among his cast of characters
Endodiegetic	*Lodge*: integrates a lecture on deconstruction by a specific character at an academic conference
Metadiegetic	*Wagner*: provides a commentary on poems which contains various theoretical perspectives
Allegorical	*Draesner*: shows an intersex character representing questions of gender studies
Dialogical	*Duncker*: has the protagonists discuss various elements of Foucault's discourse analysis

FUNCTIONS OF THEORY IN LITERATURE

The third step of a second-order literary theory is to understand the *function* of theory in a literary text. Whereas the level essentially encompasses the form or structural tier at which the theory becomes part of a literary text, its function pertains to the specific objectives or goals of theory within literature. This is a hermeneutical perspective: what kind of interpretive processes and premises are shown? What do the elements of theory add to or effect for the story? Are the elements of theory presented with a certain attitude, for example, in an affirmative or critical way? Is there a move away from theory toward a pre- or post-theoretical world?

Four functions of theory within literature can be differentiated: a presentation, a dynamization, an evaluation, and a rejection of theory. Quite often, these evolve from each other, in the form of a circle or spiral (if theory is modified): at first, there is just a presentation of theory, which then leads to a dynamization of the story. At some point, theory is evaluated, be it by a character, narrator, or others. This may lead to its rejection—which, then, leaves room for other or new theories to come into the novel (Fig. 2.6).

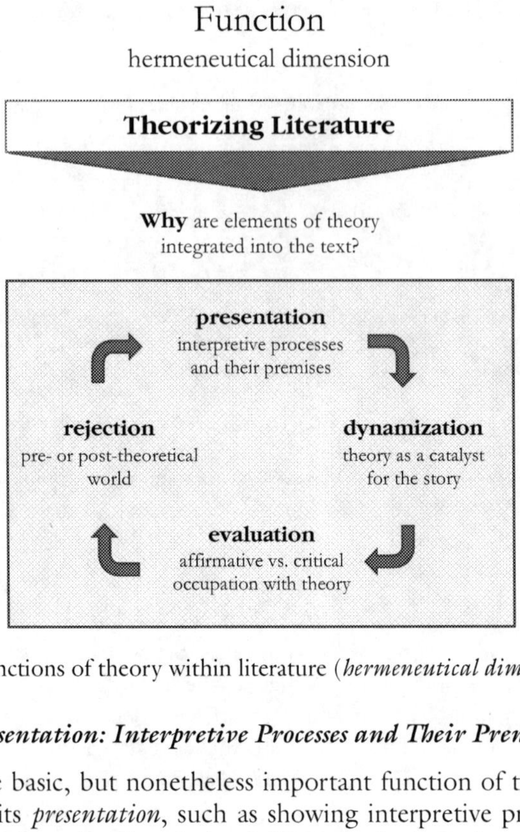

Function
hermeneutical dimension

Theorizing Literature

Why are elements of theory integrated into the text?

presentation
interpretive processes and their premises

rejection
pre- or post-theoretical world

dynamization
theory as a catalyst for the story

evaluation
affirmative vs. critical occupation with theory

Fig. 2.6 Functions of theory within literature (*hermeneutical dimension*)

Presentation: Interpretive Processes and Their Premises

A first, quite basic, but nonetheless important function of theory within literature is its *presentation*, such as showing interpretive processes (and their premises) on the diegetic level. If so, the basic business of theory—providing a methodology for the analysis and interpretation of (literary) texts or phenomena in general—is mirrored in the diegetic world. The function of theory in literature is thus not only to present its conceptual character, but also its actual practice and functioning (and, potentially, its limitations). This might be used in terms of an extrapolation of theory: for applying a 'praxeological' perspective, as has been discussed recently,[20] to 'doing theory' in particular.

---

[20] For example, by Martus and Spoerhase (2022).

Within a literary text, there may be, for example, a fictitious text for which one of the characters provides interpretive hypotheses according to explicit or implicit theoretical premises, or the interpretive process may be presented in relation to a non-textual phenomenon (as in a detective story). In any case, the interpretive process forms part of the story. As a consequence, someone approaching the novel using literary theory may be confronted with the functional question: what does the presentation of an interpretive process within a literary text mean for a theoretically informed interpretation of the text itself?

In David Lodge's *Small World*, for example, the protagonist's hunt for the woman he imagines himself in love with can be understood as a hermeneutical perspective on readers hunting for a particular sense in texts. Umberto Eco's *Foucault's Pendulum* shows its characters performing different interpretations of the same text, presenting the implicit or explicit assumptions the interpretations are based on. And in Laurent Binet's *The 7th Function of Language*, two characters try to decode a cryptic sentence by applying different theoretical concepts to it. In all these cases, there is a presentation of theory that can be analyzed in its function for the text as a whole—and, as a consequence, also for further considerations on theory itself.

Dynamization: Theory as a Catalyst for the Story

The second function of theory in literature lies in its shaping the narrative arc: a *dynamization*. In this context, theory serves not merely as a passive framework, but as an active catalyst that propels the plot forward. Theory offers the literary text a framework that it can explore within its diegetic world. Whether grappling with the post-structuralist notion of 'killing the author' as an organizational principle or contemplating a society unshackled from gender and racial categorizations, novels can function as experimental spaces. These narrative laboratories allow for the integration of theoretical concepts into lived experience, thus offering insights into their applicability or limitations in the real world. Theory serves as the nucleus around which such an explorative narrative is constructed, providing both depth and direction to the text.

I have already pointed to the symbiotic relationship between literary theory and the detective genre in particular. Literary theory supplies conceptual tools that enable the formulation of hypotheses aimed at organizing various phenomena in a coherent manner. Similarly, the investigator in a detective story employs a methodological approach to synthesize disparate pieces of evidence into a compelling hypothesis about the perpetrator. Hence, the utilization of theory serves to invigorate and structure the narrative of the crime plot.

This dynamization through theory is most evident in Binet's *7th Function of Language*. Without theory as a catalyst, the story would not develop at all. The novel would lack Jakobson's functions of language, which are at the center of the scavenger hunt that many characters undertake; it would lack Roland Barthes's suffering an actual 'death of the author' in addition to the metaphorical death he proclaimed; it would lack the methodological foundations for the debating duels in the secret rhetoric club. Theory, in other words, brings dynamics to the novel; it provides central patterns, leads to various complications in the diegetic world, and also leaves room for solving the mazes it has previously created.

Patricia Duncker's *Hallucinating Foucault* would not work without theory as a catalyst either. Michel Foucault's theoretical writings provide a key dynamic to almost every level and plot line of the novel. In the realm of Duncker's fiction, the author Paul Michel would not have written his novels without Foucault. Similarly, without Foucault's theories, the narrator and his girlfriend would not have been able to argue about the difference between author and author-function—and thus would not have advanced the plot in the first place. And without Foucault, there would be no theoretical basis for the various facets of the relationship between the narrator and the author Paul Michel—a relationship that can be seen as the core of the novel around which the narrative experiment unfolds.

Finally, Mithu Sanyal's novel *Identitti* also draws its key dynamic from theory. The scandal at the center of the novel—a seemingly Indian professor of postcolonial studies turning out to be white—would lose much of its controversial potential if it were not grounded in the various facets of critical race theory. Again, theory provides a basic idea around which the narrative revolves and from which it draws the issues it addresses. Moreover, in the case of *Identitti*, theory also dynamizes the plot in the long run, since much of the novel recounts the debates over the scandal, debates that are substantially grounded in theory.

In summary, the dynamization of literature through theory extends beyond mere intellectual ornamentation or background context—which the presentation of theory may be seen as. Theory not only provides the intellectual scaffolding that shapes a story's plot, but also furnishes the narrative with conceptual or ethical dilemmata. This creates a reciprocal relationship between theory and narrative, each stimulating the other in a symbiotic loop. The circular or spiral layout of the four functional aspects underlines this. Thus, the engagement with theory emerges as a dynamic component in the literary experiment, guiding the narrative structure and enriching the thematic depth, while simultaneously extending the boundaries of theoretical discourse itself.

Evaluation: Affirmative vs. Critical Presentation of Theory

The third function of theory in literature consists in the *evaluation* of theory. Corresponding questions include: are the elements of theory built into the text affirmatively, neutrally, or critically? Are there several ways of dealing with theory, in the case of integrating theory as a character's trait, for instance? Is one theory—if handled critically—replaced by another?

Literature is not bound to academic procedures and may therefore eschew logical arguments for dealing with theory in favor of more literary ways such as irony or ambiguity. In terms of an evaluation of theory within literature, this becomes particularly useful: whereas, for example, describing authorship from a theoretical point of view requires clearly defined concepts and terms, the literary presentation of authorship may be characterized by plurality with various (and even contradictory) forms of authorship being valid at the same time.

In its observation of theory, literature can also illustrate the limits of a certain theory—limits arising from the necessary simplification of any conceptual model. At the same time, literature demonstrates what specific theoretical concepts mean for literature: it can, for example, exemplify the consequences of the 'death of the author' for a diegetic world. In doing so, literature does not only criticize or ironize theory, but also embraces theory for its own purposes in an affirmative way.

The detailed analysis of literary texts undertaken in this book reveals various forms of an evaluation of theory. Binet's *7th Function of Language* confronts semiotics and deconstruction as both a methodology of dealing with a literary text and an attitude toward the world in general. The novel demonstrates a preference for the construction of meaning and, therefore, for interpretation—as long as the interpretation is grounded in a careful consideration of context. The same is true for Jan Wagner's collection of poems augmented by various interpretive tools (glossary, commentary, etc.). Some of these means of interpretation are presented as helpful (as semiotics in Binet's novel), while others are put into an ironic perspective (such as deconstruction in Binet's case).

Christoph Ransmayr's *The Last World* reduces the importance of author and reader in favor of an all-embracing text. It is, therefore, difficult to interpret the text from a distanced, academic point of view; the reader becomes a participant in its literary game, as part of the text. Lodge's *Small World* takes an ironic stance toward the theories allegorically personified by its characters—and can thus be understood to take a critical approach toward theory in general. Yet the novel does not deny the value of theory entirely; it offers a rather playful perspective on theory as a worldview that takes itself too seriously. Daniel Kehlmann's *F*, finally, presents a critical and, at the same time, affirmative stance toward theories of authorship. On the one hand, the novel shows the limits of authorship attribution, revealing, for example, discrepancies between real and attributed authorships. On the other hand, the novel reaffirms the power of the author as a figure able to create fictional worlds for people to believe in.

All in all, literature building on literary theory often does not do so in a strictly neutral way. Usually, a certain attitude with regard to the theory presented can be identified, be it through certain characters, through the role of a narrative entity, or through the story itself (e.g., by one theory proving more powerful than another). Therefore, a second-order literary theory describing the function of theory in literature must identify the various perspectives through which the elements of theory are viewed.

Rejection: Postulation of a Pre- or Post-Theoretical World

A fourth function of theory in literature can be a critical stance toward theory altogether: a *rejection* of theory. In contrast to an evaluation of theory, this does not entail a critical position toward a specific methodology or concept, but toward theory in general. Is theory necessary for a better understanding of texts (and the world) at all? Or should one aim for conceptual frameworks that are more intuitive and less hermeneutically focused?

Hans Ulrich Gumbrecht brought forward such an idea in his book on *The Production of Presence*, in which he looks at forms of reception that take place before any analytical, rational, and/or hermeneutical processes have occurred.[21] The approach offered by Gumbrecht can prove useful for

---

[21] Gumbrecht (2004); see also Gumbrecht (2012).

understanding several texts analyzed here. They offer a resigned outlook on the role of theory, particularly when it falls short in capturing the nuances of reality or becomes ensnared in an endless loop of mutual reflexivity between literature and theoretical discourse. This criticizes the limitations inherent in theoretical frameworks, questioning their capacity to fully comprehend or represent the complexities of the lived experience.

Lodge's *Small World* has its character Morris Zapp identify with a number of theoretical approaches one after another, before ultimately turning toward a non-theoretical worldview. Shaken by a kidnapping and brush with death, Zapp wants to experience the world 'as it is', without any theory mediating his perception. Similarly, Umberto Eco's protagonist in *Foucault's Pendulum* sees a pre-hermeneutic, sensual experience as the only chance of getting out of a game of interpretations over which he has lost control. For him, the only way to stop the infinite (and destructive) chain of ascribing meaning to phenomena is 'just' to experience them without trying to interpret them. Ulrike Draesner's *Dowry*, too, presents the limits of theory by confronting it with 'real world experience'. In her case, the protagonist feels their being intersex as an existential condition that cannot be coped with by describing it in theoretical terms.

All these texts, therefore, opt for an interruption of the vicious circle of infinite interpretations. They proclaim a way of accessing the world which works without theory. Again, this is a solution that literary texts are arguably better equipped to provide than theoretical ones. If theory wanted (as, for example, in Gumbrecht's case) to explain non-rational experiences of the world, it would nevertheless be forced to use rational instruments to describe them (the terms, concepts, etc. that constitute a theoretical approach). Yet to theoretically describe an experience that exists *before* any application of theory is in itself a paradox, one that can be 'solved' by literature working with elements of theory. These texts are able to build on a theoretical basis to illustrate such a paradox, without losing the capacity to describe experiences in a way that does not rely on theoretical instruments at all. Thus, a critical reflection upon theory in literature may strive away from theory and toward a pre- or post-theoretical world.

Overview of the Literary Texts in Terms of the Functions of Theory

As an overview, Table 2.3 links these different types of functional reflections on theory to the novels discussed in the case studies:

Table 2.3 Examples for different functions of theory in literature

Function	Example
Presentation of theory	*Eco:* considering the correct interpretation of a 'secret message'
	Lodge: integrating interpretive processes into the story
	Binet: trying to decode a cryptic message by applying different theoretical concepts to it
Dynamization of theory	*Binet:* integrating theoretical patterns (functions of language, death of the author, etc.) brings forward the plot
	Duncker: harking back to Foucault's theories provides the narrative quandaries the novel evolves from
	Sanyal: grounding the central dilemma in critical race theory gives room for the narrated debates and conflicts
Evaluation of theory	*Binet:* confronting semiotics and deconstruction
	Wagner: ironizing certain perspectives on literature
	Ransmayr: deconstructing the importance of author and reader
	Lodge: presenting allegorical characters that live theory in various (and ironized) ways
	Kehlmann: questioning the role of the author
Rejection of theory	*Lodge:* leaving theory behind altogether
	Eco: focusing on a pre-theoretical experience
	Draesner: limiting theory by confronting it with 'real world experience'

EXTRAPOLATION OF THEORY FROM LITERATURE

The fourth and final step of a second-order literary theory is to analyze elements of theory within literature that may themselves be understood as innovative contributions to theory: does the literary text present conceptual ideas for theory and thereby contribute to the academic discourse? These ideas may serve as a creation of theory within literature and be *extrapolated* from there. In this case, the theoretical discourse must not be understood as limited to so-called theoretical texts, but as pervading different text genres, including literature. There are good arguments for not limiting discussions about theory to theoretical texts: why should literature not be able to offer convincing frameworks for approaching notions of authorship or semiotic processes? Are there not ways of presenting concepts that simply cannot be achieved through common academic methods (as is the case with irony or ambiguity)?

Two forms of an extrapolation of theory from literature can be differentiated, a metaization and a creation of theory (Fig. 2.7).

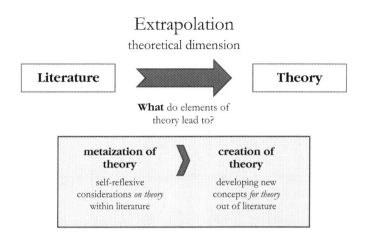

Fig. 2.7 Extrapolation of theory from literature (*theoretical dimension*)

Metaization of Theory: Self-Reflexive Considerations on Theory

A first form of extrapolation of theory from literature can be based on meta-theoretical, self-reflexive forms of theory in the text: a *metaization* of theory. The allegorical or the endodiegetic presentation of theory discussed previously do not necessarily indicate a self-reflexive stance toward the theories in question. If, for example, the characters do not show any awareness of their representing some specific theoretical approach, they may be said to live out a theory without self-reflexively realizing it. The same is true for interpretive processes being represented without questioning their premises or implicit assumptions. In both (and other) cases, however, a self-reflexive presentation of theory may also appear—one that does not only apply theory, but also questions the premises that underpin its application. Such approaches display a critical, self-conscious attitude toward (the literary integration of) theory that can have consequences for an extrapolation of theoretical ideas from the literary text.

A theoretical approach interested in the process of interpretation and its underlying premises could productively use the series of interpretations performed in Umberto Eco's *Foucault's Pendulum*. Presenting different interpretations of a text following various interpretive methods, the novel self-reflexively illustrates the limits of interpretation. An interpretation can be too broadly oriented (thus arbitrary) or too narrow (thus ignoring important options of understanding the text), or 'simple', as Eco puts it in the novel (following an economical approach that aims at an apt complexity of interpretation for the relative text). A theory of interpretation can build on these critically differentiated forms of interpretation in the novel—just as Eco himself does in his theoretical book on *The Limits of Interpretation*.[22]

A theory of fictionality, too, could use ideas developed in texts that self-reflexively work with literary theory. Juli Zeh's *Dark Matter* offers an analogy between the construction of multiple worlds in quantum physics and the multiple worlds of narration. In doing so, Zeh comes to understand fiction by its ability to offer a plurality of options at the same time. While a fictional text presents a limited number of options on the one hand (specific narrative spaces, specific characters, etc.), on the other, it hints at the fact that everything could be different—because the text is nothing more than a construct. A theory of fiction working with this idea could, therefore, view fiction as the result of a negotiation process in which both determination and contingency play an important role.

Creation of Theory: Developing New Concepts for Theory

Finally, there is no reason to exclude literary texts as original contributions to theory: to see them as a room for the *creation* of theory. An innovative concept of authorship can well be based on suggestions made in theory *and* in literature. As a consequence, literary texts should be taken seriously as 'participants' in debates about theory—(new) theory can build on literature just as it builds on existing theoretical concepts.

Out of the texts discussed in this study, one could start from Patricia Duncker's *Hallucinating Foucault* to elaborate a modified concept of authorship. Duncker's novel uses Foucault's replacement of authorship with the author-function (an ascription without any bearing on interpretation), but shows that, from certain perspectives, it may be

[22] Eco (1990). For a detailed analysis, see Schilling (2012).

fruitful for the role of the author to be re-established. Taking up Duncker's considerations in a theoretical debate about authorship might, therefore, lead to a modified understanding of what an author is—an understanding that captures the author neither (naively) as an original genius, nor (critically) as completely extraneous to the interpretation of texts, but as a concept that can be of use in specific interpretive perspectives.

A similar plea for differentiation can be seen in Italo Calvino's *If on a Winter's Night a Traveler* with regard to the reader. The novel presents various forms of reading that could be taken as a basis for a theory of reading. In picturing a multitude of approaches toward reading literary texts, the novel can be understood as a plea for a plurality of interpretation that sees different reading perspectives as adequate for dealing with literary texts. A theory of reading seeking to build upon Calvino's novel would have to pluralize 'the' reader into a variety of readers, their individual readings and the respective premises they rest upon, their particular worldviews, and the specific interpretive decisions made while reading. Calvino's theory of reading could, therefore, be part of a sociological approach toward the reception of literature—an approach that empirically differentiates between various forms of reading.

A historically oriented perspective on theory (or, in particular, on the development of French theory) could, finally, work with Laurent Binet's *7th Function of Language*. Dealing with a crucial moment in twentieth-century history of theory, the novel can provide insights into the reconstruction of the past—not through the inclusion of specific historical details, but through its self-reflexive approach to historiography that continuously questions its own premises and hypotheses.

Overview of the Literary Texts in Terms of an Extrapolation of Theory

The examples discussed underline the fact that theorizing literature can be considered a valuable contribution to debates in theory. Theory, therefore, is not only taken up in a playful manner for the purposes of illustration or ironization, but also in order to develop new concepts of theory or to shed light on subjects that cannot be grasped by common theoretical approaches. As an overview, Table 2.4 links these different extrapolations of theory from literature to the novels discussed in the case studies:

Table 2.4 Examples for different extrapolations of theory from literature

Extrapolation	Example
Metaization of theory	*Eco:* illustrating the limits of interpretation (too broad vs. too narrow)
	Zeh: using fiction theory as a meta-level to competing physical theories
Creation of theory	*Duncker:* re-establishing the role of the author for texts
	Calvino: presenting various forms of reading
	Binet: writing a history of theory

THE FOUR DIMENSIONS OF SECOND-ORDER LITERARY THEORY

Literary theory has always reacted to tendencies in literature. It has created or modified instruments for the analysis of texts and their contexts or developed concepts for writing literary history. The final overview of second-order literary theory on the following page (Fig. 2.8) brings together its four main dimensions as outlined in this chapter: mode, level, function, and extrapolation. The scheme may serve as an orientation for the case studies in the next chapters. As they will show in detail, numerous literary texts of the last fifty years can be understood in the light of interpretive theories. They integrate, reflect upon, or ironize elements of theory within their fictional world. In doing so, they also participate in doing literary theory.

2 SECOND-ORDER LITERARY THEORY   47

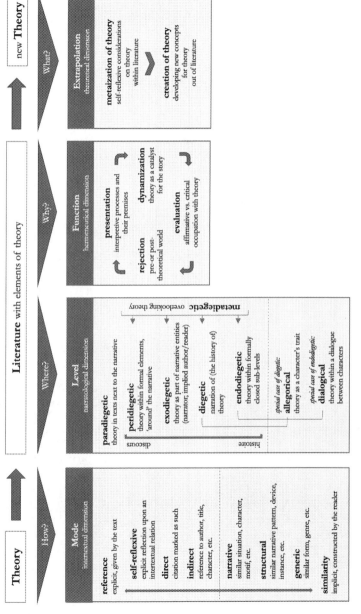

Fig. 2.8 The four dimensions of second-order literary theory (detailed)

Bibliography

Agostini, Giulia (2021): *Nach der Literatur. Studien zu einer Theorie der Literatur.* Heidelberg.

Bal, Mieke (2017): *Narratology: Introduction to the Theory of Narrative. Fourth edition.* Toronto.

Bhatti, Anil, and Kimmich, Dorothee (2018): Introduction. In: Anil Bhatti and Dorothee Kimmich, eds.: *Similarity. A Paradigm for Culture Theory.* New York, 1–22.

Booth, Wayne C. (1961): *The Rhetoric of Fiction.* Chicago.

Ceserani, Remo, and Zanotti, Paolo (2008): The Fragment as Structuring Force. In: Gerald Gillespie, Manfred Engel, and Bernard Dieterle, eds.: *Romantic Prose Fiction.* Amsterdam/Philadelphia, 452–475.

Croce, Benedetto (1902): *Estetica come scienza dell'espressione e linguistica generale: Teoria e storia.* Bari.

Eco, Umberto (1990): *The Limits of Interpretation.* Bloomington et al.

Genette, Gérard (1980): *Narrative Discourse: An Essay in Method.* Ithaka.

Genette, Gérard (1982): *Figures of Literary Discourse.* New York.

Gumbrecht, Hans Ulrich (2004): *Production of Presence: What Meaning Cannot Convey.* Stanford.

Gumbrecht, Hans Ulrich (2012): Vom Wandel der Chronotopen: Ein mögliches Nachwort. In: Klaus Birnstiel and Erik Schilling, eds.: *Literatur und Theorie seit der Postmoderne. Mit einem Nachwort von Hans Ulrich Gumbrecht.* Stuttgart, 229–236.

Habermas, Jürgen (1988): Philosophie und Wissenschaft als Literatur? In: Jürgen Habermas: *Nachmetaphysisches Denken: Philosophische Aufsätze.* Frankfurt/Main, 242–263.

Hempfer, Klaus W. (1973): *Gattungstheorie: Information und Synthese.* München.

Lang, Simone Elisabeth: Between Story and Narrated World: Reflections on the Difference between Homo- and Heterodiegesis. In: *Journal of Literary Theory* 8/2 (2014), 368–396.

Lenz, Jakob, and Schilling, Erik (2023): Gipfelblick – und dann zurück: Intertextuelle Reflexionen auf Räume, Erkenntnis und Politik in Thomas Manns "Zauberberg" und Platons "Politeia". In: *Thomas-Mann-Jahrbuch* 36, 81–95.

Luhmann, Niklas (1994): Observing Re-Entries. In: *ProtoSociology* 6, 4–15.

Martus, Steffen, and Spoerhase, Carlos (2022): *Geistesarbeit: Eine Praxeologie der Geisteswissenschaften.* Berlin.

Michler, Werner (2015): *Kulturen der Gattung: Poetik im Kontext, 1750–1950.* Göttingen.

Pfister, Manfred (1985): Zur Systemreferenz. In: Ulrich Broich and Manfred Pfister, eds.: *Intertextualität: Formen, Funktionen, anglistische Fallstudien.* Tübingen, 52–58.

Schilling, Erik (2012): Umberto Eco zwischen Theorie und Literatur. In: Klaus Birnstiel and Erik Schilling, eds.: *Literatur und Theorie seit der Postmoderne. Mit einem Nachwort von Hans Ulrich Gumbrecht.* Stuttgart, 67–80.

Spencer-Brown, George (1969): *Laws of Form.* London.

Wolf, Werner (1989): Literaturtheorie in der Literatur: David Lodges "Small World" als kritische Auseinandersetzung mit dem Dekonstruktivismus. In: *AAA: Arbeiten aus Anglistik und Amerikanistik* 14, 19–37.

CHAPTER 3

Narrating Literary Theory

Certain novels narrate literary theory at various levels, thus playing a central role in the theorization of literature. In David Lodge's *Small World*, various characters allegorically represent major schools of theory. The novel's cast of characters includes a daily life structuralist, a deconstructivist who loses faith in deconstruction, a Marxist who drives a Bentley, and a meta-theorist, among others. Together they form a panorama of twentieth-century literary theory transferred onto the diegetic level of the literary text.

Laurent Binet's *The 7th Function of Language* is a historical novel about all the important representatives of twentieth-century literary theory. Similarly to *Small World*, the characters behave allegorically according to their theoretical approach. In addition, however, a dialogical presentation of theory (in the form of debating duels) plays an important role in Binet's novel. This allows for various theories to be presented 'in action'. Moreover, *The 7th Function of Language* 're-theorizes' its fictional reality, offers a metaization of theory, and thus constitutes a first step toward a possible extrapolation of (modified or new) theory from literature.

© The Author(s), under exclusive license to Springer Nature Switzerland AG 2024
E. Schilling, *Theorizing Literature*,
https://doi.org/10.1007/978-3-031-53326-6_3

Presenting Theory as a Character's Trait: David Lodge's *Small World* (1984)

David Lodge, born in 1935, is a British writer and academic known for his novels and literary criticism, which often focus on intellectual settings. Among his most popular novels are *Changing Places* (1975), *Small World* (1984), and *Nice Work* (1988), which explore the intricacies of academic life through the lens of satirical humor. Lodge's combined expertise in narrative technique and academic subject matter has made him a major figure in British literature of the late twentieth and early twenty-first centuries.

Small World is the second in the series of three campus novels mentioned above. The main characters of *Changing Places*, Philip Swallow and Morris Zapp, return to play an important role in *Small World*.[1] Yet now the stage is no longer restricted to one (or two) university campus(ses),[2] but rather encompasses the whole world as a playground for academics jetting from conference to conference. In addition, each of the main characters allegorically represents a literary theory, which renders the novel particularly interesting for a first analytical approach toward theory in literature.

The novel is a mosaic of multiple scenes, plots, and detours. Its most important structural element is a focus on various 'grails', elusive objects of desire derived from the medieval literature on the Holy Grail, for example, by Chrétien de Troyes or Wolfram von Eschenbach.[3] There are two modern 'grails' in *Small World*, structurally similar to the medieval one: love and academic recognition. Love is the aim of Persse McGarrigle, who has just finished his MA and teaches modern English literature at the University of Limerick in Ireland. At a conference organized by the British scholar Philip Swallow, he meets Angelica Pabst and falls in love with her. By analogy with the medieval grail stories, however, Persse cannot reach her. She deliberately and/or by chance escapes his advances, so that he is

---

[1] For an overview of the whole trilogy, see Seligardi (2013).
[2] As Zapp and Hilary Swallow, Philip's wife, put it "'[T]he single, static campus is over.' – 'And the single, static campus novel with it'" (63). Quotations from the novel here and in the following are taken from Lodge (2011 [1984]). For a comparison with *Changing Places*, see Mews (1989).
[3] On the grail references, see Hermann-Brennecke (2001, 241–243); for other intertextual references, see ibid., 243–247 and Holmes (1990, 49), who calls the novel "a fiction that contains a myriad of other fictions".

forced to chase her from conference to conference, flying around the world in search of her. A further complication arises in Angelica's having a twin sister, Lily, whom Persse mistakes for Angelica several times. Even when he finally seems to have found Angelica and made love to her, it is Lily lying in bed with him.

The second 'grail' pursued in the novel is that of academic recognition. *Small World* sets its characters the ultimate goal: a "UNESCO Chair of Literary Criticism" (120), endowed with the highest salary of all professorships and unburdened by duties of any kind.[4] The professors who strive for this chair represent different literary theories and therefore compete not only on an individual, but also on an allegorical level: which theory will prove worthy of being awarded the most prestigious post of all? Theory, therefore, drives and dynamizes a great deal of the story. In the end, there is a debate between the protagonists representing the different theories at a Modern Language Association (MLA) conference panel in New York. The panel's host is emeritus professor Arthur Kingfisher, a name that refers to the Arthurian literature of the grail: it is the so-called fisher king whom—in Chrétien's and Wolfram's version—Perceval relieves of his suffering by asking the right question. The conference mirrors the grail legend by having Persse ask a question which leads to Kingfisher regaining his physical and intellectual power. As a consequence, he assigns the UNESCO chair to himself, to the meta-perspective on competing theories, instead of giving it to one theory in particular.[5]

At the end of *Small World*, there is thus a plurality of grails both of amorous and academic recognition, represented by the different theories the novel showcases. Theory is present on various levels: in the form of academic talks (thus 'endodiegetic' in my terminology), in the form of debates between scholars ('dialogical'), and—most importantly—as a trait of the main characters ('allegorical'). The characters represent certain forms of theory to such an extent that they could almost be considered stock characters of a postmodern comedy of manners. It is this aspect that makes *Small World* distinctive within my corpus, and I will therefore place

---

[4] "[N]o students to teach, no papers to grade, no committees to chair" (121).
[5] A similar meta-perspective is identified by Mews (1989, 726) for the novel as a whole when he calls it "a serious questioning of the purpose of literary studies and of the institution of academic criticism itself".

a particular focus on it by analyzing the main characters as allegorical personifications of theory.[6]

The Anti-Theorist

Philip Swallow, chair at the fictional Rummidge University in England, is an anti-theorist both in word and deed. When he learns that Morris Zapp is going to deliver a talk on theory, he says: "Theory? [...] That word brings out the Goering in me. When I hear it I reach for my revolver" (24). Consequently, his latest book is entitled *"Hazlitt and the Amateur Reader"* (78), possibly referring to a socio-cultural reconstruction of amateur readers reading Hazlitt; at the same time, however, and more plausibly, (involuntarily) revealing Swallow as an amateur reader himself. During the MLA conference panel in New York, he explicitly stands for this form of reading:

> It was the job of the critic to unlock the drawers, blow away the dust, bring out the treasures into the light of day. Of course, he needed certain specialist skills to do this: a knowledge of history, a knowledge of philology, of generic convention and textual editing. But above all he needed enthusiasm, the love of books. (317)

Just as the other MLA participants, Swallow lays open what drives him as a scholar. He is a 'philo-logist' in the original sense of the word: a lover of words and literature. Yet his love hinders a critical distance toward his objects of research. What Swallow—deliberately—lacks is a critical stance toward books, a stance that would make his approach an academic one, driven by method and/or theory.

Apart from Swallow's allegorical and dialogical occupation with theory in *Small World*, he demonstrates an endodiegetic presentation of his antitheory as well. Characteristic for this is his short, yet intense love affair with a woman named Joy. When he meets her right after having survived a plane accident, he lusts after her with all his body and mind. They have

---

[6] For an overview, with slight differences to my analysis in detail, see Selejan (2016, 61), who identifies: "post-structuralism (Morris Zapp), liberal humanism (Rudyard Parkinson), Marxism (Fulvia Morgana), Freudian theory (Sybil Maiden), reader response theory (Siegfried von Turpitz), anti-theoretical views (Philip Swallow), Computational Linguistics (Robin Dempsey), structuralist narratology (Michel Tardieu), deconstruction (Angelica Pabst), Arnoldian criticism (Rodney Wainwright), etc."

sex just once, but it is enough for Joy to conceive a child (without Philip knowing). His affair with Joy exemplifies the fact that Swallow transfers the "enthusiasm" and "love" he espouses as the adequate mode of reading to his personal life, too—another example of his allegorical presentation of (anti-)theory.

When he (endodiegetically) tells Morris Zapp about this episode, his way of dealing with literature is mirrored in a narrative fashion. Swallow becomes the 'author' of (the narration of) his affair with Joy and he decides to tell it in the romantic fashion in which he lived it. Although even the setting suggests a critical distance to what he is telling ("all the time [when undressing Joy] I was looking at myself reflected in the dressing table mirror", 73), Swallow is just as engaged as a narrator as he is as a reader: "now in the mirror I could see her face, reflected in another mirror on the other side of the room, and, my God, there was an expression of total abandonment on it" (73).

Philip Swallow thus tells and lives his anti-theoretical approach toward literature and life. He clings to his old-fashioned way of reading as an enthusiastic 'amateur' (again, also literally: a lover, not an expert). And despite his affair with Joy, he ultimately returns to his wife of twenty-five years, Hilary. In doing so, he turns out to be far more consistent in his actions than his friend and rival Morris Zapp, as I will outline in the following.

The Deconstructivist Losing Faith in Deconstruction

While Swallow remains—beside a few rule-proving exceptions—the same in his words and actions, Zapp is constantly on the move, not only physically traveling from one conference to another, but also in his intellectual and personal views. At the beginning of *Small World*, he gives an important deconstructivist talk at the Rummidge conference.[7] In the talk, he speaks openly about his personal development:

> [I] once believed in the possibility of interpretation. That is, I thought the goal of reading was to establish the meaning of texts. [...] Then I began a commentary on the works of Jane Austen, the aim of which was [...] to examine the novels from every conceivable angle—historical, biographical,

---

[7] Accordingly, Wolf (1989, 23 and 25–30) considers deconstructivism the most important theory for *Small World*.

rhetorical, mythical, structural, Freudian, Jungian, Marxist, existentialist, Christian, allegorical, ethical, phenomenological, archetypal, you name it. (24)

Zapp expresses two fundamental steps in his path to becoming a methodologically flexible scholar. He started as a classic adherent of hermeneutics, believing "in the possibility of interpretation". At some point, however, he discovered that there is not just one interpretation, but that interpretation depends on the perspective, on—as Derrida put it—a "point of presence, a fixed origin"[8] which may change. As a consequence, in his commentary he tries to consider all the contexts and "transcendental signifiers"[9] one could possibly think of for interpreting the works of Jane Austen. His personal development thereby illustrates the institutional development of the 1950s, '60s, and '70s, adding various theories and methods of interpretation to traditional hermeneutics.

At a certain point, however, Zapp finds this no longer fulfilling, which leads him to go one step further and become a deconstructivist. He says: "To understand a message is to decode it. Language is a code. *But every decoding is another encoding*" (25). Quoting Roland Barthes's metaphor of reading as striptease,[10] Zapp states that the pleasure in reading does not consist in finally revealing the one and only meaning of a text. On the contrary, what makes reading (and striptease) exciting is the infinitely postponed meaning—the idea that you always move toward a revelation yet never arrive at a *telos*: "The text unveils itself before us, but never allows itself to be possessed; and instead of striving to possess it we should take pleasure in its teasing" (27).

After the three steps of hermeneutics, theoretical plurality, and deconstructivism, however, Zapp reaches a fourth form of methodological approach toward literature (and life). After being kidnapped by an Italian left-wing terrorist group and confronted with his own mortality, he no longer accepts an endless, playful deferral of meaning, at least not in his personal life. He discusses the matter with Persse at the MLA conference: "'I've rather lost faith in deconstruction.' [...] [Persse:] 'You mean every decoding is not another encoding after all?'—'Oh it is, it is. But the deferral of meaning isn't infinite as far as the individual is concerned'" (328).

---

[8] Derrida (1978 [1967], 278).
[9] Ibid., 280.
[10] Barthes (1972 [1957]).

Having been confronted with existential experiences in 'real' life, particularly with his fear of death, Zapp becomes a convert once more, turning against theory in a way not unsimilar to the one represented by Swallow from the very beginning.[11]

This conversion of Zapp is already hinted at when he listens to Swallow's narration of his love affair with Joy: "Morris [felt] slightly piqued at the extent to which he had been affected, first by the eroticism of Philip's tale, then by its sad epilogue" (76). When Swallow says in the same conversation that, growing older, he finds books are no longer able to satisfy him, he proves to be one step ahead of Zapp, who will undergo the same experience a little later. Theory can no longer satisfy him; instead, he takes up a romantic life himself: "Thelma and I are thinking of getting married" (329). *Small World*, thus, not only presents, dynamizes, and evaluates, but also signals the limits of its scope, rejecting theory.

The Daily Life Structuralist

In addition to Swallow and Zapp, three more professors speak at the MLA panel on "The Function of Criticism" (316). Among them is French structuralist Michel Tardieu. He stresses the link between scientific knowledge and its underlying structures:

> If literary criticism was supposed to be knowledge, it could not be founded on interpretation, since interpretation was endless, subjective, unverifiable, unfalsifiable. What was permanent, reliable, accessible to scientific study [...] were the deep structural principles and binary oppositions that underlay all texts [...]. (318)

Tardieu allegorically represents a structuralist approach as developed, for example, by Claude Lévi-Strauss or in the early work of Roland Barthes—and as presented as an academic overview by David Lodge himself in a volume entitled *Working with Structuralism*, published in 1981.[12] As Michel Tardieu's name suggests, his theoretical approach is enriched by Michel Foucault's research on (the history of) knowledge. In his life as presented in *Small World*, he resembles Foucault (and Barthes) as well,

---

[11] Wolf (1989, 31) considers Zapp incapable of living deconstruction in the face of the power of reality. Peters (2007, 354) speaks—very similarly to Wolf—of a "deconstruction of deconstruction".

[12] Lodge (1981).

not only in his being French, but also in his preference for young, male lovers).

In addition, Tardieu re-enacts the 'eternal' structures of world and narrative in his daily life, as exemplified in his treatment of his lover: every morning, Tardieu asks him to go out and buy some breakfast rolls and a copy of *Le Matin*. When Albert, the lover, complains about this task, Tardieu explains him that "[i]t is a quest, *chéri*, a story of departure and return: you venture out, and you come back, loaded with treasure. You are a hero" (112). The grail legend, a basic structural pattern of *Small World*, is here—in typical structuralist manner—interpreted as an anthropological constant, as a way of organizing human life that does not only apply to literature, but equally to daily life, in a rather similar way to Barthes's research on everyday culture.

Using Reception-Theory as Method

The fourth person to speak at the MLA panel is Siegfried von Turpitz, a German professor focusing on 'Rezeptionsästhetik', reader-response theory as inspired by Hans Robert Jauß and Wolfgang Iser.[13] Contradicting Tardieu, Turpitz states that

> a definition from the formal properties of the literary art-object as such was doomed to failure, since such art-objects enjoyed only an as it were virtual existence until they were realized in the mind of a reader. (318)

Turpitz's professional focus on reader-response theory is taken up in two aspects of his life and behavior. First, he wears a black leather glove on one hand that he never takes off. People speculate what kind of injury he is concealing: "a repulsive birthmark, a suppurating wound, some *unheimlich* mutation such as talons instead of fingers, or an artificial hand made of stainless steel and plastic" (96–97). The black glove invites wild speculations—much like the various speculations about the literary texts analyzed by reader-response theory. At the end of *Small World*, however, Persse shakes Turpitz's hand and gets hold of the glove by accident, "revealing a perfectly normal, healthy-looking hand underneath" (335). The episode illustrates what Turpitz had stated in his talk: the actual hand is not important, unless it is "realized in the mind of a reader". In this case

---

[13] Turpitz is "not much more than an epigone of Iser and Jauß" (Wolf 1989, 24).

it means: various observers imagine some kind of hand underneath the glove according to their liking.

In addition to wearing his glove, Turpitz can be said to 'live' reader-response theory by plagiarizing a paper Persse has sent to a publishing house for peer review. Turpitz gives the paper a bad review and proposes not to publish it. Yet he himself uses the ideas for a talk at a conference and thus gives an example for a 'misled' understanding of reception. The story has another twist (typical of *Small World*), in that Persse's paper had originally focused on intertextual phenomena, thus marking it out as reception-oriented in a broad sense, by analyzing Shakespeare's influence on T.S. Eliot. Inspired by the post-structuralist spirit of the Rummidge conference, however, Persse had playfully inverted the line of influence ("the influence of T.S. Eliot on Shakespeare", 51). By picking up this a-historical approach (in my terminology: looking at similarities rather than references), Turpitz deconstructs his own (historically oriented) method of reception analysis, just as the revelation of his intact hand destroys the simulacrum (created in the mind of the observer) of a mysterious hand hidden underneath the black glove.

The Marxist Driving a Bentley

The fifth person to speak at the MLA panel is Italian Marxist Fulvia Morgana. In her view, "the function of criticism [is] to wage undying war on the very concept of 'literature' itself, which was nothing more than an instrument of bourgeois hegemony" (318). Morgana speaks of "so-called aesthetic values erected and maintained through an élitist educational system" (ibid.). By terming values "so-called", Morgana implies a critical perspective on the world and its interpretation—a perspective that, in her case, is linked to a specific idea of what has to change.

Due to her knowledge of historical processes, however, Morgana does not have a problem with living a bourgeois life herself. When Zapp asks her how she can reconcile living like a millionaire with her Marxist beliefs, Morgana calls this question "very American":

> I recognize the contradictions in our way of life, but those are the very contradictions characteristic of the last phase of bourgeois capitalism, which will eventually cause it to collapse. By renouncing our own little bit of privilege [...] we should not accelerate by one minute the consummation of that process, which has its own inexorable rhythm and momentum. (128)

Despite the contradiction between her theoretical approach toward literature and her own life—a contradiction that is not typical for other characters of *Small World*—Morgana lives what she preaches, not from a superficial point of view, but regarding the historicity of values. If she—as a proper Marxist—believes in a change of the capitalist system, she may also wait for that process to take place. Morgana sees her wealth as arbitrary, as something that may not last forever, but is there (contingently) at this proper moment and therefore not per se good or bad, but simple reality. Thus, the contradiction between her theory and life turns out to be an illusion; in some way, she lives 'her' theory just as the other characters do.

Linking Hermeneutics to Literary Criticism

A further guest at the MLA panel, prevented from attending by virtue of him missing his plane, is Rudyard Parkinson. He is "the Regius Professor of Belles-Lettres" at the prestigious "All Saints'" College at Oxford and portrayed as a doyen of literature and criticism in England, having written "innumerable books, articles and reviews" (98). In order to promote his own aspirations for the UNESCO Chair, he writes a joint review on the latest books of Philip Swallow and Morris Zapp for the *Times Literary Supplement*. In it, he proclaims an "English School of Criticism" (164) with Swallow being its most prominent representative. Implicitly, however, he aims at destroying Zapp's prospects of the chair and increasing his own, as he considers himself the most important literary scholar and does not regard Swallow a serious competitor.

Parkinson disrespects Zapp's "pretentious critical jargon" (100) and can therefore be considered someone who focuses on literary history and traditional hermeneutics, just as he himself "believes in keeping up old traditions" and has, being from South Africa originally, "perfected an impersonation of Englishness that is now indistinguishable from authentic specimens" (99). It is not only for reasons of the plot, but also plausible with regard to his methodological approach, that he does not make it to the MLA panel in time. Just like himself, his academic approach is outdated and therefore not able to compete with the other professors' theories.

The Meta-Theorist

The last person involved in the MLA debate is Arthur Kingfisher. He does not, however, appear as a participant, but as the host, a caesarian primus inter pares who will, at the end, reclaim the prestigious Chair for himself.[14] During the discussion following the talks, Kingfisher is visibly bored: he "yawned and glanced at his watch" (318). As the recurrent allusions to his lack of sexual potency underline, he has lost his professional and personal stamina—he is suffering from an unknown disease just as the fisher king in the grail legend.

It is at this point that Persse—the modern Perceval—asks his question: "What follows if everybody agrees with you?" (319). While the panel members suspect "some sort of trick" or disregard it "a fool's question", Kingfisher declares it a "very in-ter-es-ting question". He himself provides the answer in the form of a re-entry:

> [W]hat matters in the field of critical practice is not truth but difference. If everybody were convinced by your argument, they would have to do the same as you and then there would be no satisfaction in doing it. To win is to lose the game. (ibid.)

What seems to rephrase Zapp's deconstructivist approach turns out in fact to be a plea for plurality. Responding to Persse's question, Kingfisher claims that answers in the sciences and the humanities are never of eternal value. They are perspectives that work for a certain time and within a certain context, before being replaced by the next perspective—a paradigm shift, as Thomas S. Kuhn put it.[15] If there were eternal truths to be discovered, this would mean the end of research: an end of striving for new ideas, new perspectives, new theories. It is therefore not disregard for the theories presented that makes Kingfisher claim the UNESCO Chair for himself. It is his insight into what research is about: constantly gaining new perspectives on relevant objects such as literary texts by applying a new theory or method to them.

Right after the panel discussion, the same switch in perspective applies twice to Kingfisher's personal life. First, he regains his sexual abilities; second, he learns that he is the lost father of the twin sisters Angelica and Lily,

---

[14] "Arthur Kingfisher, unlike the other critics in the novel, does not profess to belong to a particular school of thought, but is a near-mythical persona" (Selejan 2016, 68).
[15] Kuhn (1962).

born 27 years ago to a colleague named Sibyl Maiden. And, in the end, the switch of perspectives applies to other characters as well, for example to Persse, who restarts his quest for love by projecting his affections for Angelica onto another woman named Cheryl.

Dealing with Sex and Gender in Theory and Life

Sibyl Maiden, a self-declared "respectable middle-aged spinster" (334), is the long-lost mother of the twin sisters. As she reveals at the MLA party, she gave birth to them in secret and pretended to have found them in the toilet of an airplane, ashamed of having gotten pregnant at a summer school. At the end of *Small World*, therefore, what Maiden had stated at the very beginning proves true: "It all comes down to sex, in the end" (12).

With regard to theory, Maiden represents Gender Studies, building particularly on Jessie Weston's remarks on the Grail legend made famous by their being quoted by T.S. Eliot in *The Waste Land*.[16] Maiden's interpretation of symbols, as performed at the Rummidge conference when she learns about Persse's MA thesis on *The Waste Land*, turns out to be a structural constant not only of her life, but of the novel as a whole:

> The Grail cup, for instance, is a female symbol of great antiquity and universal occurrence. [...] And the Grail spear [...] is obviously phallic. *The Waste Land* is really all about Eliot's fears of impotence and sterility. (12)

In these sentences, Maiden explains several things about the *Small World* inside and outside the novel. Understood as literary criticism, her comment applies to T.S. Eliot's poem. Within Lodge's novel, it proves true for Persse's quest for Angelica, for Kingfisher's impotence, for the actions of many other characters, and for her own life as well, a life that has been marked by the 'phallic' experience of conceiving the twins from Arthur Kingfisher. However, the problematic character of this experience and the length of time required before she can tell Angelica and Lily about their mother and father hint at substantial problems of transferring theory to life.

---

[16] For details, see Holmes (1990, 52–55). Wolf (1989, 24) calls her a representative of a mythical-archetypal approach.

The Computer Philologist Mistaking Artificial Intelligence

A form of interpretation missing at the MLA panel is computer philology, as represented by Robin Dempsey, a former colleague of Philip Swallow's at Rummidge. Dempsey claims to "precisely quantify the influence of Shakespeare on T. S. Eliot" (51), that is, what Persse did in his MA thesis, by having the computer list everything the two writers have in common. Using a similar method of quantification, he—unwillingly—gives the author Ronald Frobisher a severe case of writer's block by unveiling to him that his favorite word in his novels is "grease".

Yet the computer does not only prove of little use to Persse and Frobisher, it also turns out to be a threat to Dempsey's personal life: at his institute, he works with a computer that can be considered an early form of 'artificial intelligence'. The 'intelligence' mainly consists of picking up key words from sentences typed into the computer and rephrasing them in the form of questions. Triggered by these questions, Dempsey 'abuses' the computer as a personal therapist for his frustration with both his marriage and his job. He tells the computer about his life as if it were a diary. What he does not notice, however, is that at some point a colleague takes over the computer and mocks him by providing problematic advice: "SHOOT YOURSELF" (309). Following a scuffle between Dempsey and his colleague, the computer starts to endlessly print the word "ERROR".

Theory—And the World

This reserved conclusion does not only apply to computer philology, probably the method evaluated most critically in *Small World*. With its prominent position at the end of Part 4—immediately before the showdown at the MLA conference in Part 5—its somewhat cautious character also refers to the limits of theory in general. Philip Swallow and Morris Zapp both recognize the limits of applying theory to their personal lives. Arthur Kingfisher and Sibyl Maiden note the importance of theory for their lives, and yet the transfer does not happen without problems. In the end, therefore, Lodge's novel is not only a book about literary theory, but also a book about what is more important than theory: life.

Narrating a History of Theory: Laurent Binet's *The 7th Function of Language* (*La Septième Fonction du Langage*, 2015)

Laurent Binet, born in 1972, is a French writer best known for his debut novel *HHhH* (2010; an acronym for the German *Himmlers Hirn heißt Heydrich*), which explores the assassination of Nazi leader Reinhard Heydrich and won the Prix Goncourt du premier roman in 2010. Binet's work often blends historical fact with metafictional elements, questioning the role of fiction and the ethics of representation. Subsequent works such as *The 7th Function of Language* (*La septième fonction du langage*, 2015) continue to showcase his innovative approach to historical fiction, weaving in intellectual history and speculative elements to examine the complexities of language and power.

The 7th Function of Language is a historical novel set in the milieu of French intellectuals of the early 1980s. The title—forming an indirect reference—is a fictitious extension of Roman Jakobson's six functions of language by an alleged seventh, performative function, supposedly capable of convincing any interlocutor of one's point of view. In both politics and the intellectual scene, this 7th function of language becomes the object of frenzied pursuit—a very tangible example for a dynamization through theory: François Mitterand wants to use it to win the 1981 presidential election against Valéry Giscard d'Estaing; the writer Philippe Sollers, husband of Julia Kristeva, wants to use it to reach the top of a secret rhetoric club (the 'Logos Club').

Roland Barthes has obtained the 7th function from Jakobson; at the beginning of the novel, he is killed (thus suffering the 'death of the author' he himself proclaimed), though his killers fail to acquire the function. A wild scavenger hunt begins, spanning several continents, which not only shares similarities in historical setting and personnel with David Lodge's *Small World*, but also makes a guest appearance for Lodge's character Morris Zapp, complementing the tableau of historical speakers at a conference.

A History of Theory

First and foremost, *The 7th Function of Language* is a novel about a crucial year in the history of twentieth-century theory: the year 1980. Many elements of the novel are historically accurate, for example, Roland Barthes's incident with a van in Paris on February 25 and his death in a hospital four weeks later. Equally historically accurate is the account of Louis Althusser strangling his wife Hélène Rytmann on November 16, as well as the fact that Roman Jakobson is still alive in 1980, which surprises some characters of the novel.

At the same time, however, Binet freely adapts historical facts. In doing so, he builds on the metahistoriographic reflections[17] on the possibilities (and limits) of historical accounts he had presented in his earlier (also historical) novel *HHhH*. In *The 7th Function of Language*, Binet uses both fictional additions to historical knowledge and metahistoriographic considerations, which characterize his method. Where the historical sources do not give sufficient information, Binet volunteers explanations. These explanations are often ironic: they stand for a certain distance toward both the historical events of 1980 and the underlying debates about theory. Nonetheless, the explanations are reasonable conjectures filling in the 'blind spots' of history.

As the novel states from a metahistoriographic perspective at various points of the story, fictional accounts of the past may be even more accurate than factual ones. Within fiction, there is the chance of looking into people's minds, understanding their motivations, and combining these elements to reach plausible explanations of their (known) actions. Right at the beginning of the novel, for example, there is an internal focalization of Roland Barthes, self-reflexively broken by the narrator: "The reasons I mention to explain Roland Barthes's anxiety are all well known. But I want to tell you what actually happened" (4).[18]

The logical contradiction arising between what historically happened and what, according to the novel, "actually happened" emphasizes the metahistoriographic tension of Binet's approach in an ironic way. What the novel relates may be 'true' as it is based on historical facts, yet—as historiography itself—it works with narrative elements, conjectures, even speculations to such an extent that the idea of historical truth is compromised. Reasonable conjectures about the past might therefore be more

---

[17] The term 'metahistoriographic' denotes a (historical) novel that self-reflexively considers chances and limits of re-constructing historical events. Cf. Hutcheon (1988); Nünning (1995); Hutcheon (2005); Schilling (2012).

[18] "Les raisons que je viens d'évoquer pour expliquer l'attitude soucieuse de Roland Barthes sont toutes attestées par l'Histoire, mais j'ai envie de vous raconteur ce qui est vraiment arrivé" (11). Quotations from the novel here and below are taken from Binet (2018) [English translation] and Binet (2015) [French original], respectively.

desirable than historical truth, as the novel elaborates when speculating about what Barthes did immediately before his incident:

> This story has a blind spot that is also its genesis: Barthes's lunch with Mitterand. [...] Jacques Bayard and Simon will never know, never knew what happened that day, what was said. [...] But I can maybe ... After all it's all a question of method, and I know how to proceed: interrogate the witnesses, corroborate, discard any tenuous testimonies, confront these partial memories with the reality of history. And then, if need be ... You know what I mean. (138)[19]

Here, the narrator explicitly reflects upon his method, a method that may, metafictionally, also be ascribed to the novel as a whole. There is a tension between "the reality of history" and the "need" for something which is not explicitly named, yet guessable: the need for fiction, the need for a good story which, again, needs good conjectures and good narrative and structural elements. In directly addressing the audience in the last sentence, the narrator establishes a kind of conspiracy between novel and readers, a conspiracy that is not only based on the concretely outlined limits of historiography, but also on the theoretical knowledge about these limits. In this ironic apostrophe toward the reader, *The 7th Function of Language* also refers to a shared knowledge about theory, a knowledge that comprises, for example, Hayden White's postulates about the narrativity of historiography.[20]

An exciting story may thus be more important than a historically accurate one. *The 7th Function of Language* raises the question of whether the history of (twentieth-century) theory can be told better within a fictional frame than in a historiographic one. The novel stresses two possibilities of fiction reaching further than historiography: first, it may look at history from an ironic point of view, putting into perspective debates that, at some moment in the past, may have seemed incredibly important. Second, the

---

[19] "Cette historie possède un point aveugle qui est aussi son point de départ: le déjeuner de Barthes avec Mitterrand. [...] Jacques Bayard et Simon Herzog ne sauront jamais, n'ont jamais su ce qui s'était passé ce jour-là [...]. Mais moi, je peux, peut-être... Après tout, tout est affaire de méthode, et je sais comment procéder: interroger les témoins, recouper, écarter les témoignages fragiles, confronter les souvenirs tendancieux avec la réalité de l'Histoire. Et puis, au besoin... Vous savez bien" (200–201).

[20] Cf. White (1973).

historical novel may invent elements that make for an even better story than history can provide.

The possibilities of fiction can be seen, for example, in Binet's decision to have Derrida die in 1980 as well as Barthes, being attacked by two dogs that John Searle sets on him at a cemetery at Cornell University, where the two of them have come head-to-head to try and get hold of the 7th function of language. In reality, Derrida died peacefully in Paris in 2004; however, in the novel the rivalry between Searle and Derrida, between philosophy of language and deconstruction, is taken to (fictional) extremes in the cemetery scene. The dogs, however, have their basis in historical fact, as Searle was known for his passion for dogs, referring to them at various points in his philosophical works and even thanking them in his acknowledgments.

An Allegorical Presentation of Theory

The scene at the cemetery is the culmination of a (fictional, yet highly plausible) conference on theory organized by Jonathan Culler at Cornell University in 1980. The conference program as presented in the novel serves as a 'very short introduction to theory' itself.[21] However, as with many aspects of history and theory within *The 7th Function of Language*, the conference is ironically broken, as signaled in its title ("Shift into overdrive in the linguistic turn", 223). The (supposed) talks cover topics such as "Degenerative grammar" by Noam Chomsky, "Phallogocentrisme et métaphysique de la substance" by Luce Irigaray, "Stayin' Alive, structurally speaking" by Roman Jakobson, "Fake or feint: performing the F words in fictional works" by John Searle, and—last and least—"Fishing for supplement in a deconstructive world" by Morris Zapp (223–224). The talks themselves are not described at any length, with one exception: the talk given by Derrida, which is used to underline the differences between speech acts and deconstruction. Thus, in addition to the abundant diegetic theory, there is endodiegetic theory in *The 7th Function of Language* as well.

More important is that—similarly to *Small World*—the characters behave according to their theoretical approach, serving as allegorical

---

[21] Just like the whole novel, as Rodríguez Higuera (2020, 205) points out: it "sets the scene for the reader to dive into the world of deconstruction, power relation discourses, illocutionary and perlocutionary acts, and so on".

personifications of theory. Characteristic is the party concluding the Cornell conference: Julia Kristeva dances with Paul de Man, hinting at the implications of intertextuality for deconstruction. Hélène Cixous unsuccessfully tries to speak to Derrida, Foucault is masturbating in front of a poster of Mick Jagger, Jonathan Culler looks like Andy Warhol writing poetry (but is just filling in financial receipts). The party culminates in the scene at the cemetery where Searle tries to prevent Derrida from getting hold on the 7th function (in order to destroy it).

A key difference between *Small World* and *The 7th Function of Language* with regard to the allegorical presentation of theory, however, is that the latter presents theory in a much more (endo)diegetic and also dialogical way. While the main characters exhibit certain traits typical for their respective theories (as analyzed above), these determine their lives to a lesser extent than can be seen in *Small World*. Here the difference between a historical novel with some fictional elements and a clearly fictional novel with some (hidden) historical references becomes obvious. With this, the integration of the two non-historical protagonists Bayard and Simon can be explained.

A Novel Presenting Interpretive Processes

The non-historical protagonists of the novel include policeman Jacques Bayard and doctoral student Simon Herzog, an expert of semiotics whom Bayard asks for help with investigating Barthes's death. As with the indirect references to *Small World* within the novel, the protagonists work as an intertextual relation, too. In their complementing an old, worldly-wise policeman and young, smart, yet learning novice they offer a narrative similarity to both Arthur Conan Doyle's pair of Sherlock Holmes and Dr. Watson and Umberto Eco's pair of William of Baskerville and Adso of Melk—which itself can be seen as a narrative similarity to Sherlock Holmes. Binet, however, attributes the semiotic potential not to Bayard, but to the young Simon—and thus plays with the literary tradition by slightly altering it.[22] When they first meet, Simon surprises Bayard by drawing conclusions about his biography from his appearance:

---

[22] In addition, the novel presents the "clash between both wings of general semiotic theory and the search for the ultimate function of language as discovered by semiotics" (Rodríguez Higuera 2020, 206); something that cannot be analyzed in detail here.

The young postgrad thinks fast, attentively observing the man facing him, and proceeds methodically: [...] "You fought in Algeria; you have been married twice; you are separated from your second wife; you have a daughter [...]; you voted for Giscard in both rounds of the last presidential election [...]." [...] "What makes you say that?" "Well, it's very simple! [...] When you came to see me at the end of the lecture earlier, you instinctively placed yourself in a position where you wouldn't have your back to the door or the window. You don't learn that at police school, but in the army. [...] You're in the police, so you're bound to be right-wing [...]. You wear a wedding ring on your right hand, but you still have a ring mark on your left ring finger. (31–32)[23]

In presenting this masterpiece of semiotic deductions, *The 7th Function of Language* extends its intertextual similarities from the narrative to the structural level. The function of the scene can be considered an illustration of interpretive processes, similar to Eco's *The Name of the Rose, in which* William draws conclusions about a runaway horse by interpreting signs. Consequently, Simon's approach is doubled by the 'real' Umberto Eco, whom Simon and Bayard meet in Bologna. Much like Simon, Eco starts to deduct Bayard's biography from his external appearance, until Bayard stops him briskly: "All right! I know how it works" (160).[24]

This semiotic perspective is supplemented and ironized by the cars certain characters drive. Bayard himself drives a Peugeot 504, a standard and unremarkable vehicle that corresponds to his unremarkable life. Two members of the Bulgarian secret service drive a Citroën DS, the so-called déesse, meaning goddess in French. This choice is iconic (and ironic) in two respects: a secret service may be thought of trying to avoid attention. It is quite plausible, therefore, to presume the choice of the Citroën has been meant to be a 'typical' French car of the time. Yet the car is not typical, but exceptional, and it is so, secondly, for readers of Barthes in

---

[23] "Le jeune thésard [Simon] réfléchit vite, observe attentivement l'homme qu'il a en face de lui, procède méthodiquement [...]: 'Vous avez fait la guerre d'Algérie, vous avez été marié deux fois, vous êtes séparé de votre deuxième femme, vous avez une fille [...], vous avez voté Giscard aux deux tours de la dernière élection présidentielle [...].' [...] 'Qu'est-ce que vous fait dire ça ?' —Eh bien, c'est très simple ! [...] Lorsque vous êtes venu me voir à la fin du cours, tout à l'heure, dans ma salle de classe, vous vous êtes spontanément placé de manière à ne tourner le dos ni à la porte ni à la fenêtre. Ce n'est pas l'école de la police qu'on vous apprend ça mais à l'armée. [...] Vous êtes dans la police, donc forcément de droite [...]. Vous portez une alliance à la main droite mais vous avez encore la marque d'un anneau à l'annulaire gauche'" (48–50).

[24] "C'est bon ! Je connais" (227).

particular, as he referred to it in his publications about signs in everyday life. Finally, two Japanese characters (who serve as 'dei ex machina') drive a Renault Fuego, an extremely modern, even futuristic car that can be understood as a sign for both Japan as a technologically oriented, modern nation and the function of the characters within the novel who seem to possess near-omnipotent power and save Simon's life twice.

Despite being a good semiotician (or perhaps because he is one), Simon is aware of the limits of interpretation. With the help of a clearly defined context (cultural, historical, etc.), the infinite chain of signifier and signified may be traced down to an end point, for example, to Bayard's biography as a determining explanation for the signs of his external appearance. At least in theory, however, every sign is polysemous and, thus, every interpretation a never-ending process, as Simon reminds his students: "Don't forget that one interpretation never exhausts the sign, and that polysemy is a bottomless well where we can hear an infinite number of echoes" (27).[25]

The infinite echoes, metaphorically representing the infinity of interpretation, are picked up in a polysemous way some pages later. A lover of Roland Barthes, Hamed, supposedly owns a copy of the 7th function of language. While driving a car, Simon and Hamed are attacked by the Bulgarian secret service, who want to obtain the function for themselves. Hamed is shot and tries to say something to Simon: "just before dying, while the sirens scream in the distance, he has time to whisper: 'Echo'" (91–92).[26] In this passage, it remains unclear what Hamed means by this final utterance. One way of ascribing meaning to his last word would be to relate it to the approaching sirens resounding between the tall buildings of Paris. Nonetheless, Simon and Bayard suspect a hidden meaning of the word and question Tzvetan Todorov about it:

> [Bayard] asks Todorov if "echo," the last word pronounced by Hamed, means anything to him. And the Bulgarian replies: "Yes, have you heard from him recently?" Bayard does not understand. "Umberto. How is he?" (129)[27]

---

[25] "Rappelez-vous qu'une interprétation n'épuise jamais le signe, et que la polysémie est un puits sans fond d'où nous parviennent des échos infinis" (42–43).

[26] "[J]uste avant de mourir, tandis que des sirènes retentissent dans le lointain, il a le temps de murmurer: 'Écho'" (135).

[27] "[Bayard] demande à Todorov si 'écho', le dernier mot prononcé par Hamed, lui évoque quelque chose. Et le Bulgare de répondre: 'Oui, vous avez de ses nouvelles ?' Bayard ne comprend pas. 'Umberto, il va bien ?'" (187).

Out of the polysemous meanings of the word "écho", Todorov picks another one (Umberto "Eco"), one that, being a semiotics expert himself, comes naturally to him. During the rest of the novel, it remains unclear whether or not Hamed actively wanted to refer to Eco (an illustration of the fuzzy boundary between reference and similarity). However, for Simon and Bayard the newly gained signified to the signifier "écho" gives rise to a whole chain of interpretations, leading them to further investigations into the Logos Club, the secret rhetoric society of which Eco is the president. Hamed's last word, therefore, illustrates (at least) two theoretical aspects in the context of the novel: the potential polysemous character of any sign and the independence of an ascribed meaning from the intention of the author of the sign.

A Dialogical Presentation of Theory

Umberto Eco plays a central role in *The 7th Function of Language*. Bayard and Simon travel to Bologna to find him and ask him about Barthes. What they do not know at this moment, however, is that Eco is the president of the Logos Club (the 'Great Protagoras'), the secret debating society they have already encountered in Paris. During their trip to Bologna, Bayard and Simon visit a debate, in which Eco is later challenged in his capacity of Great Protagoras by Sollers. Sollers believes himself in possession of the 7th function and thus rhetorically invincible. Yet he does not know that he has only gotten to know a variant of the function falsified by Derrida. For this reason, the debating duel between Sollers and Eco turns into an exchange of blows between deconstruction and (historically informed) semiotics—probably the most striking example of a dialogical presentation and evaluation of theory.

The cryptic topic of the duel is "*On forcène doucement*" (307). Sollers uses associative language play to approach the topic he has not understood:

> Forcène... forcène... Fort... Scène... Fors... Seine... Faure (Félix)... Cène. [...] La force. Et la scène. La force sur scène. [...] Rodrigue, basically. Forêt sur Seine. (308–309).[28]

---

[28] "Forcène... forcène... Fort... Scène... Fors... Seine... Faure (Félix)... Cène. [...] La force. Et la scène. La force sur scène. Rodrigue, quoi. Forêt s/Seine" (432).

Eco, on the other hand, whose position the narrator sympathizes with not just in this scene, specifies the question by means of structuralism, (historical) semantics, and semiotics:

> *Allora*, the question that I would have discussed, if my honorable opponent had raised it, is this: Is '*forcèner doucement*' an oxymoron? Is this an association of two contradictory terms? *No*, if one considers the true etymology of *forcener*. *Si*, if one accepts the connotation of force in the false etymology. [...] he who '*forcène doucement*' is the poet, *ecco*. (311–312)[29]

Eco, as the intellectual and institutional center of the Logos Club, does not refrain from ultimately setting himself as the *telos* of his speech with "ecco". In addition, this illustrates that his speech reaches an end. While Sollers—in Derrida's manner—jumps from signifier to signifier, illustrating an infinite movement of *différance*, Eco performs a teleologically oriented semiosis. Eco, too, moves from signifier to signifier, but his process aims at the generation of meaning. Thus, he is finally able to formulate a plausible hypothesis regarding the meaning of the cryptic phrase "On forcène doucement". The debating duel between Sollers and Eco, therefore, is a striking example of evaluating theory within literature, critically in the first, affirmatively in the latter case.

In general, the debating duels—culminating in the one between Sollers and Eco—play an important role in Binet's novel. They serve as a dialogical presentation of theory with the combatants using different theoretical methods for approaching a topic or (cryptic) text. This allows various theories to be presented 'in action', especially deconstruction and semiotics. In addition to the (endo-)diegetic explanations of the respective theories given in other scenes (e.g., in Simon's talk on semiotics, Eco's explanations to Bayard, or Derrida's talk at the Cornell conference), the dialogical integration of theory sheds light on ways of interpreting texts (and reality).

---

[29] "*Allora*, la question que moi, j'aurais discutée, si mon honorable adversaire l'avait soulevée, aurait été la suivante : est-ce que 'forcèner doucement' est un oxymore ? Y a-t-il ou non association de deux termes contradictoires ? Non, si l'on considère la vraie étymologie de *forcener*. *Si*, si l'on admet la connotation de la force dans la fausse étymologie. [...] celui qui 'forcène doucement', c'est le poète, *ecco*" (436–437).

A Self-Reflexive Presentation of Theory

All the novels in question in this study are, in some way or another, intertextually linked to literary theory. Theory is transferred into a diegetic world, for example, by characters allegorically enacting it. *The 7th Function of Language*, however, goes one step further by 're-theorizing' its fictional reality. This may be regarded a metaization of theory, forming a first step of a possible extrapolation of (new or modified) theory from literature. In several moments, the protagonist Simon considers his life to be fiction-like. Thus, *The 7th Function of Language* not only presents theory as corresponding to fictional life, but also fictional life as corresponding to theory. In doing so, the novel further complicates the 'spiral of influence' between theory and the real.

The relevant passages of the novel all refer to Simon questioning his state of reality. This happens for the first time after he smokes a joint at the Cornell conference. To a group of students, he says: "I think I'm trapped in a fucking novel", eliciting the response: "Sounds cool, man. Enjoy the trip" (248).[30] In this scene, Simon's mixing of 'diegetic' levels could be easily ascribed to the effects of the cannabis. Yet he has similar experiences while completely sober. After winning a debating duel with an Italian in Venice, Simon is attacked by three masked thugs who have—as he learns later—been sent by the Italian for revenge. Simon is trapped in an impasse:

> While he retreats, Simon thinks: in the hypothesis where he is truly a character from a novel [...], what would he really risk? A novel is not a dream: you can die in a novel. Then again, the central character is not normally killed. Except, perhaps, at the end of the story. But if it *was* the end of the story, how would he know? How can he know what page of his life he is on? How can any of us know when we have reached our last page? (286–287)[31]

Similarly to Morris Zapp in *Small World* after he has been kidnapped, Simon arrives at ontological reflections about his existence. Whereas Zapp renounces theory as a consequence of his experience, however, Simon

---

[30] In the French original in English: *"I think I'm trapped in a novel"* – *"Sounds cool, man. Enjoy the trip"* (348).
[31] "Simon réfléchit pendant qu'il recule : dans l'hypothèse où il serait vraiment un personnage de roman [...], qu'est-ce que qu'il risquerait vraiment ? Un roman n'est pas un rêve : on peut mourir dans un roman. Ceci dit, *normalement*, on ne tue pas le personnage principal, sauf, éventuellement, à la fin de l'histoire. Mais si jamais c'était la fin d'histoire, comment le saurait-il ? Comment savoir à quelle page de sa vie on en est ? Comment savoir quand notre dernière page est arrivée ?" (401).

once more intensifies his dealing with theory. Zapp performs another methodological 'conversion' (after several conversions as a theorist before). Simon's actions, however, can be seen to offer an ironic view over (the history of) theory in general. He has been so strongly socialized in the context of theory that he cannot turn to reality even when confronted with an existentially threatening situation.

Yet the situation is not just ironic. In rather a postmodern way of using irony in earnest as well as in jest,[32] Simon arrives at existential considerations not *despite* but *because of* his training in theory. He turns to the idea of God as the author of everyone's life, the author who decides when and how the individually narrated biography comes to a conclusion. On the one hand, his thoughts are meta-theoretical and twist the spiral of theory and reality even more tightly. On the other hand, the journey from theory to life and back again can also result in a more solid grip on what being human may actually mean.

In a similar fashion, Umberto Eco arrives at ontological questions in his book *Kant and the Platypus*, having gone through the labyrinth of postmodern thought in his earlier works. Binet's decision to frame Eco as the 'secret hero' of his novel (he is the 'Great Protagoras', he wins against Sollers, he is the figure Simon identifies with), might indicate that Binet ultimately opts for a similar route through theory as Eco: a route that leads from empirical facts to their conceptualization within theory, to the transformation of theory into a fictional world (within novels), and finally to a modified view on theory—a view that integrates, for example, ontological questions which have been neglected by (parts of) post-structuralist thinking.

Consequently, in the last scene of the novel, Simon refers to God. Again, this is framed in an ironic fashion, through which, however, some serious aspects appear. The situation is comparable to the one in Venice: the same Italian rival threatens Simon, this time even more seriously. Simon once more thinks about the hypothetical 'author' of his life:

---

[32] See, for example, Umberto Eco's 'postmodern declaration of love' in Eco (1984, 67–68): "I think of the postmodern attitude as that of a man who loves a very cultivated woman and knows he cannot say to her 'I love you madly,' because he knows that she knows (and that she knows that he knows) that these words have already been written by Barbara Cartland. Still, there is a solution. He can say, 'As Barbara Cartland would put it, I love you madly.' [...] he will nevertheless have said to her what he wanted to say to the woman: that he loves her, but he loves her in an age of lost innocence."

He must deal with this hypothetical novelist the way he deals with God: always act as if God did not exist because if God does exist, he is at best a bad novelist [...]. [T]he ending of a story is in the hands of his character, and [...] that character is me. I am Simon Herzog. I am the hero of my own story. (357)[33]

This final scene is important for the novel as a whole in various respects. First, there is the turn to God. Even if it is not an actual turn toward God, but a hypothetical, ironized one, it shows that, in a moment of existential pressure, the idea of God springs to the character's mind. Second, there seems to be a self-empowerment of the character against his author, comparable to the Promethean self-empowerment of the human against God. Yet it remains unclear whether any of these self-empowerments are successful. Within the laws of the novel, the character remains in the hands of his author until the last letter of the book—which raises the question of whether a human being similarly remains in the hands of God until their last breath.

The 7th Function of Language does not offer an answer to this question. Yet by raising such questions, and doing so in an ironic way, Binet's novel allows for the possibility of various (and even contradictory) answers to exist at the same time. Binet's novel, therefore, does not only provide an account of a crucial year in the history of modern literary theory with amusing fictional amplifications, but also offers provocative reflections about what it means to be human.

Bibliography

Barthes, Roland (1972 [1957]): *Mythologies*. New York.
Binet, Laurent (2015): *La septième fonction du langage*. Paris.
Binet, Laurent (2018): *The 7th Function of Language*. Translated from the French by Sam Taylor. London.
Derrida, Jacques (1978 [1967]): *Writing and Difference*. Translated by Alan Bass. Chicago.
Eco, Umberto (1984): *Postscript to "The Name of the Rose"*. Translated from the Italian by William Weaver. San Diego et al.

---

[33] "Il faut faire avec ce romancier hypothétique comme avec Dieu : toujours faire comme si Dieu n'existait pas car si Dieu existe, c'est au mieux un mauvais romancier [...]. [L]a fin est entre les mains de son personnage, et ce personnage, c'est moi. Je suis Simon Herzog. Je suis le héros de ma propre histoire" (493).

Hermann-Brennecke, Gisela (2001): "Every Decoding is Another Encoding": A Didactic Discovery of David Lodge's "Small World". In: Wolf Kindermann and Gisela Hermann-Brennecke, eds.: *Echoes in a Mirror: The English Insitute after 125 Years*. Münster et al., 231–258.

Holmes, Frederick (1990): The Reader as Discoverer in David Lodge's "Small World". In: *Critique* 32, 47–57.

Hutcheon, Linda (1988): *A Poetics of Postmodernism: History, Theory, Fiction*. New York.

Hutcheon, Linda (2005): 'The Pastime of Past Time': Fiction, History, Historiographical Metafiction. In: Michael J. Hoffman and Patrick D. Murphy, eds.: *Essentials of the Theory of Fiction*. 275–296.

Kuhn, Thomas S. (1962): *The Structure of Scientific Revolutions*. Chicago.

Lodge, David (1981): *Working with Structuralism: Essays and Reviews on Nineteenth- and Twentieth-Century Literature*. Boston.

Lodge, David (2011 [1984]): *Small World*. London.

Mews, Siegfried (1989): The Professor's Novel: David Lodge's "Small World". In: *MLN* 104, 713–726.

Nünning, Ansgar (1995): *Von historischer Fiktion zu historiographischer Metafiktion. Vol. 1: Theorie, Typologie und Poetik des historischen Romans*. Trier.

Peters, Henning (2007): Metaisierungsverfahren und ihre Funktionspotentiale in postmodernen Romanzen: John Barth "Sabbatical. A Romance", David Lodge "Small World. An Academic Romance", Niall Williams "Four Letters of Love". In: Janine Hauthal et al., eds.: *Metaisierung in Literatur und anderen Medien: Theoretische Grundlagen – Historische Perspektiven – Metagattungen – Funktionen*. Berlin/New York, 340–360.

Rodríguez Higuera, Claudio Julio (2020): Semiotics to Die for: Review of Laurent Binet's "La septième fonction du langage". In: *Semiotica* 233, 205–210.

Schilling, Erik (2012): *Der historische Roman seit der Postmoderne: Umberto Eco und die deutsche Literatur*. Heidelberg.

Selejan, Corina (2016): "C'est la vie, c'est la narration": The Reader in Christine Brooke-Rose's "Textermination" and David Lodge's "Small World". In: *American, British and Canadian Studies* 26, 52–71.

Seligardi, Beatrice (2013): Retracing the Dynamics of 'University Fiction': Formula and Hybridization in David Lodge's "Campus Trilogy". In: Michael Basseler et al., eds.: *The Cultural Dynamics of Generic Change in Contemporary Fiction: Theoretical Frameworks, Genres and Model Interpretations*. Trier, 271–284.

White, Hayden (1973): *Metahistory: The Historical Imagination in Nineteenth-Century Europe*. Baltimore et al.

Wolf, Werner (1989): Literaturtheorie in der Literatur: David Lodges "Small World" als kritische Auseinandersetzung mit dem Dekonstruktivismus. In: *AAA: Arbeiten aus Anglistik und Amerikanistik* 14, 19–37.

CHAPTER 4

Topics in/of Theory

The novels analyzed in this chapter incorporate thematically oriented forms of theory. Patricia Duncker's *Hallucinating Foucault* integrates parts of Michel Foucault's discourse analysis and queer theory. The novel presents various options (of desire, sex, the 'normal', etc.), destabilizing their authority and hinting at the fluidity between the seemingly clear-cut boundaries—something that, again, might be extrapolated from the novel for new concepts of literary theory.

Ulrike Draesner's *Dowry* integrates gender theory by putting an intersex character at the center of the novel. This character serves both as a diegetic presentation of theory and as a checkpoint for the other characters' tolerance of ambivalence—thus using the other characters' opinions for an evaluation of theory. Moreover, the central ideas of gender theory are applied to peridiegetic aspects of the novel. This can be understood as a metaization and creation of theory.

Finally, Mithu Sanyal's *Identitti* (as well as Bernardine Evaristo's *Girl, Woman, Other*) can be seen, first, as an 'introduction' to critical race theory, presenting the current state of the debates. Second, the novel demonstrates a critical approach to theory by affirming certain positions or tendencies and devaluing others. Third, it offers perspectives that go beyond theory, for example by highlighting moral, emotional, or epistemological aspects not covered by (critical race) theory.

© The Author(s), under exclusive license to Springer Nature
Switzerland AG 2024
E. Schilling, *Theorizing Literature*,
https://doi.org/10.1007/978-3-031-53326-6_4

Queering Desire and Discourse:
Patricia Duncker's *Hallucinating Foucault* (1996)

Patricia Duncker, a British author and academic born in 1951, is known for her contributions to contemporary fiction, focusing on themes such as identity, gender, and the complexities of human relationships. Her works include *Hallucinating Foucault* (1996) and *The Deadly Space Between* (2002). Duncker's writing is characterized by intricate plotting, vivid characterizations, and a strong undercurrent of psychoanalytical and philosophical inquiry, establishing her as a significant voice in modern British literature.

Hallucinating Foucault is a narrative elaboration of Michel Foucault's ideas. Foucault's theories become part of the novel's diegetic world and transform it into a 'Foucaultian' universe. In particular, this is true for Foucault's concepts of (1) author, reader, and text, (2) discourse and intertextuality, (3) 'queer' voices within the text, and (4) the fuzzy boundary between the 'normal' and the 'pathologic' or 'mad'.

The novel is told by an anonymous first-person narrator. He studies at Cambridge and writes a doctoral thesis on the (fictional) French novelist Paul Michel, a contemporary author strongly influenced by Michel Foucault. In the library, the narrator meets "the Germanist" (who remains anonymous as well), a student writing a thesis on Schiller. They become a couple, and after some time the narrator notices that the Germanist is very familiar with Paul Michel's work. She has read all of his novels several times. When the narrator sees the Germanist writing a 'love letter' to Schiller, they argue about whether one has to remain neutral with regard to the object of one's research or whether—as the Germanist puts it—one has to fall in love with it. As a consequence, the Germanist urges the narrator to travel to France to look for the 'real' Paul Michel who is said to suffer from schizophrenia and live in an asylum in Paris.

The narrator travels to Paris, where he is told that Michel has been transferred to a hospital in Clermont-Ferrand. In the French national library, he finds some letters from Michel to Foucault. Michel tells Foucault that he writes his novels just for him. Soon, however, the narrator notices that the letters were never actually sent; even the letters in reply to Foucault's supposed responses are just part of a fictive game. The narrator continues to Clermont where he meets Michel in the hospital. After a rough start they become friends and spend long afternoons in the hospital garden, talking about authorship or the differences between 'sane' and 'mad'.

After two weeks, Michel's psychological condition has strongly improved, so much so that he is allowed to leave the hospital for two months. Michel and the narrator rent a car and drive south to the hinterland of Nice. The narrator's interest in Michel's texts is already mixed with a growing interest in their author. In the Midi, this culminates in Michel and the narrator becoming lovers. As a consequence, the narrator comes to learn of the details of Michel's past: Michel regards his authorship as a secret complicity with Foucault, claiming that they had been writing for each other as mutual readers. In addition, Michel tells the narrator that he met the Germanist when she was a child. In the last night before he has to return to the hospital, Michel suffers a fatal car accident under the influence of drugs and alcohol. After the funeral, the narrator returns to Cambridge and finishes his thesis, without ever mentioning his acquaintance with Michel.

Author, Reader, and Text

Right from the beginning, *Hallucinating Foucault* questions the relationship between author, reader, and text, using theory for a dynamization of the story. The novel, however, does not simply follow Foucault in exchanging the author for the "author-function".[1] It addresses authorship and readership through a shift in the differentiation of author and text. In the beginning, the narrator works on his doctoral thesis and insists on keeping text and author separate. In doing so, he is challenged by the Germanist:

> [The narrator:] "I'm not writing about his life. I'm studying his fiction."
> [The Germanist:] "How can you separate the two?" [...]
> [The narrator:] "You can't interpret writing in terms of a life. It's too simple. Writing has its own rules." (23)[2]

The narrator insists on distinguishing between author and text, as is common in literature studies. He refutes the Germanist's objection by declaring an interpretive focus on the author "too simple" and insisting on the characteristics of (fictional) writing. A little later, though, the Germanist persuades the narrator to travel to Paris in search of the author Paul

---

[1] Foucault (1998 [1969], 305–306). As Ryan (2011, 131) stresses, "the novel brings together the author-theories of Barthes and Foucault".
[2] Quotations from the novel here and in the following are taken from Duncker (1996).

Michel—who is as much 'an' author within the realm of Duncker's fictional world as 'the' author with regard to the theoretical position of authorship. When the narrator meets Michel, the boundaries between life and literature become unclear:

> [Paul Michel:] "You're too young to be writing a book about me. You're too young to be reading me." [...]
> [The narrator:] "Remember—I'm writing about your fiction, not you." [...]
> [Paul Michel:] "Then—what in God's name, mon petit, are you doing here?" (98)

The narrator lands in a contradiction between his scholarly attempt to work on texts and his personal dealings with their author. A little later, the narrator observes: "All the grant money I had been given to study his writing was spent on him" (110). He realizes that "the two [author and text], which I had always held in my mind, distinct and separate, were now no longer separate" (112). The culmination of this process is, of course, the narrator's falling in love not only with the novels but also with their author.

On the one hand, this process could be seen as a reconstruction of the author, explicitly contradicting Foucault's author-function. On the other hand, one might consider it a renunciation of the traditional categories of author and text in general—a renunciation that rather focuses on the discourses[3] which are a basis of both an author's life and works. Michel himself hints at the parallels:

> I make the same demands of people and fictional texts, petit—that they should be open-ended, carry within them the possibility of being and of changing whoever it is they encounter. (111)

For Michel, there is no difference between people and texts, at least in certain respects. The important aspect for him is a structural openness—for the interaction with a recipient. In one more dimension, the novel blurs boundaries: authors become readers, and vice versa. The focus lies on the discourse, not on the question of who speaks and who listens.

Both the Germanist and Michel 'invert' the traditional position of the reader. The Germanist justifies her love letter to Schiller by stating: "If

---

[3] According to Reiling (2021, 112) the novel presents the 'textual practices' of the various characters. Matthies (2016, 263) observes that all main characters are presented as reading and writing persons.

you're not in love with the subject of your thesis it'll all be very dry stuff" (14). Just as in concepts of love based on reciprocity, the position of author and reader is not clearly marked. When the reader loves the author (and vice versa), their positions may change. Similarly, Paul Michel writes about Foucault:

> The love between a writer and a reader is never celebrated. It can never be proved to exist. But he [Foucault] was the man I loved most. He was the reader for whom I wrote. (154)

Later on, Michel argues that he and Foucault wrote most of their work as a private communication—a secret game of lovers who subsequently exchange the positions of author and reader, demonstrating their mutual affection by reacting to the other's texts. Duncker's novel does not state whether this is 'true' (within the realm of the fictional world) or just a hypothesis of Michel who might also be 'hallucinating Foucault' as his reader. Yet this does not change the way authorship and readership are presented in *Hallucinating Foucault*: as fragile, ever-changing constructs (or 'functions'), linked to each other by texts (or 'discourses'), originating in life, but not definitely reducible to it.

Intertextuality and Discourse Analysis

Intertextuality is a fundamental compositional principle of *Hallucinating Foucault*, manifesting in various forms. For example, Paul Michel is not only the full first name of the real Paul-Michel Foucault, Michel as a fictional character also explicitly quotes Foucault in the novel:

> [He] read from [...] Foucault's preface to *La Volonté de Savoir* [...]. *There are times in life when the question of knowing if one can think differently than one thinks and perceive differently than one sees is absolutely necessary if one is to go on looking and reflecting at all.* (31)

Foucault's idea of a change of perspective is not only endodiegetically presented (in the sense of a self-contained element of theory within the novel), but it also has implications for the actions of certain characters and thus plays a dynamizing role as well. For example, one of the doctors states that working in the psychiatric system has taught her "to see things differently" (92). Moreover, Michel does not only quote Foucault; he also lives and writes similarly to him. Michel publishes "five novels [...] between 1968 and 1983" (5–6), exactly the timeframe in which Foucault's major works were published; and the "two writers explore similar themes: death, sexuality, crime, madness" (31). Thus, there are self-reflexive, direct, and indirect references to Foucault's theory in Duncker's novel.[4]

As the novel illustrates in various fashions, discourse—understood as the utterances themselves—is independent from the people who create or pursue it. At a given moment in a given culture, certain discourses about sexuality, crime, or madness may be dominant. What is not important, however, is who produces these discourses.[5] In his letters to Foucault, Michel points out:

> [T]he writer and the Muse should be able to change places, speak in both voices so that the text shifts, melts, changes hands. The voices are not owned. They are indifferent who speaks. (61)

That "voices are not owned" is one of the main insights of discourse analysis, harking back to Mikhail Bakhtin's idea of 'dialogism',[6] of different voices being present in the same utterance, blurring its seemingly unambiguous meaning toward a 'polyphony' of senses. Consequently, both Michel and Foucault renounce the use of names. Michel does not get to know his lover's name,[7] just as Foucault self-critically sketches namelessness as an ideal he should have followed in *The Order of Things*: "[W]hy did I use the names of authors in *The Order of Things*? Why not avoid their use altogether?"[8]

Instead of names, both Foucault and Michel are interested in the (verbal, formal, societal) structures they identify as the basis of discourses. Foucault says that his "objective in *The Order of Things* had been to analyze verbal clusters as discursive layers".[9] In one of his letters to Foucault, Michel writes: "You take the matter of history. I take the raw substance of

---

[4] Reiling (2021, 113) stresses that Duncker's text explicitly refers to the relations between Michel and Foucault through the novel's paratext, a list in which the biographies and works of both are correlated.
[5] As Matthies (2016, 264) points out, the different voices do not 'belong' to anyone, but are present in the form of discourses and power.
[6] Bakhtin (1981 [1934/35], 276–277).
[7] "What did you say your name was? [...] No, don't tell me" (96).
[8] Foucault (1998 [1969], 300).
[9] Ibid. 299.

feeling. Out of both we make shapes" (62).[10] These shapes—discursive structures and concepts—are the link between Michel, Foucault, and Duncker's novel. All three go back to a certain material (history, feelings, texts) in order to re-arrange it and to have people see it differently. Different perspectives arise according to the different ordering concepts established. The basis of this perspectivity lies in the separation of voices from their speakers, which allows for the simultaneous presence of different meanings and contexts in the same utterance—and therefore for a plurality of interpretation.

'Queer' Voices Within the Text

Among other aspects, *Hallucinating Foucault* is a novel about the narrator's coming out—or at least about queering his (sexual and intellectual) desire.[11] The novel does not give any information as to whether the narrator ultimately 'is' gay (he returns to his girlfriend in some way, at least)— and this question is also not important. Far more interesting is that his development from a heterosexual, 'straight' person to a homosexually interested, queer one is a key part of the novel's unfolding. This is quite obvious on the diegetic level, yet it is accompanied by a series of 'discursive' hints right from the beginning: words and sentences that refer to a first-level meaning (mostly within the context of the story), while also offering a second-level meaning if understood in the context of (homo-) sexual discourses. Thus, the novel presents various 'queer' voices within the text—and illustrates Foucault's (as well as Bakhtin's and Kristeva's) understanding of a novel (or communication in general) as polyphonic.

The narrator's affair with the Germanist already allows for a reading of ambiguities. His observation about the start ("that was how the affair between us began. She was a very good linguist. She spoke fluent French", 10) is at first a statement about their mutual interests and profession: an

---

[10] Michel's statement "Out of memory and desire I make shapes" (64) is one of the crucial examples of this literary technique. As explained above, it links to Foucault's scholarly principles. In addition, it gives important topics of Duncker's novel: memory, which might be extended to mind and thus fictional worlds, and desire, which is fundamental for the novel in many ways, as I will show in the following paragraph. Finally, "memory and desire" is, of course, a quote from T.S. Eliot's poem *The Waste Land* which provides a third resonant cavity for its use in Duncker's novel.

[11] For some—yet partially freely speculating—remarks on Paul Michel's homosexuality, see Kriston (2010, 80–85).

occupation with languages and literatures. Yet within the context of a sexual relationship, made explicit by the word "affair", the words "linguist" and "French" gain other connotations as well. They may now be understood as a hint to certain sexual practices inextricably interwoven into the main statement.

This double coding is even more obvious for the narrator's rising homosexual interest. When he first meets the Germanist's father—who is gay—the father mocks him and his daughter by saying: "If she doesn't give you a good time, boy, cruise down to us in London" (20–21). The sentence is more openly double-coded than the one about 'French' activities. The father offers an invitation to London—teasing his daughter by insinuating that she might not treat her boyfriend well. In addition, the father offers a sexually coded invitation by using the verb "to cruise", which does not only refer to a drive itself but also to the activity of looking for a short-term sexual partner.

This process comes to a head with the narrator's arrival in Paris. He undertakes a seemingly innocent walk through the city: "On Sunday morning I walked straight through the Marais [...] and came out on the rue de Rivoli" (53). On the one hand, this could be construed as a simple piece of sightseeing. On the other hand, the route described mirrors the fundamental process the narrator undergoes in the novel as a whole, compressed into just one sentence. When he starts his walk, he is "straight", that is, heterosexual. Then he passes through the Marais, the gay quarter of Paris. And at the end he "comes out" which in the context of the sentence and the novel as a whole may very well be read as the 'coming out' of a homosexual person.

The last step of this process is the actual relationship between the narrator and Paul Michel. It is initiated by a discussion about the unimportance of sex. Shortly before they sleep with each other, Michel says to the narrator: "Listen, petit. Sex isn't an issue between us. I don't usually sleep with friends" (143). As in the other cases, this statement can be understood in reference to the 'obvious' meaning of the word "sex", namely that of sexual intercourse. However, in the discourse on homosexuality and/or in the renunciation of clear categories, "sex" may also be understood as "biological sex", converting the possible meaning of "Sex isn't an issue between us" into "We don't care what sex the other is".

When Michel later tells the narrator about his meeting the Germanist ten years earlier, he also tells him that he initially mistook her for a boy:

The child was waiting for me [...]. I saw him first [...]. His ambiguity suddenly broke over me with all the force of the sea against the great rocks. I had not mistaken the nature of this child. But I had mistaken her sex. (161)

Thus, for Michel as well as for the narrator, biological sex is not important.[12] They do not only express a 'queer' desire in terms of the opposite to 'straight'. They also queer their own desire by keeping it ambiguous—a queering that pervades the whole novel and reflects on Foucault's writings about hermaphrodites.

The 'Normal' and the 'Mad'

Foucault's writings play an important role in *Hallucinating Foucault* with regard to authorship, discourse analysis, and queerness. In addition, spatial aspects of the novel mirror Foucault's theories about the heterotopia.[13] In his text about *Other Spaces* (1967), Foucault states:

There are [...], probably in every culture, [...] real places [...] which are something like counter-sites, [...] in which the real sites [...] are simultaneously represented, contested, and inverted. [...] The heterotopia is capable of juxtaposing in a single real place several spaces, several sites that are in themselves incompatible.[14]

In Duncker's novel, the hospital in which the narrator looks for Michel is built as a heterotopia in the sense of Foucault:

The hospital was like a city within a city. There were gardens, car parks, walkways, cafés, shops [...]. Hospitals are strange intermediary zones where sickness and health become ambiguous, relative states. (76)

On the one hand, the hospital is a real place within the world surrounding it, taking up several of its characteristics, so that the "real sites" are "represented". On the other hand, some crucial conditions are "inverted" and, as such, opposed to the "real", such as sickness and health being no longer clearly separated within the hospital. The ambiguity of the 'sick'

---

[12] On the question of masculinity in the novel, see Griffin (2000, 76–78).
[13] Spatial aspects play an important role for the novel in general. Cf. Reiling (2021, 121–122).
[14] Foucault (1986, 24).

and the 'healthy', though, does not only appear within the heterotopia of the hospital. The boundaries of what is 'sane' are gradually eroded in general. This can be observed in a—once more seemingly 'innocent'—remark of the narrator at the beginning of the novel:

> Writing a thesis is a lonely obsessive activity. You live inside your head, nowhere else. University libraries are like madhouses, full of people pursuing wraiths, hunches, obsessions. The person with whom you spend most of your time is the person you're writing about. (4–5)

The terminology used to describe the activities of a doctoral student is comparable to that used for psychiatric patients. Both suffer from obsessions, both pursue seemingly irrational hunches, both spend time with 'imaginary' people. Another similarity between academia and psychiatry is opened up in the French word "tutelle". One of the doctors informs the narrator that Paul Michel "has an administrative trustee. The system in France is called 'la tutelle'" (48). In an academic context, the same word is used for the supervision of a doctoral thesis.

Thus, right from the beginning it is unclear whether the narrator is 'sane' and Michel 'mad', or the other way round—or whether these categories do not make a lot of sense at all (in arguably the same way as the categories of straight and queer). This is not only true for the context of academia, but also for love—thereby recalling a tradition that goes back to antiquity, especially Plato. Michel says to the narrator: "Listen, petit, [...] you are twenty-two and very much in love. I am forty-six and a certified lunatic. You are much more likely to be insane than I am" (149). There is no clear difference here between 'normal' and 'lunatic', since it all depends on the definition of 'normal'—as Foucault illustrates in his writings by using the examples of sexuality, psychiatry, and prisons.

Literature as a 'Counter-Site'

At the end of the novel, Paul Michel turns this observation into a poetological comment on the powers of fiction. He says: "All writers are, somewhere or other, mad. [...] Because we do not believe in the stability of reality. We know [...] that reality can be invented, reordered, constructed, remade" (124). As stated in Foucault's *The Order of Things* (quoted above): reality is subject to its perception and description. Depending on one's perspective, terminology, or structuring concepts, 'the real' may look very different.[15]

Through her various references to Foucault, Patricia Duncker illustrates that literature can act as a counter-site to reality—a place in which, to paraphrase Foucault, the real is simultaneously represented, contested, and inverted. The aspect of simultaneity is important, as I have shown with the examples of queering desire and sex: literature can not only invent diegetic worlds that are different from the 'real', but also present various realities at the same time. By integrating key ideas from Bakhtin's concept of 'dialogism' and Foucault's ideas on discourse analysis, *Hallucinating Foucault* functions as a novel that simultaneously presents different options (of desire, sex, the 'normal', etc.), destabilizes their authority, and suggests the fluidity between seemingly clear-cut boundaries—something that, in turn, could be extrapolated from the novel for new concepts of literary theory.

Questioning the Gender of People and Texts: Ulrike Draesner's *Dowry* (*Mitgift*, 2002)

Ulrike Draesner, born in 1962, is a contemporary writer and scholar known for her contributions to German literature through her novels, essays, and poetry. Her work often explores historical and familial narratives, linguistic experimentation, and themes of identity and displacement, as in *Sieben Sprünge vom Rand der Welt* (2014). Celebrated for their narrative complexity and interdisciplinary reach, Draesner's writings have garnered critical acclaim and positioned her as a central figure in the landscape of twenty-first-century German literature.

Her novel *Dowry* (*Mitgift*, 2002) presents various processes of interpretation within the fictional world—in particular, as a diegetic and peridiegetic elaboration of theory. At the center of the interpretations is the gender ambivalence of Anita, one of the main characters.[16] Different characters in the novel adopt different ways of interpreting this ambivalence,

---

[15] Reiling (2021, 113), therefore, calls the novel a hybridization of reality and imagination, as well as of fact and fiction.

[16] Research has pointed out that other characters' perspectives are portrayed rather than Anita's. Cf. Vedder (2013, 415–416). Bartl (2014, 298) emphasizes that Anita remains a blind spot to be interpreted. Similarly, Catani (2009, 76) underlines that the information the reader receives about Anita is constructed in two ways: through the perspective of Aloe and through the process of remembering the sister.

with varying consequences. Some of the interpretations are reductionist, eliminating ambivalence or avoiding interpretation altogether. Others illustrate a preference for either categorization or a deliberate rejection of categorization.

Dowry is about two sisters, Anita and Aloe. The novel is told from Aloe's perspective and covers the present—Aloe in her early thirties—while also including a number of retrospective passages. Her sister Anita is born intersex—something her parents do not accept, but treat as a defect. Through hormone therapies and operations, Anita is turned into a 'perfect' woman who works as a model for swimsuits. Anita gets married to Walter, and they have a son, Stefan. At some point, however, Anita decides to live the other side of her gender identity: she wants to become a man. Her husband cannot bear this and kills Anita and himself. Aloe works as an observer of Anita's biography, witnessing the various steps that turn Anita into a woman. She develops an interest for ambivalent phenomena in art and falls in love with Lukas, a physicist who deals with ambiguity in the sciences. In the end, it is she who is left to care for Anita's son Stefan.

Anita can be considered the center of the novel. As I will explore in detail, Anita's gender ambivalence provokes a variety of reactions among the other characters. Her parents try to turn her into an unambiguous woman. Anita sees herself as a bivalent[17] person, becoming first female, then male. Aloe, on the other hand, tries to ignore gender categorizations altogether. Other characters are fine with accepting various interpretive options at the same time, some even with contradicting ones. Gender theory thus offers the literary text a central quandary that it can explore within its diegetic universe—theory dynamizes the story. The different possibilities of interpretation are mirrored on the peridiegetic level of the novel, which integrates elements of novel, novella, and drama, thereby blurring its own genre (or gender) identity. *Dowry* thus works with ambivalent gender/genre structures on the diegetic and peridiegetic levels.

One Interpretive Option

From Anita's birth onward, her parents Holger and Ingrid try to turn their intersex child into a definitive daughter. They send her to hormone

---

[17] Details on the various terms describing ambivalence and similar concepts (bivalence, ambiguity, etc.) will be laid out in a publication by Jakob Lenz and Erik Schilling, probably in 2025.

therapies and surgeries: "Anita became an unambiguous, operated little animal in a state of men and women, in a blissful world of two sexes."[18] The parents never wonder whether there might be a third sex or gender besides men and women. To them, Anita's being intersex is a 'mistake' of nature that must be corrected. The 'mistake' is taken care of by doctors who follow an (almost) binary logic as well: "They bent over Anita. It's a quick operation, they said, and then everything will be normal, up to 93 percent normal, even 95, 98 percent. That's as much as they would manage, but then 100 percent normal isn't normal, no one is that normal."[19] The doctors' statement implies that there could be a spectrum of the sexes—but their confidence in clearly assigning Anita to a given end of the spectrum implicitly negates the assumption of its existence.

In order not to cause a stir, Anita's being intersex is kept silent both inside and outside the family. Any form of standing out is undesirable to the parents. The mother's remark to Aloe that she is so 'simple' (i.e., unambiguous) is the highest form of compliment conceivable from her mouth. Only in a moment of rage, when Anita has set fire to her parents' house, does the mother say aloud what Anita is in her eyes, namely a "fucking hermaphrodite".[20] With the word "hermaphrodite", she names the phenomenon for the first time in the novel. However, using the radically pejorative attribute "fucking" she positions herself very clearly with respect to the tolerance of ambivalence. Ingrid does not regard ambivalence as something interesting, but as a threat. It is something to be avoided at all costs, something that will bring shame.

The same applies—to an even more extreme degree—to Anita's husband Walter. Anita tells him that, after her life as a woman, she wants to live the gender (and sex) variant 'man', which is part of her as well. When Walter learns that Anita wants to take hormones and finally have an operation, he kills Anita and himself. Gender ambivalence is unbearable for him. In contrast to Anita's parents, he is not fine with the doctors

---

[18] "Anita wurde ein zurechtoperiertes, eindeutiges Tierchen im Staat der Männer und Frauen, der seligen Zweigeschlechtlichkeit" (105). Quotations from the novel here and in the following are taken from Draesner (2002) [the English version is my translation].

[19] "Sie beugten sich über Anita. Das ist schnell operiert, sagten sie, und dann ist alles normal, normal zu 93 Prozent, zu 95, 98. Höher kämen sie nicht, aber 100 Prozent normal sei nicht normal, das sei niemand" (104–105).

[20] "Scheißzwitter" (213).

'transforming' Anita into either one or the other unambiguous variant of sex; he wants Anita to remain unambiguously female. For him, the preference for the unambiguous is thus also connected to a preference for one specific manifestation of the unambiguous.

Two Options Following One Another

Anita sees herself as bivalent. Having been transformed into a woman, she works as a model for swimwear. This can be read as a 'hyper-femininity',[21] which is underscored by her motherhood. With her decision to have herself operated into a man, however, Anita points out her bivalence:

> [Aloe:]—But it is an illusion to assume that one can return to anything.—I know, whispered Anita, I know. But I am not at all interested in returning. I know it all, the new conceptions of authenticity and theories of the body, Butler, Foucault, Barthes, the whole post-modern up and down. Let the theory just spin its loops, it's fun in and of itself. But for me, quite simply, [...] it's about my everyday life. For me, it's about a possibility that's been in me all along. I want to finally realize it. Otherwise, there'll always be a part of me that I'm not really living, you know? (359)[22]

Anita aims for a life in which—seen as a whole—she would have spent the first half as a woman, the second half as a man. However, in both halves of her life she would have been clearly assigned to one sex and gender each, thus not being ambivalent in the sense of simultaneity, but bivalent in the sense of two possible options, of which only one is realized at one moment in time.[23]

---

[21] Cf. Willer (2004, 94); Vedder (2013, 415).

[22] "[Aloe:] – Aber es ist eine Illusion anzunehmen, daß man zu irgend etwas zurückkehren kann. | – Ich weiß, flüsterte Anita, ich weiß. Doch mir geht es gar nicht darum zurückzukehren. Ich kenne das alles, die neuen Authentizitätsauffassungen und Körpertheorien, Butler, Foucault, Barthes, den ganzen postmodernen Auf- und Abwasch. Soll die Theorie sich nur in ihren Schleifen drehen, das macht ja Spaß, für sich genommen. Aber mir geht es, ganz einfach, [...] um mein alltägliches Leben. Mir geht es um eine Möglichkeit, die in mir angelegt war. Sie will ich endlich auch verwirklichen. Sonst lebe ich doch immer an einer Hälfte von mir vorbei, verstehst du?" (359).

[23] The simultaneity of (at least) two contradictory options is what Berndt and Kammer (2009) see as the central aspect of ambiguity.

Avoiding Categories

While Anita lives her gender ambivalence as a bivalence—two different but clearly defined options—Aloe tries to completely abolish sex and gender as categories for herself. Her preference not to interpret phenomena on the basis of gender is expressed, for example, in her admiration of Spencer Tunick's photographs, photographs that "pulled the meaning out of bodies. Masculine, feminine—this too began to dissolve."[24] A more extreme form of avoiding gender categories is Aloe's anorexia. It does not only reduce her weight, but also her femininity, for example by shrinking her breasts. When she is admitted to a clinic, Aloe explicitly refers to herself as a "neuter", exhibiting neither female nor male characteristics.[25] At the clinic, however, she learns that it is not possible to avoid gender categories, at least in the case of anorexia; on the contrary, the doctor informs her that the female body develops male characteristics in response to anorexia, such as an increased production of androgens.

Aloe's pregnancy also proves to defy categories in terms of sex and gender.[26] At the end of the third month, the embryo in her womb dies and has to be removed in surgery. The child dies before it has a clearly identifiable sexual identity. Of course, the sex could be determined genetically, but this possibility is not realized and the unborn child remains sexually indeterminate.

The Unambiguous in a Polyvalent World

Erick is a colleague of Aloe's boyfriend Lukas. Together with Lukas, he works as a theoretical physicist. Erick is characterized by the fact that he "always answers a question five minutes later, because beforehand, like the chess computer Deep Blue, he has to let hundreds of thousands of possible answers and their possible effects rattle through his head. It's only

---

[24] "[S]augten die Bedeutung aus Körpern. Männlich, weiblich – auch dies begann sich aufzulösen" (243).

[25] "Aloe wasn't the only one here. Many practised being a neuter"; "Aloe war hier ja nicht die einzige. Viele übten Neutrum sein" (151).

[26] Draesner first develops this perspective on the embryo in her "Hermaphroditic proem", published a few years before the novel. This poem can be read as a proem to the novel; it adds a fourth genre category (poetry) to the three genres blended in the novel (novel, novella, and drama). See Schilling (2024) for details.

mathematical formulas and results [...] that he speaks at a normal pace" (140).[27] With regard to a theory of ambivalence in interpretive processes, Erick's behavior is more than a mere quirk.

He distinguishes two variants of attributing meaning: in some cases ("mathematical formulas"), he immediately states the unambiguous result. With ambiguous options, however, he hypothetically plays through a multitude of variants. This seems strange, since in everyday life people have usually learned to distinguish relevant from less relevant variants of meaning. But just as certain mental disorders (e.g., manias) invalidate the hierarchization of relevant or reasonable attributions of meaning, Erick rightly assumes a potentially infinite polyvalence of the world.

With his quasi-avoidance of clear statements where the unambiguous is possible only as an approximation, Erick, without explicitly stating it, draws attention to disambiguation in everyday life. This can be related back to the disambiguation of sex and gender, which is also constantly done in everyday life.

An Overwhelming Number of Options

Patrizia, a friend of Aloe, represents a form of gendering that encompasses an overwhelming number of options. Patrizia is an expert of gender and feminist theory, knowing "all the post- and cyberfeminist jargon".[28] She recommends reading material to Aloe: "Kristeva, Cixous, Irigaray", but "Aloe's head was buzzing [...], she was reading, but none of these theories had anything to do with her experience".[29]

Thus, a conflict arises between the overwhelming number of options in gender theory and the actual experience of gender. Where gender, in Judith Butler's formulation, is not thought of as biologically given, but as a performative action, there are—at least in theory—no limits to the attribution and the performance of gender. Yet in everyday life, these are

---

[27] "Er [...] antwortet immer erst fünf Minuten später auf eine Frage, weil er zuvor wie der Schachcomputer Deep Blue Hunderttausende von möglichen Antworten und ihre möglichen Auswirkungen durch seinen Kopf rattern lassen muß. Nur mathematische Formeln und Ergebnisse [...] spricht er in normalem Tempo" (140).

[28] "[D]en gesamten post- und cyberfeministischen Jargon" (26). As Catani (2009, 79) puts it: Patrizia, like Butler, understands biological sex not as a bodily given, but as a regulating norm.

[29] "Kristeva, Cixous, Irigaray"; "Aloe schwirrte schon nach dem Telefonat der Kopf, sie las, doch keine dieser Theorien hatte mit ihren Erfahrungen zu tun" (242).

limited by cultural and practical factors, among others—and can thus be seen as a rejection of theory. In the novel, these limits are underscored by Aloe's distinction between theory and experience, but also by Patrizia's confession to Aloe that she longs to be radically reduced to her biological sex for once: "You understand: to be taken properly. According to the worst clichés. Like the feminists always forbid. Submission and all that. That's exactly what's fun."[30]

Ambivalence

The novel's characters perceive (sex and gender) ambivalence as a problem. This is particularly clear in the case of those who strive for one interpretive option or two options after one another. Yet even Erick's approach, differentiating between unambiguous and ambiguous options, or that of Patrizia, which allows for an overwhelming number of options, equally have their limits. And Aloe's preference of avoiding categories completely can be understood as a strategy to avoid interpretation at all. In neither case is ambivalence appreciated. But the characters' comparatively low tolerance for ambivalence is not the ultimate statement offered in the novel: in its form, mediality, and title, the novel shows appreciation for ambivalence—and thus recaptures on a peridiegetic level what the characters 'fail' to achieve on the diegetic one.

With regard to its form, the novel combines the genres of novel, drama, and novella.[31] At first glance, the text is clearly a novel. However, the novel is divided into five sections that correspond to the five-act structure typical for many plays, a structure widely discussed in drama theory:[32] the first act presents an introduction of the problem, the second its complication, the third the climax, the fourth a retarding moment, and the fifth the catastrophe. All these structural elements can be found in Draesner's novel as well. Genre similarities to the novella are present through direct and indirect references to Heinrich von Kleist's novella *The Earthquake in Chili*. Its end, for example, is taken up verbatim in *Dowry*. And just like *Dowry*, Kleist's novella is concerned with norms and their ruptures, with biologi-

---

[30] "Verstehst du: richtig genommen werden. Den schlimmsten Klischees entsprechend. Wie die Feministinnen es immer verbieten. Unterwerfung und so. Genau das macht Spaß" (112).
[31] Stritzke (2011, 192–206) has analyzed this in detail.
[32] Cf. Freytag (1900).

cal and cultural processes (an 'illegitimate' child), and with the narrative similarities of 'natural' and 'cultural' families when, at the end of Kleist's novella, a child is adopted. By drawing on dramatic structure and references to Kleist's novella, Draesner illustrates that her novel—just like her protagonist—can be seen as a mixture of different genres.

This mixture applies to questions of media as well. *Dowry* continuously incorporates references to art. Art (and literature) thus creates what the characters fail to achieve: a presentation of the world that allows ambivalence to exist as such. Virtually all of the artwork referred to in the novel emphasizes gender ambivalence, such as the two artworks compared to Anita in order to characterize the gender fluidity: "Anita, the feminine boy from an early Raphael painting, no: Giotto's Madonna that hung in the Uffizi, a *maestà* with slightly parted lips, fine long nose, and a face like ebony and milk, so straight cut, so symmetrical and interwoven—so androgynous."[33] With the media change from literature to art, representations of both sexes can equally be found in Anita as an androgynous figure: the boy as well as the Madonna. The same holds true for the photographs by Spencer Tunick the novel refers to.

Finally, ambivalence is represented in the title: the multi-layered term "Dowry" ("Mitgift" in German) forms a link between familial, legal, and biological forms of inheritance.[34] In addition, 'Mitgift', as the gift a bride receives from her family for her wedding, carries strongly gendered connotations. Aloe's boyfriend Lukas generalizes the meaning of 'dowry' to any gift one receives from one's family: a dowry is not only material, but can also be construed in social, cultural, or genetic terms, among others. In addition, Aloe points out that such a gift can be a burden as well: "The lot you get given by your dear ancestors. Actually, a gift ... and a little poison."[35] In the case of the dowry, its significance depends on what the recipients make of it, and the many ways in which it can be interpreted.

Thanks to the novel's ambivalence with regard to form, mediality, and title, at least, the readers find themselves in a situation comparable to that of its characters. While each of the characters somehow has to deal with

---

[33] "Anita, der feminine Knabe aus einem frühen Raffaelbild, nein: Giottos Madonna, die in den Uffizien hing, eine Maestà mit leicht geöffneten Lippen, feiner langer Nase und einem Gesicht wie aus Ebenholz und Milch, so gerade geschnitten, so symmetrisch und durchwirkt – so androgyn" (97).

[34] Vedder (2013, 417).

[35] "Die Portion, die du abbekommst von deinen lieben Vorfahren. Eigentlich ein Geschenk, oder ...? – ... und ein bißchen Gift" (46). The term 'Gift' in German means 'poison'.

Anita's ambivalence, the readers have to deal with manifold options for interpreting the novel and the ambivalence it contains. Of course, readers are free to take steps toward a more definitive categorization of the novel, by regarding it as a novel, for example, and nothing but a novel. In doing so, however, they show the same reductionist approach typical to some of the characters striving for unambiguity. The novel, therefore, similarly to its protagonist Anita, is better dealt with by an interpretive culture that accepts its ambivalence and does not try to categorize it or explain it in seemingly unambiguous ways.

Due to this, the novel may be understood as a handling of theory in two ways: first, gender theory is integrated by putting an intersex character at the center of the novel. This character serves both as a diegetic presentation of theory and as a checkpoint for the other characters' tolerance of ambivalence—thus using the other characters' opinions toward being intersex for an evaluation of gender theory. Second, the central ideas of gender theory are, as shown, applied to peridiegetic aspects of the novel. This can be understood as a metaization and even creation of theory: the novel provides the basis for a transfer of theoretical concepts from one field (gender) to another (genre). Theoretical reflections on the chances and limits of genres in literature could easily follow that, for example, by noting the reductionist aspects of genres and keeping an openness toward phenomena situated on the borders of established categories.

COLORING THE WORLD(VIEW): MITHU SANYAL'S *IDENTTITI* (2021), WITH A SIDE GLANCE TO BERNADINE EVARISTO'S *GIRL, WOMAN, OTHER* (2019)

Mithu Sanyal, born in 1971, is a writer, journalist, and cultural critic known for her work on gender, language, and identity politics. She gained recognition for her non-fiction books *Vulva*, which explores cultural and historical perspectives on female sexuality, and *Rape: From Lucretia to #MeToo*, which critically examines the discourse surrounding sexual violence. Sanyal's contributions extend beyond traditional literary formats to include op-eds, radio features, and public lectures, making her an important voice in contemporary discussions of gender and social issues.

Her novel *Identtiti* (2021) tells the story of a seemingly Indian professor of postcolonial studies at the University of Düsseldorf, Germany. The professor, named Saraswati, is known for her controversial views on race theory and even bans white students from her classes. At some point, however, someone leaks information to the press that Saraswati is actually the daughter of a German family who has gone through a 'racial transition': she has spent several years in India, immersed herself in Indian culture, adopted Indian customs (such as dress), and even changed her skin color. When people find out that she is 'transracial', she is widely accused of fraud, cultural appropriation, and stealing from an underprivileged group. Against this background, the novel deals with (literary) theory in different modes, on different levels and with different functions.

Modes of Integrating Theory in "Identitti"

In terms of its integration of critical race theory, *Identitti* can be considered a docufiction[36]: the novel gives full details of current debates in critical race theory, using the concrete (fictional) example of Saraswati as well as (real) disputes in the field.[37] Several intertextual relations in the novel are referred to, directly through a quasi-academic list of references at the end of the novel, and indirectly through the presentation of characters in the book who bear the names of real people (e.g., Kwame Anthony Apphia, Shappi Khorsandi, Jordan Peterson) and comment on the fictional debates in ways they have done elsewhere.

In an ironic and entirely fitting variation on the standard fictional 'disclaimer', Sanyal states in the novel's epilogue: "This is a novel. All characters are fictional, and some are meant to appear *almost* real" (407).[38] For example, in a fictional TV debate with Saraswati, the character Peterson states the following: "The main point of this ideology claims that the correct way of viewing the world is as a battlefield upon which different groups or races are waging war. And that negates not only the possibility of the self-sufficient, independent individual, but also the notion of

---

[36] On docufiction, see Wiegandt (2017).
[37] As a result, the novel has already been read as an original contribution to theoretical debates on identity politics, for example. Cf. Moltke (2022).
[38] "Dies ist ein Roman. Die Figuren in ihm sind fiktiv, aber manche sind fiktiver und manche realer als andere. Ähnlichkeiten mit lebenden und toten Personen sind keineswegs rein zufällig" (419). Quotations from the novel here and below are taken from Sanyal (2022) [English translation] and Sanyal (2021) [German original], respectively.

individual responsibility" (74).[39] The reference list at the end of the book identifies these sentences as extracts taken from a lecture Peterson gave on personality. These direct references can be seen as rendering the novel very up-to-date. Moreover, in the manner of docufiction, they transcend the realm of the fictional, potentially lending the novel additional relevance for readers.

This self-reflexive, direct, and indirect integration of theory on the diegetic and exodiegetic levels is also linked to similarities to current debates in critical race theory as exemplified by the character of Saraswati and her (fictional) statements and writings. In the TV debate with Jordan Peterson, for example, Saraswati responds in a way that shows narrative and structural similarities to critical race theory:

> The fact that in Germany, people like me are two times more likely to live below the poverty line than *white* people is structural racism. [...] The fact that it's harder for us to work toward our life goals, let alone even develop any in the first place, is structural racism. (74)[40]

The game of factual remarks and fictional amplification established here is elaborated in many ways throughout the novel. In addition to incorporating intertextual references to already existing texts, Sanyal asked people actively involved in public debates to contribute to the novel: how would they have reacted if Saraswati's case had been a reality? Paula-Irene Villa Braslavsky, Chair of Sociology at the University of Munich, for example, highlights the cultural and semiotic background of a 'racial transition':

> [W]hen a person so radically switches places [in the world], when they play with the keys that determine these signifiers, and do so with such virtuosic skill, then it becomes clear that these signifiers [rooted in our corporeality]

---

[39] "Die Hauptaussage dieser Ideologie ist: Die richtige Art, die Welt wahrzunehmen, begreift sie als ein Kampffeld zwischen unterschiedlichen Gruppen oder Rassen. Dadurch schaffen wir jede Idee von selbstständigen Individuen ab, jede Vorstellung von individueller Verantwortung" (74).

[40] "Dass Menschen wie wir in Deutschland noch immer ein doppelt so hohes Armutsrisiko haben wie *weiße* Menschen, ist struktureller Rassismus. [...] Dass es uns schwerer gemacht wird, einen Lebensentwurf zu verfolgen, ja überhaupt einen zu entwickeln, ist struktureller Rassismus" (75).

and their meanings are highly conventionalised and tied to the time in which that person is living. (352)[41]

By explicitly revealing her compositional principles in the novel's epilogue,[42] Sanyal once again illustrates the broad spectrum of an integration of theory into literature—from self-reflexive, direct, and indirect references to narrative and structural similarities to debates in critical race theory.

Levels of Integrating Theory in "Identitti"

When the scandal of Saraswati's 'being white' erupts, Saraswati and her student Nivedita, whose perspective the novel follows, have several discussions about the case. These discussions integrate theory on the diegetic and, above all, on dialogical levels of the novel. At one point, Saraswati and Nivedita argue:

> [Saraswati:] "If I taught you anything at all, it's that *race* is a construct." [Nivedita:] "Yeah, *race*, as a concept—but not yours …" [Saraswati:] "Say it calmly: Race. *Mein Schatz*, people can [sic] be divided into different races just as well as water and light can [sic] be divided into different sexes. People aren't dogs. What is it you want—me, or the image you've conjured of me?" (104)[43]

The arguments of the debate presented in the novel could just as easily be part of an academic discussion on the subject.[44] In another conversation with Nivedita, Saraswati complains about her former supporters who have now switched sides: "Isn't it clear to them that their arguments oversim-

---

[41] "*Wenn* […] *eine Person ihren Platz* [in der sozialen Welt] *so radikal ändert, wenn sie so virtuos auf der Tastatur dieser Zeichen* [eines Körpers] *spielt, dann zeigt sie, dass diese Zeichen und ihre Deutungen hochgradig konventionalisiert und immer auch zeitgebunden sind*" (361).

[42] "Paula-Irene Villa Braslavsky [and others] specially formulated their reactions to the Saraswati Affair for *Identitti*" (408) | "Paula-Irene Villa Braslavsky [und andere formulierten] ihre Reaktionen auf den 'Fall Saraswati' extra für *Identitti*" (420).

[43] There is a mistake in the English translation: it should twice read "can't" instead of "can". In German: "[Saraswati:] 'Wenn ich dir etwas beigebracht haben sollte, dann dass *race* ein Konstrukt ist.' [Nivedita:] 'Ja, *race*, aber nicht deine…' [Saraswati:] 'Sag es ruhig: Rasse. Mein Schatz, es gibt Menschenrassen so wenig wie es die Rasse von Wasser gibt oder das Geschlecht von Licht. Menschen sind keine Hunde. Was willst du, mich oder das Bild, das du dir von mir gemacht hast?'" (105).

[44] Accordingly, Steinmayr (2022) subsumes the novel under the terms 'identity', 'intersectionality', and 'intervention'.

plify everything? People of colour is a political subject, not a racist one!" (94).[45] And Nivedita states:

> Whenever Saraswati was near, reality became distorted and truth began to melt. If you tried getting hold of anything concrete, it all started slipping through your fingers. Just as Saraswati's seminars promised: instead of complete, cold-as-steel truths, she gave them undeveloped, breathing facts and acts that required a lot of TLC in order to grow. (95)[46]

The dialogical presentation of critical race theory in its pros and cons goes on for many pages. In this respect, the novel stands out from the other texts analyzed in this book. While Lodge's *Small World*, for example, endodiegetically presents aspects of the theory in formally closed sections of the narrative, the percentage of these sections compared to the novel as a whole is rather small. In *Identitti*, on the other hand, theory at the diegetic and dialogical levels of the novel is present in abundance—which is why the term 'docufiction' might well apply to it. Compared to Lodge and the other theory-informed texts, Sanyal's novel has a very pared-back plot and a distinct focus on a quasi-academic presentation of theory.

This quasi-academic presentation of theory becomes particularly clear on an endodiegetic level of the novel: in Nivedita's blog posts which she publishes under the pseudonym of "Identitti". In the context of the novel, the blog posts are clearly separated from the narrative by their formatting, beginning with a new paragraph and appearing in a different font in italics. In terms of content, the posts are designed to explain aspects of critical race theory to a wider audience, for example by providing historical information:

> We still think that we've always thought people would naturally distinguish one another according to skin colour, but it turns out this idea is relatively new. By *new* I mean the eighteenth century—in other words, the period we mistakenly refer to as the *Enlightenment*. Before then, of course, people

---

[45] "Ist denen auch nur klar, dass sie essentialistisch argumentieren? People of Colour ist ein politisches Subjekt und kein rassistisches!" (94).
[46] "War Saraswati in der Nähe, neigten die Wahrheiten dazu, zu schmelzen und jedem vereinnahmenden Griff zu entgleiten. Das war das Versprechen von Saraswatis Seminaren: Anstelle von Wahrheiten wie kaltem Stahl schenkte sie ihnen unfertige, atmende Tatsachen, die Liebe und Fürsorge brauchten, um wachsen zu können" (95).

were still discriminated against and divided into an *us* and a *them*, but the distinction wasn't chalked up to their supposed 'race'. (119)[47]

Again, the novel works with a rather academic presentation of theory. Nonetheless, a diegetic integration of theory can be seen in the allegorical representation of theory in the character of Saraswati. By 'living' a 'racial transition' from white to Indian, Saraswati enacts some positions of critical race theory in the same way that Lodge's characters enact structuralism, deconstructivist theory, and so on. If race can be seen as a cultural construct, similar to gender, then there must be the possibility of changing the construct as a whole, the categories involved, and/or one's individual fit into one of the construct's peculiarities.

In a talk show, Saraswati, referring to herself and the connection between her and critical race theory, states:

> *Being white* isn't a character flaw, it's just another designation within the social hierarchy, and it's assigned—like POC, or gender. Just as other social designations are now changing, our conception of what *being white* means must also change and expand. (401)[48]

Since Saraswati has lived out this chance to be (considered) white in her own life, her 'racial transition' can be seen as an allegorical presentation of theory in the novel—complementing the integration of theory on almost all narrative levels, from the paradiegetic reference list over diegetic/allegorical presentations to endodiegetic/dialogical occupations with theory.

Functions of Integrating Theory in "Identitti"

Given the particular role of *Identitti* in the textual corpus of this book (the abundant integration of theory on almost all narrative levels), the question

---

[47] "*Wir denken ja immer, dass wir schon immer gedacht haben, Menschen würden sich essentiell durch ihre Hautfarbe unterscheiden, dabei ist diese Idee verhältnismäßig neu. Mit neu meine ich das achtzehnte Jahrhundert, also die Epoche, die wir fälschlicherweise Aufklärung nennen. Vorher wurden Menschen natürlich auch diskriminiert und in wir und ihr aufgeteilt, aber diese Aufteilung wurde nicht auf ihre vermeintliche Rasse geschoben*" (119).

[48] "*Weißsein ist kein Charakterfehler, es ist eine Menschen zugeschriebene gesellschaftliche Position – wie PoC oder Gender. In der Weise, in der sich die anderen gesellschaftlichen Positionen ändern, muss sich auch unsere Vorstellung davon, was Weißsein ist, ändern und erweitern*" (411).

of the function of theory in Sanyal's novel becomes even more important. Not surprisingly, all four functions of theory within literature highlighted in this book can be identified in Sanyal's novel: a presentation, a dynamization, an evaluation, and a rejection of theory.

As far as the presentation of theory is concerned, both interpretive processes and their premises form an important part of the text. As shown, critical race theory is integrated through various self-reflexive, direct, and indirect references—and it is present on almost all diegetic levels as well as a background layer. Therefore, the novel does not only integrate theory, but also explicitly presents theory, even with different representatives and their respective opinions. The first function of the integration of theory in the novel can thus be seen as acquainting the readers with the current debates in critical race theory, with some important figures in the field, and with its most prominent positions.

Moreover, theory serves as the linchpin of the novel's narrative dynamics. The controversy at the heart of the story derives its provocative power from its engagement with the complexities of critical race theory. In this case, theory not only provides the basic premise around which the narrative revolves, but also defines the thematic scope of the story. Moreover, theory sustains the narrative's momentum in the long run, as a significant portion of the novel is devoted to dissecting debates arising from the scandal—debates that are deeply rooted in theoretical discourse.

With regard to the evaluation of theory, *Identitti* works with both an affirmative and a critical presentation of theory. The explicit attribution of argumentative positions to different representatives contributes to a plurality of perspectives through which various aspects of theory are considered. Although the novel as a whole does not explicitly take sides in the debate, a certain preference for Saraswati's position can be observed. By the end of the novel, Nivedita and Saraswati seem to have reconciled, and Saraswati moves on to the next step in her career, a chair at the University of Oxford. Thus, if the readers' sympathies follow Nivedita and Saraswati as protagonists, a certain affirmation within the field of critical race theory can be noted: the consideration of race as performative and dependent on socio-cultural convictions, similar to Judith Butler's conception of gender. In showing this preference, however, the novel takes a rather clear stand against essentialist positions on race. As a result, the novel can even be considered an active position in the field of critical race theory. Oppositional views are presented (e.g., in the character of Oluchi) but quickly intellectually disarmed.

The only exception to this affirmation of a specific position within the field of critical race theory comes in the form of the objections that Nivedita raises in her discussions with Saraswati. These objections point to a rejection of theory, a postulation of a pre-theoretical world or experience, and are therefore relevant as another function of theory in *Identitti*. Such possible rejections of theory can be based on a moral, an emotional, or an epistemological perspective.

With regard to morality, Nivedita emphasizes that acting according to theoretical beliefs may not always be the best option in a moral and/or ethical sense. When Saraswati points out the ambivalence of race, Nivedita responds that sometimes a clear position is necessary to arrive at a convincing standpoint. Moreover, in certain didactic contexts, it may be necessary to avoid ambivalence, which is especially important for a professor who may also be perceived as a role model. However, Saraswati does not accept a moral judgment on her theoretical position: "Saraswati looked as if she'd never once, in her entire life, thought about the morality of her actions. She'd almost certainly considered the effects they might have on concrete individuals, but she'd definitely not given any thought to it on a more abstract moral level" (160).[49] This implies the possible need for a rejection of theory in favor of a moral/ethical perspective.

Furthermore, an emotional perspective on the issue may not be covered by a purely theoretical point of view. Even if (a particular) theory is convincing in describing an issue in a certain way, there may be emotional barriers to accepting the theoretical approach. While Nivedita rationally arrives at an understanding of Saraswati's 'racial transition', on an emotional basis all she longs for is an apology from Saraswati. And though she gets the apology, it is not brought on by argument or discussion, but rather by a sudden bout of tears. Only then does Saraswati embrace her and whisper to her: "I'm sorry, Nivedita, I'm so very sorry" (303).[50] Just a little later, Saraswati informs Nivedita that "your feelings sometimes are based on political parameters" (311).[51] Nevertheless, emotions have been presented as something that theory may not be able to describe or deal

---

[49] "Saraswati sah aus, als hätte sie sich noch nie in ihrem Leben Gedanken über die Moralität ihrer Handlungen gemacht. Über die Auswirkungen auf konkrete Menschen, durchaus, aber nicht auf abstrakte moralische Kriterien" (160).
[50] "Es tut mir leid, Nivedita. Es tut mir so leid" (311).
[51] "Es bedeutet nur, dass deine Gefühle auf politischen Parametern basieren" (319).

with, and therefore may require a rejection of theory, at least to some extent or under some circumstances.

Finally, an epistemological perspective might also call for a rejection of theory. For example, Nivedita brings up experiences from her youth: "You don't know what it's like when none of the cultural messaging is meant for you or *anyone like you*. You don't know what it's like to never be in the system, to always be on the outside, looking in" (180).[52] Nivedita's mention of "the system" points to a blind spot: people who are used to a certain socio-cultural perspective sometimes do not question it. In doing so, they miss out on other ways of seeing things and thus, by extension, epistemological insights. The rejection of (a certain) theory can therefore contribute to a more refined and differentiated perception of things.

A Side Glance: Bernadine Evaristo's *Girl, Woman, Other* (2019)

Among its various links to other literary and non-literary texts, *Identitti* also refers to Bernadine Evaristo's *Girl, Woman, Other* (2019).[53] The second part of Sanyal's novel begins with a paragraph called "Woman, Native, Other" (141).[54] The paragraph introduces another of Nivedita's blog posts, which offers an ironic 'test' of one's skin color: "Quiz | How brown are you?" (142).[55] In contrast to real psychological tests, the one here is a parody of categorization, starting with the unreasonable question of the test as a whole and deconstructing the desire for a clear assignment along the way. The answers that the readers have to choose from to determine their 'brownness' are largely incoherent and do not fit the question, making sense as different categories with respect to one aspect, or offering clearly separated categories as a result, for example:

On a scale of 0 to 10, how entitled are you?
a) 5.
b) Entitled?
c) 42. (144)[56]

---

[52] "Du weißt nicht, wie es ist, wenn keine der kulturellen Botschaften an dich oder an Leute wie dich gerichtet ist. Du weißt nicht, wie es ist, niemals drin im System zu sein, sondern immer draußen und sehnsüchtig durchs Fenster hineinzuschauen" (179).
[53] Evaristo (2019).
[54] In the German original in English: "Woman, Native, Other" (141).
[55] "Test | Wie braun bist du?" (142).
[56] "Auf einer Skala von 0 bis 10, wie entitled bist du? | a) 5 | b) Entitled? | c) 42" (144).

At the end of the 'test', when the alleged results are announced, the test itself is ultimately deconstructed. There are three possible outcomes (with ironic attributions of characteristics) and a fourth category for those who did not fit into the others. The reason for ending up in the fourth category is to be filled in by the readers themselves, stretching the idea of an objective test ad absurdum. Trying to come up with a categorization of one's own 'brownness' is therefore a losing game.

Read against the background of the 'test', the reference to *Girl, Woman, Other* in the headline of the paragraph takes on a clear function for *Identitti*: Evaristo's novel follows the interconnected lives of twelve black British women, most of whom are of African or Caribbean descent. The novel explores their experiences of race, gender, sexuality, class, and intersectionality, as well as their relationships with family, friends, lovers, and community. The characters include a lesbian playwright, a non-binary DJ, a working-class single mother, a feminist activist, and an elderly farmer, among others. Through their stories, the novel presents a kaleidoscopic view of contemporary black British life and challenges dominant narratives of identity, history, and culture. The power dynamics between different racial and ethnic groups is also a central theme, highlighting the ways in which racism impacts these relationships.

Similar to Sanyal's *Identitti*, Evaristo's *Girl, Woman, Other* deals with aspects of critical race theory. For example, the character Amma struggles with her identity as a black, feminist, and working-class woman, illuminating the intersectionality of race, gender, and class. The impact of colonialism and slavery is shown through Hattie's ancestry and the ongoing effects it has on her life and the lives of other black characters. The novel also examines how race shapes identity, as seen in Yazz's experiences as a mixed-race woman.

Linking Evaristo's novel back to the test of 'brownness' in *Identitti*, the test shows in a condensed way what *Girl, Woman, Other* works out for twelve characters: there are no clear-cut categories that apply to individuals, neither for color nor for gender, class, or other. Categorization may be necessary in some contexts, such as sociological studies. At the same time, however, any categorization is a form of discrimination that streamlines individual phenomena according to predefined patterns.

In this context, the 'test' of skin color can be understood as a deconstruction of categorization and therefore a rejection of theory—an attempt that *Identitti* underscores through several other aspects of its story, such as Saraswati's unclear racial categorization or the theoretical discussions of race. *Girl, Woman, Other* does not undermine attempts at categorization on a theoretical level, but rather by telling the stories of twelve individuals who do not fit into the patterns—thus illustrating the need for a new perspective on (seemingly) well-established ways of ordering things. Again, this could be used for an extrapolation of theory: as a starting point for a modified version of theory or even new forms of theory.

Critical Race Theory—And Beyond

Mithu Sanyal's novel *Identitti* can be seen as a contribution to critical race theory. It presents existing debates in the field by quoting prominent proponents or even integrating them as characters into its fictional world. Moreover, it amplifies the debates by linking them to a specific (allegorical) character who not only discusses the theory but also lives it. Nevertheless, the novel stands out from the other texts analyzed in this book for its particularly theoretical approach to critical race theory, for example, by meticulously presenting arguments on an endodiegetic or dialogical level.

As a consequence, Sanyal's novel can be understood, first, as an 'introduction' to critical race theory, presenting the current state of the debates. Second, it demonstrates a critical approach to theory by affirming certain positions or tendencies and devaluing others. Third, it offers perspectives that go beyond theory, for example by highlighting moral, emotional, or divergent epistemological aspects not covered by (critical race) theory.

In doing so, the novel also paves the way for possible extrapolations of theory from Sanyal's novel. These might consist, for example, of refining concrete debates in critical race theory, such as valuing the individual choice in terms of racial ascription over apparent genetic, cultural, or other 'authenticity'.[57] Another extrapolation might be to highlight once again the limits of the theory: there are potential clashes between the need to conceptualize things and the individuality of single phenomena, or between academic/scientific worldviews and others, such as moral or emotional ones.

---

[57] On the topic of authenticity, see Schilling (2020).

Bibliography

Bakhtin, Mikhail (1981 [1934/35]): Discourse in the Novel. In: Mikhail Bakhtin: *The Dialogic Imagination: Four Essays*. Translated by Caryl Emerson/Michael Holquist. Austin, 259–422.

Bartl, Andrea (2014): Androgyne Ästhetik: Das Motiv des Hermaphroditismus in der deutschsprachigen Gegenwartsliteratur, erläutert am Beispiel von Ulrike Draesners "Mitgift", Michael Stavaričs "Terminifera" und Sibylle Bergs "Vielen Dank für das Leben". In: Christian Baier et al., eds.: *Die Textualität der Kultur: Gegenstände, Methoden, Probleme der kultur- und literaturwissenschaftlichen Forschung*. Bamberg, 279–301.

Berndt, Frauke, and Kammer, Stephan (2009): Amphibolie – Ambiguität – Ambivalenz. Die Struktur antagonistisch-gleichzeitiger Zweiwertigkeit. In: Frauke Berndt and Stephan Kammer, eds.: *Amphibolie – Ambiguität – Ambivalenz*. Würzburg, 7–30.

Catani, Stephanie (2009): Hybride Körper: Zur Dekonstruktion der Geschlechterbinarität in Ulrike Draesners "Mitgift". In: Stephanie Catani and Friedhelm Marx, eds.: *Familien – Geschlechter – Macht: Beziehungen im Werk Ulrike Draesners*. Göttingen, 75–93.

Draesner, Ulrike (2002): *Mitgift. Roman*. München.

Duncker, Patricia (1996): *Hallucinating Foucault*. Chatham.

Evaristo, Bernardine (2019): *Girl, Woman, Other*. London.

Foucault, Michel (1986 [1967]): Of Other Spaces: Utopias and Heterotopias. In: *Diacritics* 16, 22–27.

Foucault, Michel (1998 [1969]): What is an Author? In: Donald Preziosi, ed.: *The Art of Art History: A Critical Anthology*. Oxford et al., 299–314.

Freytag, Gustav (1900): *Freytag's Technique of the Drama: An Exposition of Dramatic Composition and Art. An Authorized Translation from the 6th German ed. by Elias J. MacEwan*. Chicago.

Griffin, Gabriele (2000): The Dispersal of the Lesbian, or Re-Patriating the Lesbian in British Writing. In: *Journal of Lesbian Studies* 4, 65–80.

Kriston, Andrea (2010): Madness and Marginality in Patricia Duncker's "Hallucinating Foucault". In: *Gender Studies* 9, 74–88.

Matthies, Hanna (2016): "Hallucinating Foucault": Patricia Dunckers Auseinandersetzung mit Foucaults Theorien. In: Christiane Solte-Gresser and Manfred Schmeling, eds.: *Theorie erzählen. Raconter la théorie. Narrating theory: Fiktionalisierte Literaturtheorie im Roman*. Würzburg, 259–270.

Moltke, Johannes von (2022): The Metapolitics of Identity: Identitarianism and its Critics. In: *German Studies Review* 45, 151–166.

Reiling, Laura M. (2021): *Academia: Praktiken des Raums und des Wissens in Universitätserzählungen*. Bielefeld.

Ryan, Judith (2011): *The Novel After Theory*. New York.

Sanyal, Mithu (2021): *Identitti. Roman*. München.
Sanyal, Mithu (2022): *Identitti. A novel. Translated from the German by Alta L. Price*. Berlin.
Schilling, Erik (2020): *Authentizität: Karriere einer Sehnsucht*. München.
Schilling, Erik (2024): Geschlechter von Menschen und Texten: Zur Vielfalt der Genera im Werk von Ulrike Draesner. In: Monika Wolting and Oliver Ruf, eds.: *Gegenwart aufnehmen: Zum Werk und Wirken von Ulrike Draesner*. Leiden, 175–189.
Steinmayr, Markus (2022): Identität, Intersektion, Intervention: Mithu Sanyals "Identitti" und Jasmina Kuhnkes "Schwarzes Herz". In: *Weimarer Beiträge* 68, 217–239.
Stritzke, Nadyne (2011): *Subversive literarische Performativität: Die narrative Inszenierung von Geschlechtsidentitäten in englisch- und deutschsprachigen Gegenwartsromanen*. Trier.
Vedder, Ulrike (2013): Ulrike Draesner: "Mitgift" (2002). In: Roland Borgards et al., eds.: *Literatur und Wissen: Ein interdisziplinäres Handbuch*. Stuttgart/Weimar, 415–419.
Wiegandt, Markus (2017): *Chronisten der Zwischenwelten: Dokufiktion als Genre. Operationalisierung eines medienwissenschaftlichen Begriffs für die Literaturwissenschaft*. Heidelberg.
Willer, Stefan (2004): Literarischer Hermaphroditismus: Intersexualität im Familienroman, 2002. In: Bettina von Jagow and Florian Steger, eds.: *Repräsentationen: Medizin und Ethik in Literatur und Kunst der Moderne*. Heidelberg, 83–97.

CHAPTER 5

The Fragile Relationship of Author, Reader, and Text

This chapter deals with the fragile relationship of author, reader, and text—thus putting a particular emphasis on the relation of diegetic and exodiegetic integration of theory into literature (after the analysis of a mostly diegetic/allegorical and endodiegetic/dialogical integration in the previous chapters). The novels analyzed all start from a 'traditional' hermeneutic understanding of the reception process, which they reflect upon and subvert.

In Daniel Kehlmann's *F*, each of the main characters serves as an author, presenting various and competing forms of authorship. Throughout the novel, the question of who is an author of what remains uncertain in many respects: it is a question of perspective and choice rather than immutable fact. Italo Calvino's *If on a Winter's Night a Traveler*, in contrast, multiplies the readers. The novel presents a plurality of readings, showcasing a multitude of diegetic readers, introducing the model of an implied reader, and arriving at the real readers' readings. In Christoph Ransmayr's *The Last World*, finally, everything turns out to be text, even author and reader as diegetic and exodiegetic entities. The novel presents ever-new scraps of narratives and textual remnants, reforming the existing knowledge of the world. It thereby develops into a palimpsest, dispensing with a hierarchical order such as that offered by the author.

Kehlmann, Calvino, and Ransmayr, therefore, integrate debates about authorship, readership, and textuality into their texts. Are there authors at

© The Author(s), under exclusive license to Springer Nature Switzerland AG 2024
E. Schilling, *Theorizing Literature*,
https://doi.org/10.1007/978-3-031-53326-6_5

all—and, if so, how to get hold of them? What kinds of readers exist—and to what extent does the interpretation of a text depend on them? Where are the borders of a text—or is the whole world a giant text? Moreover, the novels test the chances and limits of the theoretical concepts for the lives of their characters and pave the ground for an extrapolation of modified or new literary theory.

Eliminating the Author: Daniel Kehlmann's *F* (2013)

Daniel Kehlmann, born in 1975, is a contemporary German-language author best known for his international bestseller *Measuring the World* (*Die Vermessung der Welt*, 2005), a fictionalized account of the lives of Carl Friedrich Gauß and Alexander von Humboldt. His literary works frequently explore themes of reality, illusion, and human cognition, often employing metafictional and historical narrative techniques.

In Kehlmann's novel *F* (2013) the author dies, as in Binet's *7th Function of Language*, yet in a more subtle way. And not only does he die, but he is also resurrected. The novel is about a father, Arthur Friedland, and his three sons, Martin, Eric, and Iwan. The latter are identical twins, whom even their father cannot tell apart. The novel starts with a background story set in 1984. Arthur and his sons go to watch a hypnosis show, during which first Iwan and then Arthur are asked to come onto the stage. During the hypnosis, Arthur, despite being reluctant at first, reveals very personal details about his (deficient) ambition of becoming a successful author. The same day, after driving home, Arthur suddenly leaves his family to focus fully on his writing. His sons do not see him again until they have grown up.

The main part of the novel consists of a chapter each on the sons, now in their mid-thirties. Martin has become a catholic priest, yet does not believe in God. Eric works as a financial advisor, but has lost most of the money his clients entrusted to him. Iwan makes a living out of forging art and selling it under the name of his dead lover, an artist Iwan has helped to make famous. All three chapters play out over the same day, August 8, 2008, some days before the financial crisis. Martin's chapter is entitled "The Lives of the Saints" (33), Eric's "Duties" (107), and Iwan's "Beauty" (165).[1] In addition to these three chapters on the lives of the brothers,

---

[1] "Das Leben der Heiligen" (51); "Geschäfte" (159); "Von der Schönheit" (245). Quotations from the novel here and below are taken from Kehlmann (2015) [English translation] and Kehlmann (2013) [German original], respectively.

there is a short chapter "Family" (91)—the same title as one of Arthur's most famous novels—and a concluding chapter entitled "Seasons" (217), which again is divided into three parts, each focusing on a different moment of the years 2009–2012.[2] The final chapter picks up from the prologue and relates a number of events after the crucial day in August 2008 which forms the center of the plot.

Intertextual Authorship: Multiple Authors as a Background Choir

Before turning to the various forms of authorship diegetically presented in *F*, one might look at the texts intertwined with Kehlmann's novel in the form of intertextual references or similarities, effectively splitting up the notion of his own authorship. As in other cases, the titles of Arthur's novels (within Kehlmann's novel) are a good starting point for the interpretation.

Arthur's first novel is called "*My Name Is No One*" (51),[3] offering two indirect references and/or narrative similarities at the same time, one to Max Frisch's novel *My Name Be Gantenbein* (*Mein Name sei Gantenbein*, 1964) and the other to the famous scene in the *Odyssey* in which Odysseus, upon meeting the Cyclops Polyphemus, calls himself "nobody". In both cases, the reference is to a text that deals with authorship and identity. Frisch's protagonist is known for saying that he tries on stories (of his life) as he tries on clothes. He invents alternative biographies to better cope with his real life in which he has been left by his wife. In doing so, he regains power over his life; he becomes the author of his biography.

In the case of Odysseus, the Greek hero deceives Polyphemus, who wants to eat him, by giving him a false name. After Odysseus has escaped, Polyphemus calls other cyclopses for help, saying that "nobody" has hurt him. The other cyclopses, however, understand 'nobody' as a pronoun instead of a name for a person and do not come for support. In deceiving Polyphemus, therefore, Odysseus is not only the 'author' of a fictional story of his life (under a different name) but also the 'author' (in the sense of creator) of his real life, in that he saves it.

By noting the similarities between the two texts and the title of Arthur's first novel, Kehlmann's *F* may be understood as hinting at two things: first, that authorship is something one can acquire. Much like Gantenbein and

---

[2] "Familie" (137); "Jahreszeiten" (321).
[3] "*Mein Name sei Niemand*" (77).

Odysseus, Arthur, by writing his first novel, becomes the author of his life. He escapes the 'captivity' of family life that hinders his creativity; he focuses on fiction to start a new life. Second, however, the novel hints that authorship is something one cannot acquire—because originality is, as Roland Barthes puts it, never as innovative as one might think. Arthur's novel self-reflexively discloses its obligations to previous texts in its very title. It would not have been possible without the long tradition of literature (dealing with authorship) in which it stands.

The same is true for Kehlmann's *F*—a fact that the self-reflexive play with intertextuality and authorship around Arthur's fictive book lays bare. Kehlmann, like Arthur, is indebted to the literary and cultural tradition. His novel contains numerous references: to Henry James and Arthur Schopenhauer;[4] to the Bhagavad Gita; and to Ludwig Tieck.[5] Out of these and others, I will shortly elaborate on two intertextual relations that are particularly important for my argument: to Orson Welles's film *F for Fake* (1973) and to Jorge Luis Borges's short story *The Garden of Forking Paths* (*El jardín de senderos que se bifurcan*, 1941).

It is from Welles's film that Kehlmann's novel draws its title—just as the title of Arthur's novel self-reflexively draws on works of the past. While Welles's film, however, uses an unambiguous explanation for the letter "F" (*F for Fake*), Kehlmann does not give a single explanation for his "F", but rather offers multiple possibilities. Fake, as I will show, is one of them, but equally plausible are "Family", "Friedland" (the name of the family), "Freedom", "Fate", "F." (the protagonist of Arthur's novel *My Name Is No One*), and—last but not least—"Fiction" as the determining condition of everything Kehlmann's novel is about (and of Kehlmann's novel itself). In addition to the indirect reference to its title, the novel *F* also contains narrative similarities to the film *F for Fake*: first, Eric attends a screening of the film with his lover; in the cinema, however, they meet an acquaintance of Eric's wife who threatens to blow the cover on Eric's affair. Second, Welles's film is about an art forger, just as Eric's twin brother Iwan is an art forger.

Even more important for the intertextual construction of authorship in the novel *F* is its structural similarity to Borges's *The Garden of Forking Paths*. In this story, Borges invents a writer whose aim is to create a book with the structure of a labyrinth. The character in the book does not have

---

[4] For details, see Chraplak (2017).
[5] For details, see Meissner (2014).

to decide on one manner of living but can choose all possible variants of his life at the same time: "He thus *creates* various futures, various times which start others that will in their turn branch out and bifurcate in other times."[6] In doing so, Borges's (fictional) author creates a character who is the author of his life in all its possible variants. Thus, fiction—in contrast to reality—provides a narrative universe not bound to time or choice: the author may have their characters live different lives one after another (or even at the same time); they may undo choices and opt for alternatives. In creating this kind of fiction, the author is as omnipotent as God.

Arthur: Writing Novels that Blur Fiction and Reality

The first and probably most important figure with respect to authorship and its blurring of fiction and reality is Arthur, the father. His name not only harks back to the King Arthur of legend, an indirect reference made even more blatant by his sons Eric and Iwan being named after knights of the Round Table as well,[7] but the name Arthur also bears a striking phonetic similarity to 'author': Arthur is both an author by profession and an author in the sense of creator, being the father of the three main characters. If—as I will argue in the following—the ontological status of Arthur's three sons is doubtful, Arthur's authorship can be said to span the notions of fictional and fatherly authorship and even conflate the two.

Arthur is already an author at the beginning of the novel. At this point, however, he is not successful, and his novels are unpublished. During the hypnosis show he attends in the first chapter, he either comes to a realization or expresses what he has realized before: namely, that he wants to be an 'actual' author. The same day, he leaves his children and focuses only on fictional creations. However, the ontological status of these fictions is unclear within *F*. As I pointed out above, Arthur's novels serve as a narrative and structural mirror of Kehlmann's *F* as a whole. Moreover, they are intertwined with *F* as a novel. The third chapter of Kehlmann's novel, for example, is called "Family", just like one of Arthur's short stories. Arthur's story "Family" is about:

---

[6] Borges (1962, 98); "*Crea, así, diversos porvenires, diversos tiempos, que también proliferan y se bifurcan*" (Borges 1997, 112–113).
[7] They are represented, for example, in the epics *Erec* and *Iwein* by Hartmann von Aue, the first one going back to the French *Erec et Enide* by Chrétien de Troyes.

his [Martin's] father, his grandfather and his great-grandfather, it was the story of our ancestors, generation by generation [...]. Most of it is pure invention, for according to Arthur right at the beginning, the past is unknowable: *People think the dead are preserved somewhere.* [...] *But it's not true. What's gone is gone. What once was, is forgotten, and what has been forgotten never returns. I have no memory of my father.* (80)[8]

In this chapter of *F*, the focalization point is Martin's. The passage in italics can be regarded as a quotation from Arthur's short story, which is endodiegetically integrated into the story. Yet just a few pages later, the quoted part forms—in completely identical words—the beginning of the chapter "Family" on the diegetic level of Kehlmann's novel. At this moment, it is presented in the same layout as the other chapters of *F*, thus forming an integral part of it.

In addition, the following paragraph starts with a paradox. Having just stated that he does not have any memory of his father, the narrator continues: "He [my father] wrote poems" (93).[9] Subsequently, he tells substantial parts of his father's life which—as he said before—he does not remember. Of course, the narrator may have reconstructed his father's biography on the basis of texts and other sources. More plausible, however, is that the substantial parts of the family history are made up, just as Arthur stated at the beginning of the short story (a beginning that, ironically, is *not* presented as a quotation, but through Martin's focalization). Looking back at his past, his family, and his 'authors', Arthur uses fiction as a principal means of creation. He tells a story about what may have been there before him. Just like the fictional novel in Borges's short story, Arthur creates "various times": various pasts instead of futures.

This making and mixing up times and ancestors can be seen as a reflection on the interplay of (intentional) authorship and (contingent) fate. What may at first seem a deliberately lived life, aiming for certain goals and based on individual morals, may just as well be a series of accidental events, even an ordered fate, constructed from the outside. In every case, it

---

[8] "[S]einen Vater, seinen Großvater, seinen Urgroßvater, es war die Geschichte unserer Vorfahren, Generation um Generation [...]. Das meiste ist reine Erfindung, denn über das Vergangene, so Arthur zu Beginn, weiß man nichts: *Man meint, die Verstorbenen wären irgendwo aufgebahrt.* [...] *Aber das stimmt nicht. Was dahin ist, ist dahin. Was war, wird vergessen, und was vergessen ist, kommt nicht zurück. Ich habe keine Erinnerung an meinen Vater*" (121).
[9] "Er schrieb Gedichte" (139).

5 THE FRAGILE RELATIONSHIP OF AUTHOR, READER, AND TEXT   115

remains unclear whether there is a structuring authorial entity, and—if so—who it is. Is Arthur the author of his life—or his ancestors? Are the ancestors the authors of their individual lives—or is it Arthur recounting and inventing them? The follow-up question is: do the observations regarding Arthur's family *past* also hold true for his family *future*, for his sons' lives?

Martin: Conjuring up a God He Does Not Believe In

Martin is introduced in a scene that presents—referring to Borges's idea of forking paths—two different futures for his life at the same time:

> Martin ran [...] across the street—so fast he didn't even see the speeding car coming at him. Brakes squealed inches away from him, but he was already in the passenger seat, hands clasped above his head, and only now did his heart leap for a moment. "My God," Arthur murmured. [...] "How can anyone be so dumb?" asked one of the twins from the backseat. Martin felt as if his existence had split in two. He was sitting here, but he was also lying on the asphalt, crumpled and still. His fate seemed yet undecided, both outcomes were still possible, and for a moment he too had a twin—one there outside, slowly fading away. "He could be dead," the other twin said matter-of-factly. (4)[10]

In this short incident from Martin's childhood, there are two possible futures present at the same time. One of these futures is the one that has, within the 'reality' of fiction, already started: Martin has not been hit by the car and continues to live. The other possible 'future' is the one that is not an actual future: he has been hit by the car and lies on the street, probably dying, as the fading image of his "twin" indicates. The doubling of the twin metaphor (the twins Eric and Iwan on the back seat, and Martin

---

[10] "Martin lief [...] über die Straße – so schnell, dass er das heranrasende Auto nicht sah. Bremsen quietschten neben ihm, aber schon saß er auf dem Beifahrersitz, die Hände über dem Kopf zusammengeschlagen, und jetzt erst setzte sein Herz einen Augenblick aus. 'Mein Gott', sagte Arthur leise. [...] 'Wie kann man so blöd sein?', fragte einer der Zwillinge auf der Rückbank. Martin war es, als hätte sein Dasein sich gespalten. Er saß hier, aber zugleich lag er auf dem Asphalt, reglos und verdreht. Ihm schien sein Schicksal noch nicht ganz entschieden, beides war noch möglich, und für einen Moment hatte auch er einen Zwilling – einen, der dort draußen nach und nach verblasste. 'Hin könnte er sein', sagte der andere Zwilling sachlich" (8–9).

and his imaginary twin) underlines the multitude of options present at the same moment.

Consequently, the last sentence of the quoted paragraph has a certain ambiguity: it is not entirely clear which twin is speaking. This already holds true for Eric and Iwan, whom Martin keeps mixing up, but it also—more importantly—gestures toward an ambiguity between these living twins and the fictional, dead twin who might be the one speaking as well (within Martin's mind). The idea of a multitude of futures is, therefore, mirrored in the seemingly unimportant statement by the (doubly doubled) twin.

Later in his life, Martin makes a living as a priest. However, he does not believe in God, causing him to create a fiction once again: the fiction of God for the believers of his church. In doing so, he is an author of narratives all the time. These narratives are arguably lent a particular strength by the performative way in which they work. In one instance, while Martin holds mass, he feels "surrounded by a force field" (38) while chanting "*Holy, holy, holy*" (38),[11] as if this force were created in this very moment by his authorship—or, put differently, as if it were a force coming upon him as a form of divine inspiration. Moreover, Martin fulfills performative speech acts when absolving people from their sins. Again, his authorship is presented as very powerful, relieving the sinners' consciences and easing their spiritual burden. Martin, however, does not believe in this power either: he is distracted by solving a Rubik's cube and eats chocolate bars during confession.

Yet even though he does not believe in the fiction of faith he creates, others do—and that is what, to them, is important. During mass, the faithful believe in Martin's words about Christ; during confession, the sinners believe in their being absolved; and, at the very end of Kehlmann's novel, the readers of *F* (possibly) believe in what they have been told. It is quite striking that *F* ends with Martin's words (spoken during a mass for the late Iwan): "'And now,' he [Martin] said, 'the Profession of Faith'" (258).[12] Of course, this "profession of faith" refers mainly to the Apostles' Creed pronounced during mass. At the same time, however, it may also refer to a 'profession' of Kehlmann's readers: they have, as Samuel Coleridge famously put it, had to consent to a 'willing suspension of disbelief' for the duration of the novel. Kehlmann's readers 'have' to profess their belief in what they are told—even though they have learned that they

---

[11] "[A]lls umgäbe mich ein Feld von Kraft"; "Heilig, heilig, heilig" (57).
[12] "'Und jetzt', sagte er [Martin], 'das Bekenntnis des Glaubens'" (380).

cannot be sure which part of the novel is made up and by whom. The faithful and the readers are, thus, put in parallel, just as—in a long tradition of the poet as a 'divine creator', most prominently represented by Shaftesbury[13]—the author has been put in parallel to God.

Eric: Fabricating Money out of Nowhere

While Martin is an author of fictions in faith, his brother Eric is an author of fictions in finance. Eric works as an investment banker, but has lost most of his clients' money. In a classic pyramid scheme, he has used the money of new clients to pay out older clients, faking high returns and thereby attracting new clients again. The system is about to collapse when Eric's most important client, Adolf Klüssen—whose name can be seen as an indirect reference to both *Thyssen* and the Thyssen family's support of *Adolf Hitler*—wants to withdraw his money. However, Eric is saved by the coincidence of the financial crisis of 2008. After the insolvency of Lehman Brothers, none of Eric's clients expect their money back; they all suppose it has been lost in the crisis and do not hold Eric responsible.

In addition to his 'professional' fiction of creating money, Eric creates fictions in his private life. He tries to fake a functioning marriage with his wife Laura, for example, by inviting her on spontaneous trips abroad, hoping to cover up the problems in their marriage. Moreover, he convinces his lover Sibylle that his wife suffers from cancer, providing a convenient excuse for his reluctance to leave her. The fiction is threatened when—as noted above—Eric runs into an acquaintance of his wife while watching a film at the cinema with Sibylle. But, as the film title (*F for Fake*) indicates, he successfully comes up with another story, thereby (most likely) concealing his betrayal.

The most problematic fiction Eric comes up with, however, is one of self-betrayal, with a tendency toward schizophrenia. The manifold co-existing options of his life, founded in his being a twin and his private double life, are driven to the extreme by a form of mental instability. His partial inability to distinguish the real and his thoughts points to an extreme form of 'forking paths'. At various moments in the novel, Eric does not know whether he has said certain things aloud or just thought them in his head. Furthermore, during lunch with his brother Martin, Eric is so busy with his phone that Martin—in an ironic move—sends him

---

[13] Ashley-Cooper (1710).

a message instead of directly talking to him. Eric, however, does not understand the irony, but questions the reliability of his perceptions. He is not sure whether he is actually having lunch with his brother or just imagining Martin sitting opposite at the table: "I look up, there he is, sitting in front of me. Martin. My brother. I look at the phone. Is it my imagination after all? Am I sitting here alone?" (134).[14]

Following this episode, Eric repeatedly imagines people he is talking to, for example, two children on a bench or an old man in the elevator. On the one hand, these experiences could easily be explained by Eric's weak mental state. On the other hand, many of these experiences seem to be linked to a certain 'truth' or 'reality', as becomes evident when reading the other parts of Kehlmann's novel. Martin's perspective gives the explanation for Eric's insecure grip on reality during their lunch date. And a figure Eric believes to see in the elevator resembles the figure Iwan sees in the moment before his death. Even more strikingly, the moment Iwan is fatally wounded by a street gang, Eric suffers a breakdown in the elevator:

> It's just going up again when my knees give way and my head slams against the wall. [...] I don't know what it is, but something terrible has happened. Something that should never have been allowed to happen. Something that will never come good again. (146–147)[15]

Eric cannot know about Iwan being hurt in this very moment. Nonetheless, the novel has established the idea of a mental connection between the twins right from the beginning ("[w]e always think exactly the same thing", 8),[16] so that it is—within the conditions of Kehlmann's fiction— not implausible to assume a mental connection to his brother, especially in a moment of great danger and pain.

In the case of Eric, the playful-inventive aspect of fictions thus turns into an existentially problematic one. It is because of the fictions he creates that Eric loses his clients' money, his wife, and his awareness of reality. *F for Fake*, as Eric learns in the cinema, is—in his case—not limited to

---

[14] "Ich blicke auf, da sitzt er vor mir. Martin. Mein Bruder. Ich blicke aufs Telefon, die Nachricht steht noch da. Ich blicke in sein Gesicht. Ich blicke aufs Telefon. Ist es doch Einbildung? Sitze ich allein hier?" (200).

[15] "Kaum fährt er weiter, knicken meine Knie ein, und mein Kopf prallt an die Wand. [...] Ich weiß nicht, was, aber etwas Schreckliches ist geschehen. Etwas, das nicht hätte geschehen dürfen. Etwas, das nie wieder gut wird" (217–218).

[16] "Wir denken ständig dasselbe" (14).

literature, religion, or art, as in the case of his father and his brothers. In Eric's case, the fakes turn into an existential crisis, threatening his life and his identity in a fundamental way. Ironically, though, Eric is the only character who, at the end of the novel, is content with his life. He has lost his money, his family, and his twin brother, but he has made peace with his new life, has turned to faith and moved into Martin's parsonage. His daughter "had never known him to be in such a good mood" (222).[17] Eric is thus a character who experiences consequences of fakes but, thanks to the hard reality of these consequences, ultimately finds ways of coping with them. In the end, Eric is—in the words of the existentialist Albert Camus—to be imagined as a happy Sisyphus.

Iwan: Creating Art in the Name of Another

In Iwan's case, authorship is negotiated on different levels. The first is found within the novel's fictional world. As a student of art history writing his dissertation, Iwan travels to interview the aging painter Heinrich Eulenböck. They become a couple in life, but also in art, as Iwan takes over Eulenböck's artistic production. He amends Eulenböck's conventional mode of painting by introducing an element of irony (by referencing a piece of modern art within a traditional setting, such as Dalí's melting clocks within a still life). He produces various paintings in this style under the name of Eulenböck and appears as an art historian, art critic, and art seller charged with the care of Eulenböck's works.

When Eulenböck dies after some years, Iwan has already prepared and published a list of 'existing' Eulenböck paintings that he plans to paint and sell in the future. Iwan reflects on his authorship during the afternoon of August 8, the day in the center of Kehlmann's novel:

> I don't know if I'm a forger; it depends, like everything in life, on how you define it. Nonetheless Eulenböck's most famous paintings, all the ones on which his reputation rests, were created by the same person, namely me. (188)[18]

---

[17] "[H]atte ihn noch nie so gut gelaunt erlebt" (328).
[18] "Ich weiß nicht, ob ich ein Fälscher bin, das hängt von der Definition ab wie alles im Leben. Immerhin stammen die bekanntesten Bilder Eulenböcks, alle Werke, auf denen sein Ruhm beruht, von ein und demselben Urheber: nämlich mir" (279).

Iwan raises a fundamental question about authorship: is the author the one who *has an idea*, who *executes the idea* by writing or painting, who *integrates the original idea into a new context*, or whom *authorship is ascribed to*—to name just a few options.[19] Again, Kehlmann's novel presents and considers all these options at the same time. According to most definitions, Iwan is the 'author' of Eulenböck's paintings, and yet he is not their author in the view of the public. Authorship, therefore, is presented as something that is not an essential part of an artwork, but attributed to it by the people who read or see it—nothing more than an "author-function"[20] in the sense of Michel Foucault.

The second level on which Iwan's authorship can be put into question is that of creativity and/or originality. On the one hand, Iwan's Eulenböck paintings are a mere combination of two previous artworks: the traditional Eulenböck style and the playful integration of an item by a famous artist (e.g., Dalí's clock). None of these components is innovative. On the other hand, it is precisely the combination of two conventional items that makes Iwan's paintings something new. These thoughts can equally be applied to Kehlmann's novel, especially with regard to the intertextual references that make it a combination of used components as well, yet a combination that deals with its components in an innovative, 'authorial' way.

A third variant of authorship consists in a combination of the two forms of authorship presented in Iwan: Iwan is an art forger, and the idea behind his paintings is an 'intertextual' one. Both aspects apply to Iwan as a character as well. Iwan is modeled after one of the most notorious art forgers in postwar Germany, Wolfgang Beltracchi. For several decades, Beltracchi created 'lost' or 'newly discovered' paintings by famous (mostly twentieth-century) artists, e.g., Max Ernst or Wassily Kandinsky. One of Beltracchi's preferred artists was the expressionist painter Heinrich Campendonk. It is, therefore, probably not a coincidence that Kehlmann's forged painter is called Heinrich Eulenböck, alluding to Campendonk both by his first name and by the rhythm of his surname. In addition, Beltracchi's fictitious collection was called the "Jägers collection", whereas Iwan has his atelier in the "Jägerstraße" (317). Thus, Iwan can be seen as an alter ego of Beltracchi, just as Eulenböck is a double of Campendonk.

---

[19] Options that are regularly discussed; see the recent debate about Damian Hirst's formaldehyde works.
[20] Foucault (1998 [1969], 306).

At the same time, Iwan mirrors the protagonist of a short story by German author Ludwig Tieck from 1821. The protagonist is an art forger called Eulenböck, producing, for example, paintings by Salvator Rosa. When confronted with his forgeries, Tieck's Eulenböck says:

> It's no lie at all [...]; it is as genuine a Salvator Rosa as I ever painted. Thou hast never seen me at work upon it, and therefore canst not know who the author is.[21]

Tieck's Eulenböck uses similar arguments to Kehlmann's Iwan: authorship is not (only) a question of making, but also one of ascription—and it is a fragile construct in any case. The fragility of authorship is probably the most important aspect of Kehlmann's novel, offering the basis for an extrapolation of theory that draws on its reflections on authorship (and as will be undertaken in the final chapter of this book): in *F*, authorship is subject to construction, to changes over time, to different conceptualizations. Authorship is thus no less a fiction than the artworks it produces. And this holds true even for the 'authorship of life'—coming back to the idea of narrating one's biography, as I will recapitulate in the last paragraph on *F*.

Daniel Kehlmann: Faking Fiction Within Fiction

Near the end of the novel, when standing in front of one of Iwan's Eulenböck paintings together with Eric's daughter Marie,[22] Arthur speaks about the inseparable link between fate and chance:

> "Fate," said Arthur. "The capital letter F. But chance is a powerful force, and suddenly you acquire a Fate that was never assigned to you. Some kind of accidental fate. It happens in a flash." (248)[23]

---

[21] Tieck (1825 [1823], 14); "Ist keine Lüge, [...] ist ein so veritabler Salvator Rosa, wie ich nur noch je einen gemalt habe. Hast mich ja nicht daran arbeiten sehen und kannst also nicht wissen, von wem das Bild herrührt" (Tieck 1963 [1823], 12).

[22] Linked to the Grail legend which is present in *F* via the names of Arthur, Eric, and Iwan, Marie may be understood as a—partially ironic—'modern' continuity of the legend as, for example, presented in Dan Brown's *The Da Vinci Code* which invents a role for Mary Magdalene within the story of the Grail.

[23] "'Fatum', sagte Arthur. 'Das große F. Aber der Zufall ist mächtig, und plötzlich bekommt man ein Schicksal, das nie für einen bestimmt war. Irgendein Zufallsschicksal. So etwas passiert schnell'" (364).

This paragraph summarizes several important aspects of *F*. By emphasizing the importance of fate, Arthur points to a structure that determines the basis of each individual life. At the same time, as Arthur's references to chance illustrate, fate is (perhaps) nothing more than a narrative construction wrapped around contingency and chance.

Throughout Kehlmann's novel, the question of who is the author of what remains uncertain and unresolved in many respects. It is a question of perspective and choice rather than an immutable fact. The same holds true for the various parts of Kehlmann's novel. While they may be seen as (fictionally) 'accurate' narrations of four lives (of Arthur and his three sons), they may also be understood as fiction within fiction: as narratives invented by Arthur, just as Arthur is explicitly named as the author of the integrated short story "*Family*". Maybe, therefore, the sons do not even exist in the diegetic world—just as the fictions they create do not exist.

In the end, both authorship and fiction remain blurred in terms of their scope and boundaries. The novel questions both the concepts of (original) authorship and a clear distinction between fact and fiction. It may, therefore, be understood as a plea for a narrative freedom which goes beyond clear-cut categories of theory or criticism.

CREATING THE READER: ITALO CALVINO'S *IF ON A WINTER'S NIGHT A TRAVELER* (*SE UNA NOTTE D'INVERNO UN VIAGGIATORE*, 1979)

In his *Postscript to 'The Name of the Rose'*, Umberto Eco states that "writing means constructing, through the text, one's own model reader".[24] Italo Calvino's novel *If on a Winter's Night a Traveler* (*Se una notte d'inverno un viaggiatore*, 1979) creates not just one but a multitude of (model) readers. Calvino (1923–1985) was an Italian writer, renowned for his genre-defying works that blend elements of fantasy, postmodernism, and metafiction. His most famous works include *Invisible Cities*, a poetic exploration of imagined urban landscapes with echoes of Dante's *Divine Comedy*, and the *Cosmicomics*, which delve into metaphysical questions through the lens of science fiction. Calvino's oeuvre, which also encompasses essays and literary criticism, has had a lasting impact on twentieth-century literature, illustrating the malleability of narrative form and the limitless possibilities of storytelling.

[24] Eco (1984, 48).

If on a Winter's Night a Traveler was published at a time when conceptualizing the relationship between text and reader was high on the agenda.[25] Some years after the main debates about post-structuralism, authors could expect readers experienced in literary theory. Such readers, due to their familiarity with a specialized interpretive toolkit, potentially read more critically and are therefore more resistant to attempts by literary texts to shape their recipients in a way that they become—Eco again—"the prey of the text".[26]

Calvino's novel deals with such readers—readers who possibly do not expect an experience of immersion while reading but are open to ruptures and self-reflexivity. *If on a Winter's Night* is not a holistic text, but a series of beginning, yet never-ending novels (told on an endodiegetic level of Calvino's novel)—a plot device which may be seen as a peridiegetic integration of theory when captured in the light of its structural similarities to deconstructivist ideas. In this conception, it is also structurally similar to Morris Zapp's activity at the end of David Lodge's *Small World*, when Zapp is in a hotel room, watching the first five minutes of various films:

> They give you five minutes of a movie for free, to get you interested. […] Then if you want to watch the whole thing, you call and have them pipe it to your room and charge it. […] But if you're into deconstruction, you can just watch all these trailers in a row as if it was one, free, avant-garde movie.[27]

Calvino's plot can be considered the literal execution of this strategy. It has "the reader" (who is presented as a character within the book) starting a new book, Italo Calvino's *If on a Winter's Night a Traveler*. After some pages, however, the book is corrupted: pages are repeated, so that the reader cannot continue reading the story. He walks to the bookshop to request an intact copy, but the second copy turns out to be a totally different book. Together with a female reader he has met in the bookshop, the reader starts a quest for the 'right' book. The quest leads him to a research institute at university, to the publisher, and to other people and institutions. Again and again, the reader starts to read new books, but never succeeds in finishing them. Intertwined into the reader's story, the novel presents ten beginnings of different novels. It is only at the end of the

---

[25] See, for example, Eco (1979) or Iser (1991).
[26] Eco (1984, 53).
[27] Lodge (2011 [1984], 328).

novel that the reader—now in bed with the female reader—finishes Calvino's *If on a Winter's Night a Traveler*.

Calvino's novel thus presents a multitude of 'novels' within the novel— and a multitude of readers within the fictional text, since each of the people the two readers meet has their way of reading (the publisher different from the academic and from the translator, and so on). Moreover, each 'reader type' can be understood as corresponding to one of the novels started. The reader type in question is thus considered an option before being quickly abandoned. Therefore, *If on a Winter's Night* demonstrates various approaches to reading, integrating reader-response theory on the diegetic, endodiegetic and exodiegetic levels. There is a constant interplay between fictional and real readers, between the inside and the outside of the novel, between literature and theory. As in many other cases discussed in this book, theory has an essential function in dynamizing the plot.

In the end, however, the openness of the text, which is hinted at in the multitude of readers and their individual approaches, is not transferred to the readings of 'the' reader and his female companion. The diegetic passages of the novel are comparatively 'closed' (not an 'open work' in the sense of Eco).[28] For its main story, Calvino's novel arrives at a way of reading that does not leave space for alternatives, so that a 'closed openness' or 'pretended openness' is generated.[29]

The Real, the Implied, and the Diegetic Reader

At the beginning of the novel, there is a successive replacement of the real reader by an implied reader in the fictional world.[30] The real reader seems to be the addressee of the first sentences:

> You are about to begin reading Italo Calvino's new novel, *If on a winter's night a traveler*. Relax. Concentrate. Dispel every other thought. Let the world around you fade. (3)[31]

---

[28] Eco (1989 [1962]).
[29] Parts of this argument have been outlined in Kraft and Schilling (2018).
[30] Cf. Badley (1984, 105); Guj (1989, 67); Zima (2004, 164).
[31] "Stai per cominciare a leggere il nuovo romanzo Se una notte d'invero un viaggiatore di Italo Calvino. Rilassati. Raccogliti. Allontana da te ogni altro pensiero. Lascia che il mondo che ti circonda sfumi nell'indistinto" (3). Quotations from the novel here and below are taken from Calvino (1993 [1981]) [English translation] and Calvino (2016 [1979]) [Italian original], respectively.

The following paragraphs describe in detail how the real reader (apparently) approaches the novel. They discuss the most comfortable position for reading, the best lighting, and where the cigarettes are that accompany the reading. At this point, however, the non-smoking readers of Calvino's novel may notice the difference between themselves and the "reader" within the novel—a reader they may now tentatively term 'implied' (on an exodiegetic level of the book). The implied reader is a construct based on Wayne C. Booth's idea of an 'implied author':[32] a text does not only have the real author who (empirically) writes it and the real reader who (empirically) reads it, but also an implied reader (the one the author has in mind when writing) and an implied author (the one the reader has in mind when reading), both, however, based on certain structures in the text.

One might argue that such an implied reader is the addressee here. Consequently, at the end of the first chapter the 'actual' novel seems to start at last. A new paragraph, entitled "If on a winter's night a traveler", begins as follows:

> The novel begins in a railway station, a locomotive huffs, steam from a piston covers the opening of the chapter, a cloud of smoke hides part of the first paragraph. [...] The pages of the book are clouded like the windows of an old train, the cloud of smoke rests on the sentences. (10)[33]

The novel continues like this for some pages, until the reader reaches the corrupted pages and starts his quest for an intact copy of Calvino's book. At this point, however, the discrepancy between the real and the implied reader as developed at the novel's opening[34] gains a third dimension: there is no longer just the implied reader experiencing typical reading activities, but also "the reader" as a fictional character who acts just like any other character in the novel. By the first instances of his direct speech, if not before, it is made clear that this character speaks from a standpoint of his

---

[32] Booth (1961).
[33] "Il romanzo comincia in una stazione ferroviaria, sbuffa una locomotiva, uno sfiatare di stantuffo copre l'apertura del capitolo, una nuvola di fumo nasconde parte del primo capoverso. [...] Sono le pagine del libro a essere appannate come i vetri d'un vecchio treno, è sulle frasi che si posa la nuvola di fumo" (10).
[34] This is already emphasized by Segre (1979, 177): "Solo nel primo capitolo il lettore è potenziale destinatario del libro." However, this is not simply a framework for the exodiegetic level ("cornice", ibid., 183), as Segre explains in the following, but an integral part of the entire novel.

own, which does not coincide with that of the real or implied reader.[35] The reader typology is therefore threefold, comprising the real, the implied, and the diegetic reader.

The narrative illusion created by the implied reader could be interpreted as a way of addressing the real reader in their life and drawing them into the world of the novel. Now, however, it becomes clear that the novel might be better understood as a rupture of illusion, an effect produced by an act of critical distancing and self-reflection. Such a self-reflexive distancing continues in the novel's episodes that recount the experiences of the diegetic reader, in which things happen that (most plausibly) have not the slightest connection to the reality of the real reader. As such, the latter cannot help but treat the 'reader' of the novel as a fictional character.

The distinction between the three readers is never explicitly made in the text; it is already an interpretive step. Throughout the novel, however, the tripartite structure of real, implied, and diegetic readers persists. Only on this condition is the end of the novel plausible:

> Now you are man and wife, Reader and Reader. A great double bed receives your parallel readings. Ludmilla closes her book, turns off her light, puts her head back against the pillow, and says, "Turn off your light, too. Aren't you tired of reading?" And you say, "Just a moment, I've almost finished *If on a winter's night a traveler* by Italo Calvino." (254)[36]

The final sentence leads the action of the diegetic reader back to the action of the implied reader, who, simultaneously with the diegetic reader—and with the real reader—concludes reading the novel. At the very end of the book, the variety of readers once more becomes one.

---

[35] Kablitz (1992, 79) argues that the separation of the apostrophized real reader from the fictional reader already occurs at the end of the first numbered chapter, since the real reader is already confronted with a limited identification potential with regard to his reading circumstances.

[36] "Ora siete marito e moglie, Lettore e Lettrice. Un grande letto matrimoniale accoglie le vostre letture parallele. Ludmilla chiude il suo libro, spegne la sua luce, abbandona il capo sul guanciale, dice:—Spegni anche tu. Non sei stanco di leggere? E tu:—Ancora un momento. Sto per finire Se una notte d'inverno un viaggiatore di Italo Calvino" (260).

A Multitude of Fictional Readers

The clear differentiation of a real, an implied, and a diegetic reader indicates that the novel is not—as one might think—a text particularly 'open' to multiple readings. The fact that the process of reading itself is made the subject of the narrative does not necessarily open up the variety of real readings. Calvino's novel does reveal a variety of interpretive options inspired by literary theory, but it approaches these options from the vantage point of their limitations. Moreover, as the diegetic reader is complemented by a multitude of other readers on the diegetic level, it becomes clear that the novel is comparatively 'closed': there are various characters performing different acts and methods of reading, yet they are not structurally different from a standard novel character.

Nonetheless, the different readers bring forward different forms of reading, expanding the already threefold concept. I will not analyze all the fictional readers in detail,[37] but focus on the most important ones: the diegetic reader himself; Ludmilla, the female reader from the bookstore and the protagonist's subsequent love interest; her sister Lotaria; the publisher Dr. Cavedagna; the author Silas Flannery; and the artist Irnerio. Each of them is a character in Calvino's novel; at the same time, each of them presents a methodologically different form of reading—thus presenting reader-response theory on the diegetic level.

Calvino's diegetic reader-protagonist has particular preferences for his reading, just like the other reader-characters in the novel. He looks for something ordered and does not like "to find [himself] at the mercy of the fortuitous, the aleatory, the random" (26).[38] Similarly, the first beginning of a novel within the novel expresses an inner conflict between the plan the protagonist wants to follow and the experiences that force or tempt him to abandon the plan.

Ludmilla seeks "novels [...] that bring [her] immediately into a world where everything is precise, concrete, specific" (29).[39] In analogy to her preferences, the novel-beginning Calvino presents after she has entered the scene shows a particular attention to details: "An odor of frying wafts

---

[37] For the full typology, see Kraft and Schilling (2018).
[38] "[T]rovar[si] alla mercé del fortuito, dell'aleatorio, del probabilistico" (30).
[39] "[R]omanzi [...] che [la] fanno entrare subito in un mondo dove ogni cosa è precisa, concreta, ben specificata" (29).

at the opening of the page [...]. Rape oil, the text specifies; everything here is very precise" (33).[40]

In contrast to Ludmilla's reading stands that of her sister Lotaria. Lotaria approaches literature by forcing theorems upon texts.[41] Her reading takes place at the university and is related to society and academia, whereas Ludmilla reads privately and for pleasure.[42] What might be termed an overemphasis on nature in Ludmilla's reading is replaced by an overemphasis on culture in Lotaria's. Even the body has turned into culture for Lotaria; she cries out: "The body is a uniform!" (213).[43] A similar understanding of the body as a cultural artifact is enacted in the endodiegetic novel-beginning following her appearance. Here, the protagonist experiences sexual adventures with a mother and her daughter, according to a cultural setting he does not understand.

Dr. Cavedagna, a publisher, deals professionally with the rewriting and reworking of texts. For him, literature and books have been stripped of their magic. In his world of book production, texts appear imperfect: "books are considered raw material, spare parts, gears to be dismantled and reassembled" (112).[44] To consider them as a whole, as completed, is the reader's privilege. Indeed, Dr. Cavedagna longs to read texts in Ludmilla's manner, without regard to their production and revision. Linked to him is a novel-beginning which speaks about "accumulat[ing] past after past behind me, multiplying the pasts" (102)[45] in a manner reminiscent of Dr. Cavedagna's multiple manuscripts.

Silas Flannery is an author of novels. He tries to write but cannot concentrate. Therefore, he picks up a spyglass and watches a woman reading a book on her terrace, close to Flannery's flat. While he watches her, he feels an "absurd desire: that the sentence I am about to write be the one the woman is reading at the same moment" (166).[46] As a consequence, he starts to copy the sentence the woman is going to read next into his

---

[40] "Un odore di fritto aleggia ad apertura di pagina [...]. Olio di colza, è specificato nel testo, dove è tutto molto preciso" (38).
[41] Cf. Guj (1989, 69); Zima (2004, 171).
[42] Cf. Zima (2004, 168–169).
[43] "Il corpo è un'uniforme!" (219).
[44] "[I] libri appaiono sotto forma di materiali grezzi, pezzi di ricambio, ingranaggi da smontare e da rimontare" (113).
[45] "[A]ccumulare passati su passati dietro le mie spalle, moltiplicarli, i passati" (121).
[46] "[U]n desiderio assurdo: che la frase che sto per scrivere sia quella che la donna sta leggendo nello stesso momento" (198).

5 THE FRAGILE RELATIONSHIP OF AUTHOR, READER, AND TEXT 129

manuscript, so that he can imagine her reading 'his' sentence the moment he writes it. Consequently, he expresses his admiration for a medieval scribe who "lived simultaneously in two temporal dimensions, that of reading and that of writing" (174).[47] The novel-beginning linked to Flannery mirrors the simultaneity of reading and writing:

> Speculate, reflect: every thinking activity implies mirrors for me. [...] I cannot concentrate except in the presence of reflected images, as if my soul needed a model to imitate every time it wanted to employ its speculative capacity. (157)[48]

Another character the reader encounters in his search for the lost book is the 'non-reader' Irnerio. He represents a pre-literate state, opposing the culture of writing. The reason for his stay at the university, the site of institutionalized writing, is conversation. Otherwise, Irnerio concentrates on book art. Texts are of interest to him as material, books are "a good material to work with" (144).[49]

At the end of the novel, the diegetic reader finds himself in a public library with seven other readers, all of whom share their individual insights about reading. The plurality of different ways of reading that have been elaborated in the different characters and the different novel-beginnings connected with them is taken up in a mise-en-abyme style. The first reader says he wants to be inspired by reading, the second regards reading a fragmentary process, the third reads books again and again as if he was reading them for the first time—and so forth. After the seven readers have expressed seven ways of reading, it is the diegetic reader's turn to share his thoughts. Despite having been in contact with a multitude of possible readings both during his quest for Calvino's novel and in the library with the seven readers, he comes back to the preference he expressed in the beginning:

> Gentlemen, first I must say that in books I like to read only what is written, and to connect the details with the whole, and to consider certain readings

---

[47] "[V]iveva contemporaneamente in due dimensioni temporali, quella della lettura e quella della scrittura" (208).
[48] "Speculare, riflettere: ogni attività del pensiero mi rimanda agli specchi. [...] non so concentrarmi se non in presenza d'immagini riflesse, come se la mia anima avesse bisogno d'un modello da imitare ogni volta che vuol mettere in atto la sua virtù speculativa" (187).
[49] "[U]na bella materia" (148).

as definitive; and I like to keep one book distinct from the other, each for what it has that is different and new; and I especially like books to be read from beginning to end. (250–251)[50]

Theories of Reading

The differentiated diegetic, endodiegetic, and exodiegetic readers in Calvino's *If on a Winter's Night* seem to point to the interpretive hypothesis that the novel is an 'open work', permitting a variety of readings. Accordingly, Ludmilla understands her reading as a game immanent to fiction: for her, every text and every interpretation can be exchanged for another text as well as another interpretation. In Calvino's novel, too, reading reaches beyond the limits of the textual work: the titles of the ten novels, put together, make the beginning of another book, refer to another text.

And yet, it is precisely the typology of fictional readers extrapolated from Calvino's novel that suggests a different conclusion. As previously shown, the readers are established as characters with individual traits within a fictional text—similar to the characters who allegorically represent different literary theories in Lodge's *Small World*. Thus, the text has the power to present their readings without regard for the real readers' subjective reading impression, defined solely by what the novel says about them. As the typology of diegetic readers illustrates in detail, each character is assigned an individual attitude toward reading, but this attitude remains fixed and unchanging throughout the story. These attitudes might be used for an extrapolation of theory from literature—such as creating a typology of readers—but they are hardly open to individual interpretation in detail.

In the end, the diegetic reader equally brings his reading and life to a specific end by marrying Ludmilla. He comes to a narrative conclusion, a sense in his life, just as he concludes his quest for meaning in books. The final scene, as quoted earlier, shows them both in bed, engrossed in "parallel readings" (254). The diegetic reader has not been changed by the

---

[50] "Signori, devo premettere che a me nei libri piace leggere solo quello che c'è scritto; e collegare i particolari con tutto l'insieme; e certe letture considerarle come definitive; e mi piace tener staccato un libro dall'altro, ognuno per quel che ha di diverso e di nuovo; e soprattutto mi piacciono i libri da leggere dal principio alla fine" (257).

other readers' approaches, e.g., by Lotaria's academic readings, Irnerio's non-reading, or Dr Cavedagna's focus on the production of books. His story thus comes to the conclusion he desires in his reading, an unambiguous one: the marriage with Ludmilla.

An 'Open Work'?

In the end, two diegetic readers get married, one novel character to the other. So on the diegetic level, there is not too much room for interpretation. Anyone who does not want to read the plot and the characters of *If on a Winter's Night a Traveler* wantonly against the grain—which in practice, of course, everyone is free to do—must realize that, on the diegetic level, they are dealing with a rather closed work.[51]

One could consider whether the distinction made at the beginning of the novel between diegetic, implied, and real readers leads to a plurality of interpretations. But this is not the case either: the real readers are free to do with the novel as they please; they are not bound by any restrictions in their reading or interpretive practice. But if they want to position themselves in academic discourse with an interpretive hypothesis, they have to tie it back to the structures of the text—and are thus again rather limited, as Eco later points out in *The Limits of Interpretation*.[52] For the implied reader, a "triumph of reading"[53] and thus of interpretation over the text has been proclaimed. But even this triumph is ultimately undermined and contextualized. In the end, the implied reader turns out to be a construct of the text (on an exodiegetic level) and is thereby relegated to the limits and conditions of fiction.

Calvino's novel presents a plurality of readings, beginning with the real reader, before introducing an implied reader and finally arriving at a plurality of diegetic readers. It thus illustrates the complexity of any reading process, the different levels and methods within it, and the different choices (deliberate or not) that take place during reading. However, the threshold to the outside of the text is not crossed by either the implied or one of the fictional readers. There is no openness of interpretation detached from the text. On the contrary, the novel can be understood as

---

[51] Zima (2004, 165) argues differently, stating that Calvino wanted to write an open work in the sense of Eco.
[52] Eco (1989 [1962]).
[53] Schulz-Buschhaus (1986, 77).

a plea for the limits of interpretation: a conventional yet charming love story is told, and the real reader can follow the development of this story in all its facets. However, the reader does not find his or her own personal love in it, and so the text again sets the limits of what can be told and what experienced.

BUILDING A WORLD MADE OF TEXT: CHRISTOPH RANSMAYR'S *THE LAST WORLD* (*DIE LETZTE WELT*, 1988)

Christoph Ransmayr, born in 1954, is an Austrian writer who often explores themes of memory, history, and transformation. His best-known works include *The Terrors of Ice and Darkness* (*Die Schrecken des Eises und der Finsternis*, 1984) and *The Last World* (*Die letzte Welt*, 1988), which blend myth and history to create complex narrative landscapes. Ransmayr has been praised by critics for the poetic quality of his writing and his ability to blend past and present, fact and fiction.

The Last World, set in Augustan Rome, starts with rumors of Ovid's, the author's, demise: "The statement was: *Naso is dead*" (3).[54] Right from the beginning, therefore, there is a stark contrast to the closing words of Ovid's *Metamorphoses*, in which the ancient poet proclaimed his eternal fame: "Wherever Roman power rules conquered lands, | I shall be read, and through all centuries, | If prophecies of bards are ever truthful, | I shall be living, always."[55] Moreover, the sentence can be seen as an indirect reference to the 'death of the author' declared by Roland Barthes twenty years before Ransmayr's novel.

Building on this, one might consider *The Last World* as a transfer of the death of the author from literary theory to literature—on both the diegetic and the exodiegetic level. But as the novel progresses, it becomes clearer that this is not the only key issue in the text. Instead of installing a simple dualism between the living and the dead author, between antiquity and (post)modernity, there is a continuum of literary fictionalizations between the author's death and his eternal survival in the text. Themes from the last verses of the *Metamorphoses* are directly integrated into Ransmayr's text, where they are further varied and modified. Although the author

---

[54] "Der Satz hieß, *Naso ist tot*" (11). Quotations from the novel here and below are taken from Ransmayr (1990) [English translation] and Ransmayr (1988) [German original], respectively.

[55] Ovidius Naso (1955, XV, 877–879); "quaque patet domitis Romana potentia terris, | ore legar populi, perque omnia saecula fama, | siquid habent veri vatum praesagia, vivam".

dies, he can live on by being absorbed into the medium of fiction. Ransmayr takes up this idea and intensifies it. His novel follows the idea expressed in the last verses of the epos: that fiction spans space, time, and people. In doing so, the novel offers self-reflexive thoughts on authorship and fictionality (a metaization of theory) that could be used for an extrapolation of theory from the novel (the creation of theory).

The Last World begins with Ovid exiled by Augustus to the Black Sea. His reader Cotta leaves Rome to find him and to get hold of his most famous (yet, as the novel puts it, lost) work, the *Metamorphoses*. Cotta arrives in Tomi, a small town on the shores of the Black Sea, where Ovid (whom Ransmayr refers to by his *cognomen* Naso) is said to have lived. Cotta, however, does not find Naso. But there are several characters that the reader can easily identify as part of Ovid's *Metamorphoses*: Echo, Fama, Arachne, Pythagoras, etc. They either tell Cotta stories from the epos or live their lives in a way that mirrors their role in Ovid's *Metamorphoses*.

From Tomi, Cotta continues to Trachila, a place in the mountains a few hours away, where Naso is now believed to live. Even there, however, Cotta does not find him. All that remains are fragments of his work, either written on banners or carved in stone by Naso's servant Pythagoras. Ovid's fictional world turns out to have taken possession of Trachila and Tomi and eventually of the diegetic world as a whole. There is no longer *text in the world*, but the *world has turned into text*. The novel ends with Cotta, too, striving to become a part of this narrative.[56]

Dissolving the Author

The Last World presents an author (Naso) and a reader (Cotta) on the diegetic level of the novel. Naso and Cotta, however, are not only characters but can also be understood as an allegorical presentation of author and reader in a manner reminiscent of Umberto Eco's concepts of 'model author' and 'model reader'.[57] The author Naso is absent. The remark about his death, as quoted above, already represents a loss of the author as a biographic ledger. Moreover, the idea of an independently creating author is evoked and subsequently deconstructed. The author no longer guarantees a fixed text and/or a certain interpretation. Instead, individual stories are told endodiegetically from the perspectives of different

---

[56] Parts of this argument have been outlined in Schilling (2012).
[57] Eco (1990, 55, 59, 128).

characters in the novel (Pythagoras, Echo, Arachne). These narratives cannot be assigned to an author—they are free, like mythological narratives. Authorship as a concept of literary theory is thus not only presented in the novel, but also rejected.

This impulse of deconstruction is transferred from the author to his work as well: the traditional media of transmission—books, scrolls—are lost. At no point in the novel there is a possibility (except in Cotta's subjective hopes) of obtaining a reliable transmission or even edition of the *Metamorphoses*. Cotta's attempts to locate the text fail in a similar way to the efforts of hermeneutic interpretation that have become suspect to postmodern text and reading theory.[58] Cotta's journey can be described, in Derrida's words, as a search for the "lost or impossible presence of the absent origin".[59] But the text does not simply dissolve; it becomes a multiplicity of intertextual voices that constitute the very core of the novel.[60]

The author's death in the novel is, therefore, both a form of absence and an absorption into the fiction he has created.[61] On the one hand, the author dissolves, as do the traces of all people and their works in the novel. On the other hand, this is not a disappearance without replacement, but a form of metamorphosis. The author 'goes through death' in order to create new (literary) life—just as theory goes through Ransmayr's literary text enabling new theory to be created.

Losing the Reader

The diegetic reader Cotta is likewise characterized by a multitude of metamorphoses that ultimately lead to his disappearance. From a rationally acting 'publisher' who at first can be seen as an exodiegetic (model) reader, Cotta is transformed into a diegetic character. At the end of the novel, he is no longer in search of the *Metamorphoses* as a book, but strives to inscribe himself into the textual world of the epos:

---

[58] Anz (1997, 124).
[59] Derrida (1978 [1967], 292). For this reason, Köhler (2006, 109) proposes a deconstructivist reading of the reading of the novel—which in turn raises the question of whether a book can (or cannot) be analyzed particularly well with the help of the integrated theory.
[60] Cf. Schmitz-Emans (2004, 130–135).
[61] Wilhelmy (2004, 312) states that Naso and his text have not been deconstructed, destroyed, or died, yet grown into the world. The author is not dead: his disappearance was not a going-out-of-the-world, rather a going-into-the-world, into his own, the fictional one.

5 THE FRAGILE RELATIONSHIP OF AUTHOR, READER, AND TEXT   135

One thing drew Cotta into the mountains—the only inscription he had not yet discovered. He would find it on a banner buried in the silvery lustre of Trachila or on the boulder-strewn flanks of the new mountain. He was sure it would be a small banner—after all, it carried only two syllables. When he stopped to catch his breath, standing there so tiny under the overhanging rocks, Cotta sometimes flung those syllables against the stone, and answered, *here*! as the echo of his shout came back to him. For what reverberated from the walls—broken and familiar—was his own name. (176)[62]

For a long time, Cotta's behavior is characterized by reasoning, an approach that the novel presents as typical of Rome and that contrasts with the free play of imagination in Tomi and Trachila. Cotta tries to confront his epistemology with the world of Tomi, distinguishing between reason and madness and applying the standards of Rome during his journey. Yet the more deeply he becomes entangled in Tomi's life, the more fiction begins to take hold of him. This leads to Cotta's complete assimilation into the world of Tomi, eventually becoming "hardly distinguishable" (134)[63] from the inhabitants, and finally not even distinguishable from the world as text.

This disappearance of the rational reader can be considered through a functional perspective on theory: having deconstructed the notion of an autonomous and independently creating author, the text now also problematizes the notion of a critical reader. As quoted above, Roland Barthes had replaced the author with the reader: "[T]he birth of the reader must be ransomed by the death of the Author."[64] Ransmayr, however, 'kills' both author and reader—and thus not only presents but also criticizes theory. Cotta is initially characterized as an almost exodiegetic reader, before being absorbed by Tomi's imaginative space. At first, he behaves like a modern reader who is confronted with an open text or like a philologist who is supposed to arrange the fragments of a text and assemble them

---

[62] "Die einzige Inschrift, die noch zu entdecken blieb, lockte Cotta ins Gebirge: Er würde sie auf einem im Silberglanz Trachilas begrabenen Fähnchen finden oder im Schutt der Flanken des neuen Berges; gewiß aber würde es ein schmales Fähnchen sein—hatte es doch nur zwei Silben zu tragen. Wenn er innehielt und Atem schöpfte und dann winzig vor den Felsüberhängen stand, schleuderte Cotta diese Silben manchmal gegen den Stein und antwortete *hier*!, wenn ihn der Widerhall des Schreies erreichte; denn was so gebrochen und so vertraut von den Wänden zurückschlug, war sein eigener Name" (287–288).
[63] "[K]aum noch zu unterscheiden" (220).
[64] Barthes (1967).

to a meaningful work. In both functions, however, he fails because he is consumed by the fiction.[65]

Cotta thus does not become 'mad', as he would have to be called according to Roman standards, but 'normal' in the sense of the norms of fiction that apply in Tomi and Trachila. Moreover, Cotta as reader, through his complete integration into the fiction, comes as close as possible to Naso as author, finally merging with him when he realizes that he has been assigned a central role within the fiction.[66] At the end of the novel, there is neither an empirical author/reader nor a model author/reader, just text as a holistic universe. Against this background, Ransmayr's text may well be understood as a presentation of deconstructivist theory, illustrating Derrida's claim that "there is nothing outside the text" ("il n'y a pas de hors-texte").[67]

Multiple Authors and Readers

The three most important figures besides Cotta and Naso—Pythagoras, Echo, and Arachne—transmit individual stories from the *Metamorphoses* to Cotta. They all serve as 'readers' (i.e., recipients) and 'authors' at the same time: they hear and tell stories. They do so, however, in very different ways. Pythagoras has the role of textual transmission. He erects stone monuments in Trachila, inscribes banners, and carves the last passage from Ovid's work—the immortality topos—in stone. Echo tells Cotta about transformation myths. The deaf-mute weaver Arachne reproduces the stories from the *Metamorphoses* in her tapestries, thus contributing to the tradition in an iconographic way.

With regard to their function for the transmission of the *Metamorphoses*, they all have in common that they adopt a limited perspective and pass on only the information of interest to them individually and related to their own lives.[68] Like Cotta, the other characters also offer a subjective interpretation of the *Metamorphoses*. The myths of transformation told in the novel are thus doubly fractured: by the subjectivity of the transmission perspective on the one hand and by Cotta's perspective on the other. The

---

[65] Nethersole (1992, 238).
[66] In an analysis of a detective short story by Friedrich Kittler, Horn (2022, 101) diagnoses a comparable 'structural similarity' of author and reader.
[67] Derrida (1967, 158).
[68] Cf. Fitz (1998, 230).

mythical stories link the narrative process to the actual functioning of myth: it cannot be traced back to an author who creates a text with a claim to originality, but rather creates and reshapes itself in every moment of transmission.

Other characters in Tomi also embody the myths of the *Metamorphoses*, although this is something they are not necessarily aware of. Unlike the figures mentioned so far, who actively contribute to the transmission of Naso's work, they passively transmit the *Metamorphoses* by living them. Of course, the novel does not allow for the construction of a causal relationship: the question of whether the characters have gained their traits because they have adapted to Naso's imagination or whether Cotta derives stories from their behavior, which he attributes to Naso, must remain open. If the latter were the case, this would have further consequences for the conception of authorship—similarly to the construction and transmission of myth. In any case, however, the author is once again not simply 'dead', but the "author-function",[69] as Michel Foucault put it, has shifted to multiple procedures of intertextual, collective, unconscious authorship.

Reality and Fiction Within the Novel

The novel gradually erases the boundary between fiction and reality as the distance from Rome increases: Cotta, in his search for Naso and the *Metamorphoses*, metaleptically ends up 'within' the *Metamorphoses*; for him, literature becomes reality. The novel comments on this development in a self-reflexive way that can be considered a metaization of theory. For example, one day Fama's son Battus turns into stone, and the narrator says: "there in Fama's store stood Battus, gray and cold, a dire warning, decked out in lavender and saxifrage, that the border between reality and dream was perhaps lost forever" (134).[70] At the edges of the civilized world, imagination is established as an alternative to reality. In Rome, all mythical and cultural processes are ordered and directed by the state. In Tomi, fiction allows the inhabitants to leave reality to a certain degree. Finally, in Trachila, fiction reaches the level of the absolute—and this is

---

[69] Foucault (1998 [1969], 306).
[70] "Grau und kalt stand Battus in Famas Laden, eine mit Lavendel und Steinbrechnelken geschmückte Drohung, daß die Grenze zwischen Wirklichkeit und Traum vielleicht für immer verloren war" (221).

where both Naso and Cotta get lost in the novel, where they turn into text themselves.

The motif of the metamorphosis supports this weight of fiction.[71] Documents, inscriptions, orders, and figures are transformed. Nature converts the man-made cultural landscape of Tomi back to its 'natural' form, restoring the freedom lost to the static society of Rome. The motif of transformation refers back to the ancient model of the *Metamorphoses*, whereby Ransmayr does not inscribe any motivation for the transformations in his text. The novel offers no psychological explanation, nor can gods or any other causes be identified as the originators of the metamorphoses.[72] If identity is generally changeable—and it inevitably is in the face of the absolute dominance of fiction—then the question of maintaining identity is superfluous. The motif of change is a necessary component of freely creating imagination, which is entitled to alter or destroy its creations at will.

Consequently, the textual tradition in *The Last World* is itself fragmentary, allowing for arbitrary references in its reconstruction. The novel presents ever-new narrative fragments and textual remnants, reforming the existing knowledge of the world. In this way it becomes a palimpsest, without the hierarchical order offered by the author. Tomi and Trachila, with their multiplicity of discourses and the principle of metamorphosis, also exemplify the palimpsest structure.

The dissolution of fixed references leads to the postmodern phenomena of plurality and multiple coding. Because of the different ways of accessing the novel, one can speak of an 'open work'.[73] The novel can be interpreted and understood from numerous perspectives and thus corresponds to the ideas of postmodern plurality. At the end of the novel, the whole world turns out to be text; there is neither an author nor a reader predestined to arrive at a definitive interpretation. The loss of the border between text and world may—seen from an extrapolative perspective on theory in Ransmayr's novel—also affect the observer's perspective. Taking up Luhmann, it can be argued that every interpretation of the text requires a re-entry into the text that questions the original difference between text and interpretation.

---

[71] Cf. Anz (1997); Bernsmeier (1991); Epple (1992); Fülleborn (1996); Schmidt-Dengler (1997).
[72] Bachmann (1990, 644) sees this as evidence of the totality of reification.
[73] Eco (1989 [1962]).

BIBLIOGRAPHY

Anz, Thomas (1997): Spiel mit der Überlieferung: Aspekte der Postmoderne in Ransmayrs "Die letzte Welt". In: Uwe Wittstock, ed.: *Die Erfindung der Welt: Zum Werk von Christoph Ransmayr.* Frankfurt/Main, 120-136.
Ashley-Cooper, Anthony, Earl of Shaftesbury (1710): *Soliloquy or Advice to an Author.* London.
Bachmann, Peter (1990): Die Auferstehung des Mythos in der Postmoderne: Philosophische Voraussetzungen zu Christoph Ransmayrs Roman "Die letzte Welt". In: *Diskussion Deutsch* 21, 639-651.
Badley, Linda C. (1984): Calvino engagé: Reading as Resistance in "If on a Winter's Night a Traveler". In: *Perspectives on Contemporary Literature* 10, 102-111.
Barthes, Roland (1967): The Death of the Author. In: *Aspen* 5-6, s.p.
Bernsmeier, Helmut (1991): Keinem bleibt seine Gestalt: Ransmayrs "Letzte Welt". In: *Euphorion* 85, 168-181.
Booth, Wayne C. (1961): *The Rhetoric of Fiction.* Chicago.
Borges, Jorge Luis (1962): The Garden of Forking Paths. In: Jorge Luis Borges: *Ficciones. Translated by Helen Temple and Ruthven Todd.* New York, 89-101.
Borges, Jorge Luis (1997): *Ficciones.* 2nd edition. Madrid.
Calvino, Italo (1993 [1981]): *If on a winter's night a traveler. Translated from the Italian by William Weaver.* London.
Calvino, Italo (2016 [1979]): *Se una notte d'inverno un viaggiatore. Presentazione dell'autore. Con uno scritto di Giovanni Raboni.* Milano.
Chraplak, Marc (2017): Daniel Kehlmanns "F" als mehrfach codierter bifokaler Rätselroman in der Nachfolge von Henry James und Borges. In: *Wirkendes Wort* 67, 285-308.
Derrida, Jacques (1967): *De la grammatologie.* Paris.
Derrida, Jacques (1978 [1967]): *Writing and Difference. Translated by Alan Bass.* Chicago.
Eco, Umberto (1979): *The Role of the Reader: Explorations in the Semiotics of Texts.* Bloomington.
Eco, Umberto (1984): *Postscript to "The Name of the Rose". Translated from the Italian by William Weaver.* San Diego et al.
Eco, Umberto (1989 [1962]): *The Open Work. Translated by Anna Cancogni. With an Introduction by David Robey.* Cambridge/MA.
Eco, Umberto (1990): *The Limits of Interpretation.* Bloomington et al.
Epple, Thomas (1992): *Christoph Ransmayr: Die letzte Welt.* München.
Fitz, Angela (1998): *"Wir blicken in ein ersonnenes Sehen". Wirklichkeits- und Selbstkonstruktion in zeitgenössischen Romanen: Sten Nadolny – Christoph Ransmayr – Ulrich Woelk.* St. Ingbert.

Foucault, Michel (1998 [1969]): What is an Author? In: Donald Preziosi, ed.: *The Art of Art History: A Critical Anthology*. Oxford et al., 299–314.
Fülleborn, Ulrich (1996): Ransmayrs "Letzte Welt": Mythopoesie und das Unverfügbare von Natur und Geschichte. In: Holger Helbig, ed.: *Hermenautik – Hermeneutik: Literarische und geisteswissenschaftliche Beiträge zu Ehren von Peter Horst Neumann*. Würzburg, 355–367.
Guj, Luisa (1989): "Quale storia laggiù attende la fine?" The lettore's successful quest in Calvino's "Se una notte d'inverno un viaggiatore". In: *Italian Quarterly* 30, 65–73.
Horn, Eva (2022): Kittlers Rätselmaschine. Eine Kriminalgeschichte als Literaturmodell. In: *Zeitschrift für Ideengeschichte* 16, 101–110.
Iser, Wolfgang (1991): *Das Fiktive und das Imaginäre: Perspektiven literarischer Anthropologie*. Frankfurt/Main.
Kablitz, Andreas (1992): Calvinos "Se una notte d'inverno un viaggiatore" und die Problematisierung des autoreferentiellen Diskurses. In: Klaus W. Hempfer, ed.: *Poststrukturalismus – Dekonstruktion – Postmoderne*. Stuttgart, 75–94.
Kehlmann, Daniel (2013): *F. Roman*. Reinbek.
Kehlmann, Daniel (2015): *F (a novel)*. Translated from the German by Carol Brown Janeway. London.
Köhler, Sigrid G. (2006): *Körper mit Gesicht: Rhetorische Performanz und postkoloniale Repräsentation in der Literatur am Ende des 20. Jahrhunderts*. Köln et al.
Kraft, Felix, and Schilling, Erik (2018): Zur Geschlossenheit eines 'offenen Kunstwerks': Strategien der Leserlenkung und Typologie der Leserfiguren in Italo Calvinos "Se una notte d'inverno un viaggiatore". In: *Germanisch-romanische Monatsschrift* 68, 429–449.
Lodge, David (2011 [1984]): *Small World*. London.
Meissner, Thomas (2014): Eulenböcks Wiederkehr: Über Fälschung, Kunstfrömmigkeit und Ironie bei Daniel Kehlmann und Ludwig Tieck. In: *Athenäum. Jahrbuch der Friedrich-Schlegel-Gesellschaft* 24, 175–184.
Nethersole, Reingard (1992): Vom Ende der Geschichte und dem Anfang von Geschichten: Christoph Ransmayrs "Die letzte Welt". In: *Acta Germanica* 21, 229–245.
Ovidius Naso, Publius (1955): *Metamorphoses*. Translated by Rolfe Humphries. Bloomington/London.
Ransmayr, Christoph (1988): *Die letzte Welt. Roman. Mit einem Ovidischen Repertoire*. Nördlingen.
Ransmayr, Christoph (1990): *The Last World. With an Ovidian Repertory*. Translated from the German by John Woods. London.
Schilling, Erik (2012): Der zweite Tod des Autors? Metamorphosen der Postmoderne in Christoph Ransmayrs "Die letzte Welt". In: *Textpraxis. Digitales Journal für Philologie* 4, 1–19.

Schmidt-Dengler, Wendelin (1997): "Keinem bleibt seine Gestalt": Christoph Ransmayrs Roman "Die letzte Welt". In: Uwe Wittstock, ed.: *Die Erfindung der Welt: Zum Werk von Christoph Ransmayr*. Frankfurt/Main, 100–112.

Schmitz-Emans, Monika (2004): Christoph Ransmayr: "Die letzte Welt" (1988) als metaliterarischer Roman. In: Anselm Maler, ed.: *Europäische Romane der Postmoderne*. Frankfurt/Main et al., 119–148.

Schulz-Buschhaus, Ulrich (1986): Aspekte eines Happy-Ending: Über das XII. Kapitel von Calvinos "Se una notte d'inverno un viaggiatore". In: *Italienisch* 16, 68–81.

Segre, Cesare (1979): Se una notte d'inverno uno scrittore sognasse un aleph di dieci colori. In: *Strumenti critici* 38, 177–214.

Tieck, Ludwig (1825 [1823]): *The Pictures. The Betrothing. Translated by Connop Thirlwall*. London.

Tieck, Ludwig (1963 [1823]): Die Gemälde. In: Ludwig Tieck: *Werke in vier Bänden*. Vol. 3. München, 7–74.

Wilhelmy, Thorsten (2004): *Legitimitätsstrategien der Mythosrezeption: Thomas Mann, Christa Wolf, John Barth, Christoph Ransmayr, John Banville*. Würzburg.

Zima, Peter V. (2004): Zur Institutionalisierung der Leserrolle bei Italo Calvino: "Se una notte d'inverno un viaggiatore". In: *Romanistische Zeitschrift für Literaturgeschichte/Cahiers d'Histoire des Littératures Romanes* 28, 163–183.

CHAPTER 6

Creating and Interpreting Fictional Worlds

One main functional aspect of integrating literary theory into literature is the reflection on the creation and interpretation of fictional worlds. Umberto Eco's *Foucault's Pendulum* deals with 'good' and 'bad' interpretations of texts. The various interpretations performed in the novel are gradually extended to a theory of interpretation in general. The elements of theory in the novel contribute to a critical reflection on theory and to a metaization of the interpretive procedures performed. The interpretive procedures, both 'simple' and 'hermetic', are substantiated in Eco's theory on *The Limits of Interpretation*, offering a concrete form of an extrapolation of theory.

Juli Zeh's *Dark Matter* has its protagonists trying to create a parallel world within their own, a world whose norms they control—just as every fictional work creates norms and conditions of its own. In contrast to life, though, fiction is able to present both the order and—on a self-reflexive level—the ordering principle, something that, turned into a theoretical concept, might be extrapolated from Zeh's novel as theory. Moreover, fiction can show what an ordered world looks like—and how other orders (or observers) would form the world differently. Zeh's elaboration of fiction theory may thus serve to sharpen the 'sense of possibility' in general—and it presents a metaization of literary theory within literature.

© The Author(s), under exclusive license to Springer Nature Switzerland AG 2024
E. Schilling, *Theorizing Literature*,
https://doi.org/10.1007/978-3-031-53326-6_6

Limiting Interpretations: Umberto Eco's *Foucault's Pendulum* (*Il pendolo di Foucault*, 1988)

Umberto Eco (1932–2016) has covered the field of both theory and literature like no other twentieth-century intellectual. His theoretical writings, starting with *The Open Work* (*Opera aperta*, 1962), made him a well-known representative of semiotics, for which he received the world's first chair at the University of Bologna in 1975. In his works of the 1960s and 1970s, he extended semiotics—as cultural semiotics—to almost all areas of human civilization, only to turn his focus more particularly to texts in the 1980s and 1990s, in the form of literary semiotics.[1]

Closely linked to his academic work are the novels Eco published: *The Name of the Rose* (*Il nome della rosa*, 1980) works with semiotic concepts, while his *Postscript to 'The Name of the Rose'* (1983) reacts to the reception of the novel in a theorizing way. *Foucault's Pendulum* (*Il pendolo di Foucault*, 1988), Eco's second novel, discusses conditions of a successful interpretation, which Eco takes up two years later in theory with *The Limits of Interpretation* (1990). Eco's third novel, *The Island of the Day Before* (*L'isola del giorno prima*, 1994), is closely related to the author's, reader's, and text's intentions (*intentio auctoris, intentio lectoris*, and *intentio operis*), which Eco had introduced in his academic book *Lector in fabula* (1979) and revised several times thereafter, for example in his Tanner lectures at Cambridge in 1989/90. Finally, *Kant and the Platypus* (*Kant e l'ornitorinco*, 1997) picks up questions raised by Eco in *The Island of the Day Before*, such as the question of being and the multiplicity of worlds.

Thus, if Eco's novels are inextricably linked to his theoretical works (as it has been stated many times),[2] the opposite is also true: Eco's (later) theoretical writings are based on his novels and the experiences with their reception. As a consequence, Eco's theoretical and literary works cannot be thought of as a linear movement from theory to literature, but have to be considered in light of their complex interrelationship—as a series of re-entries of theory into literature and literature into theory. I will illustrate this by analyzing *Foucault's Pendulum*, which, out of all of Eco's novels, most artfully deals with interpretive theories and practices.

---

[1] For an overview, see Nöth (2021) and Burkhardt (2021).
[2] See, for example, Richter (1986); Bennett (1988); Schilling (2021).

Foucault's Pendulum narrates a chain of events from 1970 to 1984.[3] The protagonists, Belbo, Casaubon, and Diotallevi, are three editors working for a Milanese publisher. They are bored with their work and start to invent stories parting from historical fact. In doing so, they rewrite history, to such an extent that the invented facts are first taken for reality by other characters in the novel and eventually by themselves. For example, they trace back the history of the Templars, Rosicrucians, and other secret societies from the Middle Ages to the twentieth century and construct a so-called secret plan that is supposed to have implications for the present.

The novel's plot is presented as a double reconstruction: the reader follows Casaubon as he pieces information together from his memory of a night in a Parisian museum, as well as from Belbo's computer files. In addition, events of the Second World War find their way into the novel, focalized through Belbo's point of view and concentrated on the conflicts between partisans and fascists in Piedmont during the final two years of the war.

The resulting plurality of narrations contributes to a deconstruction of any teleological form of history. Everyone comes up with their own story, and various interpretations of history and reality compete. The novel's climax takes place over six days: Belbo vanishes. Casaubon reads some of Belbo's computer files to find him and deduces that he might be in Paris. In Paris, Casaubon spends a night at the *Conservatoire des Arts et Métiers*, where he sees Belbo (possibly) being murdered by members of a secret society who tie him to a Foucault pendulum. Casaubon flees to Belbo's country house and waits to see whether the murderers will trace him down as well. Here the novel ends.

---

[3] For an overview, see Max (2021). In its temporal ambiguity, the Italian blurb offers the perfect synthesis of the plot's loops: "This novel takes place from the early 1960s to 1984 between a Milanese publishing house and a Parisian museum where a Foucault pendulum is on display. It takes place from 1943 to 1945 in a small village between Langhe and Monferrato. It takes place between 1344 and 2000 along the route of the Templar and Rosicrucian plan to conquer the world. It takes place entirely on the night of June 23, 1984"; "Questo romanzo si svolge dall'inizio degli anni sessanta al 1984 tra una casa editrice milanese e un museo parigino dove è esposto il pendolo di Foucault. Si svolge dal 1943 al 1945 in un paesino tra Langhe e Monferrato. Si svolge tra il 1344 e il 2000 lungo il percorso del piano dei Templari e dei Rosa-Croce per la conquista del mondo. Si svolge interamente la notte del 23 giugno 1984" (https://lanaveditesseo.eu/portfolio/il-pendolo-di-foucault/, my translation).

The Longing for a Fixed Point of Interpretation

In his *Postscript to 'The Name of the Rose'*, Eco calls the detective novel the "most metaphysical and philosophical"[4] genre: its appeal lies in its representing "a kind of conjecture, pure and simple"[5] that the reader has to assume. The basic question, "who is the guilty one?", is paradigmatic for many seemingly unrelated aspects of life, such as theology and psychoanalysis. This longing for someone responsible, for a center from which a whole chain of events is to be understood, is taken up in *Foucault's Pendulum* on two levels.

First, *Foucault's Pendulum* is a detective story. It deals with people haunting other people, information being hidden and revealed, somebody being killed—and others looking for the 'whodunit'. For this reason, the novel can be seen as an exemplary case of the connection between the crime plot and theory as a driving force behind it. Second, the longing for a solution, a center, a structure, is already marked as fatal in the first chapter of the novel: Casaubon reads the expression of a divine will into a Foucault pendulum, which is nothing more than a physical experiment illustrating the rotation of the earth. To Casaubon, however, the arbitrary center of the pendulum's point of suspension is "the Only Fixed Point in the universe", where "the mystery of absolute immobility was celebrated" (5).[6]

With this mystification of a banality, which is already told with a certain irony at this point, the text seemingly takes a clear stand for the renunciation of a center, as Jacques Derrida, for example, has demanded:

> There are thus two interpretations of interpretation, of structure, of sign, of play. The one seeks to decipher, dreams of deciphering a truth or an origin which escapes play and the order of the sign [...]. The other, which is no longer turned toward the origin, affirms play and tries to pass beyond man and humanism, the name of man being the name of that being who, throughout the history of metaphysics or of ontotheology [...] has dreamed of full presence, the reassuring foundation, the origin and the end of play.[7]

---

[4] Eco (1984, 53).
[5] Ibid., 54.
[6] "[L]'unico punto fisso dell'universo", "il mistero dell'immobilità assoluta" (10). Quotations from the novel here and below are taken from Eco (1989b [1988]) [English translation] and Eco (1988) [Italian original], respectively.
[7] Derrida (1978 [1967], 292).

Earlier in his writings, in *The Open Work*, Eco had argued for a similar "'openness' based on the theoretical, mental collaboration of the consumer".[8] The recipient views a work that has already been produced and thus completed, but still allows an unlimited number of interpretations. Therefore, the recipient participates in the creation of the work.

Later, however, at the time when writing *Foucault's Pendulum*, Eco stressed the 'rights' of the text in his publications on theory. To him, the text poses limits on interpretation, which a rational reader cannot trespass. A reading beyond these limits is no longer an interpretation of the text, but a mere 'use' of the text for one's own purposes.[9] Deconstruction, in Eco's view, is such a use of the text, not an interpretation.[10] To read *Foucault's Pendulum* as a plea for deconstruction would therefore certainly be mistaken, even if the protagonists act in a deconstructivist manner for large parts of the novel. The limits of deconstruction, which are at the same time the limits of interpretation, are delineated subtly in the novel, only to be played out all the more dramatically at its end.[11]

Interpreting a 'Secret Message'

For the arbitrariness of the sign, as it corresponds to the deconstructivist 'play' with meaning, no character in the novel stands out more clearly than Colonel Ardenti, who brings Belbo, Casaubon, and Diotallevi into contact with the so-called plan for the first time. He has discovered two 'secret documents' that supposedly reveal the concept of a world conspiracy by the Templar Order. Step by step, the novel shows that his reading of the fragmentary documents could easily be just a fun game, but the potentially playful approach is thwarted by the colonel's zeal. Ardenti presents a convincing plan for deciphering the first message, yet he discredits it with his reading of the second message because he describes his conjectures as "unassailable" (135).[12] Moreover, he is compromised in his objectivity by the assumption that he is "close to the truth" (139).[13]

---

[8] Eco (1989a [1962], 11).
[9] Eco (1990).
[10] This is a statement Derrida would probably have agreed with.
[11] The novel's relationship to Eco's theory of interpretation is examined by Juarrero (1992), Landrum (1995), and Bondanella (1997); its relationship to post-structuralist theories by Phiddian (1997).
[12] "[I]nattaccabili" (111).
[13] "[V]icino alla verità" (115).

Some 400 pages later, Lia, Casaubon's girlfriend, reveals that the plan as reconstructed by Ardenti is based on pure arbitrariness. She is able to prove that the plan is not a secret message but just the note of a medieval craftsman. She comes to that conclusion by developing "the simplest hypothesis" (537)[14] and finally stating:

> "[Y]our plan is full of secrets, full of contradictions. For that reason you could find thousands of insecure people ready to identify with it. Throw the whole thing out. [...] [Y]ou three have been faking. Beware of faking: people will believe you. [...] I don't like it. It's a nasty joke." (541)[15]

While Ardenti starts with a note and develops a cosmic plan, Lia starts with a cosmic plan (which Casaubon, Belbo, and Diotallevi suggest) and arrives at a note. Even though her explanation, as just one among an infinite number of possible interpretations, initially has as much justification as any of the others, its simplicity makes it preferable. This is particularly true because—unlike all other interpretations of the 'secret message'—it works without an underlying secret.

In *The Limits of Interpretation*, two years after publishing *Foucault's Pendulum*, Eco takes up precisely this idea:

> [T]he addressee-oriented theories assume that the meaning of every message depends on the interpretive choices of its receptor: even the meaning of the most univocal message uttered in the course of the most normal communicative intercourse depends on the response of its addressee.[16]

The addressees see the text as an open world in which they are free to discover connections at will. The text is reduced to the chain of responses it evokes. A meaning of the text is either negated or extended into arbitrariness. According to Eco, one of the most striking features of hermetic thought is its flexibility: "everything can be connected with everything else, so that everything can be in turn either the expression or the content of any other thing".[17]

---

[14] "[L]'ipotesi più economica" (422).
[15] "Il vostro piano è pieno di segreti, perché è pieno di contraddizioni. Per questo potresti trovare migliaia di insicuri disposti a riconoscervisi. Buttate via tutto. [...] Voi avete fatto finta. Guai a fare finta, ti credono tutti. [...] Non mi piace, è un brutto gioco" (425).
[16] Eco (1990, 45).
[17] Ibid., 24.

In Eco's view, deconstructivist approaches establish analogies between signs by way of a continuous drift, without ever coming to terms with them. Semiosis, on the other hand, is teleologically conceived: it can achieve an agreement among different readers because it aims at determining the interpreted sign as precisely as possible within a given context and recognizes the text—"the literal sense"[18]—as a parameter of possible interpretations. The (deconstructivist) game, on the other hand, runs the risk of being "nasty" and not "simple", as *Foucault's Pendulum* puts it, because it aims at eternally maintaining a mystery, not at a context-bound and thus meaningful interpretation of the text.

The Relationship Between Author, Reader, and Text

The relationship between author, reader, and text may serve as a second example to illustrate how the limits of interpretation are established as limits of deconstruction in *Foucault's Pendulum*. With Casaubon and Belbo, a fictional reader and a fictional author are present on the diegetic level of the novel when Casaubon reads Belbo's computer files. Moreover, Belbo—similarly to Binet's and Ransmayr's novels—suffers the 'death of the author' proclaimed by Roland Barthes:[19] the secret allies tie Belbo to the pendulum and kill him.

Casaubon assumes the role of an author as well: with Belbo and Diotallevi he sketches the plan of a new world history, which is taken at face value by his readers. By allowing the narrative scheme to escape its creators and take on an independent form, Eco illustrates what he had expressed in the *Postscript*: once a text is published, it is detached from its author and thus—at least hypothetically—open to any interpretation: "The author should die once he has finished writing. So as not to trouble the path of the text."[20] Any reading, whether situated within Eco's novel or about it, is thus faced with the choice of being aware of its limits (reassuring itself of its relative validity by considering the context) or moving toward the irrational. The novel clearly takes a stand here and thus exhibits the almost opposite approach to *The Name of the Rose*:[21] the development

---

[18] Ibid., 53.
[19] Barthes (1967).
[20] Eco (1984, 7).
[21] Cf. Schilling (2012b, 68–75).

in the *Pendulum* is not one from semiotics to deconstructivism, but from a deconstructivist drift to an outline of the limits of interpretation.

The function of integrating theoretical aspects into the literary text is therefore to present the procedures of interpretation in the novel in a self-reflexive way, to dynamize the narrative through them, and to evaluate existing theory critically. As a result, the novel can be understood as an active contribution to literary theory. This was underlined two years later when the theoretical insights developed in the novel were extrapolated by Eco himself in his book on *The Limits of Interpretation*.

A Moment of Presence

But the limits of interpretation are not the end of the novel. The final scene describes Casaubon taking refuge in Belbo's country house, fearfully waiting for the secret allies who (apparently or actually) pursue him. In a closet he finds some notes by Belbo, which precipitates a surprising volte-face. Belbo—he writes—had a particular experience when playing the trumpet as a boy: when he played at a funeral and tried to hold the last sound as long as possible. It was a moment of sheer presence, without thinking and interpreting, a moment of pure being. From this, Casaubon arrives at the conclusion that a metaphysical experience of any kind cannot be based on thinking and interpretation, but only on the experience of a particular moment—a rejection of theory.[22] Thus, he decides to enjoy his last moment: "So I might as well stay here, wait, and look at the hill. It's so beautiful" (641).[23]

With this reference to a pre-semiotic experience, a moment without (or before) interpretation,[24] the emphasis on literary theory shifts once again. Whereas before it was a matter of interpreting signs either well or badly (and thus implying an evaluation of theory), now there is a difference between a world of signs (and interpretation) and a signless world of presence. This turn becomes less surprising when seen in the context of Eco's other writings. *The Island of the Day Before*, for example, is built around the central metaphor of the dove, an image which also has a metaphysical component. *The Name of the Rose*, too, is marked by a longing for a metaphysical authority, which is revealed in William's search for the plan (and

---

[22] Cf. Schilling (2012a, 143–158).
[23] "E allora tanto vale star qui, attendere, e guardare la collina. È così bella" (509).
[24] For a theoretical approach to such a moment of presence, see Gumbrecht (2004).

this is remarkably similar to Belbo's search for a religious background to the plan he designed). And there is even a similar component in Eco's teleologically oriented semiotics, which does not aim at an infinite drift, but points to the cultural determinability of meaning.

Going Back to Interpretive Theory

In *The Limits of Interpretation*, Eco states that neither focusing on the author's intention (*intentio auctoris*) nor granting the reader complete freedom through a reader-centered approach (*intentio lectoris*) can do justice to a literary work.[25] In doing so, he takes up the theme of arbitrary interpretation that he had addressed in *Foucault's Pendulum*. In order to prevent arbitrary interpretations, he offers a third variant in addition to the author's and the reader's intention: the orientation toward the text's intention, the *intentio operis*. It results from the interpretive 'cooperation' of text and reader: the reader's perspective is guided by the structures of the text. Founding the interpretation on structures of the text, it becomes apparent which of the infinite number of interpretive variants are covered by the text and do not depend on the (unfathomable) intention of the author or the (contestable) intention of the reader.

In *Kant and the Platypus*, Eco draws another conclusion: he states "that it was always something resistant that moved us to invent general concepts."[26] From this, Eco surmises that there are areas of being about which one cannot speak:

> This given is precisely the lines of resistance. The appearance of these resistances is what comes closest to the idea of God or the Law before any First Philosophy or Theology. It is certainly a God who shows himself [...] as pure negativity, as pure limit, pure 'no,' as that about which language should not and cannot speak.[27]

Literature, Eco argues, is an attempt to transcend this linguistic limit. By "giving us a sense of what might be beyond the limit, writers on the one hand console us about our limitations, and on the other remind us how

[25] Eco (1990, 44–63).
[26] Eco (2000, 66).
[27] Ibid., 69–70.

often we are a 'vain passion.'"[28] Literature comes as close to the limit of human insight as possible; admittedly, however, it cannot cross it any more than theory can: "The rest is a guess."[29]

With this in mind, the hypothesis of the mutual dependence of literature and theory can be substantiated for Eco even further. His most important theoretical work on semiotics is called *La struttura assente* (1968), whereby the "absent structure" refers to the transcendent signified, which—due to the infinity of signifiers—can never be reached. The comparison with Eco's later works, which repeatedly move between theory and literature, sheds light on the longing for that absent structure in his early theory as well. Casaubon's fleeting experience of presence stands for the only way to escape the infinity of interpretation. Even though the semiotic drift is inescapable for anyone who accepts the linguistic turn, a longing for a metaphysical 'telos' remains.

Eco's theoretical and literary works therefore turn out to exist in complex interrelation to one another. Accordingly, Eco's novels can no longer be regarded as manifestations of postmodern thought only; they also present its critical questioning—a re-entry from literature into theory, leading to some concrete forms of an extrapolation of theory. In *Foucault's Pendulum*, Eco performs interpretations, both 'simple' and 'hermetic' ones, which he substantiates in his theory on *The Limits of Interpretation*. Moreover, in the novel's final scene, he sets a limit to interpretive processes in general, favoring a pre-semiotic moment over hermeneutics—just as Eco puts it some years later in *Kant and the Platypus*.

Creating Fictional Worlds: Juli Zeh's *Dark Matter* (*Schilf*, 2007)

Juli Zeh, born in 1974, is a writer and judge known for her works that explore ethical questions, socio-political issues, and the facets of contemporary conditions. She has written novels, essays, and plays, including works such as *Corpus Delicti* (2009) and *Unterleuten* (2016), which have been translated into several languages and received various awards. Her literary style is characterized by a focus on intellectual themes, complex characters, and innovative narrative structures, positioning her as an important figure in contemporary German literature.

---

[28] Ibid., 72.
[29] Ibid.

Her novel *Dark Matter* (*Schilf*, 2007) establishes a link between quantum physics and fictional worlds. The novel's protagonists, Sebastian and Oskar, are both professors of physics. They have been friends since their undergraduate studies. Some twenty years later, however, they have arrived at different physical theories and different ways of living. When they meet, they almost immediately start arguing about their respective understandings of the world.

Zeh's novel presents the culmination of this debate. Oskar wants to convince Sebastian that there are human experiences which necessarily contradict Sebastian's many-worlds interpretation, at least on a macroscopic level. One day, when Sebastian drives his son Liam to a scout camp, Oskar simulates Liam's kidnapping. In a fake phone call, Oskar has his secretary issue a demand to Sebastian: to renounce "doublethink", that is, his many-worlds interpretation. Sebastian, however, gets the message wrong and understands "Dabbelink", the name of one of his wife's friends. He suspects them of having an affair; in addition, Dabbelink supposedly plays a role in a medical scandal at the university hospital. Sebastian interprets the phone call as an order to kill Dabbelink, which makes perfect sense to him, as he has a motive (his wife's affair), so that the actual motive (the medical scandal) cannot be traced back to him. Sebastian does in fact kill Dabbelink, and it is only at the end of the novel that he learns about the misunderstanding—a misunderstanding that is the basis for an intertwining of the seemingly different physical theories. This intertwining, as Zeh presents it, is itself linked to various possibilities of fiction—so that the novel in total can be considered a metaization of theory.[30]

Different Theories and Different Lives

Sebastian supports the many-worlds interpretation of quantum mechanics, according to which there are many worlds existing in parallel. Oskar, on the contrary, strives to combine quantum mechanics and the theory of relativity in order to "make two views of the universe into one" (32).[31] The implications of the different approaches[32] are elaborated in a TV

---

[30] A German version of this paragraph is published as Schilling (2024b).

[31] "[A]us zwei Sichtweisen des Universums eine" (28). Quotations from the novel here and below are taken from Zeh (2010) [English translation] and Zeh (2007) [German original], respectively.

[32] For a detailed account of the two physical theories, see Könneker (2015). See also the thoughts of Juli Zeh herself in an interview: Heydenreich and Mecke (2015).

debate in which Sebastian and Oskar present their respective theories. Oskar criticizes Sebastian's many-worlds interpretation as a "cozy attempt to circumnavigate God" (345).[33] The key aspect of the many-worlds interpretation is that it easily explains the incredibly low likelihood of the world existing as it is. Sebastian sees this as an advantage: there is no God, no ordering force needed to explain the existence of our world. If there is a huge number of worlds, ours may exist as well: "We exist simply because everything that is at all possible exists somewhere" (345).[34]

Yet there are several problems arising from the many-worlds interpretation. First, it cannot be tested empirically, as other universes cannot be observed from inside our universe. Second, it frees the individuals from the consequences of their actions: if all possible outcomes of a given decision are bound to come true in other universes, then there is—in the grand scheme of things—little harm in behaving selfishly or maliciously in this one.

The 'advantage' of Oskar's attempt to combine quantum mechanics with the theory of relativity is that it provides an explanation for everything and a theory without negating human responsibility. The downside of his approach is its deterministic character. If there is one single explanation for everything, then there is no freedom left for individual decisions. If God has created and ordered the world according to a perfect formula, then there is no chance of changing it. Human life would then consist in performing divine will without any possibility of altering or adding to it.

The same dichotomy of Sebastian's plurality and Oskar's unambiguousness holds true for their private lives.[35] Oskar (at least in appearance) has an answer to everything: "If Sebastian were to try to describe his friend Oskar, he would say that Oskar looks like the kind of person who could answer every question put to him" (21).[36] Sebastian, in contrast, lives two different lives at the same time, at least in Oskar's view: "'You long for other worlds,' Oskar says in a low voice [to Sebastian]. 'For the notion

---

[33] "[B]equemer Versuch, um Gott herumzukommen" (298).
[34] "Es gibt uns einfach, weil alles, was irgendwie möglich ist, irgendwo auch existiert" (298).
[35] As Könneker (2015, 116–117) states, Zeh projects the divergent basic physical positions of the antagonists, Sebastian and Oskar, onto their personality traits.
[36] "Wenn Sebastian versuchen wollte, seinen Freund Oskar zu beschreiben, würde er sagen, dass Oskar aussieht wie jemand, der alle Fragen beantworten kann" (19).

that you might be able to be two different men at the same time. At least'" (43).[37]

Yet Sebastian and Oskar do not sustain their different approaches for the whole story. By staging Liam's kidnapping, Oskar (unwillingly) 'proves' that there are various worlds possible at the same time; he is thus, to some extent, converted into a master of doublethink, as he himself states: "'Sebastian. [...] You weren't the expert in doublethink. I'm afraid it was me'" (436–437).[38] And Sebastian's preference for various worlds is in danger long before Liam's kidnapping. When he meets his wife Maike and falls in love with her, he considers this as a collapse of his theory:

> It was love at first sight, precluding alternatives, reducing an endless variety of possibilities to a here and a now. Sebastian's appearance in Maike's life was—as he would express it—a wave function collapse. (18–19)[39]

There is a world full of possibilities, but love, as Sebastian experiences it, reduces plurality to one single 'hic et nunc'. The same happens to Sebastian after Liam's kidnapping, when he sees desperation as something that prevents thinking in other possible worlds. Therefore, as the novel progresses, Sebastian gradually adopts Oskar's point of view—and vice versa. In doing so, an entire span of possibilities is fictionally represented in *Dark Matter*. As I will show in the following paragraph, Sebastian and Oskar do not only stand for competing physical theories, but also for different interpretations of fictionality. The central antagonism, however, remains the same: contingency vs. determination.

Fiction as a Means of Creating and Sustaining Different Worlds

There has been a long and intense debate about fiction, the fictional, and fictionality in literary studies.[40] *Dark Matter* takes up some of its argu-

---

[37] "'Du bist süchtig nach anderen Welten', sagt Oskar leise [zu Sebastian]. 'Nach der Vorstellung, zwei verschiedene Männer zugleich sein zu können. Mindestens'" (36).

[38] "'Sebastian! [...] Du bist nicht der große Fachmann für *doublethink* gewesen. Das war leider ich'" (379).

[39] "Es war Liebe auf den ersten Blick und damit ein Verbot von Alternativen, eine Reduktion der unendlichen Menge an Möglichkeiten auf ein Jetzt und Hier. Sebastians Erscheinen in Maikes Leben bedeutete, wie er es ausdrücken würde, einen Kollaps der quantenmechanischen Wellenfunktion" (16).

[40] For a recent contribution, see Fludernik and Ryan (2020).

ments, with special attention to the ideas presented in Robert Musil's novel *The Man Without Qualities*.[41] Musil does not contribute to literary theory in a strict sense; however, the novel is characterized by a blending of fictional and essayistic (and even theoretical) discourses. By going back to Musil, Zeh thus also goes back to a longer tradition of mixing theory and literature.

In the fourth chapter of the first part of his novel, Musil establishes his concept of 'sense of possibility' (*Möglichkeitssinn*):

> But if there is a sense of reality, [...] then there must also be something we can call a sense of possibility. Whoever has it does not say, for instance: Here this or that has happened, will happen, must happen; but he invents: Here this or that might, could, or ought to happen. If he is told that something is the way it is, he will think: Well, it could probably just as well be otherwise.[42]

Musil's sense of possibility bears a considerable resemblance to the many-worlds interpretation as it is presented in Zeh's novel. In both cases, what 'actually' happens is just one option among many possible variants. The difference, however, consists in the many-worlds theory arguing that the other options do exist, while Musil's concept is little more than thought play aiming at reducing the seemingly unavoidable state of reality.

In *Dark Matter*, fiction serves as a counterpart to reality, too. When Sebastian visits Oskar in Switzerland, desperate because of his impending arrest by the police, Oskar offers two possible worlds to him:

> "Let me tell you a story," Oskar says. "The day after the kidnapping you called me on the phone. [...] We sat up talking the whole night. [...]."
> He [Sebastian] pauses, then says, "I don't want an alibi."

---

[41] *Schilf* thus ties in directly with Zeh's earlier novel *Gaming Instinct*; on the Musil references therein, see Schilling (2024a).
[42] Musil (1996, 10–11); "Wenn es aber Wirklichkeitssinn gibt, [...] dann muß es auch etwas geben, das man Möglichkeitssinn nennen kann. Wer ihn besitzt, sagt beispielsweise nicht: Hier ist dies oder das geschehen, wird geschehen, muß geschehen; sondern er erfindet: Hier könnte, sollte oder müßte geschehen; und wenn man ihm von irgend etwas erklärt, daß es so sei, wie es sei, dann denkt er: Nun, es könnte wahrscheinlich auch anders sein" (Musil 1970 [1952], 16).

"*Bien*," Oskar says. "How about another story. [...] We're in Switzerland. That gives us a couple of days. I can get my affairs in order within two weeks." (324–325)[43]

Oskar's 'stories' create two fictional worlds counteracting the world he and Sebastian live in.[44] The first is a fictive alternative for the past (an alibi for the night the murder happened), the second an alternative for the future (leaving for a safe place out of the range of German jurisdiction). Sebastian, however, decides against both fictional options and decides to confront reality, with important implications for the novel as a whole.

Fiction as a Blending of Ambiguous and Unambiguous Aspects

Zeh's *Dark Matter* builds on competing theories in physics and transfers these to concepts of fiction. The difference between physics and fiction, however, consists in a possible simultaneity of different concepts within fiction. In reality, Sebastian's and Oskar's physical theories cannot be valid at the same time. Fiction, however, offers a space in which plurality and unambiguousness can coexist. On the one hand, fiction is—as Musil puts it—a space of possible worlds. Fiction can invent events, characters, places that do not exist in reality, yet might exist. Fiction, therefore, is well described in analogy to the many-worlds interpretation. On the other hand, fiction rejects the many possible worlds in favor of the one fictional world presented in the text with certain events and characters in a certain place. These cannot be exchanged at will, but are similarly fixed by a 'divine' (authorial) will,[45] as is the world in Oskar's physical theory.

Thus, fiction is both: an open world of contingencies and a closed world of the few options which are actually realized (out of an unlimited number

---

[43] "'Ich werde dir eine Geschichte erzählen', sagt Oskar. 'Am Tag nach der Entführung hast du mich angerufen. [...] Wir haben die ganze Nacht zusammengesessen und geredet. [...]' | 'Ich will kein Alibi', sagt er [Sebastian] nach einer Pause. | 'Bien', sagt Oskar. 'Dann eine andere Geschichte. [...] Wir sind in der Schweiz. Das gibt uns ein paar Tage Zeit. Innerhalb von zwei Wochen kann ich meine Angelegenheiten regeln'" (279–280).
[44] In this context, it is interesting that Dziudzia (2016, 549–550) understands Oskar as a 'rebellious aesthete' with a 'purely aestheticizing attitude'. If Oskar does indeed aestheticize the world in this way, his creation of possible worlds for the real world fits the scheme of the aesthete very well.
[45] An interesting exception to this is the large field of fan fiction, in which readers retell or expand on their favorite literature in the way that seems best to them. However, this is done outside of the original work and thus, to some extent, outside of its fictional world.

of possible ones).[46] The turning point of Zeh's novel, the misunderstood phone call after Liam's kidnapping, illustrates this complexity. During the call, the anonymous voice says (in Sebastian's understanding):

> "Herr Professor, I've been instructed to give you a message. A single sentence. I've been told you will understand." [...] Then she says it. "*Dabbelink must go.*" (86–87)[47]

Yet the voice does not say "Dabbelink", but "doublethink", as Sebastian learns later:

> "That is *doublethink* [...]. It means holding two contradictory beliefs in one's mind simultaneously, and accepting both of them. In Orwell that is a practice of totalitarian systems." (380)[48]

For each of the novel's characters, the events turn into a catastrophe: Sebastian kills a man due to a misunderstanding. As a consequence, his wife Maike and his son Liam find their lives ruined. Oskar's life breaks down as well: indirectly, he ordered the murder and is therefore responsible for it; in addition, he loses Sebastian as his closest friend. To some extent, therefore, Oskar reaches his goal of eliminating 'doublethink'. Every main character of the novel finds themselves reduced to one brutal reality. Just like Oskar's physics, life turns out to be unambiguous.

Fiction, however, is not—and this is probably the most important aspect of Zeh's dealing with fiction theory.[49] Her novel presents the fictional world as one that offers various possibilities at the same time, out of which some are realized and others remain only hypothetically possible. In addition to the several alternatives Oskar offers to Sebastian for their flight, the novel presents the possibility of Oskar and Sebastian becoming lovers.[50] A similar variety of options is true for Liam's kidnapping: he is kid-

---

[46] Accordingly, Pause (2012, 234) understands the novel as a reflection on narrative theory.

[47] "'Herr Professor, man hat mich beauftragt, Ihnen eine Botschaft zu überbringen. Einen einzigen Satz. Es hieß, Sie würden verstehen'. [...] Dann sagt sie es. Dabbeling muss weg" (75).

[48] "'Das ist doublethink. [...] Der Zwang, zwei Dinge, die einander widersprechen, gleichermaßen für wahr zu halten. Bei Orwell ist das eine Praktik des totalitären Systems'" (330).

[49] Pause (2012, 235) describes Sebastian as a secret literary theorist, and this is certainly equally true of Oskar.

[50] Cf. Könneker (2015, 103 and 108–109).

napped and not kidnapped at the same time. Fiction allows for this paradox to be upheld—it is able to sustain various options at the same time.

The Importance of the Viewer and the Viewpoint

Fiction, however, does not work without an observer:[51] someone who reads a text and understands it as fictional. In this respect, Zeh again combines life, physics, and fiction theory. The investigating police officer,[52] for example, captures the world by means of the fictional, applying rhetorical categories to the real: "He sees coincidences as metaphors and contradictions as oxymorons, and the repeated appearance of details as leitmotifs" (194).[53] By applying his own (in this case: rhetorical) categories to the observed object, the police officer acts similarly to the observer in quantum theory. Since the Copenhagen interpretation of quantum mechanics as proposed by Niels Bohr and Werner Heisenberg, the observer has been known to influence the result.

Zeh transfers this groundbreaking theory in physics to the realm of fiction. First, as shown, she presents her characters as observing the world according to their own premises. Again, Zeh refers to Musil's *Man Without Qualities*. In Musil's famous introductory passage, the meteorological conditions of a summer's day are ironically presented as 'corresponding' to human forecasts ("were all in accordance with the forecasts in the astronomical yearbooks").[54] In *Schilf*, Liam expresses the same thought when he says: "Nature behaves in accordance with our calculations" (18).[55] Second, fiction serves as an observation without a clear differentiation between the observer and the observed. Sebastian says: "I had always suspected my mind of doing secret things—I had an inkling that it added something to my cognition, that it brought everything I perceived into a

---

[51] See also the section on 'Observation as a Perspective of Knowledge' in the interview with Juli Zeh: Heydenreich and Mecke (2015, 294–298).
[52] On the allusions to the tradition of the detective novel and the police officer as an anti-inspector, see Plettenberg (2021).
[53] "Zufälle versteht er als Metaphern, in Widersprüchen erkennt er Oxymora, das wiederholte Auftreten von Details liest er als Leitmotiv" (166).
[54] Musil (1996, 3); "entsprachen ihrer Voraussage in den astronomischen Jahrbüchern" (Musil 1970 [1952], 9).
[55] "Die Natur entspricht unseren Berechnungen" (15).

ready-made order" (241).[56] There is no 'order of things' without the ordering person and the ordering principle the person applies. Again, this can be applied to life, physics, and fiction at the same time. In contrast to life and physics, though, fiction is able to present both the order and—on a self-reflexive level—the ordering principle, something that, turned into a theoretical concept, might be extrapolated from Zeh's novel as theory. Moreover, fiction can show what an ordered world looks like—and how other orders (or observers) would form the world differently. Again, fiction proves closed (unambiguous) and open (plural) at the same time: certain viewpoints are chosen to be presented, yet their subjective and contingent character is laid open. Zeh's elaboration of fictional theory may thus serve to sharpen the sense of possibility in general—and it presents a self-reflexive metaization of literary theory within literature.

Bibliography

Barthes, Roland (1967): The Death of the Author. In: *Aspen* 5–6, s.p.
Bennett, Helen T. (1988): Sign and De-Sign: Medieval and Modern Semiotics in Umberto Eco's "The Name of the Rose". In: M. Thomas Inge, ed.: *Naming the Rose: Essays on Eco's "The Name of the Rose"*. Jackson, 119–129.
Bondanella, Peter (1997): Interpretation, Overinterpretation, Paranoid Interpretation and "Foucault's Pendulum". In: Rocco Capozzi, ed.: *Reading Eco: An Anthology*. Bloomington/Indianapolis, 285–299.
Burkhardt, Armin (2021): Spätere Schriften zur Semiotik und Sprachphilosophie. In: Erik Schilling, ed.: *Umberto-Eco-Handbuch: Leben – Werk – Wirkung*. Stuttgart, 82–106.
Derrida, Jacques (1978 [1967]): *Writing and Difference*. Translated by Alan Bass. Chicago.
Dziudzia, Corinna (2016): Konjunkturen des Ästhetisierungsbegriffs. In: *Weimarer Beiträge* 62, 535–560.
Eco, Umberto (1984): *Postscript to "The Name of the Rose"*. Translated from the Italian by William Weaver. San Diego et al.
Eco, Umberto (1988): *Il pendolo di Foucault*. Milano.
Eco, Umberto (1989a [1962]): *The Open Work*. Translated by Anna Cancogni. With an Introduction by David Robey. Cambridge/MA.

---

[56] "Schon immer hatte ich meinen Verstand heimlicher Umtriebe verdächtigt. Ich ahnte, dass er der Wahrnehmung etwas hinzufügt; dass er alles Wahrgenommene in eine vorgefertigte Ordnung bringt" (206).

Eco, Umberto (1989b [1988]): *Foucault's Pendulum. Translated from the Italian by William Weaver.* London.
Eco, Umberto (1990): *The Limits of Interpretation.* Bloomington et al.
Eco, Umberto (2000): *Kant and the Platypus: Essays on Language and Cognition. Translated from the Italian by Alastair McEwen.* New York.
Fludernik, Monika, and Ryan, Marie-Laure, eds. (2020): *Narrative Factuality.* Berlin/Boston.
Gumbrecht, Hans Ulrich (2004): *Production of Presence: What Meaning Cannot Convey.* Stanford.
Heydenreich, Aura, and Mecke, Klaus (2015): Physik und Ethik: Juli Zeh im Dialog zu "Schilf". In: Aura Heydenreich and Klaus Mecke, eds.: *Physik und Poetik: Produktionsästhetik und Werkgenese. Autorinnen und Autoren im Dialog.* Berlin/Boston, 286–308.
Juarrero, Alicia (1992): The Message Whose Message it is that there is no Message. In: *MLN* 107, 892–904.
Könneker, Carsten (2015): 'Kopenhagener Deutung' versus 'Multiversum': Narrativierte Physik in Juli Zehs Roman "Schilf". In: *GegenwartsLiteratur* 14, 103–120.
Landrum, David W. (1995): Casaubon and the Key to All Mythologies: The Limits of Interpretation in "Foucault's Pendulum". In: *Italian Quarterly* 32, 59–65.
Max, Katrin (2021): "Das Foucaultsche Pendel" ("Il pendolo di Foucault"). In: Erik Schilling, ed.: *Umberto-Eco-Handbuch: Leben – Werk – Wirkung.* Stuttgart, 166–178.
Musil, Robert (1970 [1952]): *Der Mann ohne Eigenschaften. Roman. Herausgegeben von Adolf Frisé.* Hamburg.
Musil, Robert (1996): *The Man Without Qualities. Translated from the German by Sophie Wilkins.* New York.
Nöth, Winfried (2021): Frühe semiotische Schriften. In: Erik Schilling, ed.: *Umberto-Eco-Handbuch: Leben – Werk – Wirkung.* Stuttgart, 59–81.
Pause, Johannes (2012): *Texturen der Zeit: Zum Wandel ästhetischer Zeitkonzepte in der deutschsprachigen Gegenwartsliteratur.* Köln et al.
Phiddian, Robert (1997): "Foucault's Pendulum" and the Text of Theory. In: *Contemporary Literature* 38, 534–557.
Plettenberg, Franziska (2021): Ein Spiel auf Leben und Tod: Zum Umgang mit den Konventionen des Kriminalromans in Juli Zehs "Schilf". In: Klaus Schenk and Christina Rossi, eds.: *Juli Zeh. Divergenzen des Schreibens.* München, 328–346.
Richter, David H. (1986): Eco's Echoes: Semiotic Theory and Detective Practice in "The Name of the Rose". In: *Studies in 20th Century Literature* 10, 213–236.

Schilling, Erik (2012a): *Der historische Roman seit der Postmoderne: Umberto Eco und die deutsche Literatur.* Heidelberg.

Schilling, Erik (2012b): Umberto Eco zwischen Theorie und Literatur. In: Klaus Birnstiel and Erik Schilling, eds.: *Literatur und Theorie seit der Postmoderne. Mit einem Nachwort von Hans Ulrich Gumbrecht.* Stuttgart, 67–80.

Schilling, Erik (2021): "Der Name der Rose" ("Il nome della rosa"). In: Erik Schilling, ed.: *Umberto-Eco-Handbuch: Leben – Werk – Wirkung.* Stuttgart, 147–165.

Schilling, Erik (2024a): Mit dem Möglichkeitssinn Wirklichkeit schaffen: Juli Zehs "Spieltrieb" vor dem Hintergrund von Robert Musils "Der Mann ohne Eigenschaften". In: Erik Schilling, ed.: *Juli Zeh: Text und Engagement.* Stuttgart, 19–31.

Schilling, Erik (2024b): Mögliche Welten. Juli Zehs "Schilf": In: Erik Schilling, ed.: *Juli Zeh: Text und Engagement.* Stuttgart, 33–40.

Zeh, Juli (2007): *Schilf. Roman.* Frankfurt/Main.

Zeh, Juli (2010): *Dark Matter. A novel. Translated from the German by Christine Lo.* New York et al.

CHAPTER 7

Beyond Novels—Beyond Theory?

This final chapter of case studies goes beyond theory in novels by looking at a book of poems and a film. Jan Wagner's collection of poems *The Owl Haters in the Hall Houses* presents three fictional poets and their texts—and also the first, partly ironic, partly useful steps of literary criticism working on them. An interpretation of Wagner's poems must therefore take into account that they have already been 'processed' by analysis before criticism has even had a chance to deal with them. Interpretation is thus at best possible on a second-order level, which comprises a perspective on the first level of interpretation preformed within the literary text itself.

Marc Forster's film *Stranger than Fiction* can be seen as a cinematic presentation of literary theory, dealing with the relationship between narrator, character, and reader, and ironically crossing the boundaries between the three. The film is about observations and the influence of the observer on the observation. In the end, the film emphasizes the importance of life in relation to literature and theory, and can therefore be considered a continuous oscillation between presenting theory, ironizing it, or abandoning it in favor of 'the real'.

Self-Commenting Parody: Jan Wagner's Poetry Collection *The Owl Haters in the Hall Houses* (*Die Eulenhasser in den Hallenhäusern*, 2012)

Jan Wagner, born in 1971, is a prominent contemporary poet and essayist. His work, including the poetry collection *Regentonnenvariationen* (2014), is characterized by formal rigor, linguistic precision, and an engagement with both everyday and metaphysical themes. The blend of traditional forms and modern sensibilities in his writing has led to numerous awards and critical acclaim, establishing his position as a key figure in twenty-first-century German literature.

His book *The Owl Haters in the Hall Houses* (*Die Eulenhasser in den Hallenhäusern*, 2012) offers three collections of poems, each with a very different poetic focus (nature poems, anagram, elegy). In addition, the book gives information on the three alleged authors of the poems (Anton Brant, Theodor Vischhaupt, Philip Miller) with biographical details as well as a metadiegetic commentary on the texts and quotations from the fictitious 'secondary literature'. The book is a literary game, as all the poems and the additional information are written by Wagner himself.[1] Yet the chosen form of presentation allows for experimentation with different poetic styles and different interpretive approaches toward the texts. *Owl Haters* thus adopts an ironic distance with regard to the reception of literary works, especially in literary criticism—or at least in certain, biographically oriented forms of criticism. At the same time, however, the interpretive approaches presented offer interesting and helpful comments for a better understanding of the texts.[2]

Wagner's *Owl Haters* poems and the (para-)texts that (supposedly) make them accessible reflect upon literary theory in a variety of ways. In particular, various methods of literary analysis are juxtaposed and ironized, such as the aforementioned biographical perspective on texts, but also historiographical, intertextual, or deconstructivist approaches to literature.[3]

---

[1] Specht (2020, 264–265) summarizes that the poet conceals and reveals himself in his poetry.

[2] Klimek (2017, 193) emphasizes that an old-fashioned way of dealing with literature is taken ad absurdum, ending in flat positivism and a glorifying cult of the writer. But the ironization of literary studies goes beyond flat positivism.

[3] A German version of this chapter is published as Schilling (2022).

"Owl Haters" and Biographical Literary Studies

So far, research has focused on how a biographical approach toward literature is cast ironically in *Owl Haters*. The irrelevance of the three authors' biographies for an understanding of their work is not simply asserted, but staged in the interplay of paratextual framing and the poems.[4] This can be shown in manifold ways that relate to the connection between poems and fictional biographical introductions, as well as for the comments and the references to 'secondary literature'. A mere biographical speculation, for example, is that "father" in Anton Brant's poem "The boundaries" clearly refers to "The father: Sebastian Brant, who lived from 1895 to 1960".[5] The same is true for the supposed reference of "satanic dad" to Theodor Vischhaupt's "own childhood", whose "relationship with his father does not seem to have been the best".[6] Numerous other examples could be cited, in which biographical information is given but not helpful for an understanding of the poems.[7]

Yet the 'editor' of the poems also critically addresses the construction of such a connection between literature and life, using the example of Philip Miller's elegies: "Much more fundamentally, the question can be asked to what extent Miller's twelve elegies reflect on his own experiences at all—the question, therefore, old-fashionedly speaking, of how large the share of life and the share of art in the elegies is in each case".[8] Despite his explicit problematization of a biographical procedure, however, the editor 'fails' to see that the question he poses can hardly be answered by literary criticism. Fictional texts are detached from reality, and the 'amount' of reality within them is not measurable.

---

[4] Lampart (2017, 206) asks, on the occasion of interpreting Philip Miller's "First Elegy", whether such a text can be further explained or elucidated beyond its already explained character as ironically perspectivized role prose.

[5] "Vater: Sebastian Brant, der von 1895 bis 1960 lebte" (29). Quotations from the book here and below are taken from Wagner (2012) [the English version is my translation].

[6] Das "Verhältnis zum Vater scheint nicht das beste gewesen zu sein" (80).

[7] Specht (2020, 270). Osterkamp (2016) concludes that Wagner's texts emphasize the freedom of the poem in relation to the life of the author.

[8] "Viel grundsätzlicher läßt sich vielmehr die Frage stellen, inwiefern die zwölf uns erhaltenen Elegien Millers überhaupt seine eigenen Erfahrungen widerspiegeln – die Frage also, altmodisch gesprochen, wie groß der Anteil des Lebens und der Anteil der Kunst in den Elegien jeweils ist" (99).

"Owl Haters" and a Mimetic Understanding of Literature

Similar to a biographical approach, a mimetic understanding of literature is viewed—and practiced—in *Owl Haters* from an ironic perspective. Such a mimetic understanding does not only refer to the author's biography, but assumes generally that literature depicts life. This is characteristic of various remarks in *Owl Haters*. For example, Anton Brant's poem about a birthing sow follows, according to the commentary, a "rule of thumb estimate known among bristling cattle farmers", namely that the gestation period of a sow is "three months, three weeks, and three days".[9] A similar understanding of 'fidelity to reality' is illustrated by the commentary to Theodor Vischhaupt's poem "My Heart" and its verse "a Doge, caught in his splendor": "In fact, the Venetian Doges were far less free than is commonly supposed".[10] The prominent 'in fact' suggests a mimetic understanding, a (supposedly) straightforward correspondence between verse and world.

All these elements of the poems are categorized by the commentary in terms of a mimetic perspective: the author refers 'correctly' to how it 'really' was—an understanding of literature that has often been applied to Wagner's 'own' poems as well, for example, to "The Goutweed", which seems to depict the behavior of the plant—its uncontrolled proliferation—in a mimetic way as well. Yet *Owl Haters* does not stop at these parodies. Instead, it presents forms of a scholarly treatment of literary texts that are not ironized, but nevertheless—or precisely because of this—a challenge for interpretation.

"Owl Haters" and the Scholarly Commentary

A scholarly commentary is a useful way of dealing with texts. The fictional editor of *Owl Haters* offers numerous variations on such a commentary, which begins with the "glossary of rural words" (23–27) that accompanies Anton Brant's poems. The glossary is of use for the reading of the poems, as it deciphers, for example, words in local idioms not understandable to standard German speakers. This helpful apparatus continues at points in

---

[9] "[U]nter Borstenviehhaltern bekannte Faustregel"; "[d]rei Monate, drei Wochen und drei Tage" (47).

[10] "Tatsächlich waren die venezianischen Dogen weit weniger frei, als man gemeinhin annimmt" (73).

the commentary, explaining that a "Woog [...] is a pond or a deeper place in a river"[11] or that "Helas!" in French means "Oh!".

Potentially helpful to readers, moreover, are formal aspects explained in the commentary, which correctly refer to phenomena in the texts as "pure rhymes", as "internal rhymes", or as a "system of assonances".[12] Where the commentary gives information on rhetorical elements, it does not always ironically overshoot the mark either. Sometimes it offers helpful insights into the making of the poems, as when a passage is described as a "highly rhythmic, exceedingly musical collage of diverse culinary expressions"—which then admittedly tips into the parodic when the 'scholar' subsequently evaluates this as "lush caloric chanting" and as "phonetic gluttony".[13]

In addition, the commentary provides reliable factual information about the poems. For example, it gives references to the Brussels Atomium (30), explains that "zephyr" should be thought of as a mild wind (69), or offers historical information about the Venetian Doges (73). Philip Miller's elegies are accompanied by information about Roman poets and emperors (103–104). Theodor Vischhaupt's anagrams are enriched by a short chapter on "The anagram poem" (62–64), which explains the structure of anagrams and their literary history. This information is not only accurate, but actually contributes to a better understanding of the poems, much like the factual information of a 'normal' scholarly commentary would.

Thus, as an interim conclusion, it can be stated that the paratexts to the poems ironize a certain form of literary criticism—a biographic or mimetic approach—and expose it as unsuitable for understanding the poems. At the same time, however—and on the same narrative level, namely in the (paradiegetic) commentary—the paratexts offer important information for understanding the poems. A 'proper' scholarly commentary could hardly go beyond these elements, but rather at best repeat them.

Herein lies the central challenge in interpreting *Owl Haters*: on a superficial level, scholars who do not take on a biographic or mimetic approach can enjoy the irony and mutually assure themselves that their method is of course much better, more informed, more reliable. However, they run into a problem when the text—as shown—offers sound, informed, reliable

---

[11] "Woog [...] ein Teich oder eine tiefere Stelle in einem Fluß" (35).

[12] "[R]einer Paarreim"; "Binnenreime"; "System von Assonanzen" (29–30).

[13] "[H]och rhythmische, überaus musikalische Collage diverser kulinarischer Ausdrücke" (52).

elements of literary analysis as well. In these cases, the interpretation can no longer limit itself to diagnosing the ironic aspect of the commentary but has to recognize its integral contributions of information about the texts.

"Owl Haters" and Hermeneutics

Beyond the factual-informative parts of the commentary, *Owl Haters* presents concrete suggestions for interpretation. Some remarks explicitly aim at a better understanding of the poems. They stand for a classical conception of hermeneutics that asks for the 'meaning' of a text. For example, the editor comments on Theodor Vischhaupt's verse "coxcomb breeze | nobody's zephyr" as follows: "An enigmatic passage—a breeze to be called vain, a lukewarm breeze, appearing like a complacent young man?"[14]

On the term "Hasenwehe" ("blown hares") in Vischhaupt's poem "So Close", the editor offers some hermeneutic thoughts as well, connected to a review of the corresponding 'secondary literature': "Hasenwehe: Several hares in the wind? A row of hares in the grass, looking as if blown away, as if blown there? [...] Langenscheidt proposes to see in this neologism less the woe than the blow, but has found few supporters with this theory".[15] Once again, the commentary allows for two levels of scholarly engagement with the poems. Admittedly, it ironizes the research debates, as it does for biographical or mimetic approaches. At the same time, however, it offers plausible options for an understanding of the texts—options that strive for a careful attribution of meaning.[16]

The reflections on the structure of the poems found in the commentaries on Miller's elegies can be understood as a hermeneutic procedure as well. They discuss, for example, the thesis that the third and fourth elegies are closely interwoven in content and may have originally formed one poem (107); the commentary suggests the same for the sixth and seventh elegies as well (113–114). In the latter case, the suggestion is tied back to a concrete textual observation, namely the taking up of the penultimate

---

[14] "Eine rätselhafte Passage – eine eitel zu nennende Brise, ein laues Lüftchen, das wie ein selbstgefälliger junger Mann auftritt?" (76).

[15] "Hasenwehe: Mehrere Hasen im Wind? Eine Reihe von Hasen im Gras, die wie verweht, wie hingeweht aussehen? [...] Langenscheidt schlägt vor, in diesem Neologismus weniger die Wehe als das Weh zu sehen, hat aber mit dieser Theorie kaum Anhänger gefunden" (79).

[16] This even applies to the question of whether "Wehe" [blow] or "Weh" [woe] is at issue, the latter forming a convincing perspective on the poem.

verse of the sixth elegy at the beginning of the seventh. Again, these elements are a common hermeneutic approach to texts and by no means parodic, but could also be found in some 'real' scholarly work on *Owl Haters*. Once more, Wagner's book thus blurs the line between primary and secondary literature, presenting quite serious scholarly considerations within the framework of literature.

"Owl Haters" and Intertextuality

There are numerous intertextual references in *Owl Haters*, for example, to Goethe's *Poetry and Truth* or his *Roman Elegies* as well as to Sebastian Brant as the author of *The Ship of Fools*.[17] Again, the paratexts themselves call attention to intertextualities. For example, the commentary on Vischhaupt's poems identifies some references, such as one to the Russian poet Anna Akhmatova in the verse "So close it gets, the miraculous".[18]

Philip Miller's "First Elegy" and the "Livia" addressed therein can be understood by their structural and/or generic similarities with ancient elegies.[19] Explicitly identified by the commentary are indirect references to Goethe's *Italian Journey* or to Ferdinand Gregorovius's *The History of Rome in the Middle Ages* (102). "Abraham" and the "biblical animal" in one stanza may well be, as the commentary indicates, an intertextual "reference to Genesis 1",[20] although this identification is hardly as "natural" or as self-explanatory as the commentary asserts—which again can be understood as ironizing the unwarranted confidence demonstrated by certain commentators when they claim to have 'unambiguously' identified an intertextual reference.

Common in scholarly literature are attempts to reconstruct an author's readings. The biographical introduction to Anton Brant specifies what was included in his library: "the old family Bible, a battered dictionary of the German language, an [...] encyclopedia by Meyer".[21] As the commentary

---

[17] Cf. Klimek (2017, 186–187).
[18] Accordingly, Specht (2020, 267) refers to some actual and reliable literary cross-references.
[19] "Catullus wrote his carmina for a Lesbia, Propertius dedicated his Elegies to Cynthia"; "Catull schrieb seine carmine [sic] für eine Lesbia, Properz widmete seine Elegien der Cynthia" (99).
[20] "Abraham"; "biblisches Tier"; "Verweis auf das 1. Buch Mose" (31–32).
[21] "[D]ie alte Familienbibel, ein zerschlissenes Wörterbuch der deutschen Sprache, ein [...] etwas vergilbtes *Konversationslexikon* von Meyer" (17).

states, Brant is supposed to have used the latter to inform himself about the appearance of a yak. Even an 'authentic' trace of the author's reading, the emotional pinnacle of such a scholarly approach, is presented: "The page with the small black-and-white photograph is marked with an inserted strip of paper".[22]

"Owl Haters" and Post-Structuralism

Owl Haters, however, does not only present the classical scholarly instruments of textual appraisal—from glossary and commentary to hermeneutic hypotheses and the identification of intertextual references. It also draws a link to literary theories of the second half of twentieth century, in particular to post-structuralist ones. One of the elements that can be described as post-structuralist is the 'death of the author' in *Owl Haters*, which is staged in various ways. On the one hand, one of the three authors quite literally suffers a 'death of the author' by committing suicide, "hanged by a skein of dark green merino wool that he had been knitting for months and which was extremely durable".[23] The homespun skein echoes the traditional image of text and *textum*, of textual production as the result of a weaving process. Thus, the passage can be understood not just as the death of one character in particular, but as a staging of the 'death of the author' in general.

Moreover, the author Jan Wagner 'dies' in the context of *Owl Haters* by taking a back seat as 'auctor', the author of the texts, to the authorities of editor and commentator on exo- and paradiegetic levels of the text. In combination with the ironized biographic approaches that pervade *Owl Haters*, this can be understood as a plea for a focus on the texts—instead of a focus on the author. At the same time, however—and in a certain way contradictory to this—the author experiences a rebirth precisely through the staging of three fictional authors. For the parody of a biographical approach can only be so consistent in *Owl Haters* if it is staged as an attempt to engage with the texts. In this respect, too, *Owl Haters* proves not to be a purely ironic treatment of scholarly literature, but to oscillate between parody and seriousness.

---

[22] "Die Seite mit dem kleinen Schwarzweißfoto ist mit einem eingelegten Papierstreifen markiert" (39).
[23] "[E]rhängt an einem über Monate selbstgestrickten, äußerst strapazierfähigen Strang aus dunkelgrüner Merinowolle" (60).

Equally 'post-structuralist' are the elements of the commentary that are limited to mere allusion. For example, for the terms "marble" (33), "Justitia with milk" (42), "pilgrim" (47) or "mathematics" (49), the same academic 'paper' is referenced without further comment: "See Bäumler, Prof. Dr. Miriam: 'Marble, more precious than marble. Cultural and agricultural allusions and references in Anton Brant'", which not coincidentally was published in "Cuts. Journal for Applied Cultural Studies".[24] The 'non-commentary comments' represent an associative 'cut' themselves, a signifier without a signified, a beginning chain of meaning that (at least within Wagner's fiction) is not led to an end—but potentially could, in a (fictional or real) contribution that traces the aforementioned 'allusions and references'.

"Owl Haters" and a Second-Order Literary Theory

In *Owl Haters*, Jan Wagner not only offers poems and, from a metadiegetic position, a parody of a scholarly approach to them, but at the same time—and without clear differentiation—forms of serious scholarship. The parody is obvious and refers to biographical speculations undertaken for all three poets and their works, both in the introductory texts and the respective commentary. More subtle—but no less present—are the non-parodistic scholarly elements. They are subtle because they are not surprising at all—why should readers be surprised by a helpful glossary, explanations of historical references, or translations of foreign-language terms? Nonetheless, the scholarly references place *Owl Haters* in a gray area between poets' self-commentary, as it has been cultivated since early modern times, and parody. The parody revels in the shortcomings of an exaggerated scholarly approach—an approach that does not know its limits and tries to say something not only about texts (to which it has empirical access), but also about the personality of the authors behind these texts (about which one can only speculate).

The question is, therefore, how to deal with a text that—in addition to the (apparently) 'actual' text—offers commentary, parody, and a variety of intermediate stages between these two extremes? I suggest a compromise with two components. Firstly, as pointed out in the methodological

---

[24] "Siehe Bäumler, Prof. Dr. Miriam: 'Marmor, kostbarer als Marmor. Kulturelle und agrikulturelle Anspielungen und Verweise bei Anton Brant'"; "*Schnitte. Zeitschrift für angewandte Kulturwissenschaft*" (49).

chapter of this book, the line between literature and criticism can never be drawn quite sharply anyway. This applies not only to self-commentaries, but also to self-reflexive texts that address their own interpretability, and—in particular—to literature that integrates elements of theory into its plots. When the boundary cannot be drawn sharply, literature and theory can mutually recur to each other. Seen from this point of view, it is not a problem to let a scholarly commentary or interpretive hypothesis rest on elements that are explicitly laid out in the text (in a 'scholarly' way).

Secondly, one might cast one's mind back to the functional dimension of theory in the literary text: why does Wagner's *Owl Haters* not only offer poems, but also embed them in a scholarly apparatus? First of all, this contributes to the parodist effect and can therefore be regarded as a source of dynamization for the book. But its function goes beyond the parodic: for example, the elements of literary theory enable the text to problematize the question of authorship self-reflexively—a metaization of theory. Moreover, they establish right and wrong ways of dealing with the poems and thus the basis for a reception that aims not only at an aesthetic but also at an intellectual enjoyment of texts. And they confront the scholarly hare with a literary hedgehog that is always already there (as in the Brothers Grimm's fable)—and thus may lead to self-reflection in scholarship as well.

NEGOTIATING THE PROTAGONIST'S DEATH: MARC FORSTER'S FILM *STRANGER THAN FICTION* (2006)

Marc Forster, born in 1969, is a film director known for his versatility across various genres, including drama, fantasy, and action. He gained international prominence with films such as *Monster's Ball*, *Finding Neverland*, and the James Bond installment *Quantum of Solace*. His work is characterized by its focus on character development and emotional nuance, making him a significant figure in contemporary global cinema.

His film *Stranger than Fiction* (2006) can be considered a cinematic presentation of literary theory. The film's protagonist, Harold Crick (Will Ferrell), one day hears a voice in his head that narrates his life. Having excluded the possibility that it is 'just' some mental confusion or schizophrenia, Harold consults literature professor Hilbert (Dustin Hoffman). After some time, Hilbert and Harold find out that Harold is the protagonist of the new novel by writer Karen Eiffel (Emma Thompson). The novel, however, is unfinished, as Karen has yet to work out how she will kill off her protagonist at the end. The same day the inspiration strikes, Harold calls her and asks her not to kill him. Having become aware of his possible death, he has started to change his life and live it consciously for the first time. In the end, Karen changes the end of her novel, and Harold survives.

Theory comes into the film on various levels. First of all, the film is about observations and the influence of the observer on her observations. Second, the film presents various interpretive approaches with Professor Hilbert and Harold trying to find out what (kind of) narrative Harold is in. Third, there is a self-reflexive presentation of theory at various moments of the story. And, fourth, in the end the film stresses the importance of life in relation to literature and theory—without, however, fully disregarding them—and can therefore be considered a continuous oscillation between presenting theory, ironizing it, or rejecting it in favor of 'the real'.

Observing the Observer

Right from its beginning, the film stresses the importance of observational processes. In one of the first scenes, the viewer observes the narrator observing her main character Harold observing himself in the mirror of his bathroom. At first, Harold is not aware of any of these observations. As soon as he, however, starts to hear the narrator's voice, he self-reflexively starts to observe himself and his actions. For the first time in his life, he questions his behavior and considers alternatives to what he has been doing for years.

At some point while trying to understand his situation, Harold furiously takes over the part of the narrator. He rampages around his room and speaks about himself in the third person: "Harold, incensed, shook the hell out of it [a lamp] for no apparent reason" (21:15).[25] In doing so, he questions himself and the narrator in a paradoxical way. On the one hand, he now takes hold of his own life. On the other hand, he still does not get a grip on it completely: the narrator is challenged, yet not ousted from her position of control.

In the following, however, the observed starts to have an impact on the observer. As soon as Karen learns that Harold knows about her and about being the main character of her novel (who is supposed to die), she cannot

---

[25] Quotations from the film follow the English subtitles of the DVD version (Forster 2006), with the time stamp in brackets.

continue working on her book. She is no longer a neutral figure of authority operating beyond her text and her observations, but is affected by the object she creates and observes.

When Harold stays at home one day—Professor Hilbert has asked him not to bring forward the plot by not doing anything—he watches animal documentaries on TV and applies them to his life. He sees a wounded bird killed by crabs, while the commentator says: "Its desperate attempts to escape only underscore the hopelessness of its plight" (48:10). Just as Harold watches the bird being killed, the narrator watches him before being killed.

The various observations performed and described have, if extrapolated to a theoretical level, implications for literary theory: first, theory (as the method of observations) has to reflect upon its impact on the observed. Second, theory has to learn self-reflexively during the observation process and constantly look for improvements (in Karen's case: a new ending of the novel; in the case of theory in literature: a second-order theory apt for analyzing theory in literature). Third, the levels of observer and observed (or, of author and text; or, of theory and literature) cannot be thought of as strictly separate from each other, yet have to be conceived as inextricably linked to, and mutually influential on, each other.

Trying to Understand

While Harold and Professor Hilbert try to find out more about Harold's condition and the narration he apparently finds himself in, both perform various interpretive processes, following different methodological approaches. The first is unwittingly suggested by Harold when he cites one of the phrases the narrator said about him. The phrase is "little did he know", which Hilbert immediately identifies as a commonplace formula of literature. Here, Hilbert works with an approach of discourse analysis, knowing that specific conditions of structures and truth apply for each utterance. The narrative formula 'little did he know', applying Hilbert's methodology, cannot mean that Harold suffers from a form of mental illness, but has to be taken seriously as his being part of a literary discourse.

The next methodological step Hilbert applies is testing a plurality of narrative patterns on Harold's story: "I've devised a test […] of 23 questions which I think might help uncover more truths about this narrator" (31:15). Hilbert asks Harold about mythological aspects of his life, tries to find out about intertextual references in the narration, and comes up with structuralist questions. One thing Hilbert does not reveal, but which (potentially) enriches the test for the viewer of the film, is that the 23 questions themselves can be seen as an indirect reference to the mathematician David Hilbert and his famous list of 23 unresolved problems in mathematics, published in 1900, which were central to interpretive approaches in mathematics in twentieth century.

At the end of the scene, Hilbert gives Harold the task of finding out whether the story he is in is a comedy or a tragedy. So, the next methodological approach Hilbert proposes is one of genre. He finds out that one aspect of Harold's life matches a typical element of a comedy: Harold has just met someone who strongly dislikes him, someone who might then, however, fall in love with him against all expectation. In Harold's case, it is Ana (Maggie Gyllenhaal), a young baker he is auditing as a financial agent. Hilbert tells him: "Well, that sounds like a comedy. Try to develop that" (37:05). Now Harold is not only trying to understand his life, but also to change it, which means, to return to the methodological point of view, that the observed can influence the observation.

All the different perspectives on Harold's life—mythical, structuralist, genre-oriented, etc.—provide heuristic tools which may help to better understand the biographical narration. Various approaches toward interpreting a narrative are thus presented within the film. Again, the seemingly clear-cut boundaries between the inside and outside of the narrative are blurred: while Hilbert and Harold try to interpret Harold's life, they are an integral part of it.

Questioning Oneself and the Others

This paradox intensifies when Karen learns about Harold's being alive and his actually experiencing her decisions in his daily life as her fictional character—a life which in the film is 'narrated', however, with the same state of reality as Karen's (similar to the situation Hilbert and Harold find themselves in when interpreting and—at the same time—living Harold's life, a metaleptic mixture of the diegetic and the exodiegetic level). The difference between narrator and character (the narrator has absolute power over her characters because their ontological status is different) is challenged in the case of Karen and Harold: Karen still has absolute power over the narration of Harold's life, but her decisions lead to consequences on the same ontological level she lives on. Killing Harold, therefore, no longer means killing someone on paper, but in her real world.

Changing the analytical perspective, one might postulate that Karen and Harold do in fact exist on the same narrative level: not because Harold—for some mysterious reason—metaleptically jumps into Karen's world, but because both Karen and Harold are characters in a fictional world, that of the film. Yet if, within the world of the film, the figures of narrator and character find themselves on the same diegetic (or ontological) level, why should that be different for a narrator (or author or viewer) of the film and its characters? Of course, one could argue that author and viewer are 'real'—but on a structural level there is no difference at all. Applied to an extrapolation of theory from the film, this might lead to one to question the seemingly stable differentiation of author, narrator, and character—or the different narrative levels (diegetic, exodiegetic, etc.).

Staging Interrelations of Life, Literature, and Theory

As the film unfolds, it plays out various forms of relating life, literature, and theory to each other. For example, before asking the literature professor for help, Harold sees a psychologist. When she insists that Harold's condition is schizophrenia, Harold proposes another point of view. He asks the psychologist: "What if what I said was true? Hypothetically speaking, if I was part of a story, of a narrative..." (23:08). Here, Harold suggests the classical 'fiction contract'. He tries to come up with a different (fictional) world in which the norms of the 'normal' (real) world do not apply. In fact, he succeeds in convincing his recipient (the psychologist) in a 'willing suspension of disbelief'. Once she has accepted the new worldview, she easily comes up with a solution for Harold's problem: Harold should consult an expert in literature, not a psychologist—a piece of advice that, in the long run, will turn out to have been the only adequate one.

When arguing with Professor Hilbert one day, Harold brings forward the difference between life, literature, and theory: "this isn't a philosophy or a literary theory or a story to me. It's my life" (51:50). While, at first glance, the film takes a clear stance here toward a differentiation between literature and life with a preference for the latter, a deliberate perspective shows that the one cannot be had without the other. If there were no fiction (film and literature), Harold simply would not exist. If there were no philosophy or literary theory, Harold would not understand his life, in two respects: without having asked philosophical questions (e.g., about his imminent death), he would not have started to live his life consciously. And without literary theory, he would not have come up with the interpretations of his life that improve (developing his relationship with Ana) or even save it (contacting the narrator).

The difference between life and literature—or reality and fiction—is taken up in a seemingly minor scene. Meeting Ana on a date, Harold brings her a selection of flours as a gift. The scene makes perfect sense 'in reality', as Ana, being a baker, can surely make good use of the flours. Within the range of language and fiction, though, the sound when Harold says "I brought you flours" (59:20) is the same as when saying "I brought you flowers", the traditional gift for a suitor. By linking life and literature, Harold thus offers Ana two gifts at the same time, flours in life, and flowers in fiction. A theory of interpretation can illustrate the connections between the two worlds.

The idea of double-coded words is picked up a little later when Karen is interviewed for television and says that her new book is called "Death and Taxes", which the interviewer understands as "Death and Texas" (01:07:10). In this scene, the double-coding is seemingly resolved with a clear meaning when Karen explains what she was referring to. But then Harold watches the interview, so that the interconnectivity Karen talks about is turned from fiction to reality, and the idea of various meanings is immediately re-installed. Interconnectivity is (a) the topic of her new novel, (b) the situation she and Harold are (unknowingly) in, (c) the topic the film is about, and (d) the theory needed to describe and understand both the situation the characters are in and the film as an artwork properly. At the end of the interview, Karen says she does not believe in God—and the same moment Harold rushes out to contact her, thereby destroying the position of the author as a God-like person capable of arranging her fictional world at will. By renouncing God, Karen thus implicitly renounces her own position as an author.

In Harold's (potential) death, life and literature converge once more. Professor Hilbert reads the draft Karen has written for Harold's death. Hilbert talks about it to Harold and compares it to the banal deaths he could experience one day: whatever the other (non-fictional) death might be, "it won't be nearly as poetic or meaningful as what she's written" (01:24:15). Again, there is not 'just' reality, but there are different forms and interpretations of reality: the banal ones and the poetic ones—the ones that can be understood as more than just a simple fact.

The end of Karen's novel is shown to the viewer as type-written text on paper—a shot which simultaneously forms the end of the film *Stranger than Fiction*. Thus, with a final ironic wink, various levels of reality are blended again, similar to Calvino's *If on a Winter's Night a Traveler*: the 'reality' of the novel, the 'reality' of the film, and the reality of the viewers, in which they find themselves having finished the film. What they may extrapolate from it is the same that literary theory might: to create a perspective on the world that allows for a certain order of things while, at the same time, remaining open to changes of perspectives, to re-entries into differentiations, or to a new approach in theory that sheds new light on seemingly known phenomena.

BIBLIOGRAPHY

Forster, Marc (2006): *Schräger als Fiktion – Stranger than Fiction*. Sony Pictures Entertainment Deutschland GmbH.

Klimek, Sonja (2017): Vergessene Dichter, die es nie gab: Zu Jan Wagners Gedicht "Kröten". In: Christoph Jürgensen and Sonja Klimek, eds.: *Gedichte von Jan Wagner: Interpretationen*. Münster, 175–194.

Lampart, Fabian (2017): Der verborgene Autor: Jan Wagners Variationen über Kreativität und Autorschaft in Philip Millers "Erster Elegie". In: Christoph Jürgensen and Sonja Klimek, eds.: *Gedichte von Jan Wagner: Interpretationen*. Münster, 195–209.

Osterkamp, Ernst (2016): Die stillen Helden der Kunstautonomie: Über Jan Wagners "Die Eulenhasser in den Hallenhäusern". In: Frieder von Ammon, ed.: *Jan Wagner*. München, 15–27.

Schilling, Erik (2022): Der literarische Igel und der literaturwissenschaftliche Hase: Jan Wagners "Die Eulenhasser in den Hallenhäusern" zwischen Selbstkommentar und Parodie. In: Christoph Jürgensen et al., eds.: *Natur – Form – Autorschaft: Das literarische Werk Jan Wagners*. Würzburg, 215–226.

Specht, Benjamin (2020): "Der Poet als Maskenball": Fiktive Autorschaft und literaturgeschichtliche Positionierung bei Jan Wagner. In: *Jahrbuch der Deutschen Schillergesellschaft* 64, 261–285.

Wagner, Jan (2012): *Die Eulenhasser in den Hallenhäusern. Drei Verborgene. Gedichte*. Berlin.

CHAPTER 8

Theory Extrapolated from Literature

The previous chapters have outlined the various ways in which theory enters into literature: the modes, levels, and functions of these transitions. There have also been hints at possible extrapolations of new theory from literary texts; this final chapter, however, may help to deepen further the understanding of how literature can actively contribute to the modification and creation of theory.

The chapter distinguishes three ways in which literature influences theory: (a) the advancement of theory within literature in ways that are inaccessible through traditional academic routines—what might be called 'non-theoretical' forms of theory; (b) theoretical remarks within literary texts; and (c) a general inspiration of theory by literature. Since debates about authorship have been crucial since Roland Barthes's 'death of the author', not only to theory but also to many literary texts, I will use the topic of authorship as an example of possible extrapolations of theory from literature. At the end of this chapter, I will provide a very short summary both of extrapolating authorship theory from literature and of this book as a whole.

In the years covered by the books analyzed here, the debate around authorship in literary theory has shifted toward an emphasis on the social and cultural forces that shape literary production and reception.[1] The idea of the autonomous, individual author has been challenged by various critical approaches, such as postmodernism, feminist theory, and cultural studies.[2] These approaches have emphasized the role of power, ideology, and identity in shaping literary texts and their meanings, as well as the collaborative and intertextual nature of literary creation.

In addition, the rise of digital technologies has brought new issues to the forefront of the authorship debate, such as the proliferation of user-generated content, the remixing of existing texts, and the increasing blurring of the boundaries between authors, publishers, and readers.[3] Recent years have also seen a revival of 'intentionalism' in some scholarly circles,[4] which suggests a swinging back of the pendulum toward the author's role in meaning-making—or at least the role of the author's historical context for a 'hypothetical intentionalism'.[5] And the concept of the 'writing scene' has been proposed as "the broader replacement of the traditional, legal-philological authorship, a replacement which allows for more descriptive flexibility on the one hand and new conceptual rigor on the other".[6]

Thus, while the concept of authorship has been deconstructed, dispersed, and democratized, it is far from being obsolete and remains a vibrant focal point of contention and inquiry in contemporary literary theory.

As the following paragraphs will illustrate, literature has actively participated in shaping authorship in recent decades (and before) by working on authorship theory within literature in non-theoretical ways, by integrating theoretical considerations into the fictional world, and/or by generally inspiring theory (Fig. 8.1).

---

[1] Cf. Love (2002); Spoerhase (2007); Schaffrick and Willand (2014); Berensmeyer et al. (2012); Berensmeyer et al. (2019).

[2] Some examples: for a postmodern conception of authorship, see Eco (1984); McHale (1987); Hutcheon (1988); for feminist authorship theory, see Zwierlein (2010); for conceptions of authorship in cultural studies, see McLeod (2001); Hartley (2012).

[3] Skains (2019); Weel (2019).

[4] For example, Köppe (2014, 40) makes the author's intention a central component of his definition of fictionality: "T ist genau dann ein fiktionaler Text, wenn gilt: (1) T wurde von seinem Verfasser mit der Absicht A verfasst [...]" ["T is a fictional text exactly if: (1) T was written by its author with the intention A [...]"].

[5] Spoerhase (2007); Sneis (2020).

[6] Campe (2021, 1116).

Extrapolation

of authorship concepts from literature

| Theorizing Literature | ➡ | new Theory |

examples of metaization and creation of theory

'Non-theoretical' Forms of Theory	Theory in Literary Texts	Literature Inspiring Theory
non-theoretically conceptualizing authorship within **the literary text,** e.g., as: * an act of creation * a foundation of identity * not clearly attributable * fragmentary * an interplay between text and recipients	theoretically conceptualizing authorship within **the literary text,** e.g., as: * a plurality of voices * plural voices, yet attributed to individuals * a mingling of plural and individual voices	theoretically conceptualizing authorship within **a theoretical text,** e.g., within: * a spectrum of intertextuality (from reference to similarity) * narratological levels (diegetic, endodiegetic, exodiegetic, and peridiegetic)

Fig. 8.1 Extrapolation of theory from literature: authorship concepts

'Non-Theoretical' Forms of Theory

Perhaps the most compelling, yet concurrently the most challenging for intersubjective validity, is what can be termed 'non-theoretical' forms of theory within literature. By 'non-theoretical', I refer to conceptual frameworks and ideas developed within literary works that can be considered meaningful contributions to theoretical discourse, despite eschewing conventional academic methodologies and techniques.

In traditional academic theory, elements such as ambiguous language or internal contradictions would typically be seen as shortcomings. However, in the realm of literature, an intellectual landscape exists that accommodates non-academic approaches to topics traditionally covered in theoretical discourse. Such literary explorations may creatively employ irony and ambiguity or present a diverse array of viewpoints without reconciling them into a singular, coherent perspective. This departure from academic rigor opens up a space for nuanced inquiry and interpretation, enriching dialogues between literature and theory.

To draw an analogy to Carl von Linné's ordering of biological species: under the conditions of a 'non-theoretical' form of theory, an animal might be considered both a mammal and a reptile. What would be a contradiction under standard scientific terms may, in the context of 'non-theoretical' theory, offer a new perspective or account for phenomena that do not fit into the established academic worldview. In such cases, an approach that accommodates ambiguity—within reasonable bounds—may indeed be more fitting than pursuing univocal clarity. Such a 'non-theoretical' approach not only challenges but also enriches the prevailing theoretical frameworks, fostering a more expansive and adaptable discourse capable of addressing the complexities inherent in language and meaning.

Returning to the authorship debate, I will make five observations about how literature can deepen theoretical discussions of authorship by using 'non-theoretical' forms of theory. Literary texts can present authorship in a variety of ways, organized logically as follows:

(1) *An act of creation*: Authorship often starts with the notion of creation, as this lays the groundwork for any subsequent discussion about the nature and ownership of a text.
(2) *A foundation of identity*: Following the act of creation, authorship becomes a way through which the creator's identity is defined, either by themselves or by their audience.
(3) *Not clearly attributable to a single person*: At times, literary works may present authorship as a collective endeavor or one that cannot be clearly ascribed to a singular individual, challenging the notion of a unified authorial identity.
(4) *Fragmentary*: Further complicating the issue, authorship can be presented as dispersed or fragmented, either through multiple narrators, disjointed timelines, or even through fragmented styles and genres.

(5) *An interplay between text and recipients*: Lastly, authorship can be depicted as a dynamic relationship between the text itself and its reception by an audience.

This logical sequence navigates from the creation of a literary work to its interaction with readers, highlighting the multifaceted nature of authorship as presented in literary texts. In all these cases, the thoughts on authorship are not radically different from what has been pointed out in literary theory before; what I will highlight, however, is the capacity of literary texts to engage with theoretical questions in a way that a common theoretical approach cannot.

Authorship as an Act of Creation

The idea of the author as an *alter deus*, a god-like creator, has been common since antiquity and has been carried over into the modern era, for example, when Shaftesbury called the poet a "second *Maker*, a just Prometheus, under Jove".[7] The notion of authorship as an act of creation is thus by no means a new idea in literary theory. However, some of the texts analyzed in this book point to an ambiguous aspect of the parallelization of author and creator: while the author's creatorship traditionally refers to the fictional world over which the author has absolute power, some of the novels that theorize authorship in non-theoretical ways show possible (and potentially problematic) consequences of authorship for the real world. Seen in this way, authors no longer only create their own (fictional) world, but also change the (real) world in which they live.

In Umberto Eco's *Foucault's Pendulum*, for example, three authors come up with creations they intend to be fictional and ironic. They invent stories about secret societies that have supposedly influenced history and politics. However, some of those who hear these stories believe them to be true. As a result, the authors are no longer just creators of fictional stories, but also of substantial (deadly) changes in their real world. Eco's novel thus presents authorship as something very powerful: to be an author is not just to play with fictional characters, but—potentially—to change the world in which the author lives.

---

[7] Ashley-Cooper (1710, 55).

The same is true of Juli Zeh's novel *Dark Matter*. The two protagonists, two physics professors, are presented as authors of competing explanations of the world: one opts for quantum theory, the other for multiverses. Like Eco's authors, however, Zeh's protagonists not only create narratives in theory, but these narratives also affect the world in which the authors live. When one of the professors comes up with a game to prove his theory, their lives are fundamentally changed and, in the end, torn apart. Once again, authorship is presented as an act of creation that is not limited to the playful realms of fiction or theory, but can potentially affect or even destroy the authors' real world.

Extending these non-theoretical considerations to a theory of authorship, it becomes evident that the scope of authorship transcends the act of immediate creation, be it a text, an artwork, or any other form of artistic expression. Far from a constrained understanding of authorship, the act of generating fictional constructs carries the potential to resonate within the realm of reality—a dimension of authorship that has often been insufficiently examined or even overlooked in literary theory.

By acknowledging this broader scope, a more expansive conception of authorship emerges, one that accommodates not only the creative inception but also the subsequent real-world ramifications. This extension of the authorial domain enriches existing theoretical frameworks, encouraging a more nuanced dialogue about the permeable boundaries between fiction and reality, as well as the ethical and social implications associated with acts of authorship.

Authorship as a Foundation of Identity

A concrete consequence of authorship for the real world might be to view authorship as a foundation of identity. Understanding themselves as authors can create or stabilize identity by allowing individuals to express their thoughts, experiences, and perspectives in a tangible and lasting form. Writing can provide a sense of self-discovery and empowerment, as well as a platform for showcasing one's (seemingly) unique voice and experiences. In addition, receiving recognition and validation for one's work can boost confidence and self-esteem, further contributing to a stable sense of identity. As a result, authorship—based on its representation in literary texts—could be seen as something important to authors themselves, but not to readers or scholars of literature. Authorship is thus transformed from a theoretical to a psychological concept.

In Daniel Kehlmann's *F*, being an author is the existential basis for the three brothers who are the protagonists of the novel, as it is for their father. The sons include a priest who is an author of faith for his congregation, a banker who is an author of the financial well-being of his clients, and an artist who is a creator of paintings. Their father Arthur (an author even homophonously) writes fictional texts and can therefore be considered a meta-author. Arthur and his sons regard their individual authorship as fundamental to their identity, which becomes particularly clear when they all suffer a crisis of identity. The priest loses his faith, the banker gambles away his clients' money, the artist becomes a forger, and the father abandons his sons. As a result, their lives are turned upside down: to lose one's position as an author is to lose one's identity.

With Kehlmann's *F* in mind, being an author can be regarded as more important than it has been, for example, in the post-structuralist context. The concept of authorship does not help understand a text better, nor does it help arrive at a coherent explanation for the multiplicity of authorial voices in a text. It does, however, contribute to the construction of a coherent self for the author. Without their authorship, the four diegetic authors in Kehlmann's novel lose an important part of their identity; they have to invent a completely new idea of themselves or fail to overcome the collapse of their identity at all.

In terms of an extrapolation of theory from literature, therefore, different aspects of authorship might be considered to be more important than they have been by certain currents of literary theory. While the author does not 'own' the text—neither as a solitary 'genius' responsible for its creation, nor as the exclusive authority capable of providing its interpretation—the role of authorship may nonetheless be integral to the author's identity. This dimension holds considerable relevance for investigations into the nature of authorship.

By recognizing this aspect, the academic inquiry into authorship can extend beyond textual analysis to incorporate psychological and sociological perspectives. Such multidisciplinary approaches yield fresh insights into individual preferences, motivations, and behaviors, even if they do not necessarily enhance the understanding of the literary texts themselves. This broader framework, therefore, not only enriches the existing discourse on authorship but also opens up avenues for exploring the interplay between the authors' internal landscape and the external reception of their work.

Authorship as Not Clearly Attributable

Recent debates about texts written by artificial intelligence have brought the question of clearly attributable authorship back to the forefront: does it matter who wrote a text? If so, in which contexts—for legal purposes, for reasons of authenticity, for attributing creativity to the author, etc.?[8] Many of the texts analyzed in this book take sides in the debate, mostly (but not only) by questioning the relevance of attributing authorship to literary texts.

Christoph Ransmayr's *Last World* begins with one of the characters trying to track down the author Ovid, in order to save the *Metamorphoses* for posterity. However, the author remains absent throughout the story, while his narratives are vividly present in the endodiegetic stories referred to in the fictional world and in some of the characters who diegetically live them. In Ransmayr's novel, Ovid's stories are thus saved for posterity without the need of an author as a guarantor of meaning. The stories are simply there, slowly but surely taking over the diegetic level, and whether they are considered interesting, relevant, beautiful, touching, or otherwise does not depend on who created them.

This may have consequences for the debate on authorship in literary theory that go beyond Barthes's 'death of the author'. Especially in recent years, there have been lively debates about the (necessary) connection between authors and their texts.[9] In the context of 'cultural appropriation', for example, it is disputed whether a text should be substantiated by the author's experiences.[10] An extrapolation of theory from Ransmayr's novel would come to a clear conclusion: stories are independent of who invents or tells them. Authorship is not a category that grants relevance, beauty, or ethical reliability. Thus, the pursuit of ascribing authorship could be seen as a mere pastime, not relevant to the text, the reader, or interpretation.

Seen in this way, authorship would lose much of its dominance, at least in literary theory. Investigating whether Robert Galbraith is a pseudonym of Joanne K. Rowling or Elena Ferrante is a German translator living in Rome may be important in terms of copyright, but not in terms of literary

---

[8] See Hacker et al. (2023) on legal purposes; Schilling (2020) on authenticity; Zwierlein (2010) on creativity, with a special focus on gendered creativity.

[9] This is part of a broader debate about a 'return of the author'. Cf. Jannidis et al. (1999); Nünning (2003).

[10] Young (2010); Matthes (2018).

criticism or for a simple reading of their novels. Using natural language processing to attribute a text to Shakespeare may help promote a forgotten play, but it has no bearing on its interpretation or aesthetic value.

If we were to genuinely relinquish authorship as a categorization schema, it would necessitate a radical reorganization of how to engage with literature and texts. Consider, for instance, the implications for libraries: a shift away from organizing books alphabetically by author might require a new system focused on chronology, genre, or thematic content. Similarly, the traditional quest to glean insights into a text by examining its author's biography and intent would become an obsolete practice.

Furthermore, this paradigm shift would have legal ramifications, potentially challenging existing copyright laws predicated on the idea of the author as the 'original genius' behind the creation of a text. Such legal reevaluations become increasingly salient in an era where artificial intelligence is assuming a more significant role in content creation, thereby blurring the lines between human authorship and machine-generated outputs.[11] In summary, capturing authorship as not clearly attributable, as some of the literary texts analyzed here suggest, would call for a comprehensive reassessment across multiple dimensions—organizational, interpretive, and legal—ultimately redefining the very landscape of literary studies and creative production.

Authorship as Fragmentary

Beyond the challenges of clear attribution, authorship can further be conceptualized as inherently fragmentary. This fragmentation implies that the difficulties are not confined to the notion of identifying a singular, definable individual as the author. Rather, they extend to the text itself, which often manifests as an interplay of diverse voices and influences. Key concepts such as intertextuality, dialogism, and semantic variations—shaped by distinct groups or speakers—become instrumental in decoding the layers of meaning within a text. This multifaceted approach encourages an exploration of how texts are not just authored, but also constituted and continually redefined through dialogical engagements with other texts, contexts, and interpretive communities.

Patricia Duncker's novel *Hallucinating Foucault* can be seen as an important literary contribution to theory in this context. The novel blends

---

[11] Some parts of this book have in fact been improved using ChatGPT-4.

(at least) four layers of authorship, each dealing with the same issues. First, there is the fictional novelist Paul Michel, who writes about psychiatric illness, homosexuality, and concepts of authorship. Second, there is Michel Foucault, who in Duncker's novel offers a response to Michel's novels by addressing the same issues in his philosophical and theoretical writings. Third, the narrator of Duncker's novel deals with the themes of Michel and Foucault in his dissertation. And fourth, the narrator and Paul Michel deal with the above themes when they meet in a psychiatric hospital, become lovers, and debate the relevance of the author to the understanding of a book.

In Duncker's novel, therefore, the same topics are treated by different characters and on different narratological and ontological levels. However, when reading the novel and getting to grips with the different topics at play, knowing which voice contributes which aspect to the discussions is not important. The voices are fragmentary and often difficult to attribute to a particular author or narratological entity. Many ideas mentioned in the novel could just as easily be expressed by the 'real' Michel Foucault, by a literary character named 'Michel Foucault', by a literary character named 'Paul Michel', who frequently refers to Foucault's writings, by a graduate student working on the topics of psychiatric illness, homosexuality, and authorship, or by the novelist Patricia Duncker, who invents a story about these topics and some characters (or real people) who represent them.

Ultimately, ideas exist in a state of perpetual fluidity. In extrapolating theory from Duncker's novel as it pertains to authorship, a compelling case for the deployment of more nuanced discourse analysis emerges. The focus could shift from an unwieldy effort to attribute concepts and ideas to specific individuals to a more rigorous tracing of the conceptual lineages and ideational flows that inform a given text. Embracing a fragmentary view of authorship also precipitates a significant paradigm shift in interpretive strategies. Within this new framework, the mere identification of an intertextual relationship would cease to be an end in itself. Instead, it would gain interpretive value only when it serves to deepen the understanding of the text in which it appears, and potentially, to illuminate anew the source text from which it was derived. Thus, this approach demands not only a reorientation of how to understand authorship but also a reconceptualization of the methods and objectives of literary analysis.

Authorship and the Interplay Between Text and Recipients

Should authorship be understood as not clearly attributable and fragmentary, this insight could finally be extrapolated to the attribution of meaning itself. Scholarly debates have long contended that meaning is not solely confined to the artifact—be it text, artwork, or any other form of creative expression—but is instead co-constituted through a dynamic interaction between the artifact and its audience.[12] Meaning, in this context, is influenced by an array of variables, including individual experiences, cultural backgrounds, and linguistic frameworks.

Applying this perspective to authorship theory further diminishes the centrality of the author in interpreting their own creations. Here, the act of meaning-making occurs not merely as an authorial imposition but as a reciprocal process situated at the intersection of the artifact and its interpretive community. This reorientation not only calls into question traditional notions of authorial intent but also invites a more nuanced understanding of how meaning is socially and contextually constructed.

Literary texts can illustrate this process and point to the difficulties involved. Among the texts analyzed in this book, Jan Wagner's *Owl Haters* in particular highlights the process of creating or attributing meaning to a text. Wagner's book presents poems by three fictional authors as well as tools for interpreting the poems (biographical information on the authors, a glossary, a commentary, etc.). Some of these aids to interpretation can be considered helpful, others may seem rather parodistic (depending on the recipients' perspective). In any case, however, the interplay of text and interpretation presented in Wagner's book illustrates the complex process of attributing meaning. In this interplay, authorship is probably the least important component compared to text and reception.

In terms of extrapolating theory from the literary text, Wagner's book could be used in several ways. First, the diminished importance of authors for the understanding of their texts is presented not in an argumentative way, but by means of irony. Wagner gives biographical information about the 'authors' of the poems, but this information does not at all contribute to a better understanding of the texts. Secondly, the perspective can shift toward the text and the reader, as Wagner's book also shows by offering a number of perspectives on the poems, for example in the commentary. Third, the ambiguity of attributing meaning to a text is underscored by

---

[12] Cf., among many others, Bakhtin (1981 [1934/35]); Eco (1989 [1962]).

the multiplicity of competing perspectives that cannot be summarized in a single interpretation of the poems, but remain part of a plural reception of the literary text.

Wagner's book can thus be seen as a non-theoretical contribution to literary theory: it uses non-academic means to arrive at its ideas. The idea of reducing the importance of authors for the understanding of their texts is not presented in an argumentative way, but by ironizing the attempt of a biographically based interpretation. Moreover, no clear concept is proposed as to how the attribution of meaning to a text might best function; rather, there is a plurality of options that might be transferred to a (plural) theoretical conception of authorship—a conception to which the readers contribute significantly.

Theoretical Remarks within Literary Texts

Theoretical remarks within a literary text do not occur in every literary text, but only in 'theory-informed' ones. The principal distinction between this form of theoretical engagement within literature and the 'non-theoretical' forms discussed in the previous paragraphs lies in its methodological approach. Theory-informed texts employ vocabulary, rhetorical devices, and analytical techniques commonly associated with (literary) theory. As far as the levels of theory in literature are concerned, such theoretical remarks are mostly found on the diegetic and/or endodiegetic level, that is, they are part of the narrative or marked as an interruption of the narrative flow, weaving academic discourse into the literary text.

Looking at authorship in particular, the end of Umberto Eco's novel *The Name of the Rose* may serve as an example. In the epilogue, Adso, the protagonist and narrator of his own story (many years after the events narrated), reflects on the conditions of his writing: he explicitly states that he does not know whether he, as an autonomous author, was the one telling his story or whether (and if so, to what extent) he was influenced by fragments of books he had collected and stories he had read. In the final passage of Eco's novel, authorship is presented in a post-structuralist way that no longer allows for the attribution of ideas to individual authors, but captures texts as an intertextual collage of different voices.

Even more academic in their presentation are the various debates about authorship in Mithu Sanyal's novel *Identitti*. In a detailed epilogue, Sanyal distinguishes between "real and imagined voices"[13] and

---

[13] Sanyal (2022, 407). In the German original in English: "real and imagined voices" (Sanyal 2021, 419).

reveals that her novel is not solely her creation: other people, appearing as characters under their real names, have contributed texts (e.g., tweets, newspaper articles, statements) to the novel. These texts address the question of how a range of academics and critics would react if the central conceit of the novel (a seemingly Indian professor of postcolonial studies turning out to be white) were to happen in reality. In addition, Sanyal creates collages of opinions elsewhere expressed by people who appear in the novel as characters under their real names. The theoretical remarks within the literary text are thus not only invented by Sanyal and part of the fictional world—where they are often endodiegetically marked as debates about theory—but also part of discussions about race and class that take place in the real academic world. In terms of authorship, then, Sanyal's novel oscillates between two extremes: on the one hand, the novel makes it very clear that it is not the product of an original genius who invented the story, plot, arguments, and so on. On the other hand, the plurality of voices is very transparently broken down into a number of explicitly marked individual voices. In doing so, the novel de- and reconstructs authorship at the same time.

In uncovering the fundaments of their authorship, both Eco's and Sanyal's novels can be understood as theoretical remarks on the debate about authorship. Each of the novels self-reflexively exposes its intertextual basis: the plurality of voices that speak out of the novel and cannot be reduced to a single authorial voice (of the protagonist, the narrator, or the author). Unlike Eco, however, Sanyal attributes the various voices to individual authors, often in an academic form with direct references. As a result, Sanyal's novel may be seen as another development in the debate about authorship: whereas Eco in the early 1980s primarily stresses the post-structuralist idea of losing the individual author, Sanyal in the early 2020s links the debate about authorship back to the one about identity, which is the basis for her novel.

Consequently, theoretical remarks embedded within literary texts serve as an extension of ongoing intellectual discourses, particularly those situated within the domain of literary theory and broader humanities scholarship. To accomplish this, such texts employ a sophisticated array of linguistic constructs, rhetorical devices, and methodological approaches that are traditionally attributed to theory. In the specific case of authorship, the novels engage in a balancing process, portraying authorship as both fragmentary and individualistic. In doing so, they navigate a middle ground between post-structuralism and contemporary debates surrounding identity. This multidimensional portrayal of authorship not only enriches the individual narrative but also contributes to a broader academic debate, amplifying the interconnectedness of literature and theory.

Literature Inspiring Theory

Literature inspiring theory, finally, is the most common, yet, for the purposes of this book, least interesting case of transmission between the two. In essence, this entails readers, upon an engagement with literary works, subsequently articulating new theoretical frameworks or modifying existing ones. This follows the conventional inductive methodology of concept development, wherein phenomena are observed, analyzed, and subsequently synthesized into a coherent scientific terminology. Just as Linné's taxonomies of biological species were 'inspired' by the phenomena he observed, Genette's narratological categories were formulated in response to modes of storytelling found in literature. In terms of authorship, Genette's distinction between (real) author, narrator, and character can be seen as a contribution to theory inspired (not surprisingly) by literature.

In the ambit of this publication, such an inspiration of theory through literature in terms of authorship can be seen on two levels: the intertextual and the narratological refinements. In order to capture the different intertextual relations between theory and literature better, it was necessary to suppose an intertextual spectrum, stretching from references to similarities between two (or more) texts, with the six sub-dimensions of self-reflexive, direct, and indirect references as well as narrative, structural, and generic similarities. The refinement of intertextuality inspired by the literary texts analyzed here has helped to better understand their concept of authorship (how and how openly do authors present their relation to other texts, in particular with regards to theory)—and might also be of use for the analysis of other literary texts.

Moreover, it was necessary to refine common narratological concepts in order to differentiate the various narrative levels on which theory enters into literature more precisely. As there may be various narrative levels 'above' and/or 'below' the diegetic one, this book operates with the terms 'exo-' and 'endodiegetic', which can be expanded by an unlimited number of sub-levels. This flexible nomenclature is particularly useful for novels that engage with theories of authorship or even advance their own concepts of authorship; here, a differentiated approach to diegetic levels has proven indispensable. This analytical tool may likewise be extrapolated for use in the scrutiny of other literary works.

Nevertheless, it is crucial to distinguish this form of theoretical genesis (literature inspiring theory), which is based on observing and interpreting literature, from the more intricate act of theory formation *within* literature. When literature inspires theory, theory materializes as an organizational framework, a meta-perspective that seeks to impose a taxonomic 'order of things' upon the observed phenomena. Whether the literary text in question is itself imbued with theoretical considerations becomes ancillary in this context. Consequently, this mode of extrapolation of theory from literary works assumes a position of relative subordination within the scope of this book's central inquiry.

Summary

New Perspectives on Authorship

In sum, various new perspectives on authorship can be derived from looking at literary texts. As always, there is the possibility of theory being inspired by literature. Moreover, theoretical remarks and non-theoretical forms of theory in literary texts can shed new light on established concepts of authorship. As this book shows, literary texts such as Eco's *Foucault's Pendulum*, Duncker's *Hallucinating Foucault*, Kehlmann's *F*, or Sanyal's *Identitti* participate in contemporary debates on authorship. The discussion about the diminished (or even abandoned) importance of the author for the interpretation of a literary text is thus not only addressed in theoretical texts, but also in literary ones.

Furthermore, literary texts probe the constraints and ambiguities of authorship in a manner that conventional theoretical frameworks, when confined to typical academic practices, may fail to capture. The texts analyzed here illuminate the diminishing relevance of the author as a center for interpretation. They destabilize the author as a reliable reference point by casting authorial biographies and their ties to literary works in an ironic light. Alternatively, they complexify the notion of a singular author by highlighting the multiplicity of agents involved in the text's creation, including but not limited to the 'actual' author, intertextual voices, participants in the publishing process, and the interpretations generated by readers.

In this light, numerous literary texts present authorship as unstable, fragmentary, and resistant to singular attribution. This evolving conceptual landscape is further enriched by non-theoretical engagements with theory within literature. Methods of blurring, ironizing, or pluralizing the concept of the author gain heightened persuasive power when delivered not through argumentative exposition but through narrative techniques that themselves exploit ambiguity, irony, or plurality. In doing so, the texts performatively underscore what is expressed in terms of content.

Even more salient to contemporary debates on authorship are those literary texts that reconfigure authorship not merely as an interpretive tool but also as a sociological and/or psychological construct. From a sociological vantage point, authorship gains significance through its real-world impact—such as when a text precipitates societal changes. Concurrently, a psychological lens allows to see authorship as a pivotal component of an individual's identity.

This nuanced understanding of authorship becomes doubly relevant in contexts related to self-empowerment or the amplification of marginalized voices. For instance, examining how authorship is deployed or reclaimed by certain groups can yield insights into the interplay between textual creation and social transformation. Thus, this expanded conceptualization of authorship also holds substantial implications for scientific analysis, offering a multidimensional framework through which to engage with an age-old literary question.

New Perspectives on Theory Through Literature

Literary texts engaging with theoretical constructs do more than merely incorporate existing ideas into a fictional domain through various modes, levels, and functions. Rather, such texts can be viewed as active participatory agents in theoretical discourses for two primary reasons:

First, literary texts enable the exploration of theoretical concepts within a fictional framework. For instance, fictional characters partake in academic discussions, or non-fictional statements are interwoven into the fabric of a narrative. While these conceptual engagements could potentially be presented in non-literary forms, the choice of a literary text as the medium may offer enhanced accessibility and vivid representation. Narrative settings imbued with theoretical discourses may afford readers an easier point of entry, particularly when complex arguments are embedded within a compelling storyline.

Second, and arguably more crucially, literature possesses the capacity to approach theoretical concerns in manners unattainable through conventional academic discourse. Utilizing literary techniques like ambiguity, irony, or the juxtaposition of contradictory perspectives allows for innovative treatments of established theoretical issues. Drawing upon Heisenberg's uncertainty principle—which posits that observational outcomes can vary based on perspective—literary texts can adapt this epistemological uncertainty to theoretical inquiries. In doing so, they offer not just alternative but potentially groundbreaking contributions to theoretical discussions. This is made possible through what can be termed 'non-theoretical' contributions to theory which emerge from the text itself, thereby enriching and expanding the scope of academic debate.

Consequently, a second-order literary theory serves multiple critical functions that extend beyond surface-level textual analysis. First, it facilitates an examination of the diverse *modes* through which theory is embedded in literature, offering a nuanced understanding of the literary as a theoretical space. Second, it allows to pinpoint theory across different *levels* of a literary text, from its diegetic world to its exo- and peridiegetic nuances, thereby mapping out the topography of theoretical engagement within the narrative. Third, this approach illuminates the multifaceted *functions* that theory assumes within literature, allowing for a more comprehensive grasp of theory's impact on narrative techniques and the resulting possibilities of interpretation. Fourth, it opens up avenues for the *extrapolation* of theory from literature itself, suggesting that literature can be not just an object of theoretical scrutiny but also a generative site for theoretical innovation and extension.

Bibliography

Ashley-Cooper, Anthony, Earl of Shaftesbury (1710): *Soliloquy or Advice to an Author*. London.

Bakhtin, Mikhail (1981 [1934/35]): Discourse in the Novel. In: Mikhail Bakhtin: *The Dialogic Imagination: Four Essays. Translated by Caryl Emerson and Michael Holquist*. Austin, 259–422.

Berensmeyer, Ingo, et al. (2012): Authorship as Cultural Performance. New Perspectives in Authorship Studies. In: *Zeitschrift für Anglistik und Amerikanistik* 60, 1–29.

Berensmeyer, Ingo, et al., eds. (2019): *The Cambridge Handbook of Literary Authorship*. Cambridge.

Campe, Rüdiger (2021): Writing Scenes and the Scene of Writing: A Postscript. In: *MLN* 136, 1114–1133.
Eco, Umberto (1984): *Postscript to "The Name of the Rose"*. Translated from the Italian by William Weaver. San Diego et al.
Eco, Umberto (1989 [1962]): *The Open Work*. Translated by Anna Cancogni. With an Introduction by David Robey. Cambridge/MA.
Hacker, Philipp, Engel, Andreas, and Mauer, Marco (2023): Regulating ChatGPT and other Large Generative AI Models. In: FAccT '23: *Proceedings of the 2023 ACM Conference on Fairness, Accountability, and Transparency*, 1112–1123.
Hartley, John (2012): *Communication, Cultural and Media Studies: The Key Concepts*. London.
Hutcheon, Linda (1988): *A Poetics of Postmodernism: History, Theory, Fiction*. New York.
Jannidis, Fotis, et al., eds. (1999): *Rückkehr des Autors: Zur Erneuerung eines umstrittenen Begriffs*. Tübingen.
Köppe, Tilmann (2014): Die Institution Fiktionalität. In: Tobias Klauk and Tilmann Köppe, eds.: *Fiktionalität: Ein interdisziplinäres Handbuch*. Berlin/Boston, 35–49.
Love, Harold (2002): *Attributing Authorship: An Introduction*. Cambridge.
Matthes, Erich Hatala (2018): Cultural Appropriation and Oppression. In: *Philosophical Studies* 176, 1003–1013.
McHale, Brian (1987): *Postmodernist Fiction*. London/New York.
McLeod, Kembrew (2001): *Owning Culture: Authorship, Ownership, and Intellectual Property Law*. New York et al.
Nünning, Ansgar (2003): Die Rückkehr des sinnstiftenden Subjekts: Selbstreflexive Inszenierungen von historisierten Subjekten und subjektivierten Geschichten in britischen und postkolonialen historischen Romanen der Gegenwart. In: Stefan Deines et al., eds.: *Historisierte Subjekte – subjektivierte Historie: Zur Verfügbarkeit und Unverfügbarkeit von Geschichte*. Berlin, 239–261.
Sanyal, Mithu (2021): *Identitti. Roman*. München.
Sanyal, Mithu (2022): *Identitti. A novel. Translated from the German by Alta L. Price*. Berlin.
Schaffrick, Matthias, and Willand, Marcus, eds. (2014): *Theorien und Praktiken der Autorschaft*. Berlin/Boston.
Schilling, Erik (2020): *Authentizität: Karriere einer Sehnsucht*. München.
Skains, R. Lyle (2019): *Digital Authorship: Publishing in the Attention Economy*. Cambridge.
Sneis, Jørgen (2020): Faktischer und hypothetischer Intentionalismus: Einige Bedenken aus methodologischer Sicht gegen eine inzwischen etablierte Unterscheidung. In: Andreas Mauz and Christiane Tietz, eds.: *Verstehen und Interpretieren: Zum Basisvokabular von Hermeneutik und Interpretationstheorie*. Leiden, 173–190.

Spoerhase, Carlos (2007): *Autorschaft und Interpretation: Methodische Grundlagen einer philologischen Hermeneutik.* Berlin.
Weel, Adriaan van der (2019): *Literary Authorship in the Digital Age.* Cambridge.
Young, James O. (2010): *Cultural Appropriation and the Arts.* Hoboken.
Zwierlein, Anne-Julia, ed. (2010): *Gender and Creation: Surveying Gendered Myths of Creativity, Authority, and Authorship.* Heidelberg.

Name Index[1]

A
Abrams, J.J. (Jeffrey Jacob), 12
Akhmatova, Anna, 169
Althusser, Louis, 65
Apphia, Kwame Anthony, 96
Ashley-Cooper, Anthony, 3rd Earl of Shaftesbury, 117, 183

B
Barthes, Roland, 2, 3, 7, 8, 10, 38, 56–58, 64–71, 79n1, 90, 112, 132, 135, 149, 179, 186
Beltracchi, Wolfgang, 120
Binet, Laurent, vi, 3, 7, 10, 25, 28, 32, 35, 37–40, 42, 45, 46, 51, 64, 65, 65n18, 67, 68, 72, 74, 75, 110, 149
Bohr, Niels, 159
Booth, Wayne C., 125

Borges, Jorge Luis, 112–115
Brand, Dionne, 13
Brant, Sebastian, 165, 169
Brown, Dan, 121n22
Butler, Judith, 2, 90, 92, 92n28, 101

C
Calvino, Italo, 2, 11, 27, 28, 31, 35, 45, 46, 109, 122–132, 178
Campendonk, Heinrich, 120
Camus, Albert, 119
Catullus (Gaius Valerius Catullus), 169n19
Cervantes, Miguel de, 6
Chomsky, Noam, 67
Chrétien de Troyes, 52, 53, 113n7
Cixous, Hélène, 68, 92
Coleridge, Samuel, 116
Culler, Jonathan, 67, 68

---

[1] Note: Page numbers followed by 'n' refer to notes.

© The Author(s), under exclusive license to Springer Nature Switzerland AG 2024
E. Schilling, *Theorizing Literature*,
https://doi.org/10.1007/978-3-031-53326-6

D

Dalí, Salvador, 119, 120
Dante (Dante Alighieri), 6, 122
Derrida, Jacques, 2, 10, 32, 56, 67,
    68, 71, 72, 134, 136,
    146, 147n10
Dorst, Doug, 12
Doyle, Arthur Conan, 68
Draesner, Ulrike, vi, 2, 10, 26, 28, 34,
    35, 41, 42, 77, 87–95
Duncker, Patricia, vi, 2, 8, 10, 25, 28,
    34, 35, 38, 42, 44–46, 77–87,
    187, 188, 193

E

Eagleton, Terry, 2
Eco, Umberto, vi, 2, 4, 8, 11, 12, 35,
    37, 41, 44, 46, 68, 69, 71, 72, 74,
    122–124, 131, 133, 143–152,
    183, 184, 190, 191, 193
Einstein, Albert, 32
Eliot, T.S. (Thomas Stearns), 59, 62,
    63, 83n10
Ernst, Max, 120
Eugenides, Jefferey, 13
Evaristo, Bernadine, 2, 77, 95–105

F

Felman, Shoshana, 2
Ferrante, Elena, 186
Ferrell, Will, 172
Fforde, Jasper, 13
Forster, Marc, 12, 163, 172–178
Foucault, Michel, 2, 3, 8, 10, 11, 25,
    28, 32, 34, 35, 37, 38, 41, 42,
    44, 57, 68, 77–83, 82n4, 83n10,
    85–87, 90, 90n22, 120, 137,
    143–152, 183, 188, 193

Freud, Sigmund, 7, 19, 54, 56
Frisch, Max, 111

G

Galbraith, Robert, 186
Gauß, Carl Friedrich, 110
Genette, Gérard, 18n1, 28, 29, 32,
    33n19, 192
Giotto (Giotto di Bondone), 94
Giscard d'Estaing, Valéry, 64,
    69, 69n23
Goethe, Johann Wolfgang von, 169
Gregorovius, Ferdinand, 169
Grimm, Jacob and Wilhelm, 172
Gumbrecht, Hans Ulrich, 40, 41
Gyllenhaal, Maggie, 175

H

Hartmann von Aue, 113n7
Heisenberg, Werner, vii, 159, 195
Hermes Trismegistus, 6
Heydrich, Reinhard, 64
Hilbert, David, 172–177
Hitler, Adolf, 117
Hoffman, Dustin, 172
Humboldt, Alexander von, 110

I

Irigaray, Luce, 67, 92
Iser, Wolfgang, 58

J

Jagger, Mick, 68
Jakobson, Roman, 38, 64, 65, 67
James, Henry, 112
Jauß, Hans Robert, 58

NAME INDEX 201

K
Kandinsky, Wassily, 120
Kehlmann, Daniel, vi, 2, 10, 11, 26, 28, 40, 42, 109–122, 185, 193
Khorsandi, Shappi, 96
Kittler, Friedrich, 13n21, 136n66
Kleist, Heinrich von, 93, 94
Kristeva, Julia, 2, 3, 10, 32, 35, 64, 68, 83, 92
Kubrick, Stanley, 7

L
Linné, Carl von (Carl Linnaeus), 182, 192
Locke, John, 6
Lodge, David, vi, 2, 10, 33, 35, 37, 40–42, 51–54, 57, 62–64, 99, 100, 123, 130
Luhmann, Niklas, 20, 21, 138

M
Man, Paul de, 2, 68
Meinecke, Thomas, 13
Mitterand, François, 64, 66
Musil, Robert, 156, 156n41, 156n42, 157, 159

N
Nolan, Christopher, 1

O
Oloixarac, Pola, 13
Ovid (Publius Ovidius Naso), 132, 133, 136, 186

P
Peterson, Jordan, 96, 97
Plato, 6, 86
Propertius (Sextus Propertius), 169n19

R
Ransmayr, Christoph, 2, 11, 32, 35, 40, 42, 109, 132–138, 149, 186
Raphael (Raffaello Sanzio), 94
Rosa, Salvator, 121, 121n21
Rowling, Joanne K., 186
Rytmann, Hélène, 65

S
Sanyal, Mithu, vi, 2, 10, 25, 28, 38, 42, 77, 95–105, 190, 191, 193
Schlegel, Friedrich, 7
Schleiermacher, Friedrich, 7
Schnitzler, Arthur, 7
Schopenhauer, Arthur, 112
Searle, John, 10, 67, 68
Shakespeare, William, 25, 59, 63, 187
Sollers, Philippe, 64, 71, 72, 74
Sontag, Susan, 2
Spencer-Brown, George, 21
Sterne, Laurence, 6

T
Thompson, Emma, 172
Tieck, Ludwig, 112, 121, 121n21
Todorov, Tzvetan, 70, 70n27, 71
Tunick, Spencer, 91, 94

V
Villa Braslavsky, Paula-Irene, 97, 98n42
Virgil (Publius Vergilius Maro), 6

W

Wagner, Jan, 11, 12, 33, 35,
　39, 42, 163–172,
　189, 190
Warhol, Andy, 68
Welles, Orson, 112
Wolfram von Eschenbach, 52

Z

Zapp, Morris, 41, 52, 52n2, 54–57,
　54n6, 57n11, 59–61, 63, 64, 67,
　73, 74, 123
Zeh, Juli, 3, 11, 12, 44, 46, 143,
　152–160, 153n32, 154n35,
　156n41, 184

Subject Index[1]

A
Allegorical (presentation of theory), 2, 6, 18, 28, 30, 33–35, 40, 42, 43, 47, 51–55, 57, 67, 68, 73, 100, 105, 109, 130, 133
Ambiguity/ambiguous, v, 1, 5, 39, 42, 82, 83, 85, 88–93, 88n17, 90n23, 95, 112, 116, 131, 145n3, 154, 157, 158, 160, 169, 182, 183, 189, 193–195
Ambivalence/ambivalent, 77, 87–95, 88n17, 102
Artificial intelligence, 63, 186, 187
Artistic research, 5, 5n14
Author/authorship, v, vi, 2, 3, 5, 10–13, 23–26, 28–32, 34, 35, 37–40, 42, 44–47, 55, 63, 71, 74, 75, 78–82, 85, 109–117, 119–123, 125, 127, 128, 132–138, 144, 149, 151, 164–166, 165n7, 169–172, 174, 176, 177, 179–194, 180n2, 180n4, 186n9

Author-function, 38, 44, 79, 80, 120, 137

B
Biography/biographical, 68–70, 74, 82n4, 88, 111, 114, 121, 133, 164–171, 175, 187, 189, 190, 193

C
Code, 37, 42, 56, 84, 177
Commentary, 11, 29, 33, 35, 39, 56, 164, 166–172, 174, 189
Conjecture, 65, 66, 146, 147
Context, v, vi, 10, 12, 13, 18n1, 25, 32, 33, 37–39, 46, 56, 61, 70, 71, 74, 83, 84, 86, 99, 102, 104, 120, 131, 149, 150, 157n44, 170, 180, 182, 185–187, 189, 193, 194

[1] Note: Page numbers followed by 'n' refer to notes.

SUBJECT INDEX

Contingency/contingent, 44, 60, 114, 122, 155, 157, 160
Creation (of theory), 5, 13, 42–44, 46, 47, 77, 95, 130, 133, 134, 179, 181
Critical race theory, vi, 3, 38, 77, 96–102, 104, 105

D
Death of the author, v, 3, 8, 38, 39, 64, 132, 135, 149, 170, 179, 186
Deconstruction/deconstructivist, 2, 2n1, 10, 27, 28, 31–35, 39, 40, 42, 51, 55, 56, 57n11, 59, 61, 67, 67n21, 68, 71, 72, 100, 104, 123, 133, 134, 134n59, 134n61, 135, 136, 145, 147, 149, 150, 164, 180
Deductive reasoning/deduction/deductive, vi, 4, 69
Detective novel/detective story, v, 7, 8, 13, 37, 38, 136n66, 146, 159n52
Dialogical (presentation of theory), 9, 28, 30, 34, 35, 47, 51, 53, 54, 68, 71, 98, 100, 105, 109
Diegesis/diegetic, 9, 24, 26, 26n11, 28–30, 28n15, 32–39, 33n19, 47, 51, 67, 68, 72, 73, 77, 78, 83, 87, 88, 93, 95, 97–101, 109, 111, 114, 122, 124, 126, 127, 129–134, 149, 175, 176, 181, 185, 186, 190, 192, 195
Différance, 72
Digital humanities, 10, 180
Discourse analysis, 2, 3, 10, 34, 35, 77, 81, 82, 85, 87, 174, 188
Docufiction, 96, 97, 99
Drift, 3, 149–152
Dynamization (of theory), 18, 35–39, 42, 47, 53, 57, 64, 79, 81, 88, 101, 124, 150, 172

E
Editor, 8, 11, 29, 30, 145, 165, 166, 168, 170
Endodiegetic, 28–30, 32–35, 43, 47, 53–55, 67, 81, 99, 100, 105, 109, 114, 123, 124, 128, 130, 133, 181, 186, 190–192
Epistemology/epistemological, 6, 20, 77, 102, 103, 105, 135, 195
Evaluation (of theory), 18, 35, 36, 39–40, 42, 47, 57, 63, 71, 72, 77, 95, 101, 150, 167
Exodiegetic, 24, 26, 26n11, 28–31, 35, 47, 97, 109, 124, 125, 125n34, 130–132, 134, 135, 175, 176, 181
Extrapolation (from theory), vi, 4, 6, 9, 11, 12, 17–19, 22, 27, 36, 42, 43, 45–47, 51, 73, 77, 87, 105, 110, 121, 130, 133, 138, 143, 150, 152, 160, 174, 176, 178, 179, 181, 185, 186, 188, 189, 193, 195

F
Feminist theory, 10, 92, 180
Fiction theory, 3, 46, 143, 158, 159
Four senses of Scripture, 6
Fragment/fragmentary, 31, 31n17, 129, 133, 135, 138, 147, 181, 182, 187–191, 194
Function (of theory), vi, 4, 6, 9, 17–19, 22–25, 35–37, 39–42, 46, 47, 96, 100–102, 104, 135, 143, 150, 172, 179, 194, 195

G
Game theory, 12
Gender theory, 2, 3, 5, 13, 26, 28, 33–35, 37, 62, 77, 88, 92, 95

SUBJECT INDEX 205

Genre, 10, 11, 17, 20, 20n4, 24, 27, 32, 37, 42, 47, 88, 91n26, 93–95, 122, 146, 172, 175, 182, 187
Glossary, 11, 39, 166, 170, 171, 189

H

Hermeneutics/hermeneutic, 2, 6, 7, 9, 10, 18, 19, 33, 35–37, 40, 41, 47, 56, 60, 109, 134, 152, 168–170
Heterotopia, 85, 86
Historical novel, 10, 32, 51, 64, 65, 65n17, 67, 68
History of knowledge, 57
History of science, 3
History of theory, vi, 3, 5, 9, 13, 30, 32, 45–47, 64–66, 74, 75

I

Implied author/reader, 17, 28–32, 35, 47, 109, 124–127, 131
Inductive reasoning/induction/inductive, 192
Intention/intentional, 23, 71, 114, 144, 151, 180, 180n4
Interpretation/interpretive, vi, 3–7, 9, 11–13, 26, 27, 29, 31, 35–37, 39–47, 56, 58, 59, 62, 63, 68–72, 79, 83, 87, 87n16, 88, 91–95, 101, 110, 111, 123, 126, 127, 130–134, 136, 138, 143–157, 147n11, 159, 163, 164, 165n4, 166, 168, 172–175, 177, 182, 185–190, 193–195
Interpretive community, 187, 189
Intertextuality/intertextual, vi, 3, 5, 9, 17–19, 23–28, 25n10, 47, 52n3, 59, 68, 69, 73, 78, 81, 96, 97, 111, 112, 120, 134, 137, 164, 169, 170, 174, 180, 187, 188, 190–193
Irony/ironic, v, 1, 4, 5, 8–10, 12, 18, 33, 39, 40, 42, 45, 46, 65–67, 69, 74, 75, 96, 103, 104, 114, 117–119, 121n22, 146, 159, 163–170, 173, 177, 182, 183, 189, 190, 193–195

L

Level (of theory), vi, 4, 6, 9, 17–19, 22, 26, 26n11, 28–36, 28n15, 29n16, 33n19, 38, 46, 47, 51, 53, 69, 73, 83, 88, 93, 96–101, 105, 114, 123–125, 125n34, 127, 131–133, 149, 160, 167, 170, 173–176, 179, 181, 186, 188, 190, 194, 195
Limits of interpretation/theory, 3, 5, 10, 18, 36, 37, 39–42, 44, 46, 57, 63, 70, 92, 93, 105, 110, 127, 131, 132, 143, 144, 147–152, 171, 184
Literary criticism/literary studies, 5, 12, 52, 57, 60, 62, 79, 122, 155, 163–165, 164n2, 167, 172, 186, 187
Literary theory, v, vi, 1–13, 2n1, 3n6, 6n15, 9n20, 17–28, 30–47, 51–68, 55n7, 70–75, 77–82, 85, 87, 88, 92, 93, 95–105, 109, 110, 121–124, 127, 130, 132–138, 143, 144, 146, 147, 150–153, 156, 158–160, 158n46, 158n49, 163, 164, 170, 172–174, 176–195, 182n2
Literature and theory, 1, 3, 18–23, 20n3, 27, 32, 124, 144, 152, 156, 163, 172–174, 176, 177, 182, 192

M

Marxism/Marxist, 10, 51, 54n6, 56, 59, 60
Material studies, 12
Metadiegetic, 28–30, 28n15, 32, 33, 33n19, 35, 47, 164, 171
Metafiction/metafictional, 64, 66, 110, 122
Metahistoriographic, 65, 65n17
Metaization (of theory), 42–43, 46, 47, 51, 73, 77, 95, 133, 137, 143, 153, 160, 172, 181
Metalepsis/metaleptic, 12, 137, 175, 176
Method/methodological, vi, 5, 7–9, 19, 20, 36, 38–40, 42, 44, 54, 56, 58–61, 63, 65, 66, 72, 74, 127, 131, 164, 167, 171, 174, 175, 181, 188, 190–192, 194
Mode (of theory), vi, 4, 6, 9, 17–19, 23, 24, 27, 28, 46, 47, 96, 179, 194, 195
Model author/reader, 122, 133, 134, 136

N

Narratology/narratological, 9, 18, 18n1, 19, 29–31, 47, 54n6, 181, 188, 192
Narrator, 9, 12, 18, 28–31, 28n15, 29n16, 33, 35, 38, 47, 55, 65, 66, 72, 78–80, 83–86, 114, 137, 163, 173–177, 182, 188, 190–192
Non-theoretical forms of theory, v, 41, 179, 181–184, 190, 193–195

O

Observation/observing/observer, 3, 12, 13, 17, 19–22, 22n7, 39, 59, 138, 143, 154, 159, 160, 163, 168, 173–175, 182, 192, 193, 195

P

Paradiegetic, 29, 30, 35, 47, 100, 167, 170
Paratext/paratextual, 7, 29–31, 82n4, 165, 167, 169
Peridiegetic, 24, 27, 29–31, 29n16, 35, 47, 77, 87, 88, 93, 95, 123, 181, 195
Physics/quantum physics/quantum mechanics/theory of relativity, 3, 11, 32, 44, 46, 88, 91, 146, 153, 153n32, 154n35, 155, 157–160, 184, 195
Plurality/plural, 19, 39, 44, 45, 53, 56, 61, 83, 101, 109, 129, 131, 138, 145, 154, 155, 157, 160, 174, 181, 190, 191, 194
Postcolonialism/postcolonial, 2, 3n6, 38, 95, 104, 191
Postmodernism/postmodern, 2–4, 53, 74, 74n32, 90, 122, 134, 138, 152, 180, 180n2
Post-structuralism/post-structuralist, 2, 3, 10, 31, 37, 54n6, 59, 74, 123, 147n11, 170, 171, 185, 190, 191
Post-theoretical/pre-theoretical, 35, 36, 40–42, 102
Presentation (of theory), vi, 4, 6, 8, 12, 18, 18n1, 19, 31–40, 42, 43, 47, 51, 53–55, 57, 61, 63, 64, 67, 68, 71–73, 77, 80n3, 81, 95, 99–101, 111, 116, 120, 134, 136, 163, 164, 172, 173, 175, 182–184, 189, 190, 194
Psychoanalysis/psychoanalytic, 2, 7, 78, 146
Psychology/psychological, 79, 103, 138, 176, 184, 185, 194
Publisher, 11, 30, 123, 124, 127, 128, 134, 145, 145n3, 180

Q

Queer theory/queer studies, 2, 10, 77, 78, 83, 85, 87

R

Reader/readership, 2, 3, 5, 6, 8–13, 17, 23–26, 28, 30–32, 35, 37, 40, 42, 45, 47, 54, 54n6, 55, 58, 59, 66, 69, 78–81, 87n16, 94, 95, 97, 101, 103, 104, 109, 110, 116, 117, 122–138, 126n35, 136n66, 144–147, 149, 151, 157n45, 163, 167, 171, 180, 183, 184, 186, 189, 190, 192, 193
Reader-response theory/reception theory/reception, 10, 13, 33, 40, 45, 54n6, 58, 59, 109, 124, 127, 144, 164, 172, 180, 183, 185, 189, 190
Re-entry, 21, 22, 61, 138, 152
Reference, direct, 23–25, 28, 47, 97, 98, 100, 101, 191
Reference, indirect, 23–25, 28, 47, 64, 68, 82, 93, 97, 98, 101, 111–113, 117, 132, 169, 175, 192
Reference, self-reflexive, 17, 23–25, 27, 28, 47, 97, 98, 101
Rejection (of theory), 35, 36, 40, 42, 47, 57, 88, 93, 101–104, 134, 150, 173
Rhetoric, 38, 64, 71, 159, 167, 190, 191

S

Second-order literary theory, vi, 1, 5, 6, 9, 9n20, 13, 17–47, 171, 174, 195
Self-reference/self-referential, 21

Self-reflexivity/self-reflexive, 5, 9, 18, 24, 43–45, 47, 65, 65n17, 73, 82, 112, 123, 126, 133, 137, 143, 150, 160, 172–174, 191, 192
Semantics, 72, 187
Semiotics/semiotic/semiosis, vi, 2, 4, 4n10, 39, 40, 42, 68–72, 97, 144, 149–152
Sign/signified/signifier, v, 2–4, 11, 12, 18n1, 56, 69–72, 97, 146, 147, 149, 150, 152, 171
Similarity, generic, 23, 24, 27, 28, 31, 47, 93, 97, 134, 137, 166, 169, 181, 192
Similarity, narrative, 23, 24, 26, 28, 47, 64, 67, 68, 73, 94, 97, 98, 111, 112, 121, 149, 151, 181, 192
Similarity, structural, 9, 23, 26, 28, 47, 52, 58, 69, 74, 97, 98, 112, 123, 130, 136n66, 147, 169, 178, 181, 192
Sociology/sociological, 3, 12, 45, 97, 104, 185, 194
Structuralism/structuralist, 2n1, 27n12, 29, 33, 35, 51, 54n6, 57, 58, 62, 66, 69, 72, 100, 174, 175
Systems theory, 21, 22, 27n14, 187

T

Telos/teleological, 56, 72, 145, 149, 151, 152
Theorizing literature/theory-informed literature, v, vi, 1, 4, 6–9, 19, 21–23, 27, 45, 99, 181, 190
Theory of theory, 3

W

Willing suspension of disbelief, 116, 176

Printed in the United States
by Baker & Taylor Publisher Services